Forever and Always, My Love

My Love

Book 1: Ezekeial

Renee Barton

PAGE PUBLISHING, INC.
Conneaut Lake, PA

First originally published by Page Publishing 2021

ISBN 978-1-6624-5383-0 (pbk)
ISBN 978-1-6624-5382-3 (digital)

Printed in the United States of America

We all live and learn, so never be afraid to take a leap of faith.

TABLE OF CONTENTS

CHAPTER 1

The Beginning

Making our descent down the steep, winding hill, the sound of the squealing brakes and the groaning of the old diesel engine when it is downshifted to a lower gear rocket through the open windows of the old yellow school bus, and I can feel it jerking once the brakes grab hold to slow us down. There is no room for error when driving down this stretch of treacherous road because the slightest jerk of the steering wheel or taking your eyes off the road for only just a split second can lead to a catastrophic outcome. The shoulder of the road is only about a foot wide from the outside of the white line to the edge of the pavement, and there is no kind of ground to drive on at all, just a quick drop-off from the edge right into a deep trench off the side. The other side of the road has a complete drop-off leading straight to the ground many feet below. I'm sitting on the right-hand side of the bus in my usual spot, about middleway of the length of it, the same side as the cliff face following us down the hill. Zipping around the curve, the blur of the different colors and contours of the rock and grass streak past me. The wind from the open windows is whipping my hair around my face, blowing it in my mouth and slapping me in the eyes. It is grabbing whatever is in its path, throwing it all over the place in some sort of a crazy rage, and the air around us has the musty smell of the old school bus, along with the familiar scents of the outside. Mother Earth surrounds us from every angle, and I absolutely love this smell because it is the smell of home!

At the bottom of the hill, the curve will continue sharply to the right, or continues traveling straight ahead. We're going to continue taking the curve to the right, and it gets even sharper as we descend closer to the bottom. The bus is hugging the curve even tighter when we turn onto the next road beginning at the bottom of the hill. This road is named Oak Hill. The bus begins to bounce, rattle, and jump when it hits the torn-up, uneven pavement, throwing us around in our seats like a bunch of rag dolls, so we cling to the back of the seat in front of us with a death grip, holding on for dear life. My heart begins to flutter in anticipation because my stop is next!

The pavement ends about forty feet from my stop, and the roads are all gravel from here on out. We're down in a valley, almost like being stuck inside the deep cauldron of a slumbering volcano smack-dab in the middle of farm country. And once you pass my stop, it is straight uphill, then once you hit the top, another sharp curve turns to the right.

The squealing of the brakes, along with the groaning of the motor, begins again when we brake to slow down to stop. I can hear the rocks crunching under the weight of the bus when it settles on top of them, and the dust from the gravel engulfs everything inside and out when the bus skids to a halt. My eyes are watering from it as it drifts around in the air, tormenting me from its grittiness sticking to my eyeballs. I'm breathing it in with every breath I take, and I can taste and feel the gritty earthiness it leaves inside my mouth. But the faint squeak of the bus door when it is being opened makes me forget all about the awful dust storm surrounding me.

My sister and I hop out onto the side of the road then race around the front of the bus to get to the other side. Our road is a branch off Oak Hill Road called Old Mill Road.

Reeling from excitement, I make my way home. It is the last day of the school year, and I'm so glad that it is finally over because this has been the first year that I've spent at this new school. And I've just completed the fourth grade. It really wasn't terrible, but it was sure a huge change from last year. We'll see how next year goes when I begin the fifth grade, and maybe I'll be able to enjoy it a little more with not being the new kid on the block!

Let me back up a bit and tell you a little about myself and my family. My name is Renee Marie Cox, and I was born in St. Louis,

Missouri, at St. Anthony's Hospital on August 1, 1977. I was born four weeks premature and only weighed a little over four pounds! You wouldn't know it by looking at me now! Haha! I have one sister whose name is Reese Isabella Cox. She was also born in St. Louis, Missouri, but she was delivered at St. John's Hospital on February 29, 1980. This just so happened to be a leap year! We had lived in a big old white two-story house in a quiet suburb on Lemay Ferry Road in the city, but my mama and papa had a lot of trouble in their marriage and were always fighting and arguing. One day, my mama packed up some our stuff. We got in the car and drove away, and I never saw our house ever again. They couldn't make their marriage work and decided to go their separate ways. So with this, all our entire lives would be forever changed, and nothing would ever be the same again.

I was between the ages of six and seven when they had gotten divorced. My mama was working all the time so we could get a new home of our own to live in because we had been moving around a lot when she left Papa, staying with some of her friends at times. This was the most horrible time in my life because Reese and I started going to different babysitters all the time. We would be dragged out of bed early in the morning before the sun came up and dropped off at the sitter's house, then after school, Mama would pick us up and take us to another sitter where we would stay for the rest of the evening. It seemed like, no sooner than we would get settled in for the night, my mama would be coming to collect us to take us home, and we would be dragged out of bed once again! The next morning, it would all start over again, and on the weekends, we usually stayed with the sitter all day.

Going to the babysitter's house was terrible, and I hated every minute of it! There was one sitter whose little boy, which was about three years old, would chase my sister and I all around the house, terrorizing us by biting, pinching, and scratching us the entire time we were there! We would try to hide all over the house to get away from him, but he would always find us. The only time there was any peace was when he was napping or off to bed for the night. Day after day, it was utter agonizing torture! Then soon after that, we started going to another new sitter who was an absolute witch! Her name was Shelly. She would put on a great face when everyone's parents were around, but after they were gone, all hell broke loose! If we talked too loud or got a little rambunctious, she would break out a wooden ruler and strike us with it. We weren't allowed to make any noise at nap time either because if she heard a giggle or anyone talking, she would break out that same ruler again then give us a good swat with it. Lord help you if you didn't like something that she had given you to eat because if you didn't eat it, she would shove it in your face. She did this to me with a braunschweiger sandwich one day. I'm not a picky eater by any means, but I can't even stand the smell of the stuff, let alone eat it! Shelly told me to eat the sandwich, but I told her that I couldn't. So she stood over me and told me that I had better eat it or I would have to sit in the corner for the rest of the day. I told her that I would rather sit in the corner as to eat that sandwich, and she was infuriated! Grabbing the sandwich off my tray, she proceeded to stuff it in my face and smear it all over, leaving pieces of the braunschweiger, along with the bread, stuck to my face when she had gotten finished abusing me. I guess she had gotten her kicks off that because she told me to go wash my face and then to go sit in the corner. I hated her!

The last day we had spent over there was a warm summer day, and all of us kids were playing out in the fenced-in backyard. There was a swing set out there that I was playing on that day, and I had jumped out of the swing and fell down then scraped the palm of my hand on a rock jutting out from the ground when I tried to catch my fall. There was a large gash on the palm of my hand from the rock. It was bleeding quite a bit. Plus it was all dirty, so I needed to clean it up. Not showing my hand to or saying anything to any of the other kids, I went running up to the house. Opening the doors to get in, I quickly made my way to the bathroom because I didn't want to get any blood on Shelly's floor, knowing that it would make her angry. After turning on the faucet, I started cleaning up my wound when Shelly came barreling down the hallway, then stood in the bathroom doorway and began screaming at me. She was angry because I didn't shut the back door when I came in and that I shouldn't be running in and out of the house with the air conditioning running. I didn't even think about shutting the back door at the time!

Still screaming at me, she grabbed me by the arm. Then within the blink of an eye, she slapped me across the face, not even giving me a chance to explain to her what had happened. Looking in the mirror post aftermath, I could see her handprint clearly outlined across my cheek. It was fiery red and looked like it was starting to welt up. Horrified as to what had just happened, my eyes well up with tears, and before I could even try to hold it back, I was crying. This seemed to make her even angrier, so she yanked my arm away from the sink then shoved me out in the hallway.

"Go sit down on the couch and shut that crying up!" she yelled at me hatefully. "You're not getting up until your mother comes to pick you up, and you'd better not move or even make another sound!" she continued to scream.

It felt like an eternity waiting for my mama to come, and I couldn't believe how cruel Shelly had been to me. Relieved by the sound of her car, Mama was finally here! When my mama came in and saw my face, she immediately asked Shelly what had happened. Shelly gave her the biggest, fattest lie of a story ever told because she told my mama I was outside, helping her do some yard work, and that I had tripped on a rock, so when she tried to catch my fall, her hand struck the side of my face, causing the handprint. My mama wasn't stupid and knew she was lying, so when we had gotten in the car, she asked me what had happened. Crying the whole time, I told her how it all went down. My mama stared at me for a second after I was through telling my tale, I think, because she was really ticked off and stunned, and I could tell that she was about to cry. Reese didn't know what was going on because she was outside with all the other kids when everything happened. She was sitting in the back seat all wild-eyed, with an expression of pure horror written across her face. That was the last time we ever set foot in Shelly's house ever again!

Mama finally bought a used mobile home that was already sitting on a pad in a mobile-home park. It was called High Ridge Trailer Court, and of course, it was located in High Ridge, Missouri. I loved the trailer court because there were so many places to ride my bike and lots of other kids to play with! There was also a swimming pool that we could use anytime we wanted to while it was open, and I sure wasn't a stranger there when the July heat was on! There were strict rules that had to be abided by because the owners didn't want any trash or junk lying around, and every yard had to be well-maintained. The trailers couldn't have loose or missing underpinning, and the porches and garages had to be kept in good condition. Nothing could be rotting or falling apart or have any peeling paint, and if you didn't obey the rules, they could make you move, trailer and all! Another great thing about it was, Grandma and Grandpa Wodicker only lived three streets over, and we could go visit them whenever we wanted to. I remember sitting at the island in their kitchen, and Grandma would make me some of the Lipton soup that you can buy in a box. There are two pouches inside the box containing dried noodles, chicken, and broth; then adding the required amount of water and then microwaving it for so many minutes would make an awesome and tasty cup of soup! Grandma always had the little radio sitting on the counter, playing, and it seemed like every time I was over there, the song "Glory of Love" by Peter Cetera would play. I love that song, and it makes me think of her every time I hear it. Reese and I started going to a new babysitter, but this time, it was so much different. The babysitter, whose name was Angie, lived in the trailer court too. We would ride the bus over to her house after school then stay with her until Mama got off work. Angie was really nice and never raised even a single finger to any of us kids. Sometimes we would get to stay the night at Grandma and Grandpa's house on the weekends!

Every other weekend, we get to visit Papa. He moved back to his hometown in Greenville, Missouri. It is a pretty good drive to his house from ours, but I love visiting my family down there. We always have big Sunday dinners at Grandma and Grandpa Cox's house after church, and Grandma Cox will fry up some amazing fresh catfish with all the fixings. She can fry up some of the best catfish you've ever eaten! It is the bomb! In the mornings, she whips up the best chocolate gravy in the world! We slather up a freshly baked biscuit or some bread with the stuff, and we're all in hog heaven! Yum! They live right up the road from a huge lake called Lake Wappapello, and Grandpa Cox catches all his fish right out of that lake! One time, he was in the newspaper for catching a ninety-nine-pound catfish! There was a picture of him holding it up beside him, hanging on the living-room wall, and it was huge! Fishing is his passion, and he spends all his free time up at the lake. So it is no surprise to see the old wheelbarrow parked next to the house filled with live fish and water. During the summer, Papa takes us out to the lake to go swimming, fishing, and riding in the boat. It is a lot of fun! My uncle has a speedboat, and once in a while, he'll take us out for a spin. My cousin Landry and I always go shoot some hoops around the giant oak tree standing out in my grandparent's yard, and we also ride our bikes down to the lake to go fishing. He and I always get along well together, and I love to hang out with him, even though he is a few years older than me!

One morning, when Mama was off work, which was a Saturday, she was telling us about a man she had met at her job. His name is Kent Stevens, and we were going to meet him that evening. Needless to say, I wasn't excited about it at all! I was finally getting used to all the new changes occurring in my life already and didn't want anything else to change again because it's been hard enough to adjust throughout this entire ordeal! I know that things have been tough on my Mama too, and I want for her to be happy, but Reese and I have had our own fair share of chaos and drama right along with hers!

Kent is a fairly tall man with a stocky build, has a head full of short, dark-brown hair, and piercing, dark-brown eyes. He is very light complected and has some really chubby cheeks. He was wearing bib overalls with a black pocket T-shirt and some tennis shoes, and he was not a bad-looking guy by any means. Although, I was expecting a man wearing a fancy outfit and shoes. He took all of us out to eat at the Pasta House downtown for dinner, and I've always liked eating there because they have the best fried ravioli ever! He seemed nice enough, but I must admit I still wasn't liking any of this and had my doubts. But of course, we saw more and more of Kent after that.

Several months had passed by since we had first met Kent when, out of the blue, my mama announced that we're all going to be moving in with him. Well, actually, he was going to be moving in with us. Kent owns some property in a small town called Cuba, Missouri, where his own trailer is located. They were going to move our trailer out to his property and sell his trailer, then we would all live in our trailer for the time being. This was the last thing that I ever expected to be hearing and, not to mention, wasn't thrilled with either! I didn't want to leave my new friends behind plus start a new school too! My world was falling apart yet once again, but it didn't matter what I said to my mama because she was dead set on moving. And before I knew it, our trailer was being load up for the big move. I watched them while they hooked it up to the giant tractor trailer that was going to pull it to its new location, and when they began to pull it out of its spot, my heart sank in sadness because my life was being uprooted for the second time.

After pulling into the road to where Kent's property is located, I knew right off the bat, it was going to be quite the challenge adjusting to this new life of mine. We're pretty much out in the middle of nowhere, and I didn't like the looks of any of it. Creepy old buildings sit along both sides of the road, and it reminded me of some ghost town straight out of a horror movie. I was told that this used to be a busy little town a very long time ago, and the town used to be called Oak Hill.

At the beginning of the road on the right-hand side is Kent's property, and our trailer was moved in here, with his trailer sitting right behind ours. There is a small garage with a short driveway next to our trailer, which is old and weathered, and the seasoned wood it was built with has turned gray from the elements. But even though it looks a little rickety, it was made from sturdy old barnwood and isn't about to fall down any time soon. Several feet away from the garage stands an old white two-story house. No one is living there, and it is just sitting there vacant. There is nothing really in it, just old junk furniture and peeling wallpaper, and Kent has said something about tearing it down in the future because it needs a lot of work and isn't worth fixing up. There is a huge oak tree between the garage and that old house, setting the scene for a very scary horror movie, where someone comes running out of the house with a chainsaw, ready to cut up anyone in their path.

Moving down past the house, there is an old bank building constructed out of smoothly sculpted large blocks of brown stone. It is two-stories tall and has a flight of wooden stairs built against the side of it that leads up to the second floor. It is closed in on the outside by a wooden wall that travels up the entire length of it and is covered at the top by a small porch with a tin roof that is connected to the main building. The stairs are worn and twisted from time, are rotten in some spots, and aren't very safe to be climbing. The inside of the bottom level is full of Kent's junk. He uses it for storage and has boxes and bags strung out all over the place. The original floor is gone, exposing the dirt floor beneath, and most of the walls have been removed, leaving one big, wide open area, except for a couple of the wall frames. The ceiling has the original dark bronze metal sheets lining it throughout the entire building and is sagging from the hands of time plus from not having any support, with most of the walls being removed. Some of the windows are broken, with the leftover fragments of glass just lying inside the wooden frames, along with what was left of the tattered and torn screens. The upstairs is packed with all kinds of old stuff, a huge treasure trove, and it also has the metal sheets lining the ceiling as well. I would love to venture around in there, but the floor isn't safe to walk on by any means because the old tin roof has been leaking water, causing lots of damage to the wooden floor. It is rotting and sagging down in the middle, and with most of the walls being removed on the lower level, there is no kind of support helping to hold it up. I've managed to grab a few things from the outskirts of the room, but I didn't find any kind of hidden treasures from any of it.

Kent's property ends at the corner of the old bank building but wraps around the backyard of the next house and adjoins to the next road. There is another old white house sitting beside the bank building along the corner of the road, and an elderly woman named Fannie May owns this house. She is the sweetest lady ever and has lived there almost her entire life. On nice days, you can find her sitting on her front-porch swing or walking around in her yard, petting one of her many cats or tending to her flowers. The road turns to the right or left here. So if you turn to the left, then drive a short distance; there is a huge wooden building that was once the old textile mill. A small tributary of water that branches off from the main creek upstream called the Brush Creek flows behind the old mill and runs along the outskirts of this little old town. A huge weeping willow tree stands next to the old mill beside the creek, and I love to tear off the branches and smack them around on the ground and in the air, using them like an old bullwhip or sometimes using them for a long tail.

Past the old mill, the road ends at one of the neighbors' houses. Then turning back and going down the road the opposite way past Fannie May's house, there's another small old block building that was used as a jailhouse. It is pretty tight, containing only one window, which is missing, and has a door on the end side of it. The door is barely hanging on, and the white paint along the weathered wooden doorframe has practically all faded away and peeled off. It is constructed out of smaller brown block than that of the bank building and is in pretty rough shape. I sure wouldn't have wanted to be the one staying in that little old shack!

Kent owns this little old jailhouse and down the road a small trek farther. Then it ends at the mouth of a gate leading into a huge one-hundred-acre cornfield. The cornfield wraps around the entire backside of another big old white two-story house sitting atop a small hill. It has a nice-sized front and backyard with a small garage sitting next to it and has an amazing vast open view of the surrounding area from the backyard. On the other side of the house is another gate that opens up into the cornfield too. This old white house is full of the creep factor because it is off on its own down here, secluded from the rest of the town. It was constructed out of sculpted blocks that were used to build houses with long ago, and there are two giant concrete pillars standing on each side of the porch, holding up a small roof. The white paint on it is faded and peeling just like the old jailhouse. And the door is locked, so I can't get in to check out the inside. Peering in through the window that faces the living-room side of the house, I can see the stairs that lead up to the second floor. They begin right when you enter the front door then ascend straight up. There is peeling wallpaper falling off the walls and piling up on the old hardwood floor, but I can't really see much of anything else in there. A For Sale sign is placed in the front yard, and it looks like it has been stuck out there for quite some time.

The road continues on once you pass the second gate of the cornfield, and it seems to get darker here because Mother Earth has reclaimed the surrounding area. The woods begin here, and a canopy of trees envelopes the gravel road the rest of the way down, along with thick brush lining the outer edges. At the end of this road, an old bridge crosses over the main body of water of the Brush Creek and connects to another road on the opposite side named Rutz Road. There's a narrow tunnel on that side you can walk through that travels under the road, then comes out on the opposite side of Rutz Road. I've walked through it before, but it was really scary! A bat hanging from the ceiling scared the hell out of me one day when I ventured through it because I didn't even see it until it took off, making a high-pitched squeaking noise while trying to escape.

The bridge is held up by two giant concrete slabs, one on each end, and old wooden planks line the entire floor. Back in the day, people used to drive across them. But from the unforgiving hands of time, some of the wood is rotten, and there are holes throughout the entire length of it. Pieces of tree limbs lie on top of it, along with leaves and other debris from the woods. The thick old steel frame and bolts are rusted, with some of it falling down in spots. Nevertheless, I have tested the limits and walked across it several times.

Returning to the beginning of the road at my bus stop, we'll tour the left side of our run-down little town. Kent owns a little piece of land here that has a small building sitting on it, and this building used to be the post office. It has a screened-in front porch that you walk into before entering the main part, which only has a couple of rooms inside it. One of which has a counter that extends from one of the outer walls and stops about middleway. Kent has a bunch of junk stored in here too! That guy has crap all over the place!

Several feet from the post office stands the old general store, and the neighbors own the rest of the property from here on out. The general store is a large building and is built out of wooden planks and has two floors. The top floor has a wooden porch with a tin roof along the outside that stretches across the whole length of the front of the building. Some of the windows have been broken, with the torn and tattered screens still attached to them, and are boarded up from the inside. The stairs leading up to the second floor are located within a small hallway inside the store. The upstairs level is a scavenger's dream because there are so many things stuffed inside the closets and inside the different rooms that I can dig around in there all day! I was told by Kent that the upstairs was used as a cathouse, and hopefully you know what that is because I really don't want to have to explain it to you. Luckily, the neighbors don't seem to care if I root around in there, or at least, they haven't ever said anything to my mama, Kent, or me about it.

After passing the general store is a huge yard that has another big old two-story house sitting in it as well. This house has about the same layout as the secluded house with the cornfield wrapped around it, but it has some sort of goldish-yellow-colored siding around it and is trimmed out in a dark-brown color. It too has giant concrete pillars sitting on the front porch, one on each side, except they're painted dark brown like the rest of the trim. The only real difference between the two houses is that this house has a small walk-out porch on the second floor right above the lower porch. The upper porch has two giant pillars standing on it too. The neighbors have built a shop down on the corner of this side right across the street from Fannie May's house, and they do automotive repairs and bodywork there.

The town of Oak Hill lies smack-dab in the middle of three different towns and two different counties. These three towns are called Cuba, Bourbon, and Owensville, and it is about a twenty- to twenty-five-minute drive in either direction just to even get to one of them. The towns of Bourbon and Cuba are located inside the county lines of Crawford County, and the town of Owensville lies inside the county lines of Gasconade County. We're located in Crawford County, and we go to the Cuba school district. Confusing, huh? It is like being lost in the backwoods far away from civilization. It is a lot different from being in the city where we could drive ten minutes and be surrounded by our favorite places. I hate it here! The bus ride to and from school is a little over an hour each way, and every time I'm asked to stay the night with a friend, my mama tells me that it is too far of a drive for her to come pick me up. Not to mention, we have an Owensville phone number, and everyone else has a Cuba number, which means I can't call my friends either because it is long distance. I miss the trailer park and all my old friends!

There is not much to do out here. We only get a few channels on the television, so I watch Bob Ross paint on Saturday mornings on channel 9, then Scooby Doo after that on channel 13. Most of the time, the picture is pretty fuzzy, and it is hard to see. I can ride my bike a little bit, but I can't ride it on Oak Hill Road because of all the farming traffic. Farm equipment, horse trailers, and tractors fly up and down the road all-day long, and it wouldn't take much to get plowed over by one of them. I also pass the time sometimes by drawing and coloring pictures of unicorns, dragons, and horses. They're my passion, and one day, I want to have a horse of my very own. Mostly, I go down to the creek under the bridge and play in the water. I can walk up or down the bank, fish and swim, or go hunting for frogs and tadpoles because the creek seems to go on forever. Sometimes I venture off into the woods to go exploring. Reese likes to tag along with me, but I prefer to hang out by myself because I don't want to have to babysit her the entire time.

Reese and I are your typical siblings. We fight and argue one minute, and then the next, we're playing games together or with our Barbie dolls. She gets on my nerves a lot. But in the end, she is my sister, and I love her. My mama was able to quit her job and stay at home with us after we moved out here, but that is about the only plus side to this whole thing. She works part-time at a little bakery in Owensville early in the mornings, making doughnuts, and sometimes she brings us a box of doughnuts home from there to eat for breakfast. They're delicious! I love the chocolate-iced, filled-Long-John kind the most!

Kent is not a bad man. He doesn't yell at us or hit us. Although, he is a very stern man and very set in his ways. Getting into trouble means a two-hour lecture and community service on the property. Meaning, the punishment is raking up leaves, picking up rocks, or doing some sort of odd job for days at a time until he feels that you've served your time. And whatever you do, don't lie! It is a far worse punishment than any of that! Most of the time, he is gone working the evening shift at Chrysler and has to leave pretty early in order to make it to work on time because it takes over an hour to drive from our house to Chrysler one way. Kent usually sleeps most of the day and practically gets straight up from bed then heads back to work.

CHAPTER 2

Close Encounters

"I want the two of you girls to know that Kent and I are buying the house down the road that's for sale," my mama announces one afternoon when we're on our way home from staying at our dad's house during the week of the Fourth of July. Reese and I have been down there for the past two weeks. And it was fun to go, but I'm glad that we're on our way back home. My dad is seeing a woman he was friends with years ago, and her name is Janelle. She seems nice enough, but it is way too early for me to tell if I'm ready to like her just yet. She has a daughter, whose name is Candice, and is about a year younger than me. We've all gotten along together really well during the past two weeks, and she is pretty easy to hang out with because I didn't feel like I had to be a different person in order to fit in.

"We're going to be moving into that mess down there?" I ask, feeling horrified. "It's a complete disaster!" I cry out in utter shock and disbelief because I can't believe she has just told us this terrible news! That old place is just so creepy!

"Well, we're going to move into the apartment next to the house and live there until we get the house fixed up," my mama explains. "We sold Kent's mobile home last week, and then after we move into the apartment, we're going to sell our mobile home," she continues.

"I thought the building next to that old house was a garage! It doesn't look like an apartment to me!" I gripe, shaking my head.

"Actually, it has a small kitchen and dining room area, a nice-sized living room, one bathroom, and two bedrooms," she explains.

19

"Oh, man!" Reese cries out unhappily. "Renee and I still have to share a room! That sucks!" Reese isn't happy about it at all, and neither am I because, out of all the places to buy, they just had to pick that one!

In her defense, Mama chimes in and says, "The house has three bedrooms, so once it's done, you two will have your very own bedrooms. Plus Kent plans on putting in an extra bathroom upstairs for you girls. Your bedrooms will be upstairs."

"How long will that take?" Reese asks excitedly.

"I'm not sure how long it's going to take because there's no way to be for sure. Kent plans on doing most of the work himself so we can save some money on the remodeling," Mama explains, glancing at Reese through the rearview mirror, giving her a flash of a smile.

Reese and I have shared a bedroom our entire lives, so it'll be great to finally have my own space. My tenth birthday is drawing near, so my mama asks me what I would like to have for my birthday.

"I'd like to get a new fishing pole and tackle box!" I answer happily. The pole that I have now won't tighten up when I increase the drag on it, and the eye on the very tip is broken off. "I wouldn't mind getting a few new lures to put inside the tackle box either!" I add, trying to throw her a small hint.

She chuckles a little bit and flashes me her smile too. "We'll see what you get on your birthday."

My birthday arrives, and Mama throws me a party. She loves to throw parties. It turns out to be a huge crowd, and I can't wait to open up my gifts. I'm mostly given cards and money, which is great, because this way, I can go pick out whatever I want. Mama and Kent have purchased a new fishing pole, a tackle box, and a few things to put inside it for me; and I'm ecstatic! Kent must've put it all together because there is a hook and small sinker already tied to it. It is ready to go, and I'm totally pumped because I can't wait until I can get down to the creek to try all of it out!

Getting up early the next morning, I grab a butter bowl that is sitting in the dish drainer. My mama always reuses plastic and glass containers that we've brought home, things such as butter, Cool Whip, or sauces from the store. They always come in handy to pack leftovers in, or in my case, I'm going to put my fishing worms inside it. Grabbing my new fishing pole, tackle box, and bowl, I head down the road toward the creek. I stop to dig up some worms by the mouth of the second gate of the cornfield because it is really easy to dig up tons of worms here in the soft black dirt. I fill up my bowl with enough worms to last me for the whole day then make my way down the road. It is quite a trek from the cornfield to the bridge, and you can barely see the creepy old white house that my mama and Kent have just purchased, standing at the edge of the tree canopy. The cornfield runs all the way down to the creek bank, along the side of a small patch of woods next to the right side of the road, and along the other side of the road, across the small finger of the creek, lies another cornfield. A few birds fly out of the brush while I walk down the road, giving me quite the scare, and I can hear their wings flapping frantically as they fly away, fleeing from the oncoming danger of my approach. The corn has already been harvested for the season. Peering through the trees, I can see the empty outlines of the rows from where the stalks had grown. Plus I can see and hear the black crows cawing and calling out to one another while they scavenge around on the ground for any leftover pieces of goodies. It is going to be a really nice day out today. It is already beginning to heat up as the sun rises overhead, but there is a nice breeze gently circulating the air around me.

There is a skinny trail leading from the left side of the bridge descending a small hill that takes you right down to the sandy bank of the creek, and surrounding along both sides of it is a horrible weed called sting weed, also known as itch weed. It is a terrible weed that can wreak havoc on anyone who gets in contact with it, causing red welts and an agonizing, burning itch like nothing I can describe. It only takes one small rub up against it, and the hell begins! Noticing that my little white canvas shoelace has become untied, I decide to fix it before I make my way down the trail. Lord knows I don't want to trip over it and stumble or fall right into the patches of sting weed lining the trail! Lying my fishing gear down beside me, I bend down on my knees then begin to tie my shoe. Catching a glimpse of something out of the corner of my eye moving down at the other end of the road toward my house, I turn to look at it. I can make out the figure of a large dog standing at the edge of the canopy, and it is just standing there, staring at me. At first, I think it is just one of the neighbor's boxers. They have two boxers, one male and one female. The male's name is Sam, and the female's name is Jenny. So I'm not too concerned about it because I play with them all the time, and they love to play fetch. Suddenly, the dog starts moving in closer. I can hear it growling softly underneath its breath, and I realize that it is not Sam nor Jenny. Quickly finishing tying up my shoelace, I stand up slowly, not taking my eyes off the dog for one second because I'm not sure what I should do while keeping a wary eye focused on it. Without warning, the dog darts down the road, running toward me at lightning speed, growling and barking loudly. Panicking, I bolt, turning to flee across the old wooden bridge. The fight-or-flight mode has kicked in, and I'm in full flight! *Crack!* About midway, one of the boards that I've run across has caved in from my weight, and my right leg falls right through it. My left leg buckles up underneath me, and I'm sitting on top of it. Pain wheels throughout my entire body from the wood scratching my leg as it slides down through the gaping hole, but I know that I don't have any time to waste. So crying out in pain, I try to pull my leg free. It has fallen through all the way up to my thigh, and I can feel it swinging around in the air beneath the bridge. The dog is panting heavily while it pursues me and is barking and growling while it closes in. I know there is no way or enough time to free myself, so I place my hands around the back of my head then curl my body up into itself as much as I possibly can, shielding myself from the oncoming attack. The dog's nails are tearing across the surface of the wooden planks as it descends on me, and I can only hope that it falls through a rotten patch of the bridge too. *Whoosh!* I feel a sudden rush of wind blow behind me. There is the soft sound of a thud, then the dog lets out a high-pitched yelp. Frozen in fear, I can't move and can only hear the sound of the creek gently rolling downstream from beneath me, the sounds of birds chattering up in the trees overhead, and a little rustling of the brush from the gentle breeze blowing throughout the woods; but not one sound of the dog can be heard.

"Renee, are you okay?" I hear a strange voice ask me. "Let me help you up because we need to get off this bridge," it tells me sternly. Still frozen in fear, I can't move or make a sound. "The dog is gone, and you have nothing more to worry about. Let me help you out of that hole because we must be moving on."

Looking up, I see a boy standing next to me, and he is holding his hand out for me to grab onto. Shaking violently, I can barely raise up my arm. "Here, let me help you," he says softly, staring at me. The boy reaches down, puts his arm around my waist, and then begins to pick me up. Strangely enough, he doesn't seem to have any trouble pulling me up at all. I'm not a big person by any means, but I know I'm not light as a feather either!

Lifting my body carefully upward, my leg is pulled free from the rotten hole in the plank. It is burning terribly, and blood is streaming down it from all the scratches. Plus my left leg is numb and tingling from sitting on top of it the entire time. He holds me up against him while I try to put my weight down on my sleeping leg. Then breaking free from the shock, I begin to freak out and scan the area frantically, searching for any sign of the dog.

I scream out in fear, "Where is it! Where did it go!"

Then in the same stern voice, the boy barks at me, "It is gone, Renee! There is nothing more to worry about! Let us go because we do not want to fall through anywhere else!"

My leg is still a little tingly and numb, so he holds onto me tightly then walks me off the bridge. Getting to the spot where my fishing tackle is still lying on the ground, I slowly take a seat on the gravel.

Sitting on the ground, trembling violently, I look up at him. "Thank you for helping me," I manage to spit out. "That dog was about to take a bite out of me!"

Kneeling beside me, the boy tells me, "You must be getting home to clean up that wound!" He points at the blood and dirt all over my leg.

He has a strange accent that I've heard before but can't place it. His hair is jet-black and is a little past his shoulders. His eyes are the most beautiful color of green that I've ever seen, and they seem to sparkle in a magical way when the light hits them at different angles. He is tall and sort of husky, with a really sweet smile.

"What happened to the dog?" I ask, not being able to take my eyes from his.

"I heard your screams while I was walking down Rutz Road and saw the dog getting ready to attack you. I ran past you with a big rock then threw it at the dog before it could get ahold of you. It let out a yelp when the rock struck it then ran off into the woods," he replies.

I think to myself, *There's no way he ran right past me!* I blurt my thoughts out loud. "There's no way you ran right past me!" I gripe, staring him down.

Standing up, he stoops over me, swearing that that was what had happened. Not really feeling like arguing with him, I begin to stand up, so he grabs my arm then helps me to my feet. Even though my leg is still throbbing and stinging something awful, I begin to ask him some more questions, trying to figure him out because, for one, he knows my name and I've never seen him before in my life!

"Where are you from? You have a strange accent, and how do you know my name? I've never met you before in my life!" I begin, drilling him with questions.

"I am from Romania," he replies happily.

Shocked and confused by his answer, I say, "Romania? What on earth are you doing here!"

"My family and I are here in America, visiting friends. My name is Ezekeial Michael Dragkarr, and I am thirteen years old," he answers, smiling. Then after picking up my fishing gear, he begins to lead me down the road back toward home.

"My name is Renee Marie Cox, and I've just turned ten years old two days ago!" I inform him happily.

"This I know," he replies, looking at me with those intense big green eyes of his and smiling at me. "I know everything about you."

Not knowing what else to say and a little weirded out by his comment, I don't say another word or ask him another question because I just want to get back to the trailer!

Ezekeial walks me all the way home. "How does your leg feel?" he asks me when we get closer to the trailer.

"It's pretty sore, and it burns quite a bit," I reply, gazing down at my bruised and tattered leg. I'm limping a little. But I'm always able to take a great deal of pain, so it is easy to manage.

Ezekeial places my fishing gear inside the garage where I always store it then rejoins me.

"I can't thank you enough for helping me out. Do you want to come in and hang out for a while? You can meet my mama," I suggest, dying to drill this boy with more questions.

"I must be getting back before my own mother begins to wonder where I have been, but thank you for the invitation. Would you like to meet me at the creek tomorrow afternoon, and we can hang out for a little while? You can teach me how to fish!" he suggests, looking at me with a hopeful expression.

"That sounds like a lot of fun!" I cry out excitedly. That is right up my alley because I love to fish! *Someone to hang out with besides my sister. Awesome!*

"Okay, I will see you tomorrow, sleep well," he tells me, smiling, then makes his way back down the road.

Tomorrow, I plan on drilling him with a lot more questions because I want to know how he knows me and where he is staying at!

"What on earth happened to you!" My mama asks me in horror as soon as she sees my leg. "We need to clean this up ASAP!"

Reese is standing next to my mama with the look of pure shock and terror plastered across her face. "Does it hurt, Renee?" she asks me softly, staring at my wounds.

"Yeah, but it's nothing I can't handle!" I reply happily then smile at her, and she smiles back at me.

"Go take a shower and clean that out really good! We'll take a closer look at it after you get finished, and then, while I doctor it up, you can explain to us what exactly happened!"

I nod to my mama, doing what she says, then make my way to the bathroom. The cuts and gashes burn like fire as soon as the water and soap make contact, sending a searing bolt of pain throughout my leg. I clean out the wounds the best that I can. Then after drying myself off, I take a closer look at my leg, and it is not as bad as it had looked before I had cleaned it up.

"Well, luckily, you've already had a tetanus shot! We'll have to keep a close eye on it to make sure that you don't get any blood poisoning, so if you notice any streaking red lines going along the length of your leg, you let me know right away!" she orders me while rubbing iodine all over my wounds, sending another round of terrible pain shooting along my leg. Mama uses that stuff for everything, and it burns like crazy! I think she should've been a nurse because she always seems to know just what to do in a medical situation.

My mama and Reese are standing in the bathroom with me when Mama asks me, "So what happened anyway?"

I begin to tell her all about the dog falling through the bridge then about the Romanian boy who saved me, and they're both staring me down with great intensity.

"Who did you say they were visiting here in the States?" my mama questions me.

"I'm not sure! He never did say!" I answer while recapping my conversation with Ezekeial.

"Well, it was a good thing he was in the right place at the right time! If that dog would've gotten ahold of you, we wouldn't have even known about it until you didn't make it home tonight! It may have killed you!" she cries out unhappily, looking and sounding horrified. "Make sure that you always let me know where you plan on going when you take off outside because you know as well as I do people are always dumping off their unwanted animals around here!" she barks angrily.

"I will, Mama!" I say, nodding, then tell her that I'm going to go down to the creek tomorrow to teach Ezekeial how to fish.

"Well, okay, but you be extremely careful and bring this boy to the house so that we can meet him!" she orders me while shaking her finger at me.

"I'll see what I can do!" I tell her happily.

The three of us end up lounging out around the house for the rest of the day, watching movies, and before I realize it, it is already dark. I turn my gaze toward the clock, curious to know what time it is, and see that it is already 9:42 p.m. *Jeez, where has the time gone?*

After our last movie ends and all of us go to bed, I can't seem to get Ezekeial out of my head because I keep going over and over the day's events in my mind, and I know for certain that he didn't run past me to get to that dog because I never heard any footsteps of any kind at any time! Not to mention, how did he even know anything about me, because we've only lived here a little over a year and he is not even from this continent! Exhausted, I fall asleep with my mind still racing out of control and dream wild and crazy dreams.

*****

"Yuck, these worms are disgusting!" Ezekeial gripes while baiting his hook.

"Well, if you're going to fish, you have to bait your own hook!" I inform him with a big smile and can't keep from giggling a bit because you would think that, with him being a boy, this would be a cool thing to do! "So you haven't ever fished before?" I begin to question him slyly.

"No, back home, we do not really do anything like this. My parents are very busy all the time, and usually my younger brother Sebastian and I do a lot of studying and reading. We do not really get out much," he replies.

"What do your parents do? Don't you go to school?" I continue to question him.

"We have a tutor that comes to our house five days of the week. My parents run a company and travel a lot for business, so Sebastian and I stay at home with our keeper while they are gone."

"Your keeper?" I ask, confused by his choice of words.

"Yes, I guess, here in your country, it is like your babysitter or guardian," he explains.

"I hate the babysitter!" I cry out angrily, having flashbacks of my time spent at the babysitters' houses.

"Well, our keeper has been with us for as long as I can remember. She and her son live in our house, and he and I play together all of the time. We go horseback riding and play out in the woods around my home sometimes. His name is Lazar, and he is the same age as you are."

"Ezekeial, would you mind if I call you Z for short?"

He tries to cast out the line into the water, but the entire pole ends up lying on the ground. "I do not think that I am ever going to get this right!" he mutters in aggravation then turns and looks at me with a huge smile. "No one has ever called me that before, but I like it! You can call me Z for short. I do not mind it one bit!"

"Here, let me show you how to cast this out again. You'll learn how to do it sooner or later. It just takes practice!" I assure him.

He is grinning from ear to ear. "Thank you, Ms. Renee. I am enjoying this lesson very much!"

"I'm glad that you are, but I'd like to ask you how it is that you know me." I ask him before he begins to cast out his line once again.

Giving me a serious eye, he says, "Let us just say that, in a way, I am your keeper! Someone to watch over you and to keep you safe!"

Not really getting the answer that I want, I ask him again, "You really didn't say how you know me. Where have we met before?"

His green eyes lock onto mine. "I have known you for almost as long as I have known my own life. You are something special, and you are my charge until time ends."

Wow! Am I really ever confused right now! What in the world is he even talking about? I think he is one brick shy of a full load! "How am I someone special? I'm just your average, ordinary, every-day ten-year-old!" I cry out in pure frustration, looking to him for more answers.

"You are going to become something amazing when you become of age. Something most people will never know even exists. A great figure in the time to come!"

Ezekeial's pole begins to bend down when something hooks onto his line. "I have gotten a fish!" he screams out in wild excitement.

"Reel in the line!" I yell at him, getting aggravated and frustrated with him.

He slowly reels in the line, not sure what to do. Then after pulling it up, I see a good-sized sunfish dangling off the end of it.

"Bring it out of the water so that we can get it off the hook!" I order him while the fish thrashes about frantically.

"It is huge!" he screams out loudly, ecstatically.

I grab the fish once he pulls it away from the water, trying not to bust up laughing from his overjoyed craziness. "Okay, you're going to have to take it off the hook yourself. You caught it, so you have to remove it," I bark.

He looks at me with a worried face, so I explain to him how to remove the fish from the hook. And he is able to do it without getting his hand poked by the fish's fins or jabbing the hook into his finger. "This is the most fun that I can ever remember having! Thank you so much!" he screams out joyfully, and he is so excited about it that he drops the fishing pole right into the water. "Oh, no! I am so sorry!" Z cries out unhappily while reaching down to fetch it.

"It's okay, Z. The pole will be just fine!" I assure him.

He is beaming with happiness then looks deep into my eyes. "Your eyes are very beautiful." Then looking up at the sky, he says, "It is getting late. I must be going! This has been so much fun! Can we do it again?"

"Sure, I've had a lot of fun too!" I reply, smiling.

For the next couple of weeks, Z and I hang out down at the creek and go exploring out in the woods. Enjoying his company, I look forward to it every day.

CHAPTER 3

Ezekeial

"Where have you been? You have been gone all day for the past couple of weeks!" questions Ezekeial's mother when he enters the front door of the small cabin that he and his mother have been staying in for the past month, speaking in his native tongue, Romanian.

"I am keeping an eye on Renee just like I have been doing every day. Is this not what I am supposed to be doing?" he asks his mother, getting nervous.

"You do remember that you are only supposed to observe her and not to interact with her in any way?" his mother questions him with her dark eyes fixated on him. "We need to know if she is the one that we are looking for, so have you even noticed any signs yet?"

"No, Mother, I have not seen any signs, but I am pretty sure that she is the one."

"And just what makes you think that she is the one? How do you know?" she asks him angrily.

"I just have this feeling about her. That is all," he replies, looking away from her when he says this, knowing that he has broken the rules.

"You have been interacting with her, have you not? I want the truth, Ezekeial!" She is almost screaming at him by this point. "It is not allowed at all!" She loses it and screams loudly, furious with him.

"Mother, I had to save her the other week from being attacked by a stray dog. Plus she fell through the bridge!" He tries to explain to his mother.

"This is unacceptable! If Aiden finds out, the both of us will be punished, and if you have not seen anything yet, then it is time for us to go home to begin the search once again!"

"But, Mother, I am so sorry! She is a lot of fun, and she has taught me how to fish!" Ezekeial pleads with her.

"So you have been doing all kinds of things with her! Oh, no! We cannot be having this at all! We are leaving here tomorrow!" His mother screams at him, almost livid.

He knows that he is only supposed to watch Renee, but how could he just sit back and watch her be mauled or killed by the dog? Why is it such a big deal if he wants to hang out with her anyway? It is so lonely, with it just being he and his mother.

"Whatever you do, do not speak a word to Aiden about any of this! If he asks you anything, you just tell him that you did not see anything! I mean it! Who knows what he may do if he finds out you were interacting with her!" his mother cries out hatefully, spitting while she says this. "You can never see her again, and you must stay right here until we leave! I am going to call the airline to get us the earliest flight home!"

The thought of going back home causes Ezekeial's heart to sink because he enjoys being here and being with Renee.

"We will give her a few more years, and then we will come back once more to see if there have been any changes unless we find the right one before this time," his mother explains to him while looking up the number for the airline.

Ezekeial can't stop thinking about leaving because he is supposed to meet Renee down at the creek tomorrow. They're supposed to walk all the way to the back of the cornfield to explore the valley behind it, and he wonders what she will think when he doesn't show up. Tossing and turning late into the night, he finally falls asleep.

CHAPTER 4

New Changes

"Ezekeial!" I call out loudly, making my way down to the creek bank. "Z, where are you?" I don't see him anywhere, and he isn't answering me. Pacing around the creek, I begin to wonder if maybe I've made him angry about something, but I don't remember anything bad being said. He is supposed to meet me here today, and we're going to go exploring behind the cornfield. He seemed pretty excited about going on this adventure yesterday, so I'm at a loss from his absence.

Calling out his name once again, I still don't get an answer. The birds are chirping and chattering up in the trees along with a squirrel barking, and the water in the creek is rushing past me. But I don't hear any footsteps coming toward me. School is going to be starting tomorrow, and I have to be home earlier tonight. Plus it is already 11:17 a.m., so we're running out of time! I wait around for another forty-five minutes, but still no Z. And I'm pretty sure that, by now, he isn't coming. He hasn't been late, not even once, since we've been hanging out, and I have this strange feeling that he is gone. Saddened by the thought of never seeing him again, I slowly make my way back home. I wasn't expecting him to leave like this, not even to tell me goodbye. I keep wondering if it was something that I had said or done, but I just can't think of anything that would've been an issue. I don't want him to leave because I really enjoy spending time with him, and he never even went up to the trailer to meet my family. I hope nothing bad has happened to him because he never even told me where he was staying so that I can go check on him!

"Well, we got the loan on the house, and we're going to start cleaning up the apartment just as soon as we close!" my mama announces excitedly when I walk in the front door.

"Why are you looking so gloomy?" she asks me.

So I tell her about how I was supposed to meet Z down at the creek, but he never showed up.

"Maybe they had an emergency and had to go back home unexpectedly! I never did get to meet this boy, but hopefully it's nothing terrible. And who knows, maybe he'll be back," my mama tells me, trying to make me feel better.

"Maybe, but I just feel like he won't be coming back," I reply unhappily.

Disappointed, I go to my room then grab one of my books. Sitting here, I just can't stop thinking about Z and about all the crazy stuff he said to me. He never made any sense, and he always seemed to dance around his answers when I would ask him certain things, not really explaining what he was talking about. Still, I loved his company and can't believe that I may never know what has happened to him. Maybe tomorrow he'll be down there, waiting for me after school!

*****

The buzzer goes off once we make our way to our desks, and the very first day of the fifth grade is about to start! I have the same teacher whom I had last year because he switched grades. It is okay though because I like him well enough, and he is always easy to understand. I still can't get the thought of Z standing me up yesterday out of my head, and I wonder if he is on his way back home or if he may be waiting for me down at the creek.

My day goes by in a whirl, and before I know it, it is time to get on the bus. The bus ride home is agonizing because I'm dying to get down to the creek! Flying off the bus, I race down the road to get to the creek, and I don't even stop to tell my mama where I'm going. Out of breath when I reach the path, I slow down. My heart is pounding, not only from running so fast but also in anticipation.

But to my utter disappointment, Ezekeial is nowhere in sight! There is nothing but the usual. Upset about it, I plop down on the sandy bank by the water and just sit here, listening, hoping to hear the sounds of his footsteps coming my way. But as the time passes by, there is still nothing, just the familiar sounds of the busy woods, as always. So I force myself to my feet, with my eyes welling up with tears, then walk home.

"We're closing on the house in a couple of weeks," my mama informs me after I get inside the house. "Still no sign of your friend?" she asks.

"Nope, I just wish I knew what happened!" I answer in frustration then begin to tear up. "He could have at least told me that he was going to leave!"

"It'll be okay, Renee. You'll make more friends!" she assures me. "People will come and go throughout your entire life. It's just a part of it!"

I really don't care what she has to say because I'm still pretty upset about it right now!

Reese is sitting at the kitchen table, eating her supper. "Come eat some dinner with me!" she tells me, smiling. "Maybe we can play a game together later!"

I really don't feel like eating, but I get my plate then sit down at the kitchen table with her. "What game do you want to play?" I ask her.

"How about Uno?" she questions me.

"Okay, that sounds like fun!" I reply happily because I love to play Uno. It is one of my favorite games!

I eat a little bit of my food then go get the game out, and she and I play it until it is time for bed.

"Are you feeling any better, Renee?" she asks me once we get into bed.

"A little," I reply as Z pops back into my mind.

We have a bunk bed in our room, and I sleep on the top bunk. I hate having to get up in the middle of the night to go to the bathroom because it is a big pain getting up and down the ladder plus trying to be quiet so that I don't wake up Reese.

*****

A few weeks have gone by, and we've moved into the apartment next to the old white house. It is not too awfully bad because Reese and I have twin beds now, so I don't have to crawl up and down a ladder in the middle of the night to go to the bathroom anymore. Plus the apartment is a little more spacious than the trailer too. Kent's trailer has already been moved out. And they've just sold our old trailer, but it is still up there, waiting to be moved. We've been busy cleaning up the white house, trying to get it fixed up. Reese and I have already picked out our bedrooms, so I can't wait to get moved in! I think it is going to be awhile though because there is still a lot of work yet to be done. Ripping the wallpaper off the walls has been really challenging because, over the years, people have just glued wallpaper after wallpaper right over the top of the other instead of removing the old first. Every time one layer is peeled away, there is more underneath it. The floor has to be replaced in the living room as well, and it is going to take a lot of work to replace it. Kent is doing all the work himself, and he doesn't get much time to get anything done with having to work so much. Mama, Reese, and I do whatever we can to help out, but when it comes to the big power tools, such as the table saw, it is a no-go.

It is a couple of weeks before Christmas, and we still don't have a tree yet. "Mama, I'm going to go out in the woods to cut a tree down for us," I inform her while putting on my boots, but she doesn't say anything and just nods.

I grab a handsaw from the inside of the house then make my way across the cornfield down into the woods. I spot a small cedar tree standing just inside the wood line and decide that it is the one that I'm going to cut down. While standing next to it, my mind drifts back to the summer, and I think about Z. I wonder how he is and what it is like at his home now. Do they celebrate Christmas? We have snow on the ground, and it is pretty cold. I'm not sure what kind of weather Romania has, but I'm sure that it is probably cold there too. I cut the tree down then drag it back home, still thinking about Z.

"Well, that's a nice-looking tree!" my mama says happily while I drag it into the apartment. "We'll put it here right in front of the window. I'll grab the decorations, and you two girls can start working on it!"

Of course, she'll get the lights out and hand them to me because I always get stuck straightening out the strands of lights then replacing the bad bulbs. So when she walks into the living room and hands me the tub of lights, I laugh to myself, already knowing that I would be in charge of the light duty. Once we finish, the tree looks great, so having to go through the endless strands of lights wasn't so bad after all! I love the different sparkling and twinkling colors of the Christmas lights and the wonderful feeling that I get from the spirit of the holiday!

Christmas and the New Year fly by, and the house is coming around slowly because not much has been getting done lately. Kent has been putting in a lot of overtime and hasn't been home enough to work on anything. Spring has arrived, and everything that was ugly and brown throughout fall and winter is beginning to come to life. I absolutely love this season because everything is fresh and new. The grass is the most beautiful color of green, and the wild jonquils are blooming everywhere around the property and across the driveway. There is a fabulous color explosion of yellow bursting everywhere I look!

School will be getting out soon, and I can't wait for summer vacation. It is hard to believe how fast the time has gone by! Kent says that we should be able to move into the house by falltime this year, and I sure hope so! I have the stuff picked out for my room already, and he is building me a nice-sized closet for my clothes. Our neighbor is building the cabinets from scratch for the house, and the floor is done in the living room. The bathroom is finished downstairs, but Kent hasn't started on the one upstairs yet. He says that he isn't going to start on it until we get moved in. That is a huge bummer because the stairs leading up to the second floor are really squeaky and have a pretty steep incline, so I'm dreading getting up in the middle of the night and tackling that obstacle. I'm sure falling down them once or twice won't come as a big surprise!

"Kent and I are going to get married this year," my mama begins to tell Reese and me. "We're planning on doing it in October, out at Lost Valley Lake."

I don't really know what to say because it doesn't come as much of a surprise. "Well, that sounds like a lot of fun," I tell her.

Lost Valley Lake is a resort about forty-five minutes from our house. Kent's brother has a membership there, and we've gone out there a few times. There is a huge lodge with an indoor swimming pool, along with a game room located inside it. The lake is pretty big, and I have fished in it before. Plus it has a small island out in the middle of it. They have paddleboats down at the boating dock that you can rent for the entire day, and they're a lot of fun!

"We plan on trying to have a baby after we get married," she adds, and Reese and I lock eyes after she says this. She looks just as surprised as I feel, and I'm sure, to her, I look the same way. Neither of us say anything, so my mama looks at us and says, "What do you girls think?"

"I hope I get a little brother!" Reese tells my mama excitedly.

But I just stand here without saying a word, drawing up a mental picture in my mind what it'll be like with having another sibling in my life because I think everything is just fine the way it is! Why do they want or need to add another kid into the mix? So without thinking, I say, "Why do you want to have another baby?"

"Kent hasn't had any children of his own and would really like to have one," she answers, smiling.

"Oh, I see," I say, still not happy with the idea of having another kid in the house. So that is about all I can give to her as far as my opinion on the matter.

"You'll love it just the same," she tells me, smiling. Thinking to myself, I agree with Reese and hope it is a boy instead of another sister.

October comes, and our house is finished enough for us to move in. It is just in time before Mama and Kent's wedding. It is great having my own room, except I hear a lot of strange noises at night. Whispering and footsteps echo throughout the darkness, and it sounds like someone is walking up and down the stairs at all hours of the night. I can hear the boards creaking under someone's weight even though no one is there. I get a sense of being watched from my bedroom closet, and never ever do I leave the doors open while I'm in my room or after I go to bed. I can feel a presence all around me inside the house, and it is really unnerving. Sometimes when I'm watching a movie on my little TV in my room, the VCR will stop, rewind, play, stop again, and then shut off all by itself! One time, when I was playing Mario Bros. on my Nintendo and had gotten all the way to the end of the game to where you defeat the monster, King Koopa, and save the princess, my Nintendo just turned off all by itself! I was right in the middle of taking King Koopa out! Oh my gosh! I was so mad! It is really annoying, and sometimes I yell at whatever it is to stop and leave me alone! I've also heard my name get called out on several occasions, but there was not ever anyone there. I've told my mama about it, and she tells me that I'm just hearing things, that I'm scaring myself, that the house is old, and that it is just the sound of it creaking and settling on the foundation. But no matter what she says, I know that I'm not crazy because these things are really happening! Reese hasn't said anything about any noises nor about seeing anything either and doesn't seem to think there is anything there, so they all look at me like I'm crazy! Sometimes I can't sleep at night because I get so freaked out, so I crawl in bed with Reese. Yeah, I'm a big scaredy-cat. But there is something roaming around the house all the time, and it wants me to know it. It likes to aggravate me constantly. But no one in the house will listen to me, so I just have to deal with it all by myself. The presence doesn't really seem threatening in any way, but I still get creeped out from it. And I feel like there are more than just one of them too! Yikes!

Mama and Kent's wedding is today, and some of us get to ride the paddleboats over to the island located in the middle of the lake where they're going to exchange their vows. It is awesome! The weather is absolutely wonderful, and my mama looks really amazing and totally happy! After they exchange their vows, we go back to the lodge for the reception. Reese and I get some money, go down to the game room for a while, put on our swimming suits, and hang out at the pool. There is also a hot tub next to the pool, and I love just sitting in it and relaxing.

It is late before we get home, but we've all had a really great and an extremely long day. I'm way too tired to deal with the ghosts in the house and go to sleep in my own room for a change. I've slept with Reese almost every night since we've moved in, and I've tried leaving my radio on that sits next to me on my nightstand because it has a small light on it that is pretty bright and gives me a great sense of comfort. Plus, the music drowns out the constant nightly commotion, but my mama comes up to my room every night and shuts it off. She claims that I'm playing my radio too loud and that she can hear it in her room downstairs and can't sleep. Sometimes I turn it back on, but a little while later, as always, she'll come back up here and shut it off again! Her room is right under mine, but I don't think that I have it on too loud because I can barely hear it myself even though the radio is sitting right next to me! I think she just can't stand knowing that it is on. She also told me that I can't have my table lamp on either because it runs up the electric bill. Whatever! That is a crock of crap if you ask me! She is starting to gripe and complain about everything that I do these days, and I can't stand it!

Several months have passed by, and Mama announces that she is pregnant with a baby girl and that she is going to be born some-time in January. It is 1988 now, and our lives are about to change yet again with this newest addition. I'm not too thrilled about any of it! Mama is constantly nagging at me and never happy with anything that I do. I can't seem to do anything right! I'll be turning twelve this year, and all she seems to be worried about is, when I turn fifteen and a half, I'll have to go get my driver's permit. Then as soon as I turn sixteen, I'll have to go get my license and then a job! She informs me that I'll have to buy my own gas and pay for my own car insurance once I start working too! She tells me that if I want to go to college, I'll have to earn a scholarship to help pay for it because they won't be helping me out with any of the expenses, so I'll have to pay for all of it myself! Jeez, I'm not even twelve yet, and she is preaching to me about driving, getting a job, and going to college! I can't just be a kid because it is like she is in a hurry to get rid of me! What have I done so wrong for her to be so angry with me all the time? I don't really get into any trouble! I only go to school and do my homework. My grades are pretty good, and I do whatever I'm told. I'm starting to get very angry and resentful with her because she is becoming a real jerk, and I don't like it! I never hear her gripe at Reese hardly at all! It is always me she is after!

My little sister, Charlene Nicole Stevens, is born on January 30, 1989, and my mama and Kent are ecstatic. My mama says that she isn't planning on having any more kids and that Kent doesn't seem to mind. He has one kid now, and that makes him happy enough. I know that things are really going to start changing for the worse because they have their new child, and now I'm just sitting on the sideline, waiting to be my mama's punching bag every time she is angry or upset about something. She is not abusive physically, but the constant complaining and griping is taking its toll on me. When Charlene first came home, things weren't too bad because my mama had enough to keep her busy with the new baby, but she has been getting mad at Kent too because he is still working all the time and hasn't been spending any time with her and the baby. I can understand her point on the matter, but when Kent isn't working at Chrysler, he is working on all the unfinished stuff here at the house and doesn't seem to get much of a break! He has started putting in mine and Reese's bathroom upstairs, and I can't wait for it to get done! It'll be so nice not having to go downstairs to use the bathroom during the middle of the night because Reese and I both have fallen down the stairs numerous times while walking down them in the dark, and one night, there was a freakin' copperhead under the kitchen table!

CHAPTER 5

Coming of Age

It is summertime again! I've just turned thirteen, and I'm getting ready to head down to Grandma and Grandpa Wodicker's house for two weeks before school starts once again. Shortly after we moved out to Oak Hill, they sold their trailer at the trailer park and have moved to a town in Arkansas called Fairfield Bay. It is a resort community of older retired people. Down the road from my grandparents' house is Greers Ferry Lake, and Sugar Loaf Mountain is located right inside the middle of it. Every summer since they've moved there, after we spend two weeks with our papa, Reese or I will stay with one of our cousins at their house. Grandpa has bought a boat, and sometimes he takes us out fishing at the lake. There are also a few swimming pools located around the resort, and we'll walk to one of them every day to spend the entire day swimming. Grandpa likes to bowl, so on certain evenings, we'll all get into the car then make our way over to the bowling alley located inside the resort. I love to bowl myself, and we always have a blast.

It is late. I'm getting ready to go to bed, so I head into the bathroom, wanting to take care of business before I hit the sheets. I'm quite stunned when I pull down my panties. *Oh, no!* I cry out loud in disbelief, along with panicking, because there is blood lining my panties, and I know exactly what is happening. I call out to my mama, "Mama, can you please come in here?"

"What's wrong?" she asks me after she walks through the door, and I'm holding my panties in my hand. She looks down at them and spies my issue right off the bat. "Oh, that's just great!" she gripes unhappily while she stares at them. "You're supposed to be leaving tomorrow morning to go to Mom and Dad's house! Well, you're still going to go because it's already been arranged, and it's too late to call them now!" she tells me coldly.

"I don't really want to go now because I won't be able to swim, and we go swimming every day! What am I going to do?" I plead with her.

"You'll figure it out. It'll be just fine!" she barks in a sharp tongue, and I'm completely mortified and upset because this is going to be a terrible two weeks!

Meeting my grandparents at the drop-off, my mama begins explaining to them about my situation. They keep looking over at me, and I'm feeling so awkward and completely humiliated! I'm so embarrassed!

Getting into the car, Grandma says to me, "Well, you've become of age now, and you'll be just fine." I grin when she gives me one of her winks, even though I'm anything but happy about this whole horrific ordeal.

We make our way to their house, and it becomes the longest two weeks that I've ever spent with them. Something came up, and my cousin Mindy wasn't going to be staying with me this year either. Plus Grandma still wanted to go to the pool every day, and I just sat on the side, with my legs in the water, or in a lounge chair the entire time. It wasn't a very pleasurable experience at all. I was miserable. Then to make matters even worse, a little girl asked me at the pool one day why I wasn't getting in, and I didn't know what on earth to say. So I made up some lame excuse, and I can just about imagine the look on my face when she asked me that.

This year, I'm noticing some strange changes about myself other than the women's curse that has just begun. I get strange sensations and weird cravings, sometimes wanting to eat everything in sight. I've gained some weight and don't feel very comfortable in my own skin at all. I'm starting to get a little acne also, and it makes me feel so self-conscious. My body is filling out in certain spots, and Reese makes fun of how big my boobs are. Plus this last year of junior high has been brutal! Some of the Preppies, the popular kids, aggravate me all-day long by calling me names and giving me hateful looks. I'm not an ugly person. And I may be a little bit heavy right now, but I'm not obese by any means. I wear decent clothes plus fix my hair every morning, and I'm not from a poor family, even though that doesn't make any difference because it shouldn't matter where you come from or who you are! I've been told my entire life about how my eyes and smile are so beautiful and that I'm going to be a beautiful woman someday, but when I stare at myself in the mirror, I just don't see it! People don't realize or even care about how much they can hurt a person's self-esteem by their constant bullying. I hate going to school, and next year, I'll be going into high school. Yikes! I can't bear the thought of all of it!

Even though, every year since I've started junior high, I've been on the B honor roll and, this year, the A honor roll, it doesn't seem to matter to my mama. The same broken record repeating over and over again about me getting my license, job, and college is played daily. I've gotten to where I can't even stand going home after school because, as soon as I get home, there is some sort of drama playing out, and the constant complaining carries on for the rest of the day. Charlene has learned how to climb up the stairs now, and every day after school, she is either in my room or has been in my room. I've found my cassette tapes ruined from her pulling out the tape, and my books with the pages torn or ripped out. I've told Mama about Charlene climbing up the stairs to mine and Reese's rooms, destroying our things while we're gone, but she doesn't seem to care. One day, while I was doodling on my sketch pad up in my room, Charlene was climbing up the stairs and fell down them, cracking her head against the front door. Mama blamed me, saying that I had shoved her down the stairs, but I had nothing to do with her falling down them!

Time is passing by so quickly! I've made it through my freshman year of high school and getting ready to start my sophomore year. Last year wasn't too bad, and my classes weren't really hard. But this year, I'm worried though because I have to take Spanish and Algebra 1 in order to earn the required credits needed to graduate. I've never been really great at math, and I'm pretty worried about it.

Plus Spanish is really confusing, and I'm not sure how well I'm going to do with it. I was on the A honor roll for most of the year last year, but I'm afraid it won't happen again this year. And my mama will be at my throat if my grades are bad. Not to mention, I've turned fifteen this past summer, and the broken record is still playing over and over again at home. I'm so dreading the day that I can go get my driver's permit because a whole new can of worms will explode!

"I can't believe you failed your written driver's test twice!" Mama yells at me on the way home. I took it once and flunked. Then they allowed me to take it once more the same day, but I had flunked it again by missing one question too many. "You should have studied your book more!" Mama continues to scold me, looking at me with angry eyes.

"I'm sorry, Mama! They reworded some of the questions, and I read the question the wrong way!" I plead with her.

"Well, we'll take you to Cuba next week so that you can take it again! So you'd better study your book!" she shouts at me loudly, and the entire ride home is agonizing because she keeps carrying on and on about how I failed my test.

I'm about to lose my mind, and once we get home, she just has to announce to everyone about me failing my test twice. Kent and Reese are just looking at the both of us, not saying a word, while we stand in the kitchen, and little Charlene is waving at me from the living room. I want to just scream at my mama and tell her to shut up and to get over it!

"You'll pass next week," Kent assures me, smiling. "I know you can do it."

"Yeah! You'll do better next time!" Reese agrees in a cheerful voice, smiling too.

"She'd better pass it!" my mama yells hatefully from behind the island in the kitchen. "You'd better get upstairs right now and start going back over that book!"

Not wanting to listen to her any longer, I go up to my room and break out my driver's book. Going over it, I can't figure out how in the world I managed to miss some of the questions because they were all so easy!

A little while later, I can hear my mama talking to Kent, and she is still griping and complaining about me flunking my test. He is getting pretty irritated with her and tells her that it is all over with and just to move on.

"Hopefully she'll pass it next week," I hear him say. I can't stand hearing about it anymore, so I just have to get out of here!

I haven't been feeling too great for the last couple of days anyway, and listening to all that just adds to the mix. So I decide to head down to the creek and take a walk to get my mind off today. Taking my time making my way down to the creek, I loaf around and enjoy the peace and quiet. It seems like a war zone at the house these days, and I'm public enemy number 1. I've thought about asking to move in with my papa, but I decide it wouldn't be any better down there either. He and Janelle had gotten married shortly after my mama and Kent's wedding, and they're way too stuck into church for my liking. I don't mind going to church, but all the preaching about hellfire and damnation turns me away because it is really scary at times! Then I begin to question my own faith, wondering if I'm sinning against God, because I'm not sure about what I actually believe in. In my opinion, there is more to religion than that. At one time, they had me so scared about going to hell that I was paranoid about everything, thinking that if I said or did something wrong, Satan would rise from the belly of hell, snatch me up, and then drag me back into the fiery pit with him. It took me awhile to get over that, and I sure don't need anything else to have to worry about right now because things are crazy enough as it is!

I embrace the calm stillness of the world around me. The inviting sights, scents, and sounds drifting through the air lure me into the vast openness of the canopy. I can hear the gentle rolling of the water from the creek as I make my way closer to its bank. The weathered old bridge was removed a few years ago, and all that is left of it are the aged concrete slabs that used to carry its mighty steel frame. The recent storms and flooding have littered the entire area of the creek bank, leaving broken, rotting tree branches with dried-up leaves strewn about, and dead brush is lying around in piles. It is a disaster down here! Most of the sand that used to be lining the bank has been washed away, and the entire area has gotten smaller. Suddenly, I hear the snapping of a downed branch somewhere a short distance away from me. Listening, I strain my ears to find the source of the noise when, suddenly, a strange sickening feeling overcomes me. My heart begins to pound, my chest is tightening up, and I can't seem to breathe. An unsettling sensation of something writhing and pulsating underneath my skin causes me to start clawing at myself. My stomach doubles over in pain, and a wave of nausea hits me like a ton of bricks. I feel like my blood is on fire, scorching my veins, while it travels throughout my body, and I'm sweating profusely. Staggering my way over to the concrete slab, I lean up against it on my back then slowly slide down to the ground, and the contact of the cool stone against my back soothes me for an instant. I drop my arms down to my sides and dig at the sandy ground with my hands while the pain becomes almost unbearable. I'm moaning in agony, and I'm totally glued to this spot while the sounds surrounding me intensify and my head starts spinning. Panic and sheer terror set in while I try to endure this awful hell because I don't have any idea what this is I'm experiencing! Will someone find me if I don't make it back home?

Salty sweat is running down along my forehead then into my eyes, causing them to burn horribly, and I'm drenched from head to toe in my own sweat. Then just as quickly as this entire horrific ordeal has begun, I realize that the pain is beginning to subside, my heart rate is beginning to slow down, and my breathing is returning to normal. Leaning over to my left side, I vomit. Then afraid to move, fearing the hellish pain will return, I decide to sit here for a while. Shaking violently all over, I grab my legs then wrap my arms around them in an effort to stop the trembling and to recover from this terrifying experience. *What's happening to me!* I scream out inside my head in silence. Wanting to cry but choking back the tears, I carefully get up from my sitting position and stand up, brushing myself off as I rise. The horrific experience, I believe, is over, and standing on wobbly legs, I slowly make my way back home. *Snap! Crack!* I can hear something stirring out in the woods, trekking across the fallen limbs and brush that litter the ground. Surveying the area around me, I see nothing. *Did someone see me?* I wonder while I walk up the trail leading toward the road. If someone did, they didn't rush to my aid or offer me any help; that is for sure! I'm hoping that, once I get back home, no one wants to bother me because I just want to take a hot shower and go to bed. Luckily, once I walk into the house, no one is around, so I quickly make my way upstairs, not speaking a word to anyone about the nightmarish hell that I've just endured.

CHAPTER 6

Punishment

Ezekeial is trying to be extremely quiet while he follows Renee through the woods. He had been eavesdropping in on the conversation that was being discussed about the driver's test earlier, and sensing that she was upset when she walked out of the house and descended onto the road, he wished he could offer her some comfort. Knowing that contact is forbidden, he reluctantly stays silent. His heart flutters when she approaches his way a little closer, and while he observes the new changes in her appearance, he can hardly recognize her! She was only ten years old then, and now she is fifteen.

Renee has grown a lot taller, and she is filling out quite nicely in certain places. Her dark hair seems to be a lighter color brown than it was before, and it is hanging down to the middle of her back. He has turned eighteen and has been sent yet once again to observe her. It has only been two days since Ezekeial has returned, but Renee has stayed up inside her room for the most part and hasn't been outside. The thick dark curtains hanging in her window block any kind of view, so last night, he climbed the tree next to her bedroom window, trying to get a good glimpse of her but couldn't make out anything. Thinking of the day he was forced to leave her years ago rips his heart into pieces because he hadn't even gotten to tell her goodbye.

Trying as silently and as stealthily as he can to stay out of sight, Ezekeial accidentally steps on some broken branches that are lying on the ground. The sound explodes throughout the stillness of the woods, and he watches Renee stop, trying to pinpoint from where it had come from while she stands motionless at the water's edge.

Sensing something is awry, he watches her intently. A look of pure terror and pain flies across her face, and he can smell her fear. Ezekeial can tell that she is panicking because her heart rate increases and her breathing has become labored. Her face twists up into an expression of severe distress and agony, and he watches in horror while she stumbles over by the concrete slab then sits down on the ground. She is absolutely petrified! This is the sign that he has been waiting for, and he knows right away that she is the one he and his mother have been sent to find!

Ezekeial begins to make his way over to her and then stops abruptly. He is dying to offer her some comfort but remembers what had happened to him the last time he had interfered, and it pains his heart while he watches her convulse and dig her hands into the ground, reeling from the intense pain. He looks away for a second because he can't stand being able to only just stand here and watch. Renee throws up beside herself and sits motionless, not moving at all, and he watches her intensely, waiting for her to show any signs of life. Slowly Renee begins to rise up off the ground, and appearing terribly shaky and unsteady, she begins to wander away toward the path. Repositioning himself so that he can follow her, he steps right on some more fallen branches littering the ground. The sound of it snapping under his feet penetrates throughout the silence of the woods for the second time, and Renee stops dead in her tracks then scans the surrounding area, straining her ears to pick up the slightest sound. After waiting for a few seconds, she slowly begins to make her way back to her house, and he pursues in toe, wanting to make sure that she arrives safely.

*****

Returning home from their trip to America the first time he had made contact with Renee, Ezekeial's stepfather, Aiden, is anxious to know the details from his weeks of observations.

"I did not see any changes in her at all, sir. Nothing has happened," Ezekeial explains. But before he can say anything else, his mother begins spilling out all the details Ezekeial had told her about interacting with Renee to Aiden. He knows he is going to be in trouble now because the anger is written all over Aiden's face. He broke the rules, and now he will be punished.

Aiden is a cruel and hateful man, and since Ezekeial is only his stepson, he treats him differently from his little brother, who is of his own blood. His mother was pregnant with him before they had gotten together because his real father was killed before he was even born, so Aiden makes sure that everyone knows Ezekeial isn't his son.

After she tells him about their trip, he is furious. "You know that you are not supposed to interact with the girl! You should have let that dog take her down because, if she was the right one, then she would not have needed your help!" he scolds him angrily, screaming in rage. "You will be punished for disobeying my orders!"

Aiden knocks Ezekeial down with a blow from his fist while his mother watches helplessly in complete horror. Dragging him by the hair out into the backyard, Aiden throws him down in front of a big tree. There is a rope lying down on the ground beside it, and Ezekeial knows exactly what it is for.

"Put your arms around the tree, boy!" Aiden demands him. So he wraps his arms around the tree like he is told to do, knowing what is about to happen, and hugs it tightly. His eyes fill up with tears, and he trembles with fear while Aiden ties his arms to the tree then walks back inside the house.

Emerging from the inside, Aiden is carrying a leather whip in his hand. "I will teach you not to disobey me one way or the other!" he cries out loud while beginning to whip Ezekeial across the back.

Screaming in pain, Ezekeial begs him to stop. Blood is running out of the gapping wounds, and the terrible pain is excruciating.

"Please stop!" begs his mother. "He is just a boy, Aiden!"

"I do not care! He is going to learn to obey me! Stay out of this and go back inside!" he screams at her hatefully, pointing toward the house.

After about five lashes of the whip, Aiden stops then removes the rope from Ezekeial's wrists. "Remember what will happen to you the next time you disobey me, boy!" he barks, spitting in his face while he talks to him.

Relieved when Aiden begins walking back toward the house and reeling from the unbearable pain, Ezekeial leans against the tree, not being able to move. The lashes that Aiden has just whipped into him burn, intensely, and are extremely, painful. He can smell and feel, the fresh blood from his wounds running down his back.

"I am so sorry, my son," his mother whispers while she begins to help him back inside the house. She has been crying the entire time, and her eyes are all bloodshot. Aiden has already gone inside up to his study, so at least, he'll be left alone for the time being.

Guiding Ezekeial into the bathroom, his mother begins cleaning up the wounds and then places bandages over them. "I did not mean to tell him, but if he would have ever found out, the punishment would have been much worse," she tries to explain to him. But he does not care what his mother has to say because he is so angry with her, and he absolutely hates Aiden! Ezekeial's blood is boiling from the hatred that he has for Aiden, and he wishes for nothing more than for him to die!

*****

Returning to the cabin that he and his mother are staying in, he begins to tell her about what he has just witnessed.

"You did not make any kind of contact with her, did you?" his mother asks in a worried voice.

"No, Mother, I only watched her from a distance," he replies unhappily. "I wanted to go to her, but I did not."

"That is good! I am glad that we have finally found the one! I am tired of traveling all over the world, searching for this girl that Aiden believes we need to find!" his mother cries out in joyous relief. "We will return home to tell Aiden this wonderful news at once!" she continues to tell him happily.

"She did not completely transform, Mother," he reminds her. "Will what happened today be enough information to satisfy Aiden and to put a stop to this endless quest?" he questions her.

"I hope so, my son, because I am ready to end this search and to be at home with my family," she answers, looking over at him with sad eyes.

Ezekeial worries about what will happen to Renee once Aiden hears this news and hopes that he hasn't just done a terrible thing by telling his mother what happened because he can never forgive himself if she will be harmed in any way.

CHAPTER 7

Strange Times

After the episode that I had down at the creek a few weeks ago, I begin noticing different things changing with me physically. I've lost some weight, and my body is beginning to change shape. I'm not complaining by any means because it is looking killer! I don't work out. But my muscle tone is giving me a subtle, athletic appearance, and my stomach has flattened out. So when I move around in certain ways, I can see a hint of a six-pack underneath my skin. My hair appears to be turning blonde on the top then gets darker underneath it in layers, leaving the bottom and longest parts of my hair almost black. I have a slight tan even though I haven't been out in the sun much. And my boobs have gotten more perky, so I don't really even need to wear a bra to hold them up. It is awesome! My acne has cleared up, and my skin seems to be glowing. I'm finally feeling comfortable in my own skin!

I managed to get my permit, and now my mama is already at my throat about getting my driver's license. I do have a friend who lives in town, and every once in a while, I get to stay the weekend with her. It is the greatest escape ever! I'm afraid to give my mama my report card because I'm failing algebra class, but I don't understand the work that we've been doing. And I have a D in Spanish too. I just can't seem to get the hang of the language at all, and I'm struggling!

"These grades are terrible!" my mama yells at me angrily when I manage to work up the courage to hand her my report card. "You're grounded and can't go anywhere until these grades are brought up!" she adds.

53

"I'm trying, Mama, but I don't understand the work that we've been doing in algebra class at all! The teacher has gone over it with me several times, but I just don't understand it!" I plead with her. "I'm also having trouble trying to figure out Spanish too because I just don't understand the way that the language is spoken!" It is useless trying to explain my problems to her because she won't listen to me. Not to mention, she just wants to have a reason to complain.

There are only a few months left of the school year, so I need to figure this stuff out like yesterday. And I'm so disappointed in myself for doing so terrible because my grades haven't ever been this bad!

I'm not sure what had happened, but one day, while I was in algebra class, the work that I was having so much trouble understanding just clicked in my brain, and I couldn't believe it! It was so simple! Why was this so hard before? I'm so happy that it makes sense now, but I only have a short amount of time to bring up my grade. We have a big test over it next week, and I need to do a great job. I'm finally beginning to figure out Spanish also, and hopefully I can bring that grade up too.

I'm a nervous wreck when we sit down in class then begin our final exams, but luckily I feel pretty confident with my answers. Yes! I've passed my algebra test, and it has raised my grade up to a D plus, which is much better than a failing grade. I know my mama will still gripe about it. But I don't care because I brought it up, and that is all that matters. I also manage to bring my Spanish grade up to a C minus.

I'm hesitant to hand Mama my grades, waiting for the big lecture, but surprisingly, she doesn't say much. "Well, at least you've gotten these grades up before the end of the year," she says while studying my report card. "Hopefully, next year, they'll be better."

"I'm going to try to do my best, Mama," I reply, happy that she is not throwing a fit.

My sixteenth birthday has come and gone, so now it is time for me to get my driver's license. Mama asks me when I plan on taking my driver's test. "I'd like to take my test in Cuba whenever they're there next because I'm familiar with the streets and will feel more comfortable by going and taking my test there," I explain to her.

"Okay," she replies. "I'll find out when they're there next."

I pray that I pass this test the first time; otherwise, I won't ever hear the end of it! Of course, running a stop sign while taking my test, I automatically fail. Oh, great! Here it comes! I get into the car with my mama, and she starts yelling at me about failing my test.

"I'm sorry!" I plead to her. "It's not like I failed it on purpose! I didn't mean to run the stop sign, and I can take it again in two weeks!" I'm just about sick and tired of all her scolding, and when we get home, it is just like the driver's permit all over again.

She is making a scene in front of everyone at the house and is telling Kent all about how I've failed. "I can't believe she failed her test!" she cries out angrily.

"It's not the end of the world, Sara! She can take it again!" Kent reminds her, and at least he is trying to stick up for me because he is sick of listening to her just as much as the rest of us!

Luckily, I pass my test the second time. Thank you, sweet baby Jesus! If I were to have flunked it again, my mama would have gone over the edge!

As we're driving home, she starts to carry on about me finding a job. "You need to get a job since you have your license now," she tells me, and I almost lose my cool.

"Mama, I don't even have a car to drive," I explain to her, shaking my head in frustration and aggravation.

"Well, Kent and I have decided that we're going to give you this car to drive," she says as if they're doing me a big favor. Oh my gosh, this car sucks! It is an old Chrysler LeBaron station wagon, and it is almost on its last leg! It is the ugliest color of light beige, and it only runs on two cylinders even though it is a six-cylinder. I'm thankful that they want to give me this car, but it is a huge piece of crap! "We'll pay for one year's worth of car insurance, but after that, you'll have to pay for your own. We'll also help you pay for your gas until you get your first paycheck but only enough for you to go to school and back and to also go job-hunting," she explains. No pressure here!

I feel like it is a rat race now to get a job, so I've been driving all over Cuba, putting in applications, and hopefully someone calls me really soon! Every day, I get home and get questioned by my mama, wanting to know about my job-hunting, and she is driving me out of my mind nuts! It never ends!

The truck stop on the edge of town in Cuba has finally called me in for an interview. I get hired on the spot, and I'm starting tomorrow. Yay! Thank you, sweet baby Jesus! I'm working from 4:00 p.m. until 10:00 p.m. after school, four to five days a week plus the weekends. On the weekends, I usually work from 2:00 p.m. until 10:00 p.m.

Between working and going to school, my junior year has flown by. I've been saving up my money so that I can buy a better car because the piece-of-crap station wagon that I've been driving is just about done for and is not dependable whatsoever. I've also been checking out ways to get student loans to help me pay for my college after I graduate, but I still can't seem to satisfy my mama.

One day, I was home after school, and it was my day off. The truck stop called to ask me if I could work that evening, but I told them that I couldn't. I could have gone in, but I was exhausted and just needed a break! My mama asked me who had called, so I told her that they wanted me to go into work that night. "Well, you're not doing anything tonight anyway, so you could've gone into work!" she tells me hatefully.

"I'm ready for a break, Mama! I'm working all the time plus going to school!" I gripe, giving her an angry stare down. She was just complaining the other day because I'm never at home! Oh, my Lord! I'm so over all of it because nothing I do makes any difference! Luckily, I only need one credit to graduate next year, and I plan on taking the easiest classes that I can. Plus I'm only going to go to school for half of the day.

Starting my senior year, I begin working from 2:00 p.m. until 10:00 p.m. on my scheduled days. It is my normal shift now, and I'm still bussing tables. I'm not going to tell you that I really like the job because a lot of the truckers who come in are very rude and ignorant and say vile and demeaning things to me, and there is one guy who makes me cry every time he comes in. He gets off on getting me upset. But I need my job, so I put up with it. School hasn't been too bad, and I'm looking better than ever! The Preppies at school aren't aggravating me anymore because they know they can't compare to me at all, and I absolutely love it! After years of treating me like I was nothing, teasing, and making fun of me, they don't have shit on me now!

I'm not really interested in dating, so I keep to myself. Although, I have had some of the guys from school ask me out, including a couple of the football jocks, but I turn them all down because none of them appeal to me at all. I've noticed a few more changes beginning to happen to me again. Plus I'm hungry all the time, but nothing I eat ever seems to satisfy me. I've been eating everything in sight all-day long and never gain a single pound. In fact, if I don't eat a lot, it seems like I lose weight! My body is lean and built quite nicely now, with all my curves being in all the right places. I love to gaze at it in the mirror, knowing that I look pretty damn good! To hell with all those Preppie jerks at school who used to always make fun of me! Eat your hearts out!

CHAPTER 8

My Ascension

My senior year is coming to an end, and there are only a few weeks left before graduation. I'd taken the old station wagon a few months ago and traded it in on a different car. I've purchased a 1979 Firebird Trans Am, and it looks just like the one in the movie *Smokey and the Bandit*, although mine is a bit rough around the edges. But regardless, it can tear up the highway, and I absolutely love the sound of the engine when it screams. I'm totally in love with my new car!

I haven't been feeling quite up to par this week, and I would really like to just go home and lie down. It is only a little after 4:00 p.m., and I've only been at work for about two hours. But I'm thinking there is no why in hell I'm going to make it through my shift, so I tell my boss that I'm going to go home because I don't feel well at all. It is Friday night, fish night, a busy day of the week. He isn't very happy about me leaving, but I don't care because I feel like crap! Hopefully my mama won't gripe too much about me coming home early from work, but I'm not going to worry about that either because this is the first time that I've taken off work since I've been there. Growing up, Mama wouldn't even let us stay home from school because we didn't feel good, and we had to go no matter what!

Pulling into the driveway, I'm so relieved to see that everyone is gone and that the house is quiet. Barely stepping out of the car, I double over in pain. Then falling to the ground next to the tire, I clench my abdomen when my stomach begins to spasm with agonizing cramps. A sense of strange urgency that I need to run and find a place to hide is gripping me tightly. I'm getting hotter by the second,

58

and the sweat starts pouring out of my body. Struggling to my feet, I lean against the car. My heart is pounding fiercely, feeling like it is going to erupt right out of my chest at any given second, and I'm struggling to breathe. Then for reasons unknown, I head toward the open gate of the cornfield, feeling overwhelmed by the need to run. Taking off as fast as I can, I bolt across the cornfield, heading toward the tree line along the other side. There is a sandstone cave over there up in those woods that I had found years ago while exploring, so I dive into the tree line, tearing through the brush and thornbushes, making haste to the cave.

Lying down inside the mouth of the cave, I begin to tremble uncontrollably. The muscles underneath my skin are twisting and convulsing violently. I cry out loud when something begins to shift deep within my body. The sounds of cracking bones and ripping flesh and of my own cries of pain surround me. My skin is burning intensely, and the clothes that I'm wearing feel like pins and needles being driven into my flesh. So without thinking, I rip off my clothes. My stomach begins to cramp up again, so I try to curl up into a ball to ease the pain. I'm terrified right now, and I don't have any idea what is happening to me! My top and bottom jaws begin to throb with immense pain, and I can feel, as well as hear, my canines popping and snapping while the roots are being shoved out of their sockets. Blood fills my mouth, and my stomach bursts to life, churning and rumbling like a wild animal. Another searing pain jolts throughout my body, and I cry out again.

"Renee, I am here." I hear a deep male voice whisper softly. "Just stay calm because it will all be over with soon." I'm not sure who he is, but I recognize that familiar accent. Then I feel his hand touch the top of my head, and it starts to rub my scalp and then gently runs through my hair. "Let it out," he tells me in another soft whisper. "It wants to be free."

The next thing I know, something rips out of my back, and the agonizing pain reels throughout my entire body, causing me to jump. I can feel something else tearing out of me down by my lower backside, right above the crack of my rear. Thrashing about, sand and dirt are being thrown all over, and they are sticking to me from my sweat-drenched body. I feel him place his hand in the middle of my back, then he begins to massage me between the shoulders gently and rubs his hand tenderly up and down my spine. My legs start to crack, and I can feel them changing shape past my ankles. Deep, raspy growls are coming from my throat, and my shoes have fallen off from all the thrashing around. I'm appalled when I see that, at the end of my feet where my toes should be, they've formed into cloven hooves. *Oh my God!*

"You are just fine! I will take care of you," he assures me in a soft voice. I can smell the blood that is streaming out of my body from my wounds. "*Shhhh*, calm down," he whispers to me while rubbing his hand along my face.

Tears are streaming from my eyes while the agony of the unbearable pain and the extreme terror commences, and I thank the gods once the pain begins to subside. I can feel myself beginning to relax, my heartbeat is slowing down, and my respiration is returning to normal.

"There, it is almost over," he says happily. I want to know who this man is beside me, but I'm afraid to move, fearing that it'll awaken the painful monster once again. Lying here, completely motionless, I can hear, smell, taste, and feel this unfamiliar, new world all around me. My senses are heightened acutely, and I can hear the stranger's fiercely beating heart along with his intense breathing. I can also smell his wonderful scent too.

Working up the courage to move, I slowly roll over on my stomach then place my arms, along with the palms of my hands, on the ground to push myself up. The protrusions on my back are slightly heavy, and they shift as I move. I can feel the projecting appendage that extends from my lower backside moving around as I get up on my knees, and it has taken on a life of its own. It is curling itself around my body then rubs around in the sand, lying on the ground. Suddenly, I feel it touch the man beside me. Glancing down at my hands, I can see that the ends of my fingers have grown long black clawlike fingernails, and I can't believe all this has just happened to me!

Looking over, dying to see this stranger who has been with me throughout this entire terrifying experience, I freeze in shock because it is him! It is Ezekeial! I could never forget those beautiful green eyes and that perfectly sweet, gorgeous smile of his. He is magnificent!

Standing over me, patiently waiting, our eyes lock. "Let me help you to your feet," he says while reaching down to help me up. Putting his arm around my waist, he slowly pulls me to my feet, and I'm still pretty shaky. Plus my new legs feel really strange. There is some sort of powerful, agile spring to them, and I feel like I can leap over anything! The sounds in the woods are echoing inside my ears and are much more pronounced than ever before.

Placing my hand against the wall of the cave, I hold myself there for support. "How do you feel?" Z asks me with a curious expression. He is standing right next to me, and I can't help but stare at him because I can't take my eyes off him. He has grown extremely tall, over six feet, and has a muscular, husky-type build. His skin glows with a hint of a tan, and his jet-black hair has grown long and is pulled up into a man's ponytail. His green eyes are mesmerizing as they look into mine, and he has a five-o'clock shadow of a stubbly beard, adding to the whole sexiness factor. He is wearing a royal-blue pocket T-shirt, some straight-style faded jeans with a black leather belt, and black biker boots.

"I feel different. That's for sure!" I reply, trying to pull myself together because that is about all I can manage to say!

Snapping out of my trance, the craziness of this entire tribulation hits me like a ton of bricks when I start checking out my body. There is not a mirror, so I can't see the whole package. But I've grown long pointed teeth in my gums where my canines once were, and underneath my belly button around my lower abdomen and all the way down to where the hooves begin, I'm covered with short black hair. I try to peek around at my backside. I can see most of the tail that has projected out of me, and it too is also covered with black hair. It is long and sleek with a rounded tip. I reach over, trying to grab one of the wings that have grown out of my back beside my shoulder blade, but it sends a twinge of pain throughout my entire body. Suddenly, Ezekeial reaches over and gently places his hand on it, grasping it tenderly then hands it to me. It is dark black in color and appears to have the same shape as a bat. *HOLY COW!* I think to myself. *I should've listened to Janelle when she preached to me about the devil and the fires of hell because here I stand, looking like a demon that has just crawled right out of the pages of the Bible!*

Releasing the wing from my grasp, I look over at Ezekeial again. He is standing beside me with a pleased look on his face, and I realize, to my horror, that I'm basically standing here naked for all the world to see. I've torn off all my clothes, including my bra and panties, and my boobs are hanging out like anyone's business. But at least the black hair that I've grown is covering the rest of my womanly parts.

Z must have read my mind and takes off his T-shirt. "Here, let me tie this around you," he says, throwing me that delicious, sexy smile. To my relief, he doesn't seem to be afraid to touch me because I know I must look hideously grotesque. "There, that should do for now," he says, pleased with himself while he checks me out.

My stomach begins to rumble and growl, and it is a whole new beast that has been awakened. It is a different feeling from the terrible cramps that I was experiencing earlier. This is a feeling of hunger.

"You must feed," he says, staring at me intensely.

"What do you mean?" I question him, unable to look away from him.

"It is the only way to relieve the hunger," he answers in a serious voice. "You are now complete, and this is your entire transformation. So you will have to satiate your appetite from now on." Of course, I know he is telling me that blood is what I'll need because it is not rocket science to figure that out! This girl has watched plenty of horror movies!

My belly begins to roll again, and I can feel the hunger getting stronger. I can't stand quite all the way up inside this cave because my wings keep grazing the ceiling, so Z helps me outside. My legs are tingling with an indescribable strength, and my body pulsates with a powerful force. The heightened state of my senses is overwhelming yet absolutely amazing!

"I want for you to take your first taste from me," Ezekeial tells me while staring me down with his beautiful green-eyed gaze, and

I feel like I can melt right here in front of him. Then commanding me in a brassy tone, he says, "I want for you to look away from me."

I am feeling unsure about his demand, but by the way he has just spoken to me, I do what he says. I can hear him pulling off his boots then hear his pants unzip. His belt buckle makes a clattering noise when he removes it from the waist of his pants. I want to look at him terribly, so I try to peek over my shoulder but can't see a damned thing because my wing is right in the way! Suddenly, I can hear some familiar sounds, the sounds of bones cracking and skin ripping apart, and he makes a few small deep groans and growls then silence.

"Look at me," he commands me again, so I turn around slowly, not sure what to think about all this. To my surprise, I'm completely astonished! He has transformed into a beast and, from what I can tell, appears to be much like my own! His towering figure is ravishing. I know that I'm probably drooling right now because my mouth is hanging wide open, but I can't help myself! This guy looks absolutely delectable! His muscles and abs look like they've been sculpted right onto his body, and his beastly stature sends tingly sensations throughout my anxious body.

"Is this what I look like?" I ask him, breaking my gaze away from him to myself.

"For the most part, we are closely similar. I am just a little bigger than you are!" he laughs out loud happily.

"I guess so!" I say, shooting him a playful, wary eye. It is starting to get dark. So I look at my watch, which has survived throughout the entire trauma of the day's events, and it reads 8:32 p.m.

"I want for you to drink from me to gain some strength. I will need to show you how to take care of yourself before I leave," he explains softly. At a loss for words, I stand quietly, without moving or speaking, trying to compute his words.

Ezekeial moves in closer to me, almost on top of me, towering over me like a monstrous creature about to take down its victim, and I'm feeling a little unnerved at this moment. Standing in front of me, he extends his right arm toward me then saying to me in a demanding tone, "Take my arm and put my wrist into your mouth." I know that I must have a terrified expression written across my face because he smiles and says, "It is fine! Drink from my wrist!"

I don't have a clue how to go about this whole situation and reluctantly pull his wrist up to my mouth. I can tell that he is eager for me to get started because his eyes twinkle with anticipation. So placing my fangs delicately around the upper part of his wrist, I slowly bite down. And immediately, I can hear his heart begin to race, and his breathing quickens. When the blood begins to flow into my mouth, I forget all about the craziness surrounding me at this time as my own heart begins to race, and I begin to respire, quickly. My stomach churns with satisfaction as my hunger is satiated, and an erotic excitement is wrenching throughout my entire body.

Ezekeial places his left hand on the top of my head then pulls me into his chest gently, and I can feel the beating of his heart against my cheek plus the warmth of his bare skin. He rests his chin against the top of my head, and I can feel the stubbles of his beard poking me while he rubs it along my scalp. I don't care because I absolutely love it! Goose bumps break out all over my skin, and his heavy breathing is blowing my hair when he exhales, almost panting. He turns me slightly to the side, enveloping me within his grasp, and I can feel his burning, throbbing manhood against my thigh when it presses against me. His wet excitement runs down the side of my leg, and my inner thighs are quivering, screaming in agony to be touched. The passionate electricity in the air is swirling all around us, and I'm bathing in pure ecstasy, ready to climax.

"This is all that I can give you, my love," he tells me, whispering in my ear softly. I can feel him beginning to release his grasp from me, and I'm reeling in anguish because I don't want to stop! Delicately he pulls his arm away from my mouth then takes a step away from me, panting heavily. Our tails, at some point, have intertwined, so he pulls his from mine in a slow, tender fashion. Standing here in disbelief, I can only look at him, feeling utterly disappointed and confused!

"We must go now," he says to me as he begins to turn around then walk away.

Inside, I'm screaming, *What the hell! I'm about to have to most epic and passionate climax for the very first time ever in my life, and he just walks away!*

"Come, follow me!" he commands me while I'm still standing here in utter disbelief and disappointment, staring him down. Then looking back at me with intense, anxious eyes, I obey his orders and make my way over to where he is.

The light has gone, and the dark of the night is upon us. But with my new beastly senses, I can see clearly through the darkness. A whole new world has been awakened before me, and tonight, the night beckons me as we make our way farther into the woods. The moon is hanging high tonight, bathing the landscape in its heavenly light, along with brightly illuminating a large clearing up ahead. Along the way, I chitchat about graduation and about how I'm wanting go to college but worrying about the cost of all of it. I tell Z that I'm ready to get my life started and to make my own way, but now, I'm concerned with this new phenomenon and how it is going to affect my hopes and dreams. He listens quietly and doesn't speak a word until we stop at the edge of the tree line then survey's the area.

"We will stop here," Ezekeial says flatly. "I want to show you how to use your wings because you will need to learn how to fly. Hunting is much easier from the sky."

He flaps his ginormous wings a bit, but before he does anything else, I want answers! "First, I want to know a few things!" I gripe, with my arms crossed in front of me, sick and tired of dealing with his mysterious ways. "How did you know this was going to happen to me today? Not to mention, how did you even know where to find me, and where have you been?"

Giving me a huge grin, his large fangs glisten in the light of the moon. "So many questions," he replies, staring off into the clearing, but to my surprise, he begins to answer me. "Last night, while I was sleeping, I had visions of you transforming. I heard you crying out for help, but there was no one there to comfort you. Something inside of me told me to come to your aid because it was coming close, so I wanted to make sure that I would be here to offer you comfort. Transforming for the first time is a terrifying event, and I was lucky enough to have my mother there for me when I turned. I was only twelve when my beast was born, and that is a very young age for that to happen!

"I could sense your distress just as I pulled onto Rutz Road. Then parking next to the old bridge slab, I took off quickly to get to you. I have driven for ten and a half hours straight just to get here. And I tried to reach you before you took off across the field, but you were bolting across it so fast that I could not catch up to you! I am glad that I made it by the time it had all began. I have left Romania, have gotten my citizenship here in America, and have purchased a nice-sized farm with a few head of cattle. Does this answer your questions fully?" he asks me in a sweet tone of voice. He still didn't answer me quite the way that I want, but for now, I'll just let it be.

"How do you operate these damn things?" I ask Z, getting frustrated, because I'm trying to flap my wings together simultaneously, but they're fighting me and going every which way other than the way that I'm wanting them to.

Chuckling at me, he says, "Don't fight them so much. They are weak, so you need to build them up first. Take a moment to just relax and let them do the work. Clear your mind and concentrate."

Sure, that's easy for him to say! I think to myself. I stop, stand still, and then try it again; and flapping my wings at a rhythmic pace, I begin to get a handle on this situation.

"Let us go over to that downed tree over there so that you can climb on top of it and practice taking off." Ezekeial is pointing to a tree that is lying on the ground next to the tree line. So after climbing on top of it, I stand straight up and try to picture myself taking flight into the night sky, with my wings flapping simultaneously, lifting me higher and higher. Needless to say, trying this is an epic fail! I run across the tree as fast as I can. Then launching myself into the air, I try to fly. Of course, I fall to the ground, feeling completely mortified! "It is okay! I did not make it the first several times either!" he assures me, grinning from ear to ear, amused by my unsuccessful attempts.

He laughs at me again when I try a few more times and fail. "I'm done with this! It's so not happening right now!"

"Come, watch me," he orders me, motioning for me to come to him. I'm so aggravated that I'm ready to just go home, but his deep voice and that sexy accent are irresistible! I walk over to where he is standing. Then the next thing I know, he grabs my arm, takes off into the sky, and drags me up above the trees. It all happens so fast that I can't even scream when he releases my arm. Plummeting to the ground below, my beastly reflexes take over, and my wings begin to flap. Then suddenly, I'm beginning to ascend! The muscles of my wings are weak but are still able to carry me higher. Straining them even more, I climb higher and higher, then Z swoops in next to me. "I knew you could do it!" he cries out happily. "Let us go find something to eat!"

We fly around the moonlit sky, scanning the area for prey. "There is one!" he shouts out excitedly and, without warning, begins to descend quickly. I look down and see that there is a small herd of deer feeding on the grass below. So I watch him put his legs out down toward one of the deer, then he jumps on the top of it, thus knocking it down. It is thrashing around, trying to escape his clutches, but I don't want it to die because it has done nothing wrong.

Ezekeial is holding it down with little effort, waiting for me to drink from it. "You must drink, Renee," he tells me with a hard stare.

"I'm not going to kill it!" I scream at him angrily while the deer gasps to breathe from Z's weight holding it down. "There has to be another way without killing it!"

"Drink from it now!" he demands me coldly, so I squat down on my haunches and straddle the deer, pinning it down, while Z releases his grasp from it and stands up. I hold the deer's head down while I place my mouth around its neck, and the sound of its terrified heart is overpowering from it racing in fear. Once I begin feeding from the deer, it relaxes and doesn't fight me anymore, and I almost can't stop myself from draining it dry. But I manage to pull myself away from it then set it free before I take too much. Sitting for a moment in a daze, it staggers to its feet. Then with one giant leap, it bolts away frantically.

Ezekeial looks puzzled and stares me down. "I'm not going to kill them because if I let them go, I'll always have a steady supply of sustenance. They don't need to die," I explain.

Once he and I fill our bellies, my wings are exhausted, and I can take flight no more. I look at my watch, and it reads 3:24 a.m. The evening has flown by literally! My hunger has been satisfied for the time being, and I feel absolutely amazing!

As we make our way back to the cave, I can see Z looking at me out of the corner of his eye, and I wonder what all is running through his mind. He has left his clothes there, and now we're headed back. "You did well, fledgling. I am impressed!" he tells me, smiling, while the two of us walk slowly side by side.

"Thank you! I'm so glad that you were here to help me out! My guardian angel." Z looks at me and smiles, but I can sense some sadness stirring inside him. Once he gathers up his clothes lying next to the mouth of the cave, disappointment begins to set in because I don't want this night to end! It has been awesome!

"I must be getting dressed because it is time for me to go."

I feel a twinge of pain tug at my heart because I want him to stay with me. "You don't have to leave! You can stay with me!" I plead with him, hoping that he won't leave me.

"I cannot stay here with you! I have shown you most of what you need to know, and I must leave! You will figure out more as time goes on. You must practice flying to get those muscles built up, and you will be fine!" He steps inside the mouth of the cave while his beast slowly diminishes. Then once he is out of sight, I can hear him putting on his clothes.

"Come, it is time for you to be getting home," he tells me as he walks up to me after he emerges from the cave then places his hand on my shoulder. "The morning will be coming before long."

"I want to walk with you to your truck, then I'll go home! First, I need to stop off at my car to grab my duffel bag because I keep an extra set of clothes in it all of the time for 'just in case,' and I think that today qualifies for a just-in-case type of day!" I tell him, and he laughs at me while we make our way back to my car.

Opening the door on the car then reaching inside for my bag, I hear him say, "I really love this car of yours!"

"Yeah, I saved up all of my money from working and had bought it about four months ago. That old station wagon wasn't going to make it much longer, and when I saw this car, I just had to have it! It may look rough, but it sure can tear up the road!" Staring at my car, I run my hand lovingly along the driver-side front fender. My beast is fading away, so I walk over to the tree line next to the second gate of the cornfield to put on my clothes. Ezekeial walks over to me when I'm finished. So I hand him his T-shirt, then he and I continue on down the road toward his truck. My heart is sinking knowing that he is about to leave me because he is the only one I can talk to about this new part of my life. Plus he is the only one who can understand what I'm feeling.

His truck is parked on the grass, sitting off the road next to the old slab. We cross over a shallow part of the creek then make our way up the hill to get to it. Then standing next to the driver's side door for a moment, neither of us speak a word.

"I must be leaving now. You need to get back home and get some rest," he says while he climbs into the truck.

"You must be my guardian angel, Z, because you have two of the names of God's angels in your own name, Ezekeial and Michael, and you've been here to help me out at my worst times, and I thank you! I'll miss you!" Trying to hold back my tears, I look away from him.

"I will miss you as well, my love, and you do not have to thank me because it is my pleasure to be here for you," he replies, smiling at me as he fires up the truck. And after the engine roars to life, "Goodbye," he says softly then runs his hand along the top of my head.

"Goodbye, Z," I reply while backing away from the truck, then he slowly drives down the road. I watch it pull away until I can't see the glowing outline of the red taillights any longer. Then tears fill my eyes, and I begin to cry. Sadness and heartbreak take over my emotions because there is no way of holding it back. I want to take off after him to bring him back to me, but I know that I can't.

Walking back home, I keep replaying the few passionate minutes that we had shared when I drank from him, the rush of taking flight for the very first time, and the horror of my transformation. I can still feel his warm body against mine, the pounding, beating of his heart, his breathing, and the wonderfully erotic feelings that I had felt when we touched. I know, while I relive these moments, that I am truly, madly, and deeply in love with him.

It is now 4:18 a.m., and I'm trying to be as quiet as a mouse when I enter the house. I can't let my mama see me this way because I'm sure that I'm a complete disaster, and thankfully I can tell by the sound of her breathing that she is sleeping soundly. Getting inside the bathroom, I begin to observe myself in the mirror, and oh... my...God, I'm a flippin' hot mess! I look like I've been run over by a Mack truck! Hopping in the shower, I let the warm water soothe my aching body, and it feels wonderful. But now I have a different rumbly in my tumbly. It is the one for mortal food, and luckily I have a secret stash of groceries in my closet for times like this. So after drying off and heading to my room, I walk over to my closet.

There is a box sitting on the top shelf that I keep an emergency stash of groceries inside of because I've found that peanut butter can curve even the strongest of appetites. I grab my Peter Pan peanut butter, some Hi-Ho crackers, and a spoon, along with a packet of Capri Sun, then hop in bed. My TV remote is sitting on top of my nightstand, and there is a movie in the VCR that I had started watching the other day. So turning on the TV and VCR, I get cozy in my bed, watch my movie, and chow down on my snacks!

"Renee...Renee!" I hear my mama calling out to me while she shakes my arm. I fell asleep with my peanut butter and crackers still in my hand, and my Capri Sun is lying next to me on my pillow, empty. "It's eleven a.m.! Do you plan on sleeping all day?" Mama questions me while staring at the groceries lying in bed with me.

"I haven't been feeling that great, Mama! I just want to lie here a little while longer because I have to be at work by two p.m., so let me rest, please!" I plead with her.

"Well, you can't be feeling too awfully bad if you've been stuffing peanut butter and crackers down your throat all night!" she scolds me.

"I was throwing up until midnight, and then later on, I felt like I could eat a horse!" I explain, lying to her, and I'm hoping like hell she doesn't know that I wasn't in my room all night. Luckily, Reese had stayed the night with one of her friends, so I won't have to worry about her snitching on me.

"Are you feeling any better now?" she asks me.

"Yeah, I feel a lot better, but I'm just exhausted from the long night," I reply while picking up the food lying around then place it on top of my nightstand.

"That's good! I'll let you rest then. Kent and I are going into the city to visit my sister, so make sure that you set your clock so that you're not late for work," she bosses me.

"Will do. Thanks!" I flash her a big smile, wishing she would just get the hell out of here!

"I'll see you later. I love you!" she says, beginning to leave my room.

"Love you too, Mama. Drive safe!" I reply then snuggle back up under my covers. I hear the two of them leave the house and then the sound of the engine of the car when it starts, and I smile to myself when my mind drifts back to the evening before. And I fall asleep thinking about Z.

CHAPTER 9

New Beginnings

Beep, beep, beep. My alarm screams to life, and it is 12:30 p.m. I moan and groan, thinking about it being time for me to get ready for work because I'm not ready to get out of bed. My work clothes are all dirty, and I don't have any fresh ones to put on. So I'll just have to make do! I won't be too upset if they send me home because I'm not wearing the proper attire! Fat chance on that happening!

"How are you feeling today?" my boss asks me when I make my way into the kitchen.

"A lot better!" I reply happily. "I'm really sorry that I had to leave last night, but I wouldn't have made it through the shift."

"That's fine, Renee! I'm just glad that you've made it in today," he says happily.

I snicker to myself while replaying the events of last night in my mind because wouldn't that have been something if I had "beastied" out in front of all of them! Smiling and chuckling to myself, I get to work.

My grades aren't good enough in order for me to qualify for any scholarships, and I'm worried about how I'm going to pay for my schooling. I'm dead set on wanting to go, and I've met with a few college recruiters who have been up at the school recently. The bad part about it is, I'll have to go somewhere that I can drive from home and back because I can't afford to stay in a dorm or campus housing. As I'm driving home from work, I notice that the sky is lighting up, and I can hear rumbling all around me from the thunder booming throughout the entire atmosphere. Lightning is striking everywhere, and the wind is beginning to pick up. It looks like there is one angry storm brewing up! Leaves and debris are flying all over the road in front of me, and I can feel the strong gusts of wind shoving the Trans Am all over the road. Kent is getting out of his car just as I'm pulling up, and after I get out, the both of us walk over to the sidewalk by the house and look toward the sky. More lightning seems to be striking with a powerful force, and I can feel the electrical static all around us in the air. The hair on my arms and along the back of my neck is standing on end.

"This is some really strange weather!" I tell him, looking around.

"Yeah, I've never quite seen anything like this before! This Missouri weather is so damned crazy!" he gripes, shaking his head. Then I hear it—the magnetic sizzle of a powerful electrical force. *Crash! Crack!* The giant old oak tree in the middle of the driveway gets hit by a bolt of lightning, and the explosive sound is deafening. The sky lights up with a blinding bright burst, and the wind is blowing out of control. "We'd better go move our cars!" Kent screams over all the commotion.

His little blue Dodge Neon is parked right next to the tree, so he rushes over to get it out of the way. Just when he begins to back out of his parking spot, another explosive lightning strike hits out in the cornfield several feet away from the first gate. The old oak tree is ablaze from the first strike, so after Kent moves his car down the driveway, I hop into my car, wanting to pull it close to his.

My mama and the girls come running out of the house, freaking out. The tree is snap, crackling, and popping from the fire consuming it, and one of the big branches that had gotten cracked during the attack is about to break off it. The thunder is rolling and pounding intensely, sending waves of heavy vibrations throughout the valley.

"What's going on!" Mama cries out unhappily, looking petrified.

"I don't know, but this is crazy!" Kent replies, sounding panicked and worried while he watches the tree burn.

"I hope our house doesn't get struck!" Mama adds, still scared shitless.

Crack! The broken limb breaks free from the tree, and a loud crash echoes throughout the land. There is a small fire out in the field where the second strike has hit, but luckily the farmer's crop is already gone. There is smoke rising up from the blazing oak tree, and the scent of its burning wood is wafting through the air all around us. Catching something out of the corner of my eye, I begin scanning the area intensely because there is something coming our way through the field where the fire is burning. I can see it with my night vision, but I'm not sure what it is. There is way too much smoke drifting through the air, blocking my view.

The rhythmic pounding stride becomes louder as it draws nearer, and whatever it is, it is hauling ass! It bursts out of the field through the gate and onto the gravel road, and I can hear the rocks and dirt grinding under the weight of it when it stampedes across it. The great beast begins to advance in our direction, and my family and I are frozen in place while we watch it move in closer. I don't think that any of us have even taken in a single breath!

The sound of its labored breathing and racing heart pounds inside my ears, then it lets out a loud cry when it rears up before us. All of us stand as still as stone in complete and utter silent awe while we watch this magnificent creature rear up right in front of us. It is a beautiful huge black Friesian stallion! It is the very one that I've imagined myself having since I was a little girl. I was always picturing myself in the movies, riding along with the Vikings and knights who were also mounted up on their own elegant beasts.

Standing still after it comes down from its rear, it is breathing heavily. The old burning oak tree is still ablaze, and it crackles loudly. Bursts of flames are sent toward the sky, and ambers are drifting away silently along the light breeze. The thunder and lightning are subsiding, and the wind has died down. Still frozen, we all watch the stallion while he paces back and forth nervously in front of us. The glow from the fire reflects off its shimmering coat, giving it an eerily but totally awesome phantom effect, making this whole experience absolutely epic! Without warning, it slowly closes in on me and then stops. It is only a few feet away from me when it begins to bow down.

The mighty black beast bends down slowly then lowers his head, and it is absolutely breathtaking! My family all turn their heads in unison and look at me with perplexed expressions, but I don't have any more of a clue as to what in the hell is happening than they do! He rises from his bow then walks over to me and nudges his muzzle against my chest. *These past few weeks have been the freakiest times that I've ever had in my entire life! What in the world is going on around here! I know this just doesn't happen to everyone!* I think to myself as I reluctantly reach over to touch him.

Running my hand along his long wavy dark mane, I still can't believe what has just happened! His fur is so soft to the touch, and I can tell that he likes being rubbed along his neck when he lets out a little horse talk and presses my hand harder against him. A strange energy surges within me when I gently place my hand on the top of his forehead, and its tingling pulse radiates along my skin. He is mine and has been sent to me as a gift from the gods. That is the best way that I know how to describe it! I feel a strange, scorching pain starting below my armpit then sear down and along the right lower side of my body all the way down to the lower part of my right thigh. Not being too concerned about it at the moment, I forget all about it totally. My family is still standing with me, and everyone begins to gather around when they feel like the danger has passed.

"I wonder where he came from. Someone must have lost this horse," Mama says, staring at the horse, then looks over at Kent.

Kent runs his hand along the horse's back. "Well, we'll have to keep a lookout for anyone claiming to have lost a horse like this because he surely must belong to someone!"

Reese is standing next to me and smiles. "What are you going to call him, Renee? He seems to like you a lot, and we'll have to call him something!"

Laughing to myself, thinking about this past week's crazy events, I say, "I'm going to call him Satan."

My mama shoots me a crazy, wild-eyed look but then nods. "He did come out of a fiery flame! It sounds great to me!" she says, shrugging her shoulders while staring at the horse. Then we all look at one another and crack up laughing.

"He can stay over in the pasture because there's plenty of grass for him to eat until someone comes to claim him," Kent tells me. *No one's going to come claim him!* I think to myself while I lead him over to Kent's field. *He's mine!*

Satan follows me without trying to run off or escape. "Where did you come from?" I ask him when we walk through the gate, still going over the night's insane events in my mind. He nudges my shoulder then rubs his head along my arm as if he is trying to tell me something, so I reach over and caress his front shoulder. He has a huge stature, at least seventeen to eighteen hands high, and has a long wavy mane and tail. His body is stocky, and he has long fur flowing around his ankles and hooves. His fur sparkles in the light of the moon and reflects the light in all different directions when he walks with me. He is absolutely stunning, and I'm beaming with joy because Satan has just jumped right out of my dreams and into my reality!

Getting to the pasture, I'm afraid to leave him in fear that this is all just a dream and that he'll be gone in the morning, so I sit out in the pasture with Satan for a few hours longer, talking to him about anything and everything. I feel it getting late into the night, so I decide that I'm ready for bed and reluctantly begin to walk back to the house. "Please be here when I get up," I say to him, feeling worried, then he gives me a soft whinny as if to say he will, shaking his head up and down.

Hopping into the shower after I get inside, my right side begins to burn like fire just as soon as the warm water hits it. Then looking down toward the pain, I'm stunned when I see that an amazing tattoo of a dragon is running the length of my side, starting right under my armpit all the way down to my lower thigh. It has wings that are in a ready-to-fly position, and its mouth is gapping wide open as if it were roaring. The tongue is sticking up from the bottom jaw, and its tail is standing erect behind it, sort of twisting around to my lower back. Its arms are extended outward as if it is about to grab onto something, and the detail is exquisite, complete with scales, teeth, and claws. It is even in color! It is a dark blackish purple and blue trimmed with golden belly scales, and it is absolutely beautiful! I can't help but think to myself, *What's gonna happen next? This is just way too much!* I start thinking about Ezekeial, wishing he was here with me so that I can tell him all about everything that has happened because I miss him terribly and could really use a friend right now. There has been so many changes happening in my life that it would be wonderful to have someone whom I could talk to about it.

I'm pleasantly surprised when I awaken the next morning to find Satan peacefully grazing out in the pasture. He comes running up to me, neighing in excitement when I approach him. "Good morning to you too!" I tell him happily while running my fingers along his sleek neck.

Surprisingly, none of the neighbors have come down to see what all the commotion was about last night because they're usually pretty nosy and don't miss a thing. The oak tree that had been struck by the lightning has burnt almost completely to the ground, and the fire is just barely smoldering. And I'm still blown away by that entire spectacle!

Kent has an old saddle and bridle that we used to use when his dad would bring out his horses for us to ride, so I walk down to the old garage, the one where our trailer had been sitting next to, then gather up the tack that has been stored away inside. I approach Satan with the saddle, blanket, and bridle; and he looks at it but doesn't move.

"Can I put these on you?" I ask him, trying to sense his emotions, because I can't really read him. I don't think that he really wants me to put it on him, but he obliges me and comes forward. Getting everything placed on him and secured, I decide to mount him for the very first time. He stands motionless while I get myself situated in place, and I'm hoping Satan doesn't decide to buck me off because he is pretty tall and it would be a really nasty fall.

"Are you ready for a ride?" I ask him excitedly, thrilled with anticipation, and without warning, he begins to canter off.

His gait is wonderfully steady and smooth, and I can feel his power beneath me when he thrusts himself forward. After we make our way to the cornfield, he leaps into a full gallop, and I feel awesomely free as he dashes across the field, with the two of us being as one. Galloping down to the creek, we stop at the water's edge, so I hop off him while we proceed into the water. And when he bends his head down to get a drink, I splash him.

"You're beautiful, big fella!" I say, laughing, while getting him wet, and he looks my way then throws his head back in approval, making some horse talk. He has the greatest personality ever, and I love him already!

It is graduation day today, and everything is happening in a mind-blowing blur. My mama nor Kent have said another word about Satan's owner coming to claim him, and all is quiet around the house. It is like the whole phenomenon that had just happened the other week has all been forgotten about, and that was that! I'm nervous about graduating, and as I approach the high school, it is a bustling frenzy of chaos everywhere. People are scrambling around to find their kids or families, and some of them are taking pictures. I sit here in my car and realize that this will probably be the last time I'll ever park in this spot here at this high school ever again. I smile to myself because I'm ready to blow this pop stand and move on to bigger and better things! I see my family pull in then walk over to meet them so that I can show them where they need to go because it is all being held inside, and I have some seats reserved for them. Getting them over to their assigned seats, I begin making my way over to my chair along with the other graduates, and I just so happen to be looking around and greeting people along the way when I spot a familiar face sticking out of the crowd. It is Ezekeial! I wheel around to look again, but to my disappointment, he is not there. Scanning the entire area of the gym, I still don't see him. But it is time to begin, so I have to go to my seat. *I know he was there!* I scream silently in my mind, feeling aggravated that he doesn't seem to want me to know that he is here. What is the big deal anyway?

The graduation commences. They call my name, then I get my diploma. It seems weird knowing that I won't be coming back for the next year, but it is quite satisfying for it to all be finally over with. Although, I'm very angry with myself for not being able to get better grades, which would've helped me get a scholarship. I plan on checking into more schools starting next week.

We all get our pictures done, then I visit with everyone before I leave. My family had already left a little while ago because they're throwing me a party, and I'm really disappointed that Z didn't show his face. It saddens me a great deal because it would have been nice for him to join me at my party. *What's wrong with me? What did I do to him?* The questions just keep adding up in my mind. Walking out to my car sulking, I just can't shake my depression. As I open the driver-side door to get in, I notice a small white box with a beautiful purple bow wrapped around it sitting in the seat, and there is an envelope underneath it. Picking up the box, I remove the pretty purple silky bow then open it up. It is a golden necklace with a golden infinity charm to match attached to the center of it, and right in the center of the charm where the two bars intertwine lies a gorgeous large sparkling diamond. It is absolutely beautiful! I open the card, and it reads, "Renee, congratulations on making it through the craziest year of your life!" Underneath the words, it says, "Yours always, Z." I look around in hopes that he is waiting for me to see him, but to my disappointment yet again, he is nowhere in sight.

My graduation party is a blast, and it is really late by the time I make it home. Mama, Kent, and the girls had left early because the girls were totally exhausted, but I stay with some of my family and friends to clean up the hall. On my way home, I can't stop thinking about Ezekeial because I want to see him so badly that it consumes me.

Pulling into the driveway, I can feel a twinge of beastly hunger welling up inside me. Satan is neighing in excitement as I get out of my car, and I can hear him galloping my way across the pasture. Making my way over to him, I can hear his soft horse chatter. Then once I open up the gate, he proceeds to rub his head against my cheek gingerly, but our wonderful reunion is interrupted when my stomach begins to growl and churn, coming to life from the need to feed.

"I'm sorry, big fella, but my beast needs to be fed. And I'm going to have to go hunting," I explain to him while I rub him down.

Just when I begin to turn around so that I can get on my way, Satan nudges my arm then slings his head to the side as if gesturing for to me to get on his back. Answering his signal, I hop onto his back, and he takes off into the cornfield, trotting happily, with a springy, forceful stride. He stops at the edge of the tree line all the way at the farthest outskirts of the field, then I dismount. "I'll be back in a little bit, big fella," I tell him while standing behind some trees to remove my clothing.

Transforming is pretty uneventful these days, and it doesn't hurt near as much as it did from the start. I practice any time I get a chance to get away, wanting to perfect it. And there is still some pain involved, but I'm sure there will always be a little. I take flight and come upon the clearing in the woods. It is a beautiful night, and I enjoy bathing in the light of the midnight sun. A gentle breeze is blowing all around me, and the night air is fragrant with the amazing scents of the earth. I love it and have never felt so free! Looking below, I spy the regular herd of deer feeding off the grass in the clearing, so I swoop down then shove one of the does to the ground. She tries to escape my grasp but can't free herself from my clutches. I push her to the ground, brace myself against her, and then grasp her neck to begin to feed, and she slowly relaxes her body in submission. Not wanting to take too much from her, I satiate my hunger enough to quench my thirst then release her. The hunger pains subside, and I'm done for the evening. I could go in for another one, but I'm exhausted and ready to hit the sack!

I stay on the ground and stroll slowly while making my way back to where Satan is waiting for me. I feel the need to just take my time and to clear my head, even though it is barreling down the tracks like a runaway freight train. Looking over, I see the downed tree that Ezekeial had given me my first flying lesson at, causing my emotions to tug at my heart, and I feel a little sadness washing over me. I run my finger delicately along the lines of the infinity pendant adorning the necklace that he has just given to me today, wondering why he won't visit with me. The diamond is gleaming brightly from the light of the moon kissing it, and I admire its sparkling, mesmerizing beauty.

Walking through the woods, lost in my own thoughts, I hear, "You are doing well, Ms. Beautiful! I am very pleased with your progress!"

The sound of that delicious voice behind me sends warm, tingling sensations throughout my entire body. My inner thighs come to life with pure excitement, and I can't stop my heart from fluttering. I know that he can sense my feelings because his senses are just as sharp as mine, and I'm feeling a little bit embarrassed about it.

"Thank you. I've had a great teacher. Plus I practice all of the time so that I can make it easier and quicker!" I say while turning around then spy him leaning against a tree a few steps away from me. Z is smiling at me, and I notice that he isn't transformed. His belt buckle reflects a blinding shine from the moonlight, and I'm more than ready for him to take off his clothes. "Why didn't you let me know that you were going to come today? I could've saved you a seat at graduation, and afterwards, you could've come to my party!" I scold him with a sharp tongue.

"I did not want to intrude because these things are for you to spend time with your family and to celebrate," he replies.

"Family and friends!" I bark angrily, giving him the squinty eye.

"Do you like the gift that I have given to you?" he asks, trying to change the subject.

"Yes, it's beautiful. Thank you! I love it!" I cry out happily while running my finger along the golden chain. Then remembering Satan is still out there waiting for me, I begin to walk away. "I must be going because my horse is waiting for my return." Lifting his brow in surprise, he begins to follow me.

Satan hears our approach and begins to prance and jump around with tons of excitement. He is giving me his usual horsetalk as he trots toward me, but when he spies Z, he stops dead in his tracks. Ezekeial extends his hand out in front of him to let Satan sniff him, so Satan inhales and exhales a few deep breaths, taking in his scent then nods in approval.

"He is magnificent, Renee!" Z says, grinning.

"Yeah, he's wonderful! He's a gift from the gods!" I reply then begin explaining to Z how Satan came to be here with me and about all the craziness of that wild night. The only thing that I didn't reveal to him though was about the dragon tattoo that had been scorched into my skin on that very same action-packed night. It is my secret, and I haven't told anyone about it!

We slowly amble back to the pasture, one of us on each side of Satan's flanks. I was hoping that Z would've wanted ride back together. But of course, he never said a word about it, and I didn't either. I feel like he doesn't want to get too close to me or touch me in any way for some odd reason, and I don't think that there is anything wrong with me because I know he has the same feelings as I do. The both of us are young and dying to make love for the very first time. But of course, I don't really know anything about him, and he is a few years older than me. With as handsome and sweet as he is, I'm sure that he has been with someone already.

Once we put Satan back in the pasture, the two of us walk toward my house. "My truck is parked in the same spot as it was before. Would you like to walk to it with me? I must be going because I have a long drive home."

"Yeah, let me put my clothes on first." I reply unhappily then breathe out a soft sigh, feeling disappointed by him leaving so soon.

My beastly form is slowly disappearing, and I'm feeling a little exposed. So walking over toward the canopy of the tree line next to the second gate of the cornfield, I get dressed behind a tree. Z has turned away from me while I put on my clothes, but I'm screaming on the inside, dying for him to take me.

Walking down the road toward the creek, he asks me, "Have you gotten your college plans taken care of?"

"Not really. I'm going into the city next week to apply for some financial aid and to see if maybe I can get some sort of Pell Grant to help out with the costs. I'm going to have to stay close to home so that I can drive to and from school because I can't afford to pay for the housing or rent an apartment close by. There's plenty of work up there, so I'm going to work full-time after school lets out in the afternoon to pay for my expenses. Plus I don't want to leave Satan, and I have a place to feed when my tummy begins to get rumbly!"

"You are going to drive the Trans Am back and forth all of the time? That thing is going to cost you a ton of money in gas," Z cries out unhappily.

I reply in aggravation, "Well, what else am I going to do? I don't have many options!"

Not saying anything else, we make our way to his truck.

"I must be going now. Good luck with your college endeavor, and I know that things will work out for you. Take care of yourself and be good!" With that, he smiles at me then climbs into the driver's seat.

"Goodbye, Z, and safe travels to you," I say while searching his face for any signs of longing and not wanting to leave me behind, but unfortunately, he cranks over his truck then drives away. Feeling frustrated with all of his mysterious ways, I walk home extremely unhappy with tonight's outcome.

CHAPTER 10

College Days Are Here!

"Renee, Kent and I want to talk to you about something," my mama says when I walk through the front door. I've just gotten off work, and they're sitting in the living room, staring at me with intense eyes. Charlene and Reese are playing outside in the small stock tank that is filled up with water, using it like a swimming pool, and I can hear them laughing and screaming while they play around. I was able to work the morning shift due to one of the other bus girls quitting over the weekend.

My mama's eyes are fixated on me, making me nervous. "We're wondering if you've decided on what to do for school."

"Well, I'm off work Thursday, so I plan on going into the city to apply for some financial aid. I'm also going to see if I can qualify for a grant of any kind, but I'm going to have to stay close to home for living purposes and expenses. Is it okay if I stay here while I go to school?" I can hear all her broken recordings playing over and over in my head, so I'm getting a bit worried right now!

"Yeah, that's fine! You're always welcome here!" she answers cheerfully. Okay, so what is happening right now? Because an alien has replaced my mama with a clone!

"We want to let you know that we'll pay for your schooling for at least the next two years and give you a two-hundred-dollar-a-week allowance for your expenses. We want to make sure that you focus on your studies and don't want you worrying about working full-time," Kent informs me, smiling from ear to ear.

What the hell! What is happening right now? Since I was only about thirteen, all my mama has ever talked about is how I'm going to have to pay for my own schooling and that they weren't going to help me out at all! I can only stare at them, feeling totally perplexed, because basically they've just shocked the shit out of me!

"Fill out whatever applications you may have and get the ball rolling!" my mama orders me while I stare at her in utter disbelief and confusion.

"Okay, I'll get on it right away!" I reply then race up to my room to get started on my paperwork, and I still can't believe what has just happened!

I start at Missouri College, up closer toward the city, the following semester, and it is so much different than high school. The other kids are great, and I really like my teachers. Internet schooling is beginning to be born, and I hope it takes root soon so that I can stay at home more often because traveling all the time is getting old. A few of the other school kids and I sometimes go out after classes are over and hang out at the city park, and it is nice to feel a little bit normal, even though my life is anything but normal. A boy named Darren has asked me out a few times, but I'm reluctant to go because tons of thoughts invade my mind, trying to decide if it is safe or not. Not to mention, I think about Ezekeial constantly, and there is no man out there who can ever compare to him. Still yet, it is lonely at times, thinking about romance and sex. Plus my lust is getting stronger. These are college days, so making out and sex are a part of it!

"Renee, do you want to catch a movie before you go home tonight?" Darren asks me while I'm walking to my next class. It is Friday night, and I'm ready to head home to see Satan. I feel like I've been neglecting him too much since school has started a few months ago. Plus my need to feed is beginning to creep up on me.

"Well, which movie is it?" I ask him, not really wanting to go.

"I'm not really sure what's playing, but we can decide when we get there," he answers with a huge grin slapped across his face, and I can't help but laugh to myself because looking at the big grin plastered across his face reminds me of the time when Grandpa Wodicker and I were at a car dealership looking at some cars. The salesman came out and said, "What can I help you folks with today?" He was smiling just like Darren is right now, and my grandpa, with his lovely choice of words, replied, "You're smiling just like an opossum eatin' shit, and I don't need your damn help!" Surprised by my grandpa's abrupt rudeness, the salesman walked off and never bothered us again the whole time we were there. I was utterly mortified and humiliated that day, and it was one that I'll never forget.

Darren is a tall thin guy, not much as far as muscular goes, with hazel eyes. He is pretty nice-looking, has an awesome head of crazy blond hair, and has a really sweet disposition. His scruffy beard makes him look a lot older than he really is, and he is really smart. He has helped me out a few times with some of my paperwork. And I feel pretty comfortable around him, not feeling like I have to impress him in any way, and I really enjoy his company. I've been taking all kinds of business classes in hopes of getting an upper-paying office job. The financing that my mama and Kent have given to me is allowing me to take better classes than I ever would've been able to before. I'm still not sure as to what all happened there, but I'm not going to complain about it at all!

"So what do you think?" he asks me, sounding anxious.

"I guess, but I have to head back home just as soon as it's over," I inform him bluntly.

"Okay, that sounds good to me!" he responds excitedly. "I'll pick you up after school, then we can grab a bite to eat before the movie starts!"

"That's fine. I'll see you then!" I tell him when I make it to my next class.

The weather is cold, and winter is coming in fast! I hate it when everything begins to die and turns brown and lifeless because it all just seems so depressing! School has let out for the day, and while I'm waiting out front for Darren, I glance over and see my car sitting out in the parking lot. Kent and I gave her a full tune-up and oil change and replaced some of the hoses that were rotting away before school had started. I still love my car and hope that, one day, I can fix her back up.

I see him coming around toward me, then he stops, and I get in. "Okay, where shall we eat? I'm starving!" Darren tells me while rubbing his stomach.

Laughing to myself, I say, "I'm starving too!" because little does he know just how hungry I really am!

We drive away, proceeding to our destination, and I'm ready for a ton of groceries! Stopping at Taco Bell, I order quite a bit of food, and he stares at me in total amazement. "Where are you going to put all of that?" Darren asks, chuckling at me.

I laugh at him and say, "In my gut, where else? I can buy my own supper. It's not a big deal."

"No, I'm paying today! Keep your money!" he barks while pulling his wallet out of his pocket. "Do you want to sit at the park and eat?" he asks me after we get our food.

"Sure, that sounds good, but it's freezing out here!" I tell him, chattering my teeth when a cold chill hits me.

"We can stay in the car!" he replies happily.

"Okay, let's go then," I say, dying to eat. I may be a vampire, so to speak, but I still don't like the cold weather. I love nice warm days and plenty of sunshine!

Arriving at the park, Darren shuts off the car, then we dive into our food. My groceries taste fabulous, and I inhale them quickly, starving to death. It is after 4:00 p.m., and the movie usually begins around 5:00 p.m. or so. And I'm thrilled when Darren finally finishes eating.

"Man, you ate that in no time flat!" he says, chuckling.

"I know. I was starving!" I agree, but I am still not feeling satisfied because my hunger hasn't been quenched. And I can't wait to get home to hunt. "The movie will be starting soon, so we should probably make our way over there," I tell him anxiously.

He fires up the car, then we head over to the movies, and it seems like the show is never going to end. My hunger is in an all-out rage by the time it is over, and I can hardly hold my composure.

"What do you want to do next?" Darren asks me when we get out to the car.

"I'm really sorry, but I must be heading home, Darren! My parents are expecting me home tonight and will worry if I'm late!" I reply, urgently wanting and needing to get home. I know that I've just lied to him, but it was necessary!

"I can let you use my cell phone if you want to call them so that we can hang out for a little bit longer!" he begs me, and I'm starting to get impatient with him as my hunger rises.

"No, that's okay. I don't want to be out on the highway too late tonight because I have a long drive home!"

Darren drops his head. "Okay, I'll drive you back to your car," he tells me, sounding really disappointed when we pull out of the parking lot.

Seeing my car parked in the school parking lot is a welcoming sight, and I'm dying to get in behind the wheel and make tracks toward home! Darren pulls in next to it then shuts off his car. I feel bad for having to bail on him like this, but I can't wait much longer.

"Thank you for taking me out. It was a lot of fun!" I say, smiling.

"I'm glad you enjoyed it!" he replies happily then leans over and kisses my cheek. This is totally unexpected, and I didn't see it coming! I feel the urge wanting to kiss him back but hesitate because I'm not sure what might happen if I lose myself in the moment. "It's okay. I don't mind," he tells me softly, so I turn my head to face him, forgetting all about my urgent need to get home.

Darren's sexual excitement is sending my body into overdrive because I can sense his lust topping out, along with his pounding heart, heavy panting, and dilated pupils. I can't stop myself from leaning over toward him while gazing deep into his eyes. Then I kiss his lips softly, so he returns my kiss with one of his. And before I know it, we're making out in the car! The wonderful sensations streaking throughout my entire body keeps my angry hunger at bay, and I'm hot as hell, along with Darren. He gently pulls up the dress that I'm wearing and runs his fingers up my leg, so I grab his pants, begin to unbutton them, and then pull the zipper down, feeling an intense need to have him inside me. I'm ready, and I want to start this lovemaking session right now! His manhood is as hard as rock, so I grab it with my hand, dying to squeeze it. Darren moans while

I caress his hardness then begins to lay me down on the seat. But suddenly, without warning, the car door flies open on my side, and someone is yelling at me while I'm hanging out of the car!

"What the hell are you doing, Renee!" Ezekeial is standing over me, screaming, and he is livid!

Darren leaps away from the top of me and zips up his pants quickly, and I'm stunned while trying to compute what has just happened, feeling confused and angry all at the same time!

"Renee, get out of the car!" Z orders me, screaming loudly, and I can hear a menacing growl coming out from under his breath.

"What are you doing!" I scream back at him, mad as hell, demanding answers. "Where did you come from, and why are you here?" I continue to question him while he stares me down with mad jealousy in his eyes and fuming with anger. His eyes are as big as saucers, and he is definitely not in his right mind!

"You cannot be doing this!" he screams at me while he pulls me out of the car.

Darren is sitting in the driver's seat, watching him with pure terror written across his face, and his mouth is hanging wide open. His expression reminds me of what a little kid looks like when they think the boogeyman is in their closet.

I can sense Ezekeial's anger resonating all around me when he picks me up and carries me away from the car, and I'm starting to get frightened because I've never seen him like this before.

"You are coming with me right now!" he demands me while putting me back on my feet. Then feeling scared shitless, I freeze in place while standing next to him, not moving or speaking.

Pointing at his truck, he says, "Get in my truck this instant!"

I waste no time rushing over to it and hop inside, obeying his command, then he walks over to the car where Darren is watching us, sitting motionless. "You stay away from her, boy! Do you hear me?" A loud roar comes out of Ezekeial's mouth, and I'm fearing for Darren's life.

"Leave him alone. It's my fault just as well as his!" I scream at him from the driver's side window, waiving my arms around, wanting to take Z's attention away from Darren.

Turning around and looking at me, he pauses. I can feel him beginning to calm down, then he makes his way over toward the truck. Darren starts his car then races out of the parking lot like a bat out of hell, squealing tires, so I sit back, waiting for whatever is about to come, feeling a huge wave of relief that Darren wasn't hurt or killed. Watching Z approach the truck, flashes of this whole shakedown begin to crowd my mind's eye, and I'm beginning to get pretty pissed!

"I cannot believe you!" he scolds me after he gets into the driver's seat, staring at me with disappointed and angry eyes.

"I don't even understand what the problem is here! I'm going to be nineteen years old this coming up year, and the last time I checked, you're not my father nor my boyfriend! You show up out of the blue, never call me or take me anywhere. Then today I'm finally about to let someone make love to me for the very first time ever, and you just happen to appear from out of nowhere! What's your deal, anyway, and what is it exactly that you want from me, because I'm at a loss here!" I question him angrily, glaring at him.

Shaking his head, he looks away from me then starts his truck, not speaking another word. I'm so over him not being up-front with me and not answering my questions because the man has been popping in and out of my life since I was a little girl, and I still don't have a clue why!

"My car is right over there, and I can drive myself home. Thank you!" I tell him hatefully, beginning to open my door to get out. I hop out of the truck and walk over to my car. Then the next thing I know, he is standing right in front of my car door, blocking it! I'm about to lose my cool because I'm so upset with him. Plus I still can't believe what has just happened!

"You will ride with me! I will take you home!" he barks angrily, not looking me in the eye.

"I can't leave my car here all weekend! How am I going to get back to school?"

Z stands quietly while giving me a blank-faced stare. "Fine. I will follow you home then!" he replies hatefully.

Shit is about to hit the fan when I place my hands on my hips then begin to pace around in front him because I can feel my beast trying to break loose, and it is getting hard to control. She is dying to tear into the big monster standing in front of her because she has had enough of his bullshit. Not to mention, she is starving!

Ezekeial moves out of my way, so I get into my car to race home. It is late, and my tummy is growling uncontrollably. I'm so hungry! I race out of the school parking lot, heading toward home, with Z hot on my tail, and I'm so angry that I can't even focus. Putting my Rob Zombie CD into the CD player, I crank up the music and take out my anger behind the wheel, hauling ass all the way home. Z disappears onto Rutz Road, but I continue racing home with my heart fluttering in anticipation because dinner is almost at my fingertips!

After pulling into the driveway, I sit in my car for a few minutes, trying to calm myself down and not wanting to make a scene and wake everyone up because it is after 11:00 p.m. The house is quiet, and no one is stirring.

I hear Satan calling out to me as I'm getting out of the car, and my anger disappears almost immediately from the sound of his voice. Running over to the pasture, I throw open the gate then wrap my arms around him. He rubs his head up and down against me while I hold onto his neck, and I lavish my black beauty with as much lovin' as I can.

"Hey there, big fella! I've missed you bunches!" I whisper to him softly, and he whinnies as if to say, "I've missed you too!"

"I'm starving. Let's take a ride!" I tell him, so he gets into position so that I can hop on his back.

"Wait! I am coming with you!" Z cries out, racing toward us out of the darkness. "Please forgive my actions from earlier. I am very sorry," he pleads with me, not looking me in the eye.

"What the hell was all of that about? I have to go to school with that guy! How did you even know where I was, and why were you even there?" I question him while we head into the cornfield.

"Please let us go hunting! I know that you are hungry because I can hear your hunger calling. I am famished as well."

91

Totally frustrated and annoyed by him ditching my questions and still really pissed off, I reluctantly walk with him down the field. Not a word is being said, and I want answers. So I'm getting angrier by the minute, and I'm about to blow! Getting to the tree line that I always walk to, I remove my dress and begin to transform because my need to feed is almost unbearable. It is consuming my every thought, drowning out my anger and frustrations for the time being.

"What is that on your side?" Z questions me, looking horrified.

"Nothing that you need to concern yourself about!" I reply with a growl because I'll be damned if I'm going to stand here and explain myself to him if he is not going to do the same!

I take flight then begin ascending higher and higher into the moonlit sky. My anger is fueling me more than ever, but the rhythmic sound of my wings, along with the stillness of the night, begin to soothe my emotional distress because I'm free!

"Renee, please forgive me! I am sorry!" he pleads with me once again, flying in beside me. His eyes lock onto mine, and I can see them clearly in the light of the moon. And as I stare at him, I can see what I think may be a tear running down the side of his cheek, but I say nothing.

Seeing the deer herd below, I don't waste any time descending down upon them to catch my late-night snack because nothing is going to stop me now! It feels amazing once I feed my beast, finally quenching my agonizing hunger. With my hunger satisfied, I turn my attention toward him, but he is still feeding, letting one deer go and then going after another. After finishing up, he makes his way over to where I'm standing and stops before me, hanging his head down.

"You cannot do that," he tells me in a soft voice.

"What can't I do?" I ask him angrily, feeling utterly perplexed and baffled.

"You cannot…" He stops what he is saying then continues, "You cannot make love to anyone."

Throwing my head back and growling as loud as I can, along with throwing my arms and hands up in the air, I say, "WHY NOT! I want you to tell me why I can't have sex with anyone!"

He nervously answers me, "Because you must stay pure, my love."

What the hell kind of crack has he been smoking! I can't believe that I'm hearing this shit! At a loss from it all and knowing that he is not going to give me an answer, I begin walking away from him, growling softly and shaking my head. I am so done with all his secretive bullshit. I can hear him following close behind me, but nothing is being said. And after getting my belly full, I'm exhausted and ready for bed. There is no point in drilling Z with any more questions because it is not going to get me anywhere other than pissing me off some more.

"Please, may I stay with you tonight?" he asks me in almost a whisper, and I can't stop myself from losing my tongue.

"Do what? You want to stay with me at my house and in my room with me all night? Am I hearing you correctly!" I yell out into the darkness, mad as hell, and even more confused than ever!

"Yes, I would really like to," he replies timidly.

I look over at him. His head is still hanging down, and he kicks his feet a bit while he walks with me. Even though he has never answered any of my questions, I'm loving the fact that he is groveling right now because it makes me feel a lot better.

"So may I stay with you please?" he asks, almost begging.

Thinking about what my mama would say if she found him in my room, I almost say no! Not to mention, I'm wondering what his intentions are because he is telling me that I can't have sex with anyone, so that must include him too! "I guess, but you'll have to make sure that my mama nor Kent find you there," I reply, still feeling unsure about all this.

Looking up at me with a huge smile, he says, "They will not even know that I am there. I promise!"

Satan is standing at the edge of the wood line, waiting patiently for us to return, and does his little happy dance when we emerge from the trees. And I'm quite surprised to find my dress hanging from a tree branch next to him.

"Did you hang my dress up, big fella?" I ask him, and he nods then looks over at it.

"Wow, he is pretty smart!" Z says, smiling.

"Yeah, he's awesome," I agree, nodding in approval.

"Let us ride back through the field together instead of walking," Z suggests while we gather up our clothes.

Surprised that he is saying this, I say, "Sounds good to me!"

I send my beast back into its slumber then put on my dress while standing next to Satan, not caring about exposing my nakedness to the entire world. Ezekeial has walked behind a tree to put on his clothes too, and I know he is peeking at my naked body, trying to figure out what I have running along the length of my side. And I smile to myself, thinking about what all may be going through his mind, loving the hell out of his curiosity.

The both of us mount Satan, with Z sitting in front, then we slowly amble back toward the pasture. I test my limits and wrap my arms around him, and surprisingly he allows me to hold onto him tightly without saying a word. His body is all muscle, and I can feel the power behind them while we bounce around on the back of my horse. He smells amazing, and I catch myself rubbing my face along the middle of his back. So I abruptly stop, not wanting to press my luck and have him push me away. His body heat is thawing out my cold skin, and I can't stop grinning from ear to ear, loving the hell out of being with him like this.

Once we get back to the pasture, I'm very disappointed when Z hops down. All my warm, fuzzy feelings quickly diminish, and I'm totally bummed out! Z helps me down. Then before we bid Satan a good night, Z and I both give him a good rubdown. I can tell that Satan is in heaven while we lavish him with our affections, and I smile, enjoying having this time with him.

"You must be as quiet as possible!" I bark at Z when we get up to the front door.

"I will," he replies in a soft whisper.

We make it inside and up the stairs, but just as we're about to hit the landing at the top, I hear my mama calling out to me. "Renee, is that you?" she asks, sounding sleepy.

"Yeah, Mama, I just got in. Some of my friends and I went to a late-night show. It was a great time!" I explain, hoping she goes back to bed shortly.

"That's good. I'm going to town in the morning. Do you want to go with me?" she asks.

"No, thanks. I've got a big test next week, so I plan on studying for it tomorrow," I reply, lying to her.

"Okay, I'll see you some time tomorrow then. Love you," she says, yawning.

"Love you too, Mama. Good night!" I repeat happily.

"Good night," she tells me, then I hear her go back to her room and lie down.

"I'm going to take a shower, so you can take one when I get done if you want to. It looks like my sister's gone, so we won't have to worry about her," I whisper to Z once we get up to my room.

So he sits down on my bed and looks around quietly while I grab my pj's then jump into the shower. Oh, man! The water feels fabulous, and I crank it up as hot as I can stand it because I'm freezing!

I'm really stunned when Z barges in on me while I'm getting dressed, almost knocking me down. "Show me," he demands.

"Do what?" I ask him, not sure what in the hell he is wanting me to show him.

"Show me what is wrong with your side!" he barks, almost growling at me while burning a hole in my clothes, staring at my side.

"It's fine, Z! There's nothing there for you to see! Besides, you've never answered any of my questions from earlier." I remind him, staring him down. He comes in closer and stands right on top of me, making me feel pretty uncomfortable. I think he is going to kiss my face when he begins to bend down, but I move away from him, not giving him what he wants. "You need to take a shower!" I order him before he can do or say anything else then leave him standing in the bathroom.

The bathroom door closes, and I hear him get into the shower. Luckily, he has brought some clothes along with him, and I'm guessing that he must have planned this all along before he caught me with Darren.

When he comes into my room then shuts the door, I tell him, "Lock it, please. Just in case my mama decides to barge in on me before she goes to town in the morning." So he does what I say and closes and locks the door then sits down on my bed next to me.

He is wearing some baggy athletic shorts and another T-shirt, but I would rather see him wearing nothing at all! There is no point trying to put the moves on the guy because I sure as hell don't want to get myself all worked up then get shot down, so I turn on the TV and VCR, put the movie *The Goonies* on to play, and then make my way over to my closet. Ezekeial is tentatively watching me the entire time while I grab my groceries from out of the closet, and he chuckles when I hand him a Capri Sun.

"I'm starving!" I tell him while handing him a few crackers. "Do you want some peanut butter?" I ask him, holding the jar out to him.

Z takes the jar then spreads some peanut butter over his crackers, grinning and shaking his head slowly from side to side. "You really shock the hell out of me," he says before he shoves one of the crackers into his mouth.

I put my groceries away after I fill my belly then brush my teeth before I lie down. I can hear my mama's slumbering breaths below, so I pull the covers down and hop in bed. Z looks at me but doesn't move, so I pat the other side to let him know that he can come in with me. He slowly slides in beside me, but I stay on my side of the bed, not moving over an inch while he gets himself situated. I'm so dying to take this guy down!

He looks over at me and smiles, "I hope you can forgive me for my outburst earlier because I never usually get that upset."

"I've never seen you act like that before, and I don't like it! I thought you were going to hurt Darren!" I reply unhappily.

"I wanted to rip him to pieces, to be honest with you, because no one can touch you like that!" he says. And I can see some anger beginning to rise to the surface, so I change the subject because I definitely can't have a giant vampire going ballistic in my bedroom!

"What do you want to do tomorrow?" I ask him.

"We will figure it out after we get up," he replies, yawning. "It has been a long day."

The movie is over, so I turn off the TV and VCR. "Good night, Z," I say to him, longing for more.

"Good night, my love," he replies, and I can see him looking at me in the dark. I want to jump over on top of him, dying to feel his body against mine, but I know that I can't do that. I'm hoping that he feels the same way because not knowing how he really feels about me is driving me insane!

Suddenly, he grabs me by the waist and pulls me in closer to him, turning my back against him, and I freeze instantly, afraid to move. *Is this going to be it?* I say to myself when Z puts his head next to mine then begins to rub his chin along the back of my head, but the next thing I know, he is snoring heavily. *Why expect anything else!* I scream to myself in silence.

Dealing with the fact that he is not going to take advantage of me, I close my eyes then slip into a sleepy slumber.

The sound of my mama's car starting wakes me up, so I lift my head to look over my shoulder. Z is still lying next to me, soundly sleeping. And it is still early, so I lie back down, not wanting to wake him. Once I close my eyes, it doesn't take long before I begin to dose off. I'm lying on my left side, facing the closet door, floating away into nothingness when I feel it. He is running his hand along my right side, trying to pull up my shirt, because he is dying to know what is wrong with me. I smile while he tries to be as gentle as he can, not wanting to wake me while he pulls and tugs at my shirt and jammy shorts. I feel my shirt come up, and he stops, then he begins to pull at my shorts, wanting to see the whole thing. I hear him make a soft gasping noise when he manages to pull my shorts down enough to see my tattoo, then he runs his fingers along the length of it. So I turn over to face him, and the two of us lock eyes.

"What is this?" he questions me angrily.

"I don't have to explain myself to you for any reason!" I growl hatefully.

"Why did you do this to yourself?" he continues to question me, staring me down with his intense green eyes.

Fine. I'm just going to tell him! "I didn't do this to myself! It burned into my skin the same night Satan came out of the field! As soon as I placed my hand upon his head, I could feel it scorching into my body." I don't think he really believes me, but I don't care because there is nothing more to explain!

Placing his hand on my tattoo again then running his fingers around it, he locks his eyes with mine once more. "You are amazing," he tells me lovingly.

At a loss for words from his bipolar attitude, I lie back down. Ezekeial repositions himself and spoons me, then the two of us drift back to sleep. Luckily, I had set my clock for 11:00 a.m., wanting to make sure that I'm up before my mama gets back home. Because it begins to go off, we both jump up, so I head into the bathroom to get dressed and ready for my day.

"Let us find something to do!" Z says cheerfully while he brushes his teeth.

"To be honest with you, I'd like to just stay around here if you don't mind because I hate leaving Satan by himself all the time," I explain.

"I do not mind at all! We can walk the creek for a while if you want to!" he replies, giving me his drop-dead, gorgeous smile. "I need to check on my truck anyway."

I whistle to Satan after we get outside, and he trots down to us excitedly. He can unlock the gate to the pasture all by himself, so I don't have to walk over to do it.

"Climb aboard, young lady!" Z says happily while helping me up on Satan's back.

I'm really stunned when he hops on and sits behind me this time, but I'm not complaining about it by any means! Z holds onto my sides while we mosey down the road, and even though he isn't all wrapped around me, I'm in heaven.

The water has risen over the creek bank from all the heavy rains we've had recently, so Satan crosses the creek in a low spot, then Z hops off to go check on his truck. I stay seated on Satan's back while I wait for him, taking in the wonderful sights, scents, and sounds of the busy early afternoon because it is loaded with tons of woodsy activity. It is a cold day today, but it is not bothering me one bit because I'm lost within my own thoughts.

"Truck is good. Where to?" he asks me once he mounts back up. We take our time heading downstream while talking about this and that, and I'm quite surprised when he wraps his arms around my waist then places his chin on my shoulder. He begins to press his head against mine, and his breath is blowing in my ear, driving me absolutely batshit crazy!

"What are you doing?" I ask him angrily, wishing he would just take me.

"I want to make love to you so badly, but I cannot. I think it is time we head back because I need to be leaving."

This sends me over the edge because I'm so done with this! "I don't understand what's going on with you at all because you're not making any sense, and I'm sick of it! If this is the way that things are going to be every time you decide to show up, then just stay the hell away from me because you're the one who keeps coming around!" I hop off Satan's back, feeling so angry, frustrated, and confused by Z's twisted games, trying not to bawl my eyes out, then begin walking away, but he jumps down in front of me and grabs my arms.

"You must stay pure until you are married," he tells me with sympathetic eyes.

"Well, I don't know when or who I'm even going to marry right now because I haven't even thought about any of that! That's the last thing on my mind at the moment, and I don't plan on waiting until I get married to have sex either! I'm an adult, and I can make my own decisions!" I gripe, mad as hell.

Z is burning a hole right through my head while he stares me down. Then out of the blue, while shoving his arm out in front of me, he demands, "Drink from me."

I'm completely thrown off by this because it is quite unexpected. Not to mention, it is almost like he didn't even listen to a word I just said! WTF! This guy has some major issues! "We're standing right out in the middle of broad daylight! You're getting really weird!" I yell at him angrily, more confused than ever by his weirdness.

"I do not care. Drink from me!" he orders me again. And I heard his demand loud and clear, so picking up his arm with my hands, I put his wrist up to my mouth. I can see his pulse pumping fiercely beneath his skin while I release my fangs then place my mouth around his wrist but don't break the skin.

"Please, just do it!" he yells at me, sounding desperate.

He's gone completely off his rocker! I slowly bite into his flesh but don't take in any of his blood, and he moans while throwing his head back then places his free hand on my head and pulls me in closer. Planting the side of my face against his chest, he begins to rub my head and run his fingers through my hair, making me feel all warm and tingly inside. My body is once again screaming out with extreme erotic lust, and my inner thighs quiver with raging excitement. All this is happening just like the first time, and I'm waiting for him to bring everything to a screeching halt at any given second. I guess Satan isn't liking what is going on because he trots off down the creek then begins to nibble on the delectable, sweet grasses along the bank.

Ezekeial sticks his hand up underneath my shirt and rubs my breast with his fingers then squeezes my rock-hard nipple when he begins to kiss my lips. Butterflies flutter around in my stomach, and goose bumps erupt out of my skin from his warm hand rubbing around on my cold body. Then I drop his wrist from my mouth, dying to kiss his lips. Once we begin kissing each other passionately, he shoves one of his hands down my leggings while holding onto me with the other. Without thinking, I reach down and rub my hand along his burning, throbbing, excited member, dying to feel it inside me. It is as hard as a rock, and I want it now! I unbuckle his pants slowly, unzip them, then shove my hand inside them, and wrap my fingers around his manhood. I give it a gentle squeeze while caressing it, and when our foreplay begins to become more aggressive, I don't hold myself back. I rub Z all over with my free hand while kissing him, teasing him into madness. He is dripping wet, so I rub my fingers all over his twitching member, exciting him even more. He moans softly from my pleasing advances then rubs his fingers between my legs and touches my sweet spot. I'm dripping wet myself, and the wonderful sensations from this amazing foreplay is setting this girl on fire! We're both panting heavily, and our hearts are pounding out of our chests. I can't believe this is really happening!

I climax first. Then as my wetness increases, he climaxes, but I continue to rub him. His body trembles while he rides out his phenomenal finish, and I lavish him with my affections, feeling a great sense of relief from that amazing, sweet release.

Ezekeial kisses me on the lips some more then looks at me and smiles. "Thank you, my love. That was much needed. Sexual frustration can make a man do strange things!"

I can't help but bust up laughing because he sure hit that nail on the head with that! I'm still disappointed that he didn't make love to me, but I'll let that slide for now.

Giving him a squinty eye, I tell him, chuckling, "Really? I didn't notice a thing! Thank you, Z. That was wonderful, and I really needed that too!" I add while walking toward Satan.

Z follows behind me, grabs ahold of my arm, turns me around to face him, and then pulls me against his chest. He rocks me gently in his arms while rubbing his chin along the top of my head, and I melt within his loving embrace, wishing that this wonderful moment we're sharing would last forever.

We end up back to where his truck is parked. "Do you think that I might stay for one more night before you go back to school?" he asks me with a huge smile.

"I'll have to sneak you in," I reply happily, thrilled by the thought of having him in my bed for another night.

"I do not mind! Just open the widow next to the tree, and I will come up when it is all clear," he tells me, smiling.

"Okay, but please don't get caught!" I say, feeling worried about us getting busted.

He hops off at the bridge, then Satan and I head toward the pasture.

"This outa be interesting," I whisper to him after I dismount, and he lets out some horse talk while shaking his head. I laugh at him then give him a good scratching along his neck before I leave him.

No one is home when I get there. But there is a note on the table, and it says that they're all staying up in the city overnight.

They have tickets to some show and have a room reserved afterward. *How convenient!* I think to myself ecstatically. I yell out toward the road, but there is no answer. So I head back in then walk upstairs to my room. Looking down after I open the window, I'm devastated! Z is not there, and my heart sinks because I should've known this was going to happen!

"What is it, my love?" he says behind me, and hearing that wonderful voice makes me snap right out of my sorrow.

"My family is all gone for the night. Lucky you!" I inform him with a huge smile.

"Lucky me!" he repeats, grinning from ear to ear.

I lock all the doors, then he and I rummage around in the kitchen for something to eat. There is a chocolate sheet cake sitting on the counter, so I get a plate then grab a huge piece of it.

"Would you like some?" I ask Z.

"It looks really good. May I?"

I get him a plate of it and pour us some milk. We head up to my room, then I put the movie *Leviathan* in. It is a horror movie that I love to watch. We eat our cake and drink our milk, then I run downstairs to wash the dishes. Climbing back up, I hear the shower running, and Ezekeial is standing inside the bathroom with the door hanging wide open, motioning for me to come in. I obey without hesitation and go to him, feeling thrilled to pieces.

"I want for us to take a shower together," he says while holding his hand out to me.

I don't hesitate to grab it, then he leads me into the bathroom and closes the door. *Wow! This is totally unexpected!*

He begins to take off his clothes, and I watch in silence, enjoying every minute of it. He pulls off his shirt and then reaches over and pulls off my shirt. He unbuckles his belt and pulls it off, then he unzips his pants and pulls them off. He reaches over and pulls down my pants then my panties, but I can't move because I'm frozen in place, entranced by his magical spell. So he pulls off his underwear then scoots our clothes away from us. I can't help but stare at his naked body, wanting it so badly!

He has got chiseled abs and an amazing ripped belly. It looks like he must work out every day for hours! Not saying a word, we walk into the shower. The water feels wonderful as it cascades down my body, and before I know it, Ezekeial begins to rub my breasts, pressing on my nipples slightly. He then slowly turns me away from him and begins to rub my back and pulls me up against him. His member is standing fully at attention, and I must say it is pretty large just like the rest of him! I'm dying to feel it inside me, but he won't allow it. I rub my rear all around it then reach behind myself, tempted to stick it between my legs, but instead, I run my fingers along the length of it. I can sense his building excitement as he turns me around to face him then leans over and kisses me passionately, holding onto me tightly. I kiss him back, and my body is once again scorching with fire and overpowering sexual desire. My thighs are screaming for his touch while he slowly runs his hand down my belly and then between my legs. He touches me ever so gently, and I curl up my toes, trying to hold back my climax. So I push his hand away because I'm not ready to be finished off just yet. I rub his body gently while he pushes himself up and down against my front side.

"Put it in," I whisper in his ear, but he says nothing. So I begin to kiss his neck and then run my tongue along his chest, across his nipple, and all the way down to his manhood. I take it in my mouth, then he reaches down and places his hands around my head. Within seconds, he is finished, then I run my tongue along his member and back up to his neck. I kiss him harder when he begins to touch me once more, and I can't hold myself back for another second and climax.

"You might want to bring your clothes in here just in case some-one comes home," I suggest once he and I finish up in the shower, so Z nods then collects his clothes.

I shut my bedroom door, lock it, and then turn off the light. My movie is still playing, so I rewind it back to the beginning. And it begins to act up, so I yell out loud, "Please stop. Not tonight!" Ezekeial gives me a puzzled look, and I smile. "It's the ghosts in the house. They like to aggravate me a lot," I explain.

"If you say so," he replies, giving me a questioning eye. Once we crawl in bed and snuggle up together, Z tells me softly, "Thank you again! That was great, my love!"

"You're welcome and thank you again too! I enjoyed it a lot myself!" I reply happily while running my fingers along his arm.

"I have to make sure that I keep you well-satisfied from now on because I do not want you straying away from me to be with someone else!" he tells me, sounding angry.

"There will never be anyone else, Z. I promise," I assure him.

"I am hoping not because I do not want to have to tear someone apart, but I will for you!" he growls unhappily.

The movie goes off, so I turn off the TV and VCR. I lie down, scoot in closer to him, and then press my backside up against him; and it only takes a split second for his manhood to get hard once again.

"I have made you into a monster!" he tells me, and we both bust up laughing.

I turn over to face him and kiss his lips. Then he places his hands on my head, pulling me harder onto his lips, kissing me aggressively, so I kiss him back, returning his affections. He rolls over on his back, pulling me with him, and I end up sitting up on top of him. I want to feel him inside me something awful, but he pushes me off before I can react.

"We cannot do that. I am sorry," he tells me, lying me down flat on my back. Then running his hand along the middle of my body, he begins to make his way down to my sweet spot. I love the way he makes me feel, and I don't ever want him to stop! Bending down over the top of me, he begins to lick me from my spot all the way up to my breasts and around my nipples. Goose bumps erupt from my skin, then I place my hand firmly around his member, and we begin once again. Within a few minutes, we both climax and moan from the fabulous sexual bliss. I never want these wonderful feelings to end and wonder in silence if he feels the same way.

The alarm is going off, blaring throughout the room. I had set it for 9:00 a.m. so that we would get up before my family returns home. Z looks over at the clock. "I must be getting ready to go home. I have a long drive, and you need to visit with your family," he explains while getting up then begins to put on his clothes.

I get up to put on my clothes too, wanting to walk him back to his truck. "Thank you for the wonderful evening, Z," I tell him with a giant smile.

Turning his head to look at me, he is smiling happily too. "It was my pleasure, my love. Anything for you."

When we get back to his truck, he gives me a big kiss then rubs his hand along the side of my face. "I will be back soon and stay out of trouble! Goodbye!" he tells me after he gets behind the wheel, but I don't say a word. And after he drives away, I walk home soaring on cloud nine.

My mama and the rest of the clan pull in shortly after I get back, and I'm standing outside with Satan. They're all waving at me excitedly as they pull in, and once the car gets parked, Reese and Charlene bolt my way, wanting to take a ride on Satan. He seems content in obliging them, so I give them turns riding. And they're thrilled, screaming and laughing loudly, grinning from ear to ear. They get bored after a while and are ready to go back in. Plus Mama is yelling at us because it is time to eat. Yum! I'm ready to eat some groceries; that is for sure! We all head inside to eat dinner, and it is so nice to be able to enjoy one another's company while we visit and chitchat.

It is after 10:00 p.m., and I want to feed before my week starts. Waiting for everyone to fall asleep, I doodle in my sketch pad, reminiscing about the last couple of nights. I feel a little lonely, wishing that Z were here with me. Checking out the situation, the coast looks clear, so I make my way quietly outside. Satan is eager to take me out, so I jump on his back for our usual routine. But this time, I decide that I want to follow the creek instead of heading into the clearing.

The night is calm and really cold, but I embrace the inviting light emanating from the midnight sun. It is calling to me, begging for me to take flight into the evening sky. Leaving Satan next to the creek bank quite a trek from the house, I remove my clothes, ready to take to the sky. It is exuberating! I spy some deer below then drop down to grab one, and when its blood runs down my throat, my hungry body thanks me for the sustenance. With my hunger diminished, I feel better than ever, and being satisfied, I head back home, ready to begin the new week.

"Oh my God! Renee, are you okay?" Darren cries out loudly, heading my way, and he is anxious to get to me.

"I'm fine. Why?" I ask.

"I thought that guy was going to kill the both of us the other night! I felt horrible after I took off and left you there with him!" Darren replies all wild-eyed and distressed.

Laughing a bit, I say, "I'm fine, bud. I'm glad you aren't scared to death of me after that!"

"Of course not! You weren't the crazy psycho. He was! Who is that guy anyway? He definitely knew who you were!"

"That's my ex-boyfriend Ezekeial. He thinks he owns me," I reply, feeling bad about lying to him.

"Hopefully, he doesn't bother you anymore!" Darren replies, looking worried.

I laugh to myself. *I hope he does!*

We continue to class and go on about our day, and I'm so glad that whole nightmarish episode was easily forgotten and that he still wants to hang out with me.

Time is flying by, and I can't wait until summer break gets here once again! There is only a couple of weeks left to go, and my grades are great. Plus I've really enjoyed college! I plan on going again next year and taking some different classes for credit, so I grab some paperwork from the office then stuff them in my backpack. It is Friday afternoon, and I'm getting ready to head on home. Making my way out to my car, I notice that there are some guys gathered out in the parking lot, and they watch me while I get closer to them, grinning and chuckling among themselves, not moving. One of them steps out in front of me and asks me my name, but I ignore him then try to pass by him. But the other guys begin to encircle me, and I don't recognize any of them from this school.

"What do you boys want?" I ask them with a wary eye.

"We want to walk you to your car, baby!" one of them yells at me, and I'm getting pretty aggravated with them because I just want them to leave me alone.

"Look, guys, I'm fine! I can take care of myself. Thanks anyway!" I reply, trying to dodge around them, hoping that they'll leave.

"Baby, you can't get away that easily!" another one of them tells me with a huge grin slapped across his face.

Looking around him, I see one of the other guys slash my tire. "What the hell are you doing? Leave my car and I alone!" I scream from the top of my lungs, but they all just start laughing at me, amused by my anger. One of them advances almost right on top of me then rubs his hand down my boob, and I'm fuming, ready to explode, because his touch disgusts me! "Get the hell away from me, you jerk!" I scream at him angrily.

Most of the other college kids were gone before I had gotten out to my car, and there is no one else outside. Trying to hold my beast at bay, I warn them one more time to get away from me, but they just keep laughing and teasing me. Getting hotter by the minute, I think about knocking the one guy down when, suddenly, I feel a strange rush of energy, and something knocks him down. I think about pushing two of them together and shoving them both down at the same time when, without warning, they fall down, along with the same rush of energy like before. The wind picks up a bit as I get even angrier, and the guys begin to look around at one another with fear in their eyes. They look at me, and at that same moment, I think about all of them getting shoved out of my way. And once again, they all instantly get shoved away from me. Freaking out, they take the hint and can't tear up the pavement fast enough to get away from me. I've just realized that I have some sort of mental power, and it is totally awesome!

The tire on my car is flat from the blade of the knife, so I begin getting out the stuff to change it. "Shit!" I cry out unhappily because, for some reason, my jack is gone! I was sure it was in there! Now what! Standing here, staring at it, trying to figure out what to do, Darren just happens to come around the corner, and seeing me standing next to my car with the trunk opened, he comes to my aid.

"Hey there!" I cry out happily, feeling relieved.

"I see you have a flat tire!" he tells me while getting out of his car.

"Yeah, some jerks hanging out in the parking lot slashed it!" I explain.

"Are you okay? I'm glad they didn't hurt you!" Darren says, looking stunned.

"I'm fine! I can take care of myself!" I reply, anxious to be getting on my way.

Giving me a strange look, he tells me, "Yeah, I'm beginning to realize that!" then laughs. "Come on, let's get this thing fixed for you!" he says, smiling, then helps me change the tire. And after we're done, we stand next to my car for a while and talk.

"Well, I'm headed out of here," I tell him happily. "I'm so glad you showed up when you did, and thanks a lot for helping me out!"

"Anytime, babe! I'll see you next week!" he replies cheerfully.

Getting into his car, he smiles and waves me goodbye.

"That was some really good luck!" I tell myself as I get in my car. Thrilled with my newfound powers, I decide not to say anything to Z about it because I want to practice with it first and perfect it so that I don't look like a fool in front of him trying to show off. He has been coming often to see me these days, and I really enjoy all the time that we spend together.

Looking at my watch, it is already 8:17 p.m., and I would've been home a couple of hours ago if those guys wouldn't have punctured my tire. Finally arriving home, Satan hauls ass down the field, trying to race me. He is extremely excited, prancing around and snorting while I walk up to him after I get out of my car.

"Hey there, big fella! Did you miss me?" I ask him happily, and he snorts and whinnies while pawing at the ground. "I'll take that as a yes!"

It is not quite dark yet, but the lights are on in the house. And I can see my mama inside, walking around, busy as always. "I'm going to go in for the night, big guy. We'll hang out tomorrow, okay?" He nods and gives me some of his horse talk while I run my hand along his back then around his neck and head, and I can tell that he is loving every minute of it when he makes some soft grunting noises. "Good night, big fella. I'll see you tomorrow," I say to him softly, and again, he does more horse talk, then he turns around and walks away from me to go graze on some more delectable grasses.

"Renee!" A heavenly familiar voice calls out to me, and I know that delicious voice anywhere. "Where have you been? I have been very worried about you!" Ezekeial scolds me, standing next to my car with his hands thrown up in the air in aggravation.

"Some guys tried to jump me after school in the parking lot and slashed my tire!" I explain, and he looks stunned after I tell him this.

"What! They were lucky that I was not there because there may have been some fatalities!" Z growls angrily.

"I'm fine! I can take care of myself! I would've been home earlier, but my jack wasn't in my car. So luckily, Darren happened to drive by, and we got it changed." Z doesn't like hearing me talk about Darren, and his face instantly goes sour.

"Darren, the guy I had caught you with in the school parking lot?" he questions me, and I can see the jealousy in his eyes and sense his anger rising when he asks me this.

"Yeah, what else was I supposed to do? I didn't have any other options!" I explain while he stares me down.

Z goes silent, but I know he is still mad as hell. "We need to find your jack or buy a new one for you," he barks, frowning.

My mama must have heard all the commotion from inside. "Are you two okay?" she questions us while standing in the front doorway.

"Yeah, Mama, we're fine. Just a jealous boyfriend," I explain, and Z throws me a "whatever" kind of look then puts his head down. "Mama, I want to introduce you to my friend, Ezekeial Dragkarr." Her eyes almost pop out of her head when she gets a good look at him, and I think she may even be drooling! Haha!

"Hello, Ezekeial, my name is Sara. It's nice to meet you. Why don't the two of you come in and get something to eat!" she tells us, and I'm thrilled!

"It's a winner, Mama, because I'm starving!" I cry out ecstatically, walking toward her.

Laughing at me, she says, "Renee, you're always starving!"

Ezekeial follows me inside, and the girls instantly flock around him. They have him cornered, and I'm loving every minute of it. Kent has gone off to work for the night, so watching them melt from my vampire's presence is quite amusing. Mama has some fried chicken with mashed potatoes and gravy leftover from earlier, so Z and I dive into the delectable groceries until they're all gone.

"Thanks, Mama! That was great!" I tell her, smiling, feeling amazing with having a full belly.

"Thank you! I'm glad the two you have enjoyed it!" she replies happily.

"Yes, thank you, Mrs. Sara. The food was very good!" Z tells her, smiling, and when my mama hears him talk, she is about to lose her clothes! Her eyes fly wide open, and she and the girls are all googly-eyed, grinning at Z. It is absolutely hilarious because they're all smiling just like Grandpa Wodicker would say—opossums eating shit!

"Where are you from, Ezekeial?" Reese asks him, batting her eyelashes and blushing, and I can't help but slip out a giggle.

"I am from Romania, my dear," he answers her sweetly, and she giggles and can't stop smiling.

"Wow, you're a really long way from home!" my mama cries out, shocked as hell, and I think her jaw is about to fall off her face from it hanging open so wide.

"Yes, I love America!" he replies happily.

"How in the world did you and Renee meet?" my mama questions him, and I'm quite surprised she doesn't remember anything about my friend from Romania when I was younger.

"I met her up at school. We have a few classes together," Z answers.

"Oh, that's nice. How old are you? Where do you live?" she continues drilling him with tons of questions.

"My family owns a cattle farm in Georgia. I am twenty-one years old, and I stay at the college dorm while attending school," he answers, telling her a big, fat lie.

Being content with that, Mama says, "Well, that's great! What are the two of you up to tonight?"

"Renee wanted to show me where she lives, and it is really nice out here! We would have been here sooner, but the Trans Am got a flat tire on the way down," he explains.

"That damn car! I wish she'd get something else to drive!" my mama cries out unhappily, shaking her head.

"Mama, it's a classic! One day, I'm going to restore it!" I gripe to her.

"If you say so!" she replies, rolling her eyes at me.

"I've got to take him back up to the school, so I won't make it back until late tonight," I say, wanting to get the hell out of dodge.

"Nonsense! He may as well stay the night because there's no sense in driving all of the way back up there tonight and then turning right back around to come home! Unless he needs to be back for some reason!" Mama says, so we all look at him.

"I do not have to be back tonight, and I very much appreciate the invitation!" Z tells her happily.

"Okay, then you can stay upstairs with Renee, but there's to be no funny business!" she blurts out, shaking her finger at us. "Leave your bedroom door open too!"

"Okay, Mama. Thanks!" I tell her, thrilled to death and quite shocked she is even allowing him to stay!

"Thank you, Sara," Z says to my mama then grabs her hand and kisses it, and my mama is about to faint while melting like butter. It is hard not to die laughing while I watch her.

"Good night, kids!" she says to us when we begin walking up the stairs to my room.

"Good night, Mama! I love you!" I tell her, still trying not to laugh.

"I love you too!" she replies, trying to get one last eye full of Z.

He and I finally make our way upstairs to my room. "Shoo! I'm glad that's over!" I say to him, breathing out a huge sigh of relief.

Z chuckles, "You? I was the one being interrogated!" We both roll with laughter then Z gives me a kiss on the lips. I hear Reese coming up the stairs then going into her room. I know she is dying to peek in on the two of us, so I'm sure, sooner or later, she is going to spy in on us.

It is late, and I think the whole household has gone to bed. Z takes off his clothes then crawls in bed with me, so I get up and shut the door as quietly as I can then remove my nightgown. I climb back into bed and scoot over as close to him as I can, then he wraps his arm around me.

Leaning up on one arm, he bends down and kisses my lips. "I want to please you tonight," he whispers in my ear.

"I want more than just touching," I gripe.

"You know we cannot do that," he reminds me while rubbing his fingers along my belly.

"Why? What's the difference?" I question him, still not understanding what all the fuss is about.

"I have told you more than one time. You must remain pure before you get married," he tells me sharply.

"I don't even know what that means!" I cry out in pure frustration.

Aggravated with me, he lies back down then turns over away from me. I decide to just shut my mouth before we start arguing, so I spoon him, wanting to be close to him. Not another word gets said, and I lie awake, thinking about all his crazy talk because I'm not really sure where I stand in this man's life. Does he love me? Is he planning on asking me to marry him someday? The questions just keep piling up, and I don't have an answer for a single one of them.

A short while later, Z begins to stir then turns over and looks at me. "You do not still want to have sex with that Darren boy, do you?" he asks me.

Oh my Lord! Not again! "No, Z, I don't want to have sex with Darren," I reply unhappily then breathe out a deep breath.

"I worry, you know, that you will find someone else," he says, and I'm starting to get irritated.

"I don't want anyone else! I only want you. Besides, you may find someone else besides me that you like better!" I tell him.

"Never! I will never want anyone else!" he cries out unhappily, getting all fired up.

Great! I've gone and gotten him started! He reaches over and pulls me to him then begins kissing me, but I'm over the whole works because I know he is not going to give me what I want.

"Let's just go back to sleep," I say to him sleepily then place my hand on his head and run my fingers through his soft hair. "You can please me tomorrow," I whisper in his ear.

The morning comes, and the bustling around downstairs from the girls and my mama wakes us up. Ezekeial gets up to put on his clothes before someone comes into my room, but I lie here for a minute, taking my time getting out of bed. Z lies back down next to me then kisses my cheek. "What are your plans for today?" he asks me.

"I'm not sure. What do you have in mind?" I question him.

"I am not sure either, but I must be leaving early today because my mother is coming to visit me tomorrow. She is staying with me for the entire week," he explains.

"She's coming all the way from Romania?" I ask him, feeling quite surprised. Not to mention, he never tells me much of anything about himself or his family.

"Yes, it has been a while since I have seen her," he answers.

"What time are you going to leave?" I ask him, hating the thought of him leaving me.

"It is already ten twenty-one a.m. now, so I should probably be leaving very soon," he replies, and I can see the sadness and disappointment in his eyes.

"Well, if you must go, then go! I don't want you to worry about being here with me because I'll be fine! Family should always come first!" I explain.

He looks at me with that debonair smile. "You are right. I will just go ahead and leave now so that I can get home a little earlier. You will be all right with that?" he asks me with his eyebrows poised.

"Yes, it'll be fine!" I answer, looking deep into his eyes.

"You will have to drive me down the road to my truck since your mother thinks that the two of us rode down here together," he reminds me.

"Okay, I'll get ready," I tell him, forcing myself out of bed.

"Do not wear any panties," he tells me with a huge grin, and I return the grin then put on my sweatpants, T-shirt, and hoodie.

"Mama, I'm going to take Ezekeial home," I call out to her as we make our way downstairs.

"You're leaving already?" she asks me, sounding disappointed, and I nod. "Okay, I'll see you later then. Ezekeial, it was really great to meet you!" she tells him, smiling from ear to ear, and the girls run up to him and give him big hugs while telling him goodbye.

"It was my pleasure to meet all of you as well, and thank you for letting me stay the evening," he tells my mama, and all three of them are in a spellbinding trance while they stand and stare at him. I laugh to myself, thinking that this must have been how I looked when I first met him.

"See you guys later!" I say, trying to get out the door.

"Please come back anytime!" my mama yells to us after we get into the TA.

Pulling out of the driveway, I can't help but bust up laughing. Z looks over at me and rolls his eyes.

"Well, when you're hot, you're hot!" I say to him jokingly, even though it is the truth. He leans over and gives me a peck on the cheek then begins to rub his hand between my legs.

Getting to the truck, I pull over and turn off the car, and I know my frisky beast is ready to play!

"Let us get in the truck," he says, beginning to get himself worked up, and I'm not going to argue with him. So we hop into the back seat, and he takes off his shirt. "I want to please you before I leave because I will not make it back for a couple of weeks, and I want for you to be well-satisfied," he tells me, staring deep into my eyes. I touch his bare chest then run my fingers around the outlines of his pecs, and he laughs, "That tickles!" I look at him and grin while running my hand down to the waist of his pants, teasing my frisky beast, then unbuckle his belt and then unzip his pants while he takes my jaw and chin into his hands, pulling me to him and kissing me on the lips. Z takes off my hoodie and T-shirt then rubs his hand around my chest and around my breasts, squeezing my nipples slightly. My body is hot for him, and I want him bad! I kiss his chest then grab his manhood, which is standing at attention in the greatest of ways, and he smiles at me as he pulls me over to him then kisses my neck and face. I end up sitting on top of him, but he pushes me off to the side, resituating my body so that he can pull off his pants, then grabs mine and pulls them off too. We're both sitting naked inside the truck by the time he is done. Z rubs my sweet spot delicately while kissing all over my neck, chest, and breasts, getting me all hot and bothered, and I can't stop myself from moaning. I've got goose bumps and chills from his tender teasing and begin to tremble a little from all the built-up anticipation.

"What is it, my love?" he asks, looking concerned, but he is eating it all up because he knows he is driving me wild!

"Nothing. I'm fine," I reply softly, screaming inside for his affections while wrapping my fingers around his member, dying to feel it inside me.

He grins a devious Cheshire cat grin then begins to rub me a little harder, so I massage his rock-hard manhood a little more aggressively too. Z stops rubbing me and licks my nipples then brings his face back to mine, and we exchange passionate kisses while he runs his hands along my body. Without warning, he spins me around then begins to press his twitching, heated member along my backside while resuming rubbing me between the legs, and I can feel his wet excitement dripping down my rear. The sensation of its warmth running slowly down along my curves plus knowing that he is so excited turns me on even more, and I'm relishing in the wonderful ecstasy of it all. I can feel his member throbbing against my rear once he finishes, and the erotic sensation of it sends me into climaxing myself.

"That was wonderful, my love!" he says happily while kissing my back then wraps his arms around me and squeezes me tightly.

"Yes, it was wonderful, Z. Thank you!" I reply happily.

"It was my pleasure," he tells me, smiling, pleased with himself.

We clean up then lie together in the back seat for a few minutes. "I hate to be going, but time is passing by quickly," he informs me.

"I know, lover," I reply while running my fingers through his hair. We both get dressed, then he gets into the driver's seat of the truck. I stand next to his door, wishing that I could leave with him, missing him already.

"I will see you soon, my love," he says after he starts up his truck. Then leaning out the window, he kisses my forehead lovingly.

"See you next time, lover," I tell him while stepping away from the truck. He gives me his amazing, sexy smile then pulls away, and I watch him until he is out of sight and then head back to the TA. "Well, what should I do now? I can't go back home just yet," I say to myself out loud while getting in behind the wheel of my car. I decide to just take a drive into town and to hang out there for a while before heading home because the day is fabulous, and I'm going to enjoy it!

CHAPTER 11

Family Visits

Driving to the airport to retrieve his mother, Ezekeial can't stop thinking about Renee. He really loves her but knows that everything he has done wasn't allowed, and he would be punished severely for it. Pulling up to the pickup curb, he spots his mother waiting for him, and once she sees him, she begins flagging him down. Driving down to her then parking the truck, he gets out to open her door and to help her in. He then grabs her luggage and places it into the back seat and smiles while he stares at the back seat, remembering his morning with Renee yesterday.

"Hello, Mother!" he greets her in his native tongue then leans over to kiss her on the cheek.

"Hello, my son! How are you doing?" she asks him, smiling.

Getting back into the truck then pulling away, he replies, "I am doing well, Mother. Thank you for asking! You are looking well as always!" he tells her happily.

"Thank you, my son! You are always so polite!" she replies, smiling.

The airport is about forty-five minutes from his house, so they talk about all kinds of things, making small talk. And he knows that she is going to ask him about Renee at some point.

"So have you seen the girl lately?" she questions him, and he almost has to laugh because he already knew this was coming.

"Yes, Mother, she is well. I check in on her from time to time. Plus I sent her family the money to pay for her college tuition this year and for the next. She is taking the classes that you were hoping

117

that she would, and I have also given them enough money so that she can be a full-time student and not having to worry about working. Is this okay?" he asks his mother, hoping that she will be satisfied with his answer because he is not about to tell her much of anything else in fear of being too revealing.

"Yes, this is good news! Aiden wants me to talk to you about a few other things as well," she tells him, and his heart skips a beat from her words.

"Okay. How about we stop to grab a bite to eat and a few supplies before we drive back to the farm, then we will talk about all of it over a drink later?" Ezekeial suggests then begins to panic because it is never a good thing when Aiden wants to talk about something.

Pulling into the driveway of the farm, he gets out and opens his mother's door. He helps her out of the truck and grabs her bags, then they head inside. Ezekeial has an old yellow farmhouse that is two-stories tall and has a covered porch. The covered porch begins at the very front of the house then wraps all the way around to the right side of the house and down along the entire length of it to the back end. About middleway of the right side is the back door, which leads straight into the kitchen, and a rickety old porch swing hangs next to the door. There is a small hallway to the left after you enter, which contains a pantry and a full-sized bathroom. Then at the far end of the hallway, there is a set of stairs leading down into the cellar. Walking into the kitchen, the kitchen cabinets are on your left along the wall, including the fridge and stove, then the cabinets elbow around. And the kitchen sink is almost dead center of the adjoining wall, with a large picture window overlooking out across his property, plus a few more cabinets along the other side. A small island sits in the center of the kitchen, and looking out of the window, you can see his large barn sitting out in the open field. To the right, when you stand inside the kitchen, leads to the living room that is completely open. The front door is in the middle of the room along the wall at the front of the house, and there is a stone fireplace climbing up the wall a few feet away located on the left-hand side of the door. There are a lot of windows along the walls, and the house is full of natural light. If you pass through the kitchen going straight, there is a big entryway leading into the main dining room, which is very spacious. The stairs to the second floor run along the farthest wall of the room and lead straight up.

Ezekeial grabs his mother's luggage then takes it up to the room that she'll be using for her stay. "Our breakfast was really good!" his mother tells him happily while she looks around his house.

"Yes, the food is usually really good there," he replies, wondering what it is she needs to speak to him about.

"I never could cook very well. My mother was not a very loving woman and did not teach me the things that a woman needs to know when she becomes of age. You really need a good woman to take care of you, and I know that, right now, it is a bad time. But once everything is in place, you can get on with your life!" she says to him with an empathetic expression, and Z thinks back to Renee with a deep sense of sadness tugging at his heart.

It is already past noon, so he pours himself and his mother a tall mug of ice-cold beer, then they take a seat at the kitchen table.

"What is Aiden wanting to talk about?" he asks her, feeling a terrible sense of dread.

"He thinks that Renee needs to learn more about our kind and about the realms of the supernatural because there is a lot to learn when it comes to vampires, werewolves, the cult, magic, etc. For her, life is just the mortal way, and she has not a clue as to what the other side of her life is like. One of the things that he wants her to learn is our language. Romanian is our native tongue, and she needs to speak it. She needs to know the rules, origin, and history of all of these things. Otherwise, everything will be unknown to her later on," she's explains, looking at him intensely. "He wants for you to bring her here with you and to have her study our ways. You are very smart and can tutor her in the best of ways, my son. This way, she is familiar with all of these things, and you can always enroll her in a college here! She can go to school during the day, then you can tutor her at night. Just remember the rules because she must be pure. There should not be any physical contact between the two of you at all, or Aiden will punish you severely. You know what your mission is, and you must obey every detail of it!" she tells him with stern eyes and a sharp tongue.

How is this ever going to work? Renee will want me to please her and to touch her! I can't keep from being able to do these things, especially if she's living with me! Panic sets in, and his heart begins to pound.

"Are you okay, Ezekeial?" his mother asks him, sensing the abrupt change in his emotions.

"Yes, Mother. I am just worried about all of this. That is all," he answers nervously.

"And why should it be a problem? You have interacted with her before," she questions him.

"I know, but what if I do not teach her well enough? What if something happens to her while she is in my care?" he questions her, trying to find a good way to throw his mother off, not wanting to give away his secrets.

"The two of you will be just fine! I know you can do this!" she assures him.

"When should this take place?" he asks her, trying to compose himself better.

"After she finishes her college term for this year," she answers.

"Okay, Mother. I will go talk to her about this. I will see if I can get her to come, but what if she does not want to come here?" he questions her, feeling worried, because Renee may not even want to come and stay with him!

"She will. This I know," his mother says, and her words, along with her serious facial expression, makes him think that she must know something about them. "I am going to go up to my room to lie down. It has been a long day, and I am completely jet-lagged! We will discuss this more throughout the week," she says while making her way upstairs.

"Okay, Mother. Good night. I love you."

"Good night, my son. I love you too!"

Once she disappears up to the second floor, all Ezekeial can think about is how he plans on making all this work. He loves Renee with all his being, but he must obey his family because if they were to find out about them, he would surely pay. His emotions run wild while he decides how to handle this situation because this is totally unexpected! Never has anything like this ever crossed his mind! Damn Aiden! He has ruined his life enough, and now he plans on taking the love of his life from him as well! Sitting down at the dining room table, he ponders on how to go about doing all this. *What am I going to do?* Thinking more about the issue at hand, his anger begins to rise, swallowing up his fear, then a soft growl slips out from under his breath. *Why do they do these things to me! Have I not paid enough!* he screams in silence. Aiden knows that doing this will torture Ezekeial to death! He loves to knock Ezekeial down because he lives for it!

Agony, grief, and sadness begin to overwhelm him, and he must get out of here. Suddenly, he bolts outside then rips off his clothes while he releases his beast. Crashing through the forest and running through his farmland, he reels from the agony that he is about to endure. Then stopping at the edge of the forest, he falls to his knees and begs the gods to please help him! He is wanting mercy, something to change their minds and to let Renee be meant for him and not for anyone else! He is screaming in anguish. Roars are echoing throughout the land, and his heart is breaking. Tears fill his eyes, and he begins to weep. *What am I going to do!* Hot lava is flowing through his veins, and he is on fire with absolute rage!

Catching sight of a familiar shape trotting his way, he begins to calm down because it is his beautiful black beauty, Dutchess. She is his Friesian mare that was given to him when he was sixteen years old, and she is absolutely breathtaking while she prances up to him from below. Her mane and tail flow delicately in the wind, and her striking form is simply amazing. Stopping in front of him, she snorts and stomps her foot on the ground as if asking him what is the matter. Ezekeial tells all, needing to get everything off his chest, and Dutchess listens quietly. Once he is finished pouring out his heart and soul, she gives him her horse talk then angrily paws at the ground. Extending her sleek, elegant neck to get closer to him, she nuzzles his cheek. Ezekeial feels a little bit of relief from being able to confide in her because he knows that she can't tell on him and that she is faithful. He hasn't told Renee much of anything about himself, and she doesn't even know that he has a horse just like hers! This is going to be absolutely horrible! The gods must be punishing him for the sinful things that he has been doing! He breaks down again, and Dutchess offers him comfort. Sitting here until dark, going over and over all this crazy madness in his mind, he decides to head back to the house, broken and distraught. He'll have his revenge with Aiden someday!

CHAPTER 12

Moving Day

It is the last day of my first year in college, and I'm so relieved! I've passed all my exams with flying colors, and things are going well. I haven't seen Ezekeial in a few weeks and wonder what he has been up to. Cell phones have just become popular, and I think I may get one so that I can at least talk to him once in a while. Gathering up my stuff, I make my way out to the car, and I'm so glad that I won't have to drive up here for a while because it just gets really old driving every day to get here. I pack up my car then head for home. Maybe he'll come visit me this weekend! I'm hoping so because I really miss him. Plus my mama and the girls ask me all the time when he'll be out next, but I keep making up excuses to get them off my back.

My mind wanders aimlessly while I drive down the highway, making the drive seems shorter, and once I pull into the driveway then get out, Satan is calling out to me excitedly. He hops around like a mad jackrabbit, and I can't help but laugh at him. "Hey there, big fella!" I greet him happily then give him a huge hug. "How have you been?" He shakes his head and stomps his foot because he is ready for a ride. I am too because it has been a couple of weeks since we were out. Schoolwork has kept me plenty busy these days, and I haven't had time for much of anything. "We'll go out in a little while, okay? I want to put my stuff upstairs," I explain, and he nods his head then gives me his horse talk.

Grabbing my stuff out of the car, I begin to take it all in. "Hey there!" my mama greets me at the front door, holding the screen door open for me.

"Hey, Mama! Thanks!" I tell her happily.

"You're welcome, dear!" she replies, smiling.

"So what are your plans for the summer?" she asks me after she closes the door behind me.

"I'm not sure yet. I'm thinking about going back to the truck stop to see if I can work over the summer," I reply, not really liking the idea of going back there.

"That sounds good because at least you can save up some money to use for next year," she tells me while picking up some cups off the coffee table then accidentally spills one that had a little bit of juice left inside it. "Shit!" she cries out angrily then runs into the kitchen to grab a wet rag. After getting the mess cleaned up, she asks me, "I'm heading into town in the morning. Would you like to come with me?"

"No, but thank you, anyway. I think I'm going to spend the day with Satan and take a ride," I answer, feeling guilty about not having any time with him lately.

"Okay, I just thought I'd ask," she replies.

Her buzzer is going off for the oven. The air smells delectable from the amazing aromas of her cupcakes filling up every room in the house, and I can't wait to get one stuffed in my mouth!

Prancing down the road toward me, Satan is ready for our ride. I hop on his back, then we ride through the field. The man who owned the field passed away before the spring, so nothing was planted this year. But there is still old, dead leftovers littering the rows from last year scattered all about. It doesn't seem to bother Satan while he trots through the rows with graceful speed. He takes me down to the water's edge on the farthest, most outer edge of the field, then he walks into the water and starts pawing at it, trying to splash me. I hop off his back then begin to splash him back.

"Haha! I can splash you more!" I tell him, laughing.

He lets out a huge whinny then rushes my way and knocks me down in the water. Satan jumps away from me and does his horse cackle while looking back at me with great satisfaction because I'm soaking wet from head to toe.

"That's not fair!" I yell at him, trying not to laugh.

He snickers some more and shakes his head while he runs away from me then stops short in his tracks, so I follow his gaze to see what he is looking at. And I'm thrilled to see Ezekeial standing at the edge of the creek bank, watching us play. I smile and wave to him, dying to be in his arms.

"Hey there, stranger!" I cry out ecstatically while approaching him.

"Hello," he says to me in a strange sort of way.

"What's wrong?" I ask him, getting worried because he seems different today, and something is definitely off. I reach up to touch his face, but he steps back. And I feel a little hurt by this.

"I would like to talk to you about something," he says with a lifeless expression, and I'm very concerned about him and his strange demeanor.

"Yes, what about?" I question him, dying to know what is wrong with him.

Looking at me with an intense gaze, he says, "I want to ask you if you would like to come stay with me for a while. I want to teach you about our culture, ways, and order because you do not know anything about the history or the details of our people, and the rules and discipline involved with being our kind are very complex. I have a lot of information in my library at the house for you to study and to read up on. I was also hoping that you will want to learn the Romanian language."

I'm not sure what to say. I'm a little thrown off by this because he won't ever talk to me about himself, and now, all of a sudden, he wants me to move in with him? I'm really confused and unsure about this. Not to mention, he doesn't seem very happy about asking me to stay with him in the first place! "Well, I'm not sure. For how long will I be staying with you? I plan on going back to school next semester," I ask while my mind runs wild.

"You can transfer all of your credentials to a college near my house. They have internet so that you can do your courses online as well."

The man is talking, but it just doesn't seem like him. "Let me think about this because it's a really big decision to make," I reply, trying to pinpoint his troubles.

"I understand. Take all of the time that you need," Ezekeial says, giving me a half-hearted smile.

"What about Satan? I can't leave him behind!" I cry out, panicking.

"I can bring a horse trailer with me, and he is more than welcome to come as well," he replies, and now I'm feeling a lot better about this! It would be nice to get to be with him more often, but something just doesn't seem quite right! "Come, let us go for a walk," Ezekeial says, looking away from me.

"Okay!" I reply happily, ready to hang out with him, even though he is acting weird.

Satan comes up beside me, and I walk next to him with Z walking on the other side of him. And as we make our way closer to the house, I suggest, "Maybe we should talk to my mama about this first." Then I look over at him, but he doesn't reply. "Z, what do you think?"

"Yes, it is probably a good idea," he answers with lost eyes.

Once we get to the house, everyone greets him excitedly. He smiles and greets them back. We all sit down, then he makes up a story about me coming to stay with him because, of course, we can't give them the actual reason why. But he comes up with a great story, and they love his idea. He tells them that there is a much-better college near his home and that there are far more greater options available for me by attending this school.

I give it some thought and realize that he is right about me not having a clue about my own kind, so to speak, so I decide I'll take him up on his offer because the thought of being with him every day makes my heart soar with joy!

*****

It is moving day, and Z is supposed to be here within the hour. I'm really nervous, happy, and scared all at the same time. *What's it going to be like? How big is his house? How long will it take to get there?* Questions just keep drowning my thoughts when he finally pulls in, and I'm starting to freak out! *Is this really happening?* I start to pace up and down the sidewalk.

"What is wrong?" Z asks me when he gets out of his truck.

"I'm just nervous about all of this, and I hope that I'm doing the right thing," I answer, biting my nails. "What about my TA? Should I follow you to your house?"

Looking surprised, he says, "Oh, no! We will have to come back for it later. I will bring a big trailer some other time to haul it back to the house with," he answers, giving me his beautiful, amazing smile.

"Okay, but I don't want to be without a car for too long," I tell him sternly.

Z chuckles then kisses my forehead. "It will be fine, my love!" He seems okay today, but I get a strange sense that something is still off.

We get my stuff loaded and Satan secured inside the horse trailer. Then waving farewell to my family, we make our way to Ezekeial's house. During Z's absence, I was able to practice using my powers, and I've gotten quite good with them. The power flows like electricity running through my veins, and it surges deep inside me. I can do things that I had never thought possible! I can summon up the winds and storms and can move things around just by thinking about it. I'm not sure when I'm going to tell him about my secret. But for now, it is mine, and I'm not sharing because I want to see how things work out with this move first, then just maybe, I'll let him in on my secret.

It seems like it is taking forever to get there! It is after 8:30 p.m. already, and the time is flying by other than this trip! I can't believe how many times he has driven this just to come visit me! I look over at him, and he seems content while he stares out of the windshield, lost within his own thoughts. And I wonder what he is thinking about and, also, what this move will do for our relationship. I still have my doubts, but for now, I'll just let them be and roll with it.

Gazing out of the window, the night is almost upon us. I begin to feel drowsy because I haven't been able to sleep very good for the past couple of nights, worrying about leaving home, and my eyelids feel like heavy lead bricks. The call of slumber is so overpowering that I can't hold my eyelids open any longer and slip into the dark abyss.

I awaken to the sunlight pouring in my face. *What time is it? Where am I?* Looking around, I don't see anything familiar. My camouflage backpack/purse is sitting on a nightstand next to the bed that I'm lying on, and my luggage is sitting on top of a small couch in the room. Looking to my left, there is a set of French doors on the wall across from me that open up onto a balcony overlooking a large field, and there is a door on the wall next to me where the headboard rests, which leads into a large bathroom that has just been remodeled. The room I'm in is very spacious and has also been recently remodeled. Everything looks fantastic! I love the blueish-purply color painted on the two walls, and the opposite walls are just painted white. The combination looks awesome! There is brand-new hardwood flooring down on the floor, and it accents the walls perfectly. There is a long dresser, with a mirror facing me, along the wall straight in front of me, and it has a large flat-screen TV sitting on top of it. Everything looks brand-new. There is also a tall dresser along the wall opposite of it, with the entry door being located along the same side. The couch is parked on this side as well.

On the nightstand by my backpack, there is a brand-new iPhone sitting there with a note. It has the phone number to the phone written on it, along with a set of Beats headphones. The note also says, "To my love, keep this with you always. I know you like your music, so here are some headphones and a two-hundred-dollar iTunes card. Z." Wow! That is awesome!

I can hear some clanging outside, so I open up the French doors then step out onto the balcony. It extends out about six feet then runs along the wall past another bedroom, and I'm guessing that it is Z's room. So I walk down the balcony to peek inside, but there are thick curtains blocking the view. More clanging commences, and I hear some yelling. So I turn my gaze toward all the commotion.

I can see someone far up in the field, sitting on the ground, and it appears that they're working on a tractor. I see Satan out there too, but at a second glance, there seems to be two of him standing out there! *What the hell?* My stomach begins to rumble from hunger.

But it is not my beastly hunger; it is my mortal hunger. I decide to find the kitchen for some groceries, so I open the entry door to this room then peek out. My room is located in the front of the house at the end of the hallway, and looking to my right, I can see a couple of more doors on this side. The front and back of the house has two great big windows, one on either end, spilling tons of sunlight into the hallway. The fantastic, heavenly rays are so inviting and wonderful because they perk up my senses and make me feel so alive and happy. The opposite wall has the exit stairs leading down and a couple of more doors located along it also.

I walk across the hallway to the stairs then make my descent. The stairs end in a large dining room, and I can see into the kitchen from its entryway. Making my way over to it, I stop and take a gander around, wanting to see what all is in there. The kitchen and living room have an open floor plan, giving the whole works an amazing, spacious feel. So I walk into the kitchen then rummage around through everything, looking for some food, but I don't see much of anything. Yikes, so not good! I open up the fridge, and all there is, is a half-empty bottle of orange juice, ketchup, some eggs, milk, and butter. There is also a bag of flour sitting far in the back on the second shelf and some ice-cube trays in the freezer, but there is nothing else. I spy some cooking oil in one of the top cabinets, along with some sugar, then I also find some iced-tea bags lying next to the canister set sitting on the countertop. Well, I guess I can make some tea!

I dig around in the cabinets, and to my surprise, I find a tea pitcher, thus making a pitcher of sweet tea. I figure if Ezekeial is working on a tractor, he may want something to drink, so I find a plastic drinking bottle and fill it up with some ice and sweet tea. I also spy a bag of russet potatoes and a set of salt and pepper shakers sitting on the island in the kitchen, but other than that, there is not much to work with!

There is a door leading outside from the kitchen, so I peer out of it. I see a large oak tree standing next to a small red garage, with the driveway leading right to it, along with Ezekeial's truck parked out there. I open the door and walk out onto the wraparound, covered porch. A porch swing is hanging next to the door, so I sit down on it for a minute, looking around, trying to get a feel for this new place. I hop down the stairs then walk around toward the front of the house, and there are a few large maple trees standing in the front yard. Plus there is another driveway leading up to a large barn sitting out in the open field. The field is where Z is at, and far behind the field, I can see a dense wood line. There is a large herd of cattle grazing out in the green pastureland, and I spot the two Satans closer to me, grazing in the pasture next to the barn.

I walk up to the metal gates then open one of them to get through, and one of the Satans gets excited and dashes toward me with the other one in toe. Snorting and prancing around once they approach me, I know right away this is my big fella.

"Hey there, big fella!" I say while stroking his muzzle.

He whinnies and rubs his head against my arm while the other one slowly, as if shy, begins to walk my way. I can see that this one is a mare, and she is absolutely beautiful! Her neck is long, sleek, and slender. Not to mention, her wonderfully built body is fabulous! She is a bit smaller than my horse but is still very large in stature. Snorting a bit and giving me some horse talk, she puts her nose out to me, so I let her sniff my hand. Then after a few sniffs, she seems content with me then lowers her head down for me to stroke.

I whisper to her softly, "And who might you be, Ms. Black Beauty?" while I run my hand along her muzzle, and she must have liked this because she starts to nod and presses her muzzle against my arm, rubbing me gently. I run my hand along her sleek neck and ask her, "Are you Ezekeial's horse?" As if she understands me, she perks up then nods again. Wow! He has a horse just like mine! I don't believe it! He never mentioned this before!

I hear Z yelling some more, and he sounds pissed! I walk up to him then place my hand on his shoulder, and without warning, he wields around with lightning speed, grabs my arm, and shoves me away! I end up lying on the ground flat on my back, getting the wind knocked out of me. "What the hell!" I yell at him angrily while lying on the ground. The tea I was carrying went down with me and has rolled against my side.

"What are you doing!" he screams at me hatefully. "You should not be sneaking up on me like that!"

Standing myself up and wiping the dirt off my clothes, I say, "Well, I thought you might like some tea, but instead, I get karate chopped and smacked down! Here's some tea for you, you jerk!" Mad as hell, I grab the bottle of tea off the ground then throw it down at his feet, and he starts to laugh at me, making me even madder. "There's nothing to eat around this joint, and I'm starving! Where's the food at?" I question him.

"I have not had any time to go shopping for groceries! I have been busy here, and I am not leaving this place until I get this damned tractor fixed!" he growls.

"Well, I can go shopping! I just need some cash and to use the truck since I don't have my car!" I reply, staring him down.

"I will go with you, so you will just have to wait until I get done," he tells me coldly.

"I can't wait! I'm really hungry!" I plead with him, feeling desperate.

"You will wait for me! I will be done soon!"

"What's wrong with it anyway?" I ask, knowing a little bit about working on cars.

"You will not know," he replies coldly again, fixating his eyes on me.

"Maybe, but I do know a little bit about cars," I inform him, giving him a soft growl.

"This is not a car, Renee," he explains, trying to make me feel like an idiot.

"No shit, Sherlock! Just forget it!" I shake my head in aggravation then decide to walk back to the house, not wanting to argue with him anymore, and I can see him smiling from ear to ear while I walk away. *What a jerk!* I think to myself while ambling down the pasture mad as hell and starving. I can smell water somewhere behind where Z is working on his tractor, and even though I can't see it, I know it is there, somewhere through the forest back there.

I get down to the gate, with Satan and his friend right behind me, and I completely forgot to ask Z about the black horse he has from being so aggravated with him.

"You two had better stay here for now. Maybe we can go out later," I tell them as I open the gate, and they both snort in agreement.

Walking back around the house to the side door, I notice a fishing pole sitting on the other side of the porch swing, leaning against the wall. There is a small tackle box too. *Jackpot! I'm going to go catch some food if that's the only way to get it today!* I go inside and rummage around for something to dig up some worms with, plus a bowl to put them in. Then after I find a thick metal spoon and a plastic container with a lid, I grab the pole and tackle box.

"I better check out the gear in the box before I leave," I say to myself out loud, and I'm thrilled to pieces after I open the lid and see a stringer, hooks, and sinkers. I'm all set! I walk back up to the gate. The two horses are still there, and the both of them look at me. So I ask the mare, "Where's the water at? I want to catch some dinner!"

The elegant mare prances around in excitement then motions for me to hop onto her back. Obliging her, I hop on, then she walks back up the field close to where Z is still sitting on the ground, farting around with that damned tractor of his and cussing to himself. He must've heard us going by because I see his head shoot up, then he looks directly at us walking away from him toward the tree line but doesn't say a word and just watches. The mare takes me into the woods and through the brush, then we step out into a ginormous clearing containing a huge lake. There should be plenty of fish in there! I slide down with my gear then set it on the ground. Taking the spoon, I begin to dig for some worms under the fallen tree leaves and dirt, and finding several pretty quickly, I fill up my container with some dirt and worms in no time!

The water is pretty clear, and I can see the bottom, where I stand a few feet away from the bank, barefoot, and up to my knees. I cast out my line, hoping there isn't a bunch of stumps or brush to get hung up on out there, and within seconds, I have a good bite and jerk the pole. It is a huge rush as I reel in the line. I can't stop smiling when I see a rather large hybrid sunfish on the other end, and it is big enough to clean and eat. So I place it on the stringer then cast out again. Within about forty-five minutes or so, I have a whole mess of fish, and the stringer is full. So I pack up the gear, dying to feed my rumbling tummy.

The two horses have been patiently waiting and watching me the entire time as if they've enjoyed it. Satan motions for me to climb onto his back, but this time, I can't manage to get up that high with all this crap. So in an elegant manner, he bows down so that I can mount him. I manage to climb on. Then once I get myself situated, we make our way back toward the house.

Coming out of the tree line, Ezekeial is walking toward us. "What have you been doing?" he questions me, looking curious. Then glancing over at my stringer full of fish, a surprised expression flies across his face, and he tries to hide a smile.

"Well, if a person is desperate enough for some groceries, sometimes you have to improvise!" I hiss, still pissed at him.

He can't hide his smile any longer and lets out a muffled laugh. Then shaking his head, he says, "You never stop surprising me!"

Giving Satan a gentle nudge, he takes the hint and slowly takes off. I leave Z standing alone without speaking another word to him while he watches us walk away, and I definitely don't look back!

After getting the fish cleaned, I begin to get everything prepared. I'm limited on resources here, so I have to do some more improvising. Luckily, I've watched Grandma Cox prepare fish before, so I do have a little bit of know-how. I cut up some of the potatoes that are sitting on the counter after finding a deep fryer under one of the bottom cabinets then prepare my oil. There is a skillet on top of the stove, so I wash it then pour some oil into it as well. I get my flour and eggs ready in a couple of bowls then season the flour with some salt and pepper. My tester potato is floating around in the fryer, so this is how I know my oil is ready to fry up some fish. I dredge my fish in the flour then the egg and then back in the flour once again, thus throwing it into the deep fryer. Normally, Grandma Cox uses cornmeal for her fish, but flour and egg is the best I can do. The skillet on the stove is also ready, so I place my potatoes in it too. I use the new iPhone to time my fish for six minutes on the one side and then let it float to the top on the other side. Lining a cookie sheet with some paper towels, I then shake some salt onto it. My timer goes off, so I flip my fish, and by the time I get done, I have a whole cookie sheet filled with fried fish, along with a skillet full of fried potatoes and some sweet tea. Feeling pretty impressed with myself, I turn around to go outside to tell Z it is time to eat, but he is already standing in the kitchen, staring at me. *I wonder how long he's been standing there. If that's not creepy as hell!*

"Are you hungry?" I ask him, but he just stands over there, looking at me. "Hello, are you hungry?" I ask him again.

Breaking out of his trance, he replies, "Yes, I am very hungry!" He is still staring at me, and his intense green-eyed gaze is making me feel really uncomfortable.

"What's wrong?" I question him, but he just smiles and says, "I am fine. Thank you for cooking supper."

"No problem! Let's eat!" I cry out ecstatically because this girl is dying to stuff her face!

There is a small round table in the kitchen area, so after I place everything on it, I sit down. He joins me, but I've forgotten to get some ketchup, which I did see in the fridge earlier. So I get up to grab it then fix my plate. Luckily, my fish turns out better than expected, and I'm really impressed with myself yet again!

"This is very good!" Z tells me while he inhales his dinner.

"Thank you!" I say happily, thrilled that he likes the food. Then after we eat, I clean up the mess and wash the dishes, and he is sitting at the table, just staring at me again! It is not in a bad way, just staring, so I ignore it and go on about my business.

I smell like worms and fish, so I go up to the room that my things are in and draw up some bathwater in the tub. The bathtub looks brand-new, and it is really big. I love it! I plan on soaking for a while and listening to my new iPhone using my headphones, so while I wait on my bathwater, I download YouTube then flip through the different music, making up my own playlist.

I step into the steaming hot water after I undress and gather up my gear. *Ahh, nice!* I turn on the music, lean back, and close my eyes. Then once I soak for a while, I remove my headphones so that

I can dunk my head under the water to get my hair wet. There are some shampoo, conditioner, bodywash, and facial cleanser sitting on a small table next to the tub. Crap! I forgot to grab a washcloth! Looking around, I spy a cabinet standing against the far wall with the mirror and sink, so I get out of the tub then walk over to it. There are some towels and washcloths inside it. So after grabbing a washcloth, I turn around to get back into the tub, and he is standing in the doorway, watching me! *Oh…my…lord! What's his trip?*

"What's wrong with you?" I ask him, wanting to know what his problem is. Z looks quite shocked when I ask him this, and when he tries to speak, his words are all fumbled together. "Take off your clothes and get in the tub with me," I order him because his deep, intense gaze is driving me nuts!

He comes back to life. "I do not think I should do that."

"Well, if you're not going to get in with me, would you mind finding something else to do so that I can sit here and relax? I can't do it with you staring at me like that," I bark at him.

He walks out of the bathroom, so I put my headphones on again, turn on my playlist, sit back, then close my eyes, and relax. But the next thing I know, he is climbing in the tub with me! I jump up and look at him, shocked as hell. But he looks way too amazing to even begin griping, so I forget all about my anger and just enjoy! Z sits with his back facing me then leans back against me, resting his arms on my knees.

"I'm glad that you've decided to join me!" I tell him while squirting some bodywash in my hand then proceed to massage his shoulders.

He sits quietly and lets me rub all over him, and I can tell that he is enjoying himself quite a bit when he releases a content growl from under his breath. Without warning, he turns around to face me then places his hands around my head, pulling me to him, and rubs his face against mine. His stubbles are a little rough, but I deal with it and enjoy the affection that he is giving me.

"This is nice, and I am enjoying myself a lot! Thank you!" he tells me softly while I run my fingers through his hair and massage his head. He is in heaven right now and melts in my hands.

"We will go shopping after we get up in the morning, okay?" he says, relishing in my affections.

"Yes, that's fine," I answer.

Z and I sit in the tub for a while longer. But the water is getting cold, so I tell him that I'm ready to clean up and get out. "Okay," he says as he begins to resituate himself.

Z gets out first, but just when I begin to get out, he grabs me around the waist, lifts me up out of the tub, and then carries me to the bed. He lies me down gently even though I'm dripping wet and getting the bed totally soaked! He begins to rub his hands all over me and then climbs on top of me. *Wow! Maybe this will be it!* I can feel his member's warm hardness against my thigh. *Just do it!* I want to scream at him. He gets close enough for it to touch me, and I can feel it twitching and throbbing against my sweet spot. But suddenly, he stops. *OMG! Not again!* I'm screaming in silence.

"I cannot do this," he says then gets up and walks out of the room.

What the hell is wrong with him! Ahhhh! Feeling like I must be diseased or something, I get a towel, finish drying off, turn on the TV, and then climb into the bed, naked. To hell with it, I'm done!

It is hot in here. I've got the ceiling fan on, but it is not helping much. So I open the French doors to get more air then lie back down without any covers on. I turn over on my side and gaze out across the night sky, enjoying the fresh air and the sounds of the night. The moon hangs high tonight, spilling out its amazing, mesmerizing light across the land, and I can hear the creatures of the night doing their prowling, chattering, and calling out to one another, along with the faint cry of a pack of coyotes. A light breeze circulates through the air, making it a little bit cooler, and I love the earthy smells that it carries along with it. While I lose myself into the peaceful tranquility of the evening, I feel him climb back in bed with me then curl up around me. This guy must be really sexually frustrated! He wraps his arms around me tightly, but I just lie here, trying to decide if I should make contact or to not move at all. I can feel his manhood rising along my backside, and its warm, excited wetness is running down my naked skin. I'm not going to keep this shit up all night!

I turn over on my back, and he is staring at me with sympathetic eyes then leans over and kisses me on the lips, so I kiss him back. I place both of my hands on his head and pull him closer to me, forcing him to reposition himself, so when he begins to move over on top of me, I make my move! I pull him down on top of me and quickly reposition myself so that he enters my body then force myself upon his manhood, trying to hold him down or at least try to. Z struggles a little bit and then stops. He could very easily get away from me if he wanted to because he is much more powerful than I am, but I know that he has been dying for this just as much as myself. I roll him over then mount him without him putting up any kind of a fight because I'm going to ride this beast if it is the last thing I do! *Thank you, sweet baby Jesus!* Sitting on top of him, I begin.

At first, having him inside me hurts like hell, but the longer I ride him, the feeling becomes glorious. And I'm lavishing in all the wonderful sexual sensations. He is in rhythm with me, holding onto my sides with his hands forcing me up and down. I bend down and kiss him on the lips. Then holding my mouth above his, I breath into his face, "I love you, Z."

He pulls me down on top of him then wraps his arms around me but says nothing. Z is ready to go again, so he flips me around on my back and thrusts into me then takes his time kissing me while we move in sequence with each other. And even though his lovin' feels amazing, a tear rolls down my cheek because I was waiting to hear him tell me the same three words, but he didn't.

He is going faster, and I'm close to being finished. So I forget all about my disappointment and lose myself in the moment. Z gets done before me but doesn't stop, knowing that I haven't gotten done yet, and it doesn't take long before the fabulous sensations break free and the best climax that I've ever experienced is released. He lies on top of me for a bit and rubs his hands along my head then through my hair. "We were not supposed to do that, but I want you to know that it was wonderful and thank you," he tells me softly.

I lie here, lost in my own thoughts, feeling my disappointment setting back in. I put my hand on his face and slowly run it down along his neck then down to his chest, stopping here to feel his heartbeat while I stare off into another world, trying not to cry, because I'm tired of playing this twisted guessing game.

"I just want to tell you that whatever happens, I will always love you, my love," he whispers to me, and I can feel his heart pound harder and see what looks like tears welling up in his eyes. He wraps his arms around me again, pulls me in tightly, and then holds me for a while; so I lie here in silence with my arms wrapped around him, running my fingers along his back and thrilled by him telling me what I wanted to hear. Z releases his grip then pulls my face to his and kisses me with so much passion and love that I want him to know that I feel the same way about him, so I kiss him back harder, wanting to shower him with all my love and affections too. He lies on top of me, and we begin again. He feels amazing inside me, and I want more of him. Z licks my breasts and nibbles on my nipples, sending me into phenomenal sexual bliss. His thrusting is getting stronger, and I can't hold back anymore as another wave of pure ecstasy is released.

We finish and snuggle up for the night, then he whispers to me, "You will always be mine." Lying next to him, an ominous feeling sweeps over me, and I can't help but wonder what he is holding back and not telling me. Then he kisses my cheek. "I will love you forever." I say nothing but enjoy his sweet words while we lie next to each other, satisfied with our amazing lovemaking.

The sun's blinding light shines through the open doors, and the smell of the early spring morning is upon us. I look over at Z. He is sleeping peacefully, and a small snore escapes his mouth every so often. I lie quietly and just look at him because I love him so much and always want to be with him. Looking at every detail of his body while he rests, I can't help but want to touch him, so I reach over and gently brush away the hair that is in his face, pushing it back. He doesn't stir. So I try to go back to sleep, but I can't. Ezekeial must have awakened because I feel him run his fingers through my hair then along my face, so I open my eyes and look right into his. We lock our eyes together, and he leans in then kisses me softly.

My stomach begins to growl loudly, and he laughs. "I think someone is very hungry!"

"You know I'm always hungry!" I reply.

"Yes, my love, this I know very well," he says then laughs again.

We hop into the shower together, and he begins to go into fore-play mode. "Nope, we're not doing anymore until I get some food!" I gripe, shoving him away from me.

He looks at me and smiles from ear to ear. "Well then, let us get out of here!"

I get dressed then grab a pen and some paper to make out my grocery list. Z comes down the stairs and looks at my list. "I am going to have to get another job to keep you fed!" he tells me, laughing. So I poke him in the gut while giving him the squinty eye, and he is loving the hell out of teasing me.

We get in the truck then drive to the city, but before we hit the grocery store, we make a trip to the mall first. It has been a while since I've been in one, and I go absolutely hog wild! I need a few new clothes because my body has been changing a lot over the past few years, and I'm constantly buying new clothes that fit right. I've never looked any better than I do now, and I love to show it off. Why not? If you've got it, flaunt it! While we're looking around the stores, a gleaming glass window over at the jewelry store catches my eye, and I just have to go over there to check it out!

My eyes are stuck like glue to the contents inside because it contains a beautiful wedding ring set, which was made by Vera Wang, and I love her style of jewelry. I can't break away from it! The engagement ring has a half-karat, rose-cut diamond adorning the top, set into a platinum band, with diamonds all around it. There is a hint of twenty-four-karat gold trimming the outside of the platinum, and it is absolutely gorgeous! The wedding ring has a round two-karat diamond adorning the top of it, with two blue diamonds on either side of the top diamond set into platinum. Diamonds wrap all the way around the band with a hint of twenty-four-karat gold trimming along the edge of the band as well. Ezekeial walks over to me then takes a look at what I'm staring at.

"Wow! That is beautiful!" he cries out while staring at the spar-kly bling.

"Yes, it is! Jewelry is so expensive!" I complain once I glance at the price. The price of the whole works is eighteen thousand dollars, but I can still look at it and wish!

We stop in at Old Navy, and I pick up some pants, along with a couple of dresses that are on sale. I also find the softest, fuzziest purple blanket ever and just have to have it! I decide that I should grab two of them just for the simple fact that, when you wear one out, you'll never be able to find the same one ever again! We leave the mall then hit Sam's Club, and I can shop, let me tell you! I absolutely love Sam's Club! Z seems like he is really enjoying this expedition, and sometimes I can see him staring over at me, just watching me. I know that he is madly in love with me, and I relish in the thought of it because I feel the same way about him.

I'm not old enough to buy liquor yet, but he is. So I throw a couple of bottles of Jose Cuervo Gold into the cart.

"What are those for?" he asks, looking at me curiously.

"They're for a just-in-case type of day. Plus I'll cook with it," I explain.

"Well, if that is the case, then we will take them," he tells me happily with a huge smile.

"Can I add a couple bottles of wine too? How much money am I allowed to spend? I still need peanut butter, crackers, and Capri Suns!" I cry out frantically, and Ezekeial can't help but bust up laughing.

"My love, get whatever you want. I do not care what you spend."

"Great! I'm sure glad you have that truck!" I blurt out, and he laughs at me again, shaking his head.

By the time we get done, the truck is completely loaded down. Z makes fun of me, telling me that we should've brought the trailer while we head back to the house. "Ha, ha!" I say to him, rolling my eyes, then lean over to kiss his cheek.

I've also picked up some cookbooks because they always say, "The way to a man's heart is through his stomach!" so I want to be the best cook possible! Looking around the cab of the truck, I dread getting to the house and putting all this stuff away! We get back to the house and begin to unload the endless supply of groceries that we've just bought, and it seems like it takes a lifetime to get all the stuff put away. We're both beat by the time we finish then decide to just snack on some finger foods and to watch a little TV, so I grab one of my new blankets then we snuggle up on the couch together.

"That was quite a day!" Ezekeial tells me happily.

Laughing at him, I say, "It was a lot of fun! Thank you for buying all of that stuff!"

"Anything for you, my love!" he says with a smirk across his face.

"I'm ready for bed!" I tell him, beginning to yawn.

I start to get up, but he grabs my arm. "Wait for me! I am coming with you!" We get to my room and get ready for bed. Then that night, we have some more glorious lovemaking, and I'm loving this new chapter in my life and hope that it continues to stay this way.

Getting up in the morning, I decide to run downstairs to fix some breakfast. I begin cooking when I realize that I've forgotten to take my birth-control pill, so I bolt upstairs to take it right away. I left them lying in the bathroom vanity drawer up in my room, so trying to tread lighty, not wanting to wake him up, I sneak into the room as quietly as I can. Of course, I drop the pack on the floor, and he walks in, asking me what I'm doing.

"I'm taking my pill for the day," I answer.

Looking at me, puzzled, he says, "What do you mean by 'pill'? What is wrong?"

"I take birth-control pills daily to keep from getting pregnant because I don't want to be a mom right now in my life," I explain, and he looks at me strangely but doesn't say another word. I smell my food cooking downstairs, so I rush down to finish the breakfast.

Following me downstairs, he asks me, sounding curious, "Do you want to have children someday?"

"Well, of course, don't you?"

"I do not know because I have never really thought about it," he answers, thinking about this new conversation.

"Anyway, how do you like your eggs?" I ask, changing the subject. He smiles at me while I get his food ready. "When should I begin doing all of this studying that you want me to do?" I question him while I make his plate.

"We will begin today if you want to. We need to take a look at that college application as well," he replies when we sit down to eat.

"Sounds great!" I reply happily then dive into my plate.

Z takes me upstairs after breakfast, then we go into a room across the hall from mine. This is his library slash office. There is a computer along with all kinds of books and papers lining the walls on some bookshelves. I begin to glance through a couple of them, and there are all kinds of weird pictures and writing.

"You know how you've said that you want me to learn Romanian? Well, I could barely pass Spanish, so I'm not sure how well this is going to turn out," I explain, feeling worried.

He looks up at me from the book he is going through. "I think you will learn it easily! If I was able to learn English, you should be able to learn Romanian!"

"I guess," I reply, shrugging my shoulders. We fill out the college application, and then he grabs me a book off the shelf. It is a strange color of brownish tan, and it looks really old.

"What's this about?" I ask him.

"It talks about the different types of supernatural creatures, such as werewolves, ghosts, vampires, etc. It is not allowed for a vampire and werewolf to be together, and it is strictly forbidden because the bloodlines should not be mixed together," he explains to me while I listen intently.

"Why not? If they fall in love, whose right is it to say they shouldn't have kids? They'd be called werepires!" I say, grinning, but Z just looks at me and gives me the "whatever" look then carries on.

"Also, it is forbidden for a vampire to feed on another vampire."

"I fed from you when my beast was born!" I remind him.

"Yes, that was forbidden," he says flatly.

"I've broken the rules already! I'm going to be a terrible vampire!" I begin to laugh, but Z doesn't find this funny because he shoots me a serious, annoyed glance.

*****

Time passes by quickly, and it is almost time to go back to school. We had gone and visited my family last weekend and picked up the old Trans Am. I'm ecstatic about getting to see everyone and for getting my car back. Ezekeial and I have been going through so many books and papers that I'm filled up to the gills with knowledge! I guess so, anyway, but I don't agree with a lot of the things that their so-called Elders have to say because it is a bunch of hogwash if you ask me. Nevertheless, I read along and listen to him quietly because he seems to enjoy talking about his home plus the things that are written in all those books. This is his world, and he has the know-how of how things work and between what is right and wrong in their world. But I just don't think that I fit quite right into *their* world. I've been studying his language too. It is a bit tricky, but I think I'll be able to learn it well. Being here with him has been wonderful, and I'm really happy. Although, I do still, once in a while, get a strange sense that he is hiding something, but it'll eventually be revealed when the time is right.

School is underway, and I've gotten my new routine down pat. I get up in the morning and get ready for class, then decide what I plan on cooking for dinner so that I can lay my meat out to thaw while I'm gone. Some days I do classes at home, so I begin those days at my own leisure. After class, if I need anything from the store, I'll pick it up before I come home. I get started on supper when I get to the house then begin laundry or whatever chore needs to be done. We eat, I clean up the dishes and finish my chores that I've started earlier, and then it is time for our study sessions. Ezekeial's job is his farm, and it takes a lot of work to keep that ship running. He is out there every day, all-day long doing something, because his cattle and property are constantly needing some sort of attention. His beautiful horse's name is Dutchess. She is such a doll and lavishes on lots of affection. She and Satan have become rather close these days, just like Z and I, and are always together out in the pasture, and I'm so glad that he has someone to be with in my absence. I don't feel so bad about not being able to spend as much time with him since Dutchess is with him.

"What is for supper tonight, my love, and how were your classes at school today?" Z asks me when he comes in for the evening.

"It was pretty good today. The assignments were really easy, and I was able to get everything done before I came home." Looking at him, I can tell that he really likes it when I call this place home because his eyes shine with happiness, and I'm so glad that he is satisfied with me being here. "I'm going to fix some chicken and stuffed tortellini for dinner, along with some garlic bread. Does that sound okay?" I ask him while I'm preparing to get my ingredients all together.

"Yes, that sounds very good! I am going to get cleaned up," he tells me happily.

"Okay, you know where to find me!" I say, laughing to myself because the kitchen is my best friend!

He smiles at me then goes upstairs. The funny thing is, I've never been in his room at all, and I don't even know what it looks like on the inside. I know he has a bathroom in there, but that's it because he always comes to mine. After he comes in from outside, he'll go into his room to take a shower and change his clothes, then we always go to my room to sleep. I don't ask him about it because I'm waiting for him to volunteer the information or ask me to check it out.

Dinner is almost finished, and he comes back downstairs, ready to eat. "Smells good!" he says while he turns on the TV to watch the news because he always checks out the weather forecast for the next day. I tell him that he can look at it on my phone, but he likes to see it on the TV.

Dinner is finished, and we sit down to eat. "When school gets out, would you like to take a trip to Romania with me to visit my family?" he asks, staring me down.

"Sure! It sounds like it would be quite the adventure because I never pictured myself going anywhere like that before! Are there any werewolves there?" I ask him, dying to see one.

He laughs loudly at me. "But of course, my dear, one lives at the estate with my mother, stepfather, and half brother. His name is Lazar, and he has been with us for as long as I can remember. We used to play together as children. His mother used to be with us as well, but she was in an accident and passed away."

"Wow! Does he 'wolf out' during the full moon like in the movies?" I ask excitedly, and he laughs at me again.

"Well, he does 'wolf out' during the full moon, but I do not know all of the details about it. I have not seen him in a very long time, but you can ask him all of that once we get there," he answers but not really smiling this time.

I clean up the dinner dishes then put away the leftovers, and I'm ready for a nice, hot bath! There is no studying for me tonight, so I climb up the stairs and head to my room. It is dark out, and I can see tons of stars outside from the balcony. The moon is bright and alive, so I open the French doors with my mind's power then begin to fill up the tub. I only have the bathroom light on because I want to see the stars and the midnight sun shining up in the night sky, so I light a few candles in the bathroom then shut off the light. My water is steaming hot, and I love the heat against my tired, weary body. I lie on my stomach then look out over toward the balcony, viewing the radiant evening. A soft breeze blows through the room, setting the mood for a wonderful night's rest. It is so peaceful and calm, and every once in a while, I can hear one of the cows making some noise. But otherwise, all is quiet.

"What are you doing, my love?" Z asks while I relax, letting my mind clear and body rest.

"I'm just enjoying the night, Z. It's really nice tonight."

"Indeed, it is," he agrees softly while standing in the doorway. He comes over, sits down next to me, and then rubs my arm, looking out into the night sky himself. "It has been really nice having you here. You make me very happy," he tells me in almost a whisper.

"I'm glad that you're happy with me because I don't know what I'd do if you didn't want me! Oh! Before I forget to tell you, I have a doctor's appointment in the morning. So I'm going to class later on, and I may be a little late getting home," I explain.

"Why ever on earth are you going to the doctor?" he questions me, looking puzzled.

"I need to get my pills refilled soon," I explain.

"Pills? Oh yes, that. I understand. What time will you be making it home?" he asks me, giving me a hard stare.

"I'm not sure, but I'll text you when I'm on my way home."

"That is fine because I know you will be coming back to me." Z flashes me a giant smile then rubs my back.

"Of course, always!" I say, staring deep into his eyes while he gazes at me lovingly then kisses my cheek.

I get out of the tub then do my nightly ritual. I dry off, slather myself up with lotion, brush my hair and teeth, and then grab my phone to look at my emails while lying in bed. Z lies with me and snuggles up to me. His head is lying on my chest, and he rubs my bare belly lightly. It tickles, and I jump then laugh.

"Quit it!" I yell at him, and he laughs out loud and does it again. He is aggravating me so that I'll put my phone down and give him some attention, so I put my phone down then rub his body with my hands. He lies motionless, and I can see the goose bumps pop out of his skin. Z rubs his face against my chest then kisses my bare breast. "I love you, Z," I whisper to him then put my face on his head, smelling his clean hair.

"I know you do, and I want you to know that I will always be here for you because you are my one and only love."

With that, he turns over and faces me. Then reaching up and grabbing my face with his hands, he pulls me down to kiss my lips. I kiss him passionately while I run my hand down to his manhood then massage it lightly, just barely touching it. This pushes him over the edge, and he is ready to go. So he pulls me on top of him then begins to kiss me everywhere. He is gentle with me while thrusting himself inside me, and it feels amazing! I kiss his neck while losing myself within his wonderful lovin', then he whispers in my ear, "I will love you forever." I feel tears welling up in my eyes, and I wonder how I could have ever been so lucky to have this wonderful man in my life. A man who is so caring and loving, although mysterious at times, loves me like this. A few tears stream down my face, so I quickly wipe them away before he notices.

*****

It is morning, and my day begins once again! I want to make sure that I get squeaky-clean before I get to the doctor, so I scrub myself extra hard.

"Bye, baby! I'll see you when I get home!" I say then kiss Z on the lips while he is still lying in bed.

"Make sure that you let me know when you are on your way home. Goodbye, my love," he tells me after he gives me a few kisses.

I hop into my old TA and make tracks, and the rhythmic purr of the engine, along with the humming of the tires, sends me off into my thinking place. Thoughts race around inside my brain when I'm driving in the morning, but my mind is crystal clear once I have some time to myself.

Making it to the doctor, I get the necessary stuff done to get a refill on my pills then head for school. The day seems to drag on endlessly, and I just can't get with it today. My mind is wandering everywhere, except on school. They've called in my prescription at Walmart, so I plan on stopping to pick it up before I go home. Plus I need a few other things. It is the one-stop shop, and I love it!

Classes are over, but I stay a little later to get the paperwork done that I had missed this morning because I'm going to do school online tomorrow and won't be back until next Monday. It is Thursday today, and I don't usually attend classes on Fridays. Finishing up my work, I put my things away then head out to the car. It is getting ready to storm, and I want to make it to Walmart before it decides to pour down rain. Luckily, the rain waits until after I'm in the store, so I stop to grab my prescription first. I then take my cart and begin to shop. I can hear the rain hitting the roof violently, and it is a gusher out there! Thunder is bellowing all around outside. So I text Z to ask him if he needs anything while I'm in the store, but I don't get any response. I realize that it didn't go through because I can't ever text anyone inside this store, but I'm not about to walk outside to text. So after grabbing what I need, I make my way to the checkout to pay for my stuff. The rain has let off a little bit, so I race to the car and unload my groceries in the trunk.

Getting back on the road, I forget all about texting Z from being in such a hurry to get home. Lightning and thunder blast through the sky, and the wind is pounding the Trans Am. I can hardly see where I'm driving on the road as the rain strikes the car with such violent, raging force, so I decide to just pull over because there is no point in wrecking the car trying to get home right now. I grab my phone to text Ezekeial, but once again, I haven't gotten any service.

"That's just great!" I complain to myself out loud because it is a flooding downpour outside, and I don't think it is going to stop at any time soon! I look at my watch, and it is already 6:56 p.m. I usually get home at about 5:20 p.m. "Good, he won't worry about it much then," I say to myself, gazing out the windshield. No one drives by me the entire time I'm sitting in the car when, suddenly, a knock on the driver's side window startles me. I look over, and some guy with an umbrella is peering in at me, gesturing for me to roll my window down.

"Are you okay, ma'am?" he asks me kindly.

"I'm fine! I'm just waiting for the storm to let up a little. You should get back into your vehicle! You're soaked!" I tell him while watching the rain drench him.

"I just wanted to check on you since you're parked on the side of the road here," he tells me, smiling.

"Well, thank you, but I'm fine," I reply, so he nods and then begins to turn around.

The next thing I know, he is forcing himself into my car, and he manages to open the door then tries to drag me out. I'm so flabbergasted that I can't even function when he jabs a needle in my arm then hits me in the face. "What the hell are you doing!" I scream at him angrily. I could rip this guy's head right off if I wanted to, but I begin to drift off into the nothingness when the drug he hit me with kicks in. Shaking my head, I try to sober myself up. *What the hell did he inject into me!* I feel myself beginning to fall over in my seat, and the rain is pouring inside the car. The guy is fumbling around, trying to pick me up out of the seat quickly. I'm getting completely soaked from the rain, but I'm not able to break away from this stranger's grasp. I can hear the lightning and thunder cracking in the sky, but I can't open my eyes because they're as heavy as lead weights right now.

"Man, you're a nice one!" I hear him say while I'm going farther into the darkness, fading in and out, trying to fight off whatever this is running rampant through my veins. I can feel him carrying me somewhere, and he is slipping on the slick, wet pavement. "You and I are gonna have a lot of fun tonight!" I can barely hear him say.

"No, you are not, asshole!" A familiar voice calls out from the storm. "I am going to tear you limb from limb!" it says angrily. I don't think I can fight it anymore, and I'm gone!

"Renee…Renee…my love!" I hear him, but I can't move. I fade away again.

"Baby, wake up!" I feel a hand caressing my jaw and around my face. I'm fighting to open my eyes, but it is not working, as I plunge back into the dark abyss. "Will you please wake up!" he is screaming in my ear. I feel like there is a heavy, massive weight pressing down on top of me, and I can't move. I must be sitting in the tub because I can hear the water splashing all around me, but my body is a dead lead weight. A warm cloth is being rubbed along my face, and fighting with all my might to open up my eyes, my eyelids finally lift up. And I can see him—my guardian angel.

"Renee, talk to me!" Z is pleading with me, but I still can't move or even whisper and can only just look at him. I'm not sure how much longer I lie motionless, but I can slowly feel my body coming back to me. So I jump up, freaking out. Z wraps his arms around me, and water is flying all over while I struggle to regain control of myself.

"Renee, calm down," he tells me softly. "Calm down."

I'm still struggling and fighting, trying to catch my bearings, but it is not working. So I just stop then go limp, with Z holding me up out of the water. I'm one hell of a damned hot mess! It is the scariest feeling not being able to move like this and not being able to open your eyes or to even talk!

After what seems like an eternity, I can finally move my arm, so I put my hand on his head. And he begins to whimper a bit. "Z?" I say in a breathless whisper.

"Yes, my love," he replies, and his eyes fly wide open.

"Am I at home now?" I ask him in a breathless whisper.

"Yes, my love, I have you," he answers while lifting me out of the tub then wraps me up in a towel, and the rest of the night is history because I don't remember anything at all.

Coming to, I can hear the sound of the rain and the thunder still pounding at the earth, so I open my eyes slowly and look around. Ezekeial has a death grip on my arm. And it must be a new day, but it is still dark and gray outside from the storm. I have to pee something awful, but he is stuck to me like glue.

"Z, let me go," I tell him, feeling anxious.

His eyes fly open, and he smiles from ear to ear. Z lifts up his hand then touches my face. "I am glad that you are awake," he says happily.

"I've got to pee! Can you please help me to the toilet?" I ask, feeling like I'm about to have a urinary explosion at any time.

"Come, let us get up."

He helps me out of bed and into the bathroom just in the nick of time! Wow! That was close! I didn't think I was going to make it! My head is pounding terribly, and I have the worst case of cotton mouth ever. Z is standing in the doorway, waiting for me to finish, so once I get done, he helps me to the sink. I brush my teeth and take a drink of water from the faucet.

"Do you feel better, my love?" he asks me while I wipe my face with the hand towel.

"Not really. My head is going to burst open at any time, and I really need a Mountain Dew. I'm just a flippin' train wreck right now!"

He laughs at me. "Still my same Renee! Let me help you back to bed, and I will grab your soda and a snack," he tells me excitedly.

I lie back down. He disappears then returns with a Mountain Dew and some crackers.

"What in the hell happened?" Z questions me after I take a huge gulp of my soda.

"I pulled over to the side of the road because the rain and wind was so strong that the TA was all over the road! I didn't want to wreck it, so I pulled off to the side to wait it out. I tried to call you, but I couldn't get any service. Then some guy knocks on the window and tells me that he was just checking on me to make sure I was okay. I told him that I was fine. Then the next thing I know, my door flies open, I get stuck in the arm with a needle, and I was out cold! I could hear a little, but I couldn't move or talk. That guy was lucky he caught me off guard. Otherwise, I'd have messed him up!"

Z begins to laugh. "It is okay because I messed him up for you! No one hurts my love!"

I give him a smile, then I remember about my car. "OMG! Where's the TA!" I cry out loud then jump up frantically.

"It is fine! I have it in the driveway," Z replies, chuckling.

"Thank goodness, because that car's my boo!" I cry out again, and he cracks up laughing.

"I love you so much, my love."

"I love you too and thanks for rescuing me!" I tell him happily as he embraces me. Then we lie in bed together, listening to the rain.

Later that evening, we have the news on, and they have a special report about a serial rapist attacking women locally. He would ask them if they needed help and then force his way into their car, thus injecting them with a sedative to knock them out. He would then take them to a designated location and rape them, sometimes almost beating them to death. His body was found sitting in his car parked along the side of a dirt road with his needles stuck all over his body, and he had been severely beaten and disemboweled. I look over at Z, and he is smiling happily.

CHAPTER 13

Romania

School is over once again, and summer begins. I'm ready for it! I've been helping Ezekeial repair some of his fencing because his cattle had torn down a big section of it the other week, and we had to replace it. It was a lot of work, but we've finally gotten it done. I scratched my name into one of the new wooden posts and carved "Renee was here" onto it. I've noticed that Z has become pretty quiet these days and seems to keep to himself lately. And I've asked him numerous times if I've done something to upset him, but he tells me that everything is fine. I'm thinking that it is not. His mother had called the other day and has planned us a trip to Romania in two weeks. But I have a lot of mixed feelings about this trip, and I also get a strange, ominous, and uneasy vibe when I think about it.

"Z, how long are we going to be away in Romania?" I ask him, wanting to find out more about this dreaded trip.

"I am not sure what my mother has in mind, but I will find out," he answers without looking me in the eye.

"I'm not sure what it is, but I'm not feeling this trip at all!" he looks over at me, and his eyes are full of a strange, worried expression.

"What is wrong? Do you not want to go now?" he asks me with an intense questioning stare.

"I have to go. It's all been paid for, but...," I begin to say but stop midsentence.

"But what, my love?" he asks, staring me down with those mesmerizing green eyes of his.

"Nothing. It's nothing! I'll be fine!" I tell him after looking away from him. And I can tell that something is terribly wrong, but I don't ask because I don't want to make an issue out of it.

The time has come, and we're leaving the house tomorrow afternoon to catch our flight to Romania. I've packed some clothes and gear, went over my list, and then checked it again. I'm ready, I guess, stuck going regardless.

"Whatever you do, do not tell any of them that we have been making love, please!" Ezekeial tells me sternly, looking worried.

"I don't plan on it, because it's none of their concern or business, anyway," I reply, unhappily.

He smiles at me then looks away quickly, and after he goes to sleep tonight, I'm going to go hunting and visit the lake. Occasionally, I wait until Z is fast asleep, then I fly over to the lake. I step into the water, embracing Mother Earth and the gods, because their power pulsates throughout my veins, and under the midnight sun, I return the extra power that has built up inside me back to them. If I don't release my extra power, it becomes very overwhelming and almost impossible to control. Plus I want to feed before I go because I can't eat that dead cow in a bag shit like Z eats sometimes.

It is late, and I hear the rhythmic beating of his heart while he dreams away. So I slowly slide myself out of bed, trying not to make a sound or shake the bed then quickly make my way outside. Setting my beast free, I spread my wings and take flight. I'm free at last!

Soaring above the trees, I descend over the lake, and Satan and Dutchess meet me there because they know exactly what I'm doing. I give them both a loving rubdown and then walk down to the water's edge and step into the gentle waves. The light of the moon is beaming down upon me, and I feel like it is giving me an awesome kind of power as it kisses my body. The wind blows a bit, and the water splashes around my ankles after I stick my hands into the water. Then a pair of watery hands rise from the depths and take my hands into theirs, removing some of my unused power. I whisper to the unseen entity while it holds onto my hands in a delicate fashion, thanking the gods for this wonderful life that I'm having and for blessing me with these wonderful gifts. My power trickles out around me, leaving my body slowly, trailing throughout the lake in a glowing bluish light. The light extends upward toward me and radiates all around me while glittering light, like tiny snowflakes, shimmer out of the darkness into the light then dissipate when they fall down upon me. My power surges deep within me, and I can feel the tingly electrical sensations flowing throughout my veins. It is absolutely fulfilling, and I embrace all of it.

Once my water spirit has finished, I step out of the water then approach the two horses, and they gracefully bow in my presence. I get between them then wrap one of my arms around each of the horse's necks, giving them as much love and affection as I can give to them. They rub their heads against mine then give me their horse talk, and I love them both so much. I talk to them and tell them all about our trip, letting them know that I'll be gone for a while. Satan isn't too keen with it but nods in acceptance. I confide in him, telling him that I have a very bad feeling about this trip and that it is making me feel a little unnerved. After giving them some time, I kiss them both on the muzzle then take flight to feed.

I find my late-night snack, satiate my hunger, and then head for home but stop along the tree line and land on the ground because I can hear and smell someone or something familiar, so I scan the surrounding area, trying to pinpoint whatever or whoever it is. I'm really surprised to see Ezekeial walking out of the woods toward me, then he reaches out his arms and tangles them around me. He has totally "beastied" out, and his heavenly, loving embrace sends shivers along my spine.

"I love you, my love," he whispers to me then pulls me to his lips and kisses me ever so gently. "Please feed from me," he continues as if he is desperate for my affections.

"What's wrong? Something's wrong!" I cry out in desperation, pleading with him to tell me what is bothering him so much, but he just stands in front of me, staring at me.

"Nothing. Please drink from me, my love," he answers while holding his arm up toward my mouth.

I submit to his desire and take his arm into my mouth and slowly bite down. Once my fangs sink into his flesh, I begin to drink.

This, of course, sends me into an erotic state of mind, and it is pure ecstasy. Z pulls me into his chest and holds me tightly against him while pressing his chin into my head. Our tails intertwine around each other, then he repositions the two of us and begins kissing my neck. I'm feeling euphoric right now, wanting him so badly. He pulls his arm away from me, turns me around, grabs my sides, lifts me up off the ground, and then braces me against a tree. While holding me in place, he takes me from behind, thrusting ever so gently, but getting more aggressive as he continues. The sensation is phenomenal, setting my body ablaze, and he is rubbing his face between my shoulders, moaning from his pleased sexual satisfaction. We've never made love like this before, and I don't ever want it to end!

This amazing experience lasts for quite some time, but I can't hold out any longer and finish. Z growls out loud, climaxing at the same time, but doesn't stop and continues growling, more like purring, rubbing me everywhere. And I don't know what has gotten into him, but I love it!

After making some fantastic love long into the night, Z sets me down then turns me around and stares into my eyes while he wraps his tail around mine. I see tears running down his face, and I just can't figure out what in the hell is happening! He pulls me into his arms, then wraps his wings around us, and just holds me while he begins to sob. I'm so totally confused! I wrap my arms around him and hold onto him, waiting patiently for him to release his emotions, not to mention, his vicelike grip from me. And I can hear him softly sobbing, and his heart is racing out of control. After a short while, he finally releases me from his grasp, unfolds his wings, and then unwinds his tail from mine.

"Come, let us go to bed," he says shakily then grabs my hand and walks me back to the house.

Once we're lying in bed, he clings to me like a little boy does when he doesn't want to leave his mother, and I can't sleep a wink, worrying about what is wrong with him. The little voice inside my head is screaming at me to stay behind while he goes on this trip, but I'm torn because I don't want to hurt anyone's feelings or offend them by not joining Z. I watch the time tick by, and it seems like the morning is never going to come while I lie in bed silently, with my mind racing like an out-of-control freight train. I listen to Z's resting breathing and steadily beating heart, and he looks so handsome lying beside me while he sleeps.

I must have dosed off at some point because the morning finally arrives, and the sun bursts through the windows, bathing us in all its glory. My phone is lying on the table next to me, so I pick it up, trying not to wake Z, wanting to get a couple of shots of him, then quickly set my phone down after I snap a few pictures. Z wakes up. I can feel him staring at me, so I look over at him. "I love you!" I say, smiling, then reach over and run my fingers through his hair. He smiles back at me and then places his hand over my stomach and rubs it gently. His piercing stare is burning a hole right into me while I lock eyes with him, then he brushes the hair out of my face with his fingers. We make love again, and this time, he makes it long and slow, savoring every moment with me as if it is the last time, showering me with all the love and affection he can give to me.

The nagging voice inside my head is almost livid, but I ignore it, deciding to join Z on this trip. So after gathering our stuff together, we pack up the truck to head for the airport. It is a quiet, long ride because neither of us have said a word, and it almost seems like someone has just died. It is taking my entire will to keep myself from throwing my door open and hauling ass back to the farm, but I manage to keep my cool.

Things get crazy once we park the truck, and once we board the plane, our long journey to Romania begins. I must have dosed off after takeoff because, looking down at my watch, three hours have passed by. Z is leaning against my shoulder, lost in his own thoughts, so I close my eyes again then feel him touch my face and run his fingers through my hair. He leans over then kisses my cheek softly, and I'm trying to hold back my emotions from wanting to scream at him because I'm dying to ask him just what in the hell the problem is. But I somehow manage to hold my composure, fighting it the whole way.

We've landed at our first layover, and I'm so glad to get off the plane to stretch my legs. I realize that I've left my camo backpack back at the truck and feel really lost without it. Our layover is forty-five minutes long, then we'll board another plane headed to Bucharest, and by the time we're through, the total amount of travel time will be about fourteen hours long.

"Do you want anything to snack on?" Z asks me while we mosey around the airport.

"No, thanks. I'm okay," I answer, feeling more unnerved and jittery than ever.

Ezekeial looks at me, surprised, because I never turn down a snack ever! "Are you okay, my love?" he questions me, looking concerned.

"I just don't feel like it, that's all. Something's off about this trip, and I'm scared," I answer. And I can swear that I see his eyes tearing up, but he chokes it back. I don't say anything about it, but I'm getting really worried. "Maybe I can just go back to the house! I'll even go back home to my mama's if you want me to, but I'm not feeling this trip at all! Just sayin'!" I gripe unhappily, staring him down. My heart begins to pound, and my stress level is topping off. But he just stares at me, sensing my tenseness, at a loss for words.

"We are already halfway there," he replies softly after a few minutes.

"I know but don't care! I'll go back to work at the truck stop to pay the money back for my ticket!" I plead with him desperately, and he seems to want to tell me that he'll let me go but doesn't say anything.

After a long pause, he says, "Well, why do you not just wait and see how you like Romania first? You may really enjoy it!" I shoot him a dirty look then walk away from him, mad as hell.

We board the next plane and continue on our way to Romania, so I put on my headphones and listen to my playlist, trying to calm my nerves. Z watches me intently, wanting me to look at him. But denying him my attention, I close my eyes and ignore him because if he wants to play games, so can I.

We arrive in Bucharest at 11:39 a.m. on their time, and we're about seven hours behind them in the US. I follow Z closely while we make our way through the airport, and he keeps looking back to make sure that I'm still with him.

I see someone flagging us down. "Ezekeial! Ezekeial!" A man cries out, waving his arms around, yelling Z's name.

"Lazar! My old friend! How have you been?" Z greets him cheerfully.

"I am doing well! You are looking really good these days! This must be Renee!" the man says then looks over at me, and I could just squeeze those cute chubby cheeks of his! He is the cutest guy ever!

His hair is dark brown, a little long, and wildly curly. His eyes are dark brown, with long dark eyelashes. And his cheeks are a little chubby, but he is not fat by any means. He is just a little bit taller than I am, and I can tell that he has a well-built shape underneath his T-shirt. He is quite pale and has a well-kept short beard and mustache, and I absolutely love the British-sounding accent coming from his mouth because it fits him perfectly! I love it when he talks!

"Yes, it is!" Z replies happily.

"Hello!" I greet him when we shake hands.

"Hello, my lady. My name is Lazar, and it is very nice to meet you! This place is a madhouse, so let's get out of here!" Lazar tells us then leads us out of the airport. He takes us to the car, then we get all our stuff loaded up.

"Ms. Renee, have you ever been here before?" he asks me, smiling.

"Nope. First time!" I answer, still feeling really unnerved.

"The estate is about thirty-five minutes from here, so let's get going, shall we?" Lazar says excitedly. But I'm feeling more of a sense of dread than ever, and Z keeps looking at me with worried, questioning wide eyes.

We drive through the city then head out to the countryside, and it is absolutely beautiful! The grass is a lush-green color, and the woods dance with life as we drive by. It is not really sunny, sort of overcast, today, but the weather is nice. Z and I both sit in the back, and I still have my headphones on while I stare out of the window. I can feel Ezekeial's piercing gaze, and Lazar glances at me in the rearview mirror occasionally. Z touches my arm, so I look over at him. And he is pleased that I didn't ignore him this time and smiles at me when I touch his hand.

We turn onto a well-maintained white-chat driveway that runs a short distance off the main road, lined with tall skinny ornamental trees. We approach a massive house made from beige stone, with huge trees in the front yard and some wonderful landscaping all around it. There are a lot of windows reflecting the afternoon light, and the whole works is absolutely gorgeous!

Lazar parks the car in front, next to the main door. "I will grab your things and take them to your rooms," he tells us politely.

"Thank you!" I reply, forcing a smile.

"You are very welcome, Ms. Renee."

We walk up to the front door. Lazar opens it, then lets us go in first. Some people are walking toward us, smiling happily. And Ezekeial opens his arms to hug a woman, but I don't know who she is. She is fair-skinned, is about five foot five in height, has long straight dark-brown hair, has nice teeth, and has a thin but not very shapely build. She is a very pretty woman, and if she would fix herself up a little, she would be quite beautiful.

"My son, it is so good to have you home!" she tells Z with a huge smile.

"It is good to see you too, Mother!" he replies happily.

Another guy, who I'm guessing is Z's stepfather, is about six foot, give or take an inch; has a lean but not very muscular build; and also has dark-brown eyes. He has a hint of a tan, has nice teeth, and has a head full of short slicked-back dark-brown hair and gives me the creeps right from the start.

"Welcome home, Ezekeial!" he greets Z, smiling, but his eyes seem to tell a different story.

Another man walks up to greet Z. "Hello, brother! You are looking well these days!"

"Thank you!" Ezekeial replies then hugs him too.

"Everyone, this is Renee," he introduces me, and I feel like they're giving me a close inspection while they stare me down, checking out every inch of me. I feel really uncomfortable by their deeply intense studying eyes and can't wait to disappear out of sight.

"Renee, this is my mother, Lianna, my stepfather, Aiden, and my brother, Sebastian," Z explains.

"Hello, everyone, it's nice to meet you!" I tell them, smiling, trying to hold my composure, and they all smile back at me with strange, soulless eyes.

Looking around the house, I can feel a deep sense of sorrow and lifelessness, a home that hasn't been well-loved in. Even though the curtains on the windows have been drawn and light is spilling throughout the rooms, it is dark and cold. I'm not liking the vibe and wish that I could just get the hell out of here ASAP!

"Are you ready for some lunch?" Ezekeial's mom asks me, smiling.

"No, thank you. I'm not hungry," I reply, forcing another smile, while Z looks at me intensely because it is the second time that I've turned down food today.

"Okay, the rest of us are going to have a bite to eat," she informs me happily.

"May I go look at my room?" I ask her, dying to get out of sight.

"You sure may. Lazar will take you," she says then calls for Lazar, and he comes quickly.

"Come, my lady. I will show you to your room," he says, smiling from ear to ear. He has such a sweet disposition and bubbly personality that I can't help but like him already!

"Thanks!" I reply happily, thrilled when we leave the others.

I see Z looking at me strangely, wanting me to look at him, but I don't make any eye contact as I walk away. Lazar and I climb up a flight of stairs leading into a large hallway, then he takes me to a door closest to the front of the house.

"Here's your room, Ms. Renee." He opens the door, and my mouth drops open because the room is huge and absolutely beautiful! It has a huge bed, a large couch in front of a stone fireplace, and a spacious balcony outside; and the bathroom is just as big as another bedroom!

"I put your bags right there by the couch," Lazar informs me, smiling.

"Thank you!" I reply while scanning the entire room, still stunned by its awesomeness.

"If you need anything else, just let me know because I will do my best to please you," he tells me happily.

"You're so sweet and thank you again!" I say, embarrassing him, causing his face to turn all shades of red, and his eyes sparkle with glee. He leaves me and closes the door behind him, then I get my phone and headphones out to charge them up for later. There is a knock on the door, so I answer it. It is Z. He smiles at me, but he seems somewhat nervous.

"Are you okay?" he questions me as he closes the door behind him.

"Nope, not really. There's a really bad vibe here, and I don't like it at all!" I answer unhappily.

"I knew something was wrong when you did not want anything to eat," he replies, sounding concerned.

"My nerves are on edge, and I don't understand why because this is supposed to be a vacation, not a funeral!" I explain softly.

Z doesn't say anything when he puts his hand on my shoulder. My heart is racing, and my adrenaline is at peak level. He looks at me with sad eyes but says nothing, and then he tells me while moving in close to me, "I want to hold you, but I cannot."

I know he wants some attention, but he told me back on the plane that we can't make any contact with each other. So I just stand and stare at him. He grabs my face with his hand, rubs his thumb along my jaw, then pulls my face to his, and kisses me. He is so damned confusing! First, he says no contact, and now he is kissing me on the lips! This guy never makes any sense!

I kiss him back then rub my hand all over his front side, giving it a gentle squeeze. He is enjoying it immensely but abruptly grabs my hand and pulls it away.

"We cannot do this!" he scolds me in a loud whisper.

"You started it!" I remind him.

"I cannot help myself," he tells me, chuckling, then gives me a quick peck on the lips and leaves the room but returns quickly with a sandwich for me to eat.

"Here, eat this. It will make you feel better." Z hands me the sandwich then peers out the balcony door. "Maybe I can come visit you tonight," he tells me while looking outside.

"I don't know about that. I don't think it's a good idea because you don't want them to catch you in here, do you?"

"But I will miss you!" he whines.

"I can't help it. Your rules, remember?" I remind him mockingly, and I can read the aggravation in his eyes.

"Well, I must go visit with my family. Maybe you should come with me," he suggests. And I really just want to hold up here in this room, but I guess I can't be rude and not mingle.

"Okay, let's go," I tell him unhappily.

Z's family are all gathered together inside of a large room. The ceiling is really high up, and it is filled with all kinds of awesomely cool antiques. I mosey around, checking everything out, while they talk to me and ask me a ton of questions.

His brother Sebastian asks me, "Would you like for me to take you outside and show you the grounds?"

Oh, great! That is, for damn sure, not what I want to do!

Sebastian is a fairly nice-looking guy, having spiked black hair with the ends bleached out. He is well-built and is about five foot nine but is not near as muscular or husky as Ezekeial, with a sleeve tattoo running along the length of his right arm. His eyes are a dark brown, almost black, and they pierce right through me when he looks at me. They seem almost empty, and he makes me feel really weird, like he is undressing me with those cold black eyes of his every time he looks at me. He is well-manicured, having a well-sculpted beard, and has really nice teeth, but I don't care for him at all.

"That sounds wonderful! The two of you should get the golf cart out and go for a spin!" Aiden suggests with a huge crocodile smile.

Yikes! I don't like the sound of this, but if I don't go, they'll be mad at me. Then if I do go, Z will be mad! What does a person do in a situation like this? I guess I'll have to go!

"Okay, I'll go," I say, dreading the whole ordeal.

Ezekeial freezes in place, looking completely stunned, angry, and jealous all at the same time; but I follow Sebastian outside to the golf cart regardless. It is parked inside a large garage next to the house.

"I'm glad that you are going with me because we should get to know one another better," he tells me, giving me a creepy smile.

I'm feeling a bit unnerved right now, and I'm ready to bolt down the road then race back to the airport!

"Hop in!" he says cheerfully, so I oblige him and get in. Then he drives us all over the place, telling me about this and that.

Our little tour seems to be going on for a lifetime, so glancing down at my watch, I see that we've been gone for about three hours. I'm so ready to be done with this, but he just keeps on going!

"Do all of you go hunting back there?" I ask him, pointing to the tree line, and he gives me a crazy look.

"No, why?"

"Where do you get your sustenance from?" I ask him.

"We get blood from the local stores, so there is no need to go hunting here," he answers, still giving me a questioning eye.

"I like to hunt. The fresher, the better," I tell him.

No wonder Z always eats that frozen "dead cow in a bag shit," as I always call it!

"Don't you think we should be getting back soon?" I ask him, dying to get back to Z.

"We are not on a curfew, so we can go back whenever we are ready," he answers quickly.

It is about four and a half hours later by the time we reach the house, and I'm never so glad to see it!

I hop out quickly. "I need to go to the bathroom really bad!"

"I will see you at dinnertime!" Sebastian yells to me while I make a mad dash toward the house then bolt up to my room because I'm about to pee my pants!

Ezekeial bursts in on me, "Where have you been!"

"Well, I just took the longest ride to hell and back ever! I'm so glad that's over!" I gripe while doing my business.

"What did the two of you do?" he questions me, looking frantic and upset.

"Well, we walked deep inside the woods and made the best passionate love ever!" I tease him, trying not to bust up laughing.

Z gives me the ugliest, dirtiest look ever. "I was terribly worried about you!" he yells at me, obviously jealous as hell.

"I'm glad, but can I finish peeing now!" I bark, staring him down, because I'm still sitting on the toilet.

"I am sorry. I will wait for you out in the room," he says, turning away from me.

"Thanks!" I blurt out, annoyed with him.

After doing my business, I wash my hands then turn around, and Z is standing in front of the doorway, blocking it.

"What's wrong with you?" I question him angrily because I'm really getting aggravated with him! He shuts the door, locks it, walks up to me, and then pushes me up against the sink. He shoves his hand up under my shirt and caresses my breast softly then presses his front side against me, teasing me by rubbing it all around. I'm getting pretty turned on. But I hear someone coming, so I push him away. "Someone's coming!" I whisper to him, freaking out, so he unlocks the door then bolts out into the room just when someone knocks on my door.

"Ms. Renee, dinner is almost ready!" Lazar says through the door.

"Okay, I'll be down soon!" I yell to him while staring at Z, and once the coast is clear, I walk over to Z, shove him down on the couch, and then sit on top of his lap. "You're going to have to quit being such a tease!" I growl at him then get up to go downstairs. A huge, wide smile creeps across his face, and he is right on my tail when I head downstairs.

*****

"Renee, you will sit here," Lianna informs me while pulling out my chair, and to my utter horror and disbelief, it is right next to Sebastian's chair! *Yikes! Not again!* I'm screaming inside.

Z is sitting all the way on the other side of the table across from me. *What's the deal?* I'm thinking to myself as I look around the room. The hired help begins to bring the food out to us, and it looks like some sort of chicken breast with fresh peas, mashed potatoes and gravy, bread, and wine. Then they serve that nasty dead-cow blood for us too. *Oh no! I can't drink that shit!* I really can't force myself to eat much of anything, and of course, Ezekeial's mom is eyeballing me.

"Renee, you have hardly touched anything! You should at least drink your blood," she gripes, looking concerned.

"I'm sorry, but I just can't drink that," I tell her, and they all turn and look at me at the same time.

"What?" Aiden questions me loudly, and I can see the anger in his eyes.

"I like to hunt because I like mine straight from the vein," I answer.

"We do not hunt here! It is not allowed!" he growls angrily.

"Why isn't it allowed?" I question him.

"We do not want to be seen outside hunting. Plus there is plenty of blood coming in without having to go out and catch it!" Aiden answers, still staring me down with his cold eyes, so I don't say another word.

"Renee, I need to ask you a personal question," Aiden says, getting serious suddenly.

"Okay, what is it?" I ask him.

"I need to know if you are pure," he says, and I'm quite stunned by this! *What the hell kind of a question is this to ask your dinner guest?*

"Excuse me?" I ask him in disbelief.

"I would like to know if you are still a virgin," he questions me again. And everyone is looking at me with great intensity, waiting for my response, and I'm completely mortified!

"Well, as if it's any of your business, I really can't say for sure," I pop off. The entire room is so quiet that you can hear a pin drop, and they're all staring me down with eyes as big as saucers because they're all so perplexed!

"What do you mean?" he questions me, and I think Z is about to shit his pants.

Listen to this! I laughed to myself inside, "Well, I have my wonderful friend that I lovingly call Big Blue, if that tells you anything, or shall I go into more detail? Does that count against me?" I question Aiden, trying not to bust up laughing because the expressions written across all their faces are priceless. "A girl has her needs too!" I add, giving them the most serious look ever. Z's mom grins from ear to ear, but I don't think Aiden likes my answer very much. "Anything else you need to know about me?" I ask in a sharp tongue, wanting to tear him a new asshole, but not another word gets spoken from anyone. The room stays completely silent for the rest of dinner.

Going back to my room after dinner, Lazar meets me in the hallway. "If you get hungry later, there's some snack stuff in the kitchen."

"Thank you. I may need to hit that later!" I tell him happily, and he grins from ear to ear.

I get into my room, shut the door, and then sit down on the couch, thinking about that crazy dinner, because this is all just so freaking bizarre and insane! I was definitely not expecting any of that. I remember all the times Z had told me that I needed to stay pure until I get married, but none of it still makes any sense! The tub is calling my name, so I draw up the hottest bath that I can stand, needing some major R and R. The scalding water feels amazing as I sink down inside the tub because I'm exhausted after the long haul over here plus this entire messed-up day, but I still have six more to go! It is going to be the longest week of pure hell ever! Suddenly, the bathroom door flies open, so I whip around. Sebastian is standing in the doorway, staring at me.

"What the hell are you doing!" I scream at him angrily, but he just stands there, looking at me. "Go away!" I order him, screaming at him again, so he turns around then leaves. *This is such a friggin' freak show around here!*

I get out of the tub since my bath time has been shot to hell, put on my jammies, and then walk out into the room; but just as I begin to head toward the bedroom door, I get grabbed from behind then thrown down on the couch. *What the hell!* Flabbergasted and completely caught off guard, I begin to peel myself off the couch, but Sebastian jumps on top of me.

"What in the hell are you doing! Get off of me!" I growl loudly then shove him off me.

"I want you right now!" he cries out angrily then begins to pant heavily.

I scream at him from the top of my lungs, "I don't think so! Get out of here right now!"

Sebastian grabs ahold of me within a split second then shoves me down again, and I'm just about ready to tear him a new one when my bedroom door flies open.

Ezekeial comes barreling into the room. "What are you doing to her!" he yells at Sebastian, looking confused and pissed off.

"I want her right now!" Sebastian growls at Z, still panting, and I'm pretty shocked that Z isn't beating the hell out of the guy for basically trying to rape me. Z would have never allowed anyone else to do what Sebastian has just done to me, and while I stare at the two of them, I notice a strange understanding between them. Knowing and seeing just how jealous Ezekeial can get from my own experiences, this whole standoff is definitely unusual.

"I do not think so! You need to go to your room before I get Mother!" Z barks to him sternly, so Sebastian reluctantly steps away from me then walks out of the room. I've had just about all that I can stand and can't deal with any more of this shit and begin yelling at Z. "That's it! I want to go home! This freak show is over!"

"We cannot leave right now because it is too late!" he tells me, and I can sense his nervousness while he looks me in the eye and can hear his heart pounding almost out of his chest just as plain as day.

"What's going on around here? How many people go visit their relatives with their girlfriend and they ask them if they're still a virgin and then get molested after dinner!" I scream at him in pure rage.

"I am sorry about all of that, but you did an excellent job with your answer," he replies, chuckling, but none of this is funny in the least.

"I think your brother needs a girlfriend!" I hiss. But Z says nothing, and I can see him bite his jaw.

"I promise he will behave for the rest of the week. Come now, hop into bed, and I will sit with you for a while," he tells me then grabs my hand and leads me over to my bed. Ezekeial sits with me for a little while then goes to his room hesitantly. "I love you, my love," he whispers to me before he leaves the room.

"I love you too," I say, feeling worried about what may happen to me after he leaves me.

I can't sleep at all, with being so freaked out by this whole day, and my mind is going ninety to nothing. It is really late, and the night sky is magnificently bright from the dotted stars scattered throughout the sky. I want to go out, but I know that I can't. While lost in thought, my door creaks open slowly, and I'm going to tear that guy up if he messes with me again! I can't see whoever it is trying to creep up on me in the dark, but once they get closer to the bed, I realize it is Z.

"Hello, my love! I cannot sleep without you!" Z whines, kneeling beside the bed.

"What are you waiting for?" I ask him, then pat the bed next to me, signaling for him to join me.

Z doesn't waste any time. He pulls down the covers on the other side of the bed, crawls in, and then we snuggle up together.

"Maybe you should go lock the door," I tell him, thinking about how any one of them could walk in on us at any time.

"Yes, I had better," he agrees while climbing out of bed.

Z locks the door and is quick to slide back under the covers. He is as hard as a rock and begins to paw all over me while kissing my lips and stripping me naked. He teases me by rubbing his member all over my sweet spot but not making love to me, and it is driving me insane! My body is burning with desire and wants him inside me *now*! I give Z a low growl from being so sexually frustrated, and this does the trick because he is dripping wet with raging excitement and is about to explode. I release my fangs and scrape them along his neck and chest while he makes love to me, loving hearing him moan from my erotic play. He is close to climaxing, along with me, and begins to thrust into me harder and kiss my lips aggressively, and once he has his sweet release, I sink my fangs into his upper arm then bite down. Z throws his head into the pillow, muffling out his cries, while he rides out his phenomenal finish, and once my climax breaks free, I release his arm and plant my face into his chest, trying to keep my own cries silent.

While clinging to him, I kiss his neck and rub my face against his cheek, lavishing him with my affections, then he begins to kiss my lips delicately while holding me against his body. I smile when he begins to rub his soft manhood between my legs because I love the pleasant sensations from it, along with his tender lovin'.

"I am so in love with you," he whispers in my ear while he continues his wonderful rubbing, but I'm quite disturbed when I glance at his face and see a tear glistening down his cheek. I stare out into the brightly lit bedroom from the ghostly glow of the moon while he lies next to me after we finish, enjoying him rubbing my belly softly but still feeling quite unsettled by everything that has been going on. My troubled mind is at a huge loss, and the little voice inside my head is telling me that I should have listened to it from the start.

"I must be getting back to my room," Z says abruptly then hops out of bed. "Good night, my love."

"Good night, Z," I repeat, then he leaves me for the night.

I can sense someone staring at me before I even open my eyes, and I bolt upright, ready to fight. But I breathe a huge sigh of relief when I see that it is Lianna standing over me.

"Good morning, sleepyhead!" she says cheerfully. "I have Lazar taking you and Sebastian into town later for a few things. Will this be okay?" she asks me with a questioning eye.

Just what I don't want to hear! "Sure, what time?" I ask her then let out a loud sigh.

"In about an hour," she answers.

"I'll be ready," I tell her reluctantly. *Good morning, crazy town! Why do they keep wanting me to go with Sebastian? He's so damned creepy!*

"Good morning, my love, and just where are you off to this morning?" Z questions me when he meets me in the hallway because I'm all dressed and ready to go.

"Your mom wants me to go into town with Sebastian," I answer, and Z's face instantly turns sour.

"Why?" he questions me.

"I don't know, and I'm wondering the same thing myself! I'd rather drink that dead-cow blood than to go hang out with him for the day!" I answer unhappily.

Lazar calls for me, so I head toward him, with Ezekeial right on my heels. "Ms. Renee, are you ready?" he asks me politely, with a sweet smile.

"Unfortunately, yes," I reply unhappily.

I look at Z, and he looks totally pissed off. "See you later!" I tell him, waving him goodbye, then follow Lazar out to the car. Sebastian is waiting patiently by the door and opens it, and I get in, then he gets in on the other side.

"I just want to apologize for last night because that was very unacceptable," he admits with his head hung low.

"Yes, it was!" I agree angrily, and I can see Lazar looking at me in the rearview mirror because I'm sure he is probably wondering what had happened.

We make our way into town then stop at the places on his mother's list. "Is there anything that you need while we are here?" Sebastian asks me kindly.

"No, I think I'm good. Thanks," I answer.

We drive around the city a bit more to see some sights then finally head back to the house, and I can see Z looking out the window because I'm sure he is champing at the bit. Lazar begins to grab the groceries and other supplies we had picked up out of the trunk, so I dive in to help. "I'll help you!" I tell him happily then grab a couple of the bags, but just as I begin following Lazar toward the house, Sebastian runs up to me, mad as hell.

"That is Lazar's job!" he yells at me hatefully.

"I don't mind helping out with the groceries!" I growl angrily, staring daggers at him, then continue to walk behind Lazar.

"Put those bags down right now!" Sebastian orders me.

"What in the hell is your problem?" I'm so pissed because this guy is such a jerk! "You don't tell me what to do, and get over yourself, asshole!" I scream at him just when Z comes running out of the house.

"What is going on?" he questions me hatefully, looking stunned.

"Your brother is telling me that I can't help bring in these damned groceries! What's wrong with these people?" I yell at him, just about to lose my cool, and by this time, everyone is outside, watching the show. "I want to go home *now*!" I scream at Ezekeial as loud as I can, and they all gasp in unison when I throw dirty looks at all of them.

"We cannot leave right now!" he cries out angrily, shushing me to calm down.

"I want to go back home right now! This place is a freak show!" I scream out loud. Their mouths all drop open, and Z looks utterly mortified.

Lazar smiles at me and says, "Ms. Renee, please come with me. You need a snack that will calm you down."

I carry in the groceries whether they like it or not, following Lazar to the kitchen, then place my stuff down on the counter.

"I appreciate the help, but please, you do not have to do it," he tells me as he walks toward the fridge.

"What's wrong with all of them?" I ask him, looking for answers.

"It's just their way," he replies.

"Well, they're all a bunch of creepin' creepers if you ask me! Not you, I like you. In all the books that Z has made me study, they acted like the werewolves are the scum of the earth, but I think all of that was a bunch of horseshit! These messed-up vampires around here sure as hell aren't anything wonderful in my eyes and are all a bunch of ignorant weirdos if you ask me! There's nothing wrong with you at all! I'd rather stay in here with you than to go back out there with them!"

His eyes beam after I tell him this, then he bends over and kisses my hand. "You are one of a kind, my lady," Lazar says, smiling, so I give him a smile back while he gazes into my eyes.

Z comes running into the kitchen, mad as hell. "We need to talk!" he barks angrily, so he takes me up to my room then scolds me.

"You cannot talk like that in front of my family! Their way of doing things here is much different from the way we do things back home!"

"No one should tell me that I can't help or do something! This place is just plain freaky, and I want to go back home right now!" I scream at him, almost pleading.

"My love, please, just give it a little bit longer!" Z begs, and I'm so mad at him that I can't even focus.

"Your brother treats me like he's married to me, and he's screwing me with his eyes! Nothing makes any sense around here, and I can't deal with this shit any longer!"

Z looks down at the floor. "I will see you at dinner." He just leaves it at that then walks out the door. *I'm so confused! This is all just some kind of weird, crazy madness!*

Dinner is quiet, with no one saying much of anything, so I excuse myself early then go back to my room. I put on my headphones then scroll through my playlist. I had forgotten my camo backpack in the truck before we had left Georgia, and I feel so lost without it. My door opens, and it is Z.

"I am sorry for earlier because I know it is hard getting used to a completely different way of life," he tells me with sympathetic eyes.

"I don't think it's anything about getting used to! They think they're just too good to do any work, and they treat Lazar like he's their slave! He's just like you or I and doesn't seem any different to me!" I gripe.

"We are not back at home, and things are very different here," he tries to explain to me again then kisses my forehead. "Good night, my love."

I look away from him without speaking another word, feeling utterly helpless and distraught, because I'm stuck here until Z is ready to go, and nothing I say is going to make any difference. I listen to my music long into the night, but Z never comes in to see me. I almost lose my emotions, not wanting to be here any longer.

Morning comes. I hear some commotion going on downstairs, so I get up and sneak out of my room. Z is standing down by the front door with Lazar, and his luggage is sitting on the floor. Lazar is getting ready to pick it up, so I rush over to them because I'm ecstatic that we're leaving!

"Oh, thank the gods! I'm so ready to get the hell out of here! Let me get my stuff!" I tell Z happily, thrilled with the thought of going home.

Z is standing in front of me, looking at me with an expressionless face. Then the next thing I know, everyone is standing out in the hallway, watching us. I don't give a shit as I get ready to rush back up to my room to gather up my stuff, but then Z says to me, "You will not be going with me."

I stop dead in my tracks, wheel around, and then walk back up to him. "What do you mean?" I ask him, disbelieving what I've just heard as I grab ahold of his wrist. "I want to go home!" I plead with him desperately, not understanding what is going on.

Z looks me dead in the eyes with so much sudden rage. "The farm is not your home!" he yells at me hatefully then rips my hand away from him and looks away from me.

I can't move. Did I just hear him right? Right now, I'm absolutely appalled and totally shell-shocked, so I look away from him, trying to figure all this out. Suddenly, everything clicks, and I have one hell of a devastating revelation. And once I realize just what is going on here, it hits me like a ton of bricks because all this crazy madness, along with his strange behavior, begins to make perfect sense! I look Z dead in the eyes, wanting to punch him right in the face, but I hold my composure and end up just turning around without saying a word then casually walk back up to my room. I can't believe it because he is leaving me here, and I can't believe that I didn't figure it out any sooner!

I get to my room, close the door, sit on the bed, then draw my legs up to my chest, and wrap my arms around them. My senses go completely numb because I can't wrap my head around any of it! I've been brought here to be with his brother Sebastian, abandoned by the love of my life and left in this "house of the monsters"! All that studying and learning their language was all to prep me for this very moment. That is why they've been wanting me to hang out with him, and that is why I'm supposed to be a virgin. The reason for all the weirdness from Ezekeial is because he has been hiding the truth, and it makes me shudder thinking about him being so willing to leave me here! He has been planning this the entire time ever since he and I had first met! They wanted me for Sebastian, not Ezekeial, and I can hear all his words of love spinning around in my head just as plain as day. Him telling me how much he loves me, how much he wants to be with me, and how happy he is was all just a lie! Was all the wonderful lovemaking fake too? I'm so enraged. I'm livid!

I hear the trunk shut on the car. The car door opens, he gets in, the door closes, and then it starts up. The tires crack and pop over the gravel as it pulls away, then reality checks back in, and I'm completely freaking out! *He's really leaving me here!* The love of my life has just driven away and has left me with these monsters! *OH...GOD...HELP ME, PLEASE!*

My heart begins to pound, and my adrenaline is flying through the roof! I knew something was off about this trip! All my senses have been screaming out to me this entire time, warning me! I break down and begin to cry uncontrollably because this can't be happening to me! What did I do that was so wrong that I deserve this? They can't keep me here against my will! Pure anguish sears throughout my entire body, and I still can't believe it! My heart is breaking, and my soul has been ripped in half. Wailing from the pain of my broken heart, I have a complete nuclear meltdown. *How can he do this to me! What about my family? What about Satan? Oh no! I'm never going to see them again!* I can't stop crying! What has he done to me!

CHAPTER 14

Ezekeial's Trip Home

As Lazar drives Ezekeial to the airport, he can tell that something is very wrong, and why isn't Renee going with him? Ezekeial is reeling from the anguish of having to leave Renee behind, and he wants to cry out from the pain but holds it back. It was his job his entire life to keep tabs on her, watch her, be her keeper, and prepare her for this day. He wasn't supposed to fall in love with her, but he couldn't help it. Renee was a part of him; she always was. Now here he is, driving back home and leaving her behind. It is just too much to bear!

"Pull the car over!" he screams at Lazar. Lazar pulls the car over, and Ezekeial jumps out then falls to his knees on the ground, screaming and howling all at the same time. How can he leave her like this! "Oh my God, Lazar! What have I done! I can't leave her behind!"

Lazar isn't really sure what is happening. "Why are you leaving her there anyway, Ezekeial?" he asks him, bewildered and confused as hell.

Ezekeial looks over at Lazar. "My whole life, I have had to search the world to find the 'chosen girl,' because one of the Elders had visions that this girl, who was born on this certain day, would be blessed with great powers. I searched and searched, and when I had finally found her, I knew she was the one as soon as I met her. I never thought I would love her so much! She has been with me throughout my entire life, and now they want her for Sebastian! That was the whole reason to find her because Aiden wanted her for his son. He thinks that she is going to give Sebastian her power by bearing him a most powerful child!" Ezekeial explains then can't hide his emotions any longer and begins to roar up toward the sky. Leaving her here is what he is supposed to do because that has been his whole life's training. This is what Aiden wanted to do to Ezekeial, torment him, because it always gives him the greatest pleasure to make his life a living hell! That is why he moved to America—to get away from him! Now he has done the ultimate deed and taken her away from him for good! Crying uncontrollably, he gets back into the car then tells Lazar to continue driving to the airport. He will never be able to forgive himself, and he knows that she will never forgive him either.

"Lazar, will you give her this bag?" Ezekeial asks Lazar while he helps him with his luggage.

"Yes, I will take it to her," Lazar replies, trying to comprehend what is actually happening.

"Please make sure that she gets plenty to eat. She needs to eat a lot," Ezekeial explains, trying to choke back his tears.

"I will make sure that I do my best to make her comfortable," Lazar replies.

"Thank you! Please watch over her! She is something very special!" Ezekeial tells him, trying to pull himself together.

"Ezekeial, why don't you just go get her and take her back home with you?" Lazar questions Ezekeial, still feeling confused and disbelieving Ezekeial can just walk away the way he is.

"Because Aiden told me that if I did not leave her, he will hunt her down until the day he finds her, then he will kill her! He will not stop until she is found! She belonged to him and Sebastian, and that is how it is going to be! She and I cannot be happy like that! I do not want them to kill her, so I must obey! I do not want any harm to come to her! I was hoping and praying to the gods that they would decide they did not want her and leave her to me!" Ezekeial explains while slowly making his way inside the terminal with his head hung low, and his heart is breaking with every step he takes farther away from her. *What have I done!*

All the memories he has of her begin to flash through his mind like pictures playing in a movie, and she is everywhere but by his side. She should be sitting right next to him in this seat, listening to her playlist on her headphones while they fly back home to the farm. He wants her to be here with him, kiss her cheek, and touch her face, but that has all been taken away from him. The plane takes off, and Ezekeial goes home alone.

The flight home is agonizing, and it seems to take forever while visions of her face when he left her behind flash within his mind's eye. Upon arriving at the airport, he grabs his luggage then makes his way out to his truck. Renee had left her camouflage backpack lying in the seat, and he can't help but stare at it, knowing how much she loved it. She had forgotten it in the hustle and bustle of the trip, and his emotions take over once he picks up the backpack then breathes in her scent. He places it back down in the seat where she had left it when they had gotten out then starts his truck, having a constant reminder that she isn't going to be going home with him and that she isn't going to be waiting for him when he arrives at home either.

It is late in the evening when he approaches the house, and once he sees her TA sitting in the driveway, another wave of tears begins to stream down his face. He gets out of the truck, opens the door to her beloved boo, then takes a seat behind the wheel, and looks around; and all her stuff is right where she has left it. Her sunglasses are always in the cupholder, with her fuzzy dice hanging on the mirror and the black duffel bag that she has always kept in the back seat with clothes in it for a just-in-case type of day, as she calls it. It is all just like another day, except she won't be getting in it anymore.

"What am I going to do!" he pleads to the sky for answers.

He gets out and takes his luggage inside the house but leaves it sitting on the kitchen floor then races upstairs to her bedroom. Everything is just the way she left it, and he can picture her walking into the room to join him. Ezekeial lies down on the bed and wraps himself up in her favorite fuzzy blanket, the one that he had bought for her at the mall, then breathes in her scent and can't keep himself from sobbing because he can smell her everywhere, but she is nowhere around. The agonizing loneliness has set in already, and he is lost without her.

CHAPTER 15

Left Behind

The morning arises, and I haven't slept at all. I can't stop crying, and my mind is still trying to wrap itself around the thought of being left here. It hurts me every time I think about how Z pulled his arm away from me then told me that the farm wasn't my home like I never even mattered. I'm just a discarded piece of trash, left behind after it's past its usefulness. I didn't know this could hurt so much! I wonder what they'll do to me now that Z is gone, and I'm completely alone in this dead, lifeless dark home. *Knock...knock!* Someone is at my door, so I wipe my face then reluctantly make my way over to the door.

"Ms. Renee, may I come in?"

It is Lazar, so trying not to cry, I say, "Yeah, it's okay."

He opens the door and comes in. "I am supposed to give you this bag from Ezekeial," he says to me, but I don't even want to hear his name.

"Thank you," I reply, giving him a half-hearted smile.

"I will always be here for you if you need anything, okay?" he tells me with his sweet smile.

"Can you just hold me for a second, please? I know it's a strange request, but I need someone right now," I say, trying to choke back my tears.

Lazar walks over to me then wraps his arms around me and embraces me. "I will hold you for as long as you need for me to."

I break down and cry, letting out all my emotions, heartbroken and distraught. He holds me until I'm done and runs his hand along my back, trying to comfort me.

FOREVER AND ALWAYS, MY LOVE

"Thank you. I'm sorry," I tell him while wiping the tears away from my face.

"It is fine! I can't imagine being left behind like that! I didn't even know this was going to happen! I feel so sorry for you because you have been plucked right out of your own life, placed into something unknown and pretty scary, a whole different country and many new rules!" he tells me just when his cell phone begins to go off. He pulls it out of his pocket and answers it. "Let me ask," he says while looking at me, but I've already heard everything that has been said. "Ezekeial is on the phone and would like to talk to you," Lazar tells me, holding his phone out to me.

My anger explodes, and I'm fuming! "That mofo has left me here, and now he wants to talk to me? No, I can't! He's dead to me! Tell him not to bother calling anymore! I will never speak to him again, and he doesn't need to bother you with his cowardly issues either!" Lazar doesn't need to tell Ezekeial what I've just said because he has already heard it. "Hang it up, please!" I order Lazar almost in a whisper while choking on my tears.

"I must go," he tells Z then hangs up the phone. "I will leave you alone, Ms. Renee. Just remember, if you need anything, I will be here for you." He smiles at me then leaves the room.

My phone begins to go off, so I look over at it and see that Z has left me a text message. He is begging me to forgive him, saying that he loves me and that he misses me terribly. My eyes tear up, and I can't hold it back as I break down, crying once again. I erase the message then plug in my phone, and it begins to go off again. This time, Z is trying to call my phone, but I'm not going to answer it. So I turn it off then go lie down on the bed. My heart is shattered into a million pieces, and I feel like I'm drowning in my own sorrow and self-pity.

There are more knocks on the door, and this time, Lianna walks in then sits down on the bed next to me. "Renee, I will let you do your own thing for today, but tomorrow we will have classes."

"What kind of classes?" I ask her, sniffling.

"You will need to learn our ways of doing things around here, or else, you will be punished for disobeying," she tells me, looking at me intently. "I do not wish for you to be getting hurt, so please obey him."

"I don't understand what it is that you all want from me! I have nothing to give to any of you!" I cry out, pleading with her.

"But you do! You have so much more than you even know! You will marry Sebastian in a few weeks and forget all about your past life," she tells me with a strange expression.

"I don't want to marry Sebastian! I don't know anything about him, and I most certainly don't love him!" I shout in desperation.

"But in time, you will learn to love him. You will bear him many wonderful children!" she replies, smiling.

"What? I don't want to have any kids with that guy!" I cry out unhappily.

Lianna gives me a disapproving eye. "It does not matter what you want! It is what will happen!"

"Is that why all of you are so damned miserable, because you're always bowing down and kissing Aiden's control-freak ass? This house is full of nothing but pain and misery! It's dark and hollow!" I bark hatefully, and with that, she gets up and leaves the room. I spy the bag that Z had sent back with Lazar sitting on the couch, so I walk over to it and open it up, curious as to what he has put inside it. There is a giant jar of peanut butter, a box of crackers, and a giant bottle of Jose Cuervo Gold tequila inside it. "Gee, thanks, asshole!" I say out loud. I hide the bag in my closet for a just-in-case type of day because I don't know what these people have in store for me, but I'm sure it is not going to be anything good.

The day slowly fades away, and thankfully, no one bothers me. I'm starving, so I sneak my way down into the kitchen. It is all clear, so I open up the fridge, grab an armful of groceries, then run back to my room, and shut and lock the door. I get my food situated then pick up my phone. Turning it on, it blows up with tons of text messages and phone calls. My voice mail has twelve messages in it, and every one of them is from him—the prick who has left me behind like a whimpering dog with its tail tucked between its legs. He is begging me for my forgiveness, telling me how much he loves me and how sorry he is. His voice mails are all him bawling and crying, pleading with me, begging for me to answer his calls. I begin to erase every last one of them, but the phone goes off while I'm trying to erase all this crap. And as I do this, I accidentally hit the answer button, and I can hear him say, "Renee…Renee? Please, talk to me!" I hang the phone up on him, but he just calls back again. So I shut it off. I can't even listen to my music because the phone is going nonstop.

After putting the phone down, I make my way out onto the balcony. The day is bright, and the woods around the house are busy with activity. So I decide to go out for a walk to clear my head. Walking down the stairs and through the hallway, I barely make it to the front door when I get stopped by Aiden.

"Where are you planning on going?" he questions me, almost standing right on top of me and ready to hold the front door shut if I try to bolt.

"I just need to get some fresh air and take a walk. I'll be back," I explain to him while trying to hold back the anger welling up inside me.

"Fine, I will have Lazar accompany you! Sebastian and I are leaving town for a few days to do some business. So he must always go with you, and I will tell him this!" Aiden informs me then begins to walk down the hallway, calling for Lazar.

"Yes, sir?" Lazar asks when he approaches Aiden.

"You must accompany her everywhere she goes, and she is not to leave the grounds for any reason!" he orders Lazar. "You will be punished if anything happens!" Aiden threatens Lazar.

"It will be fine, sir! I will make sure that she doesn't run off!" Lazar assures him.

"You had better!" he screams at him while pointing his finger in his face.

"I'm all yours, my lady. Where would you like to go?" Lazar asks me politely, flashing me a sexy giant smile, and I enjoy listening to him talk with that adorable accent of his.

"Anywhere but here," I answer.

"Come then, let's go take a walk!" He grabs my hand, then we make our way outside.

It lifts my spirits getting some fresh air, but when we walk around to the back of the house, I spy a tree off toward the far end of the property with some rope tied around it.

"Why is that rope tied around that tree?" I question Lazar, feeling curious.

"That, my lady, is where some of the punishment comes from. You have to put your arms around the tree, and then they tie you up to it. Aiden has a whip that he will lash you with if you are in trouble," he explains, staring at the tree, not taking his eyes off it, and I know, right then, he has been whipped there before.

"That's terrible!" I gasp in horror.

Lazar looks at me. "Come, let's get out of here!" He leads me into the woods, and we walk through it slowly, taking in the fragrant aromas of nature. My mind is flooded with thoughts, and I'm so hungry!

"Will you tell on me if I go out to hunt really quick?" I ask him, almost pleading with him.

Lazar's eyes grow wide, and he stares at me, not sure what he should say to me. "I won't tell, but you better make it quick! They will be looking for us soon!" he gripes, and I can tell that he is really nervous about letting me do this.

"Okay, will do!" I reply, not wasting one minute to pull off my clothes.

Lazar is standing beside me, staring at my body, with his mouth hanging wide open, but at this point, I don't give a shit if I'm naked or not! My beast emerges, so I make haste to take flight, with my adrenaline pumping from nervousness and fear. I spy some deer up ahead, get my belly full, and then haul ass back to Lazar; and he is standing in the same exact spot where I had left him, gathering up my clothes. "Hurry, get dressed!" he orders me, almost throwing my clothes at me.

I get dressed in a flash, then we walk back closer to the house. "Thank you! I can't drink that dead cow from a bag shit that they drink," I explain.

"I'm glad that you have gotten what you need," he replies, walking next to me, happy as a lark, and I can tell that he is pretty pleased from me just giving him a free peep show. "I don't think the others have the same, let's just say, equipment that you have," he tells me.

"What do you mean?" I question him.

"Well, they don't have wings, furry legs, or tails from what I've seen. I've only seen fangs and the normal vampire stuff, but of course, they don't ever hunt like you do either. You're amazing, and I will never tell anyone your secrets!" Lazar says then stops in front of me and gazes into my eyes. "You must not let them know what you have!" he demands me with an intense stare.

"I'm never going to tell them anything!" I reply, thinking about how much I hate them.

CHAPTER 16

Back at the Farm

It has been a few days since Ezekeial has left Renee behind back in Romania. The house is quiet now, and nothing is stirring. He longs to hear the sounds of her rattling the dishes around in the kitchen and the constant opening up of the fridge and to watch her dance around to her music while she does this and that around the house. But there is nothing, only the deafening sounds of silence. He is lying in bed, still reeling from his agonizing pain, not being able to leave the room. Suddenly, there is a thunderous huge crash downstairs, and the house sounds like it is being ripped apart! Jumping out of the bed, he races to the bottom of the stairs and stops, frozen in his tracks. Satan has burst through the side door and is pacing around in the kitchen with a deep, growling sound emanating from deep within his throat. He is pissed and wants answers! He wants to know where she is! Walking slowly into the kitchen then falling to his knees in front of the angry giant steed, Ezekeial pleads for forgiveness.

"I had to leave her there! Please forgive me! I want her back home too, but she must stay there!" Ezekeial screams in desperation, crying uncontrollably.

Satan paces angrily around in the kitchen, his heavy footsteps vibrating the floor beneath them. He starts to scream at Ezekeial, and the sound of it is deafening as it echoes throughout the house. So Ezekeial places his hands over his ears, trying to block out Satan's cries. Backing up slowly and still pacing with rage, the mighty stallion retreats out the door, still screaming from anger. He stands on the ground next to the porch; gives Ezekeial an evil, hard stare; and then walks away back up to the pasture. His rage is almost uncontrollable.

Ezekeial lets himself fall on the floor then curls up into a fetal position. He lies here, not moving for the longest time, sobbing endlessly, because nothing will ever be the same for him ever again! He manages to peel himself up off the floor then walks back upstairs. Filling up the tub then opening the French doors to the balcony, he soaks for a while, thinking about how she always likes to do this, especially in the evenings when the moon is high. She always says that it helps her clear her mind. His mind is racing like a runaway freight train tearing up the tracks, totally out of control, because she is the other half of his soul, and without her, he is incomplete. He is the one not being able to survive without the other for all time. Feeling broken and lost, he can't stop himself from losing his emotions and breaks down once again.

CHAPTER 17

The House of the Monsters

"You will be marrying Sebastian next weekend. They will be returning from their trip in a couple of days, so we must prepare! We are only going to have a few people over, not many. We want this to be private," Lianna tells me as if I really care.

I'm losing myself in my grief and can't overcome my sorrow and pain. It has only been three weeks since I've been here, and they're in a big hurry to get Sebastian and I married. At least, Sebastian and Aiden go on their so-called business trips all the time, so hopefully, he'll be gone most of the time after this mania is over with.

She leaves my room. I run over to the closet then grab the peanut butter and crackers that Z had left for me. I was told that I was eating too much, so they won't let me eat at my own leisure, only letting me have a certain portion at a time. And I feel like I'm beginning to fade away. I need to feed my beast too, and I can't keep it all together. I used to be free to do these things whenever I pleased, but now I can't. And having to sneak around just to eat is terrible! I've been trying to ration my stash so that it lasts me awhile, but I almost can't help myself. It is not going to last for much longer at this rate. I want to just fly away, but I can't do that either. Where will I go? What will I do? I can't just go home! They'll harm my family if I disobey them! If I run off, Lazar will be beaten to death and tied to that damned tree sitting out in the backyard! My mind spins constantly with questions and is always in agonizing turmoil.

"Ms. Renee, are you ready for your afternoon walk?" Lazar asks me cheerfully, walking over to fetch me.

"Yes, I'm definitely ready!" I reply happily, relieved to see him.

We make our way out the front door then walk down the driveway and into the woods. "Let's go farther in because I can smell water," I say as I walk in deeper. We eventually come to a small clearing containing a spring-fed pond, and the wonderful smells drifting through the air, along with the heavenly, tranquil setting, rejuvenate me. The water is crystal clear, and I enjoy the feeling of just being here, away from that musty old house. "It's really nice here," I tell him then sniff the fresh, fragrant air.

"Yes, my lady, it sure is," Lazar agrees, watching me with intense emotion, anxious for me to remove my clothes. I give him what he wants when I strip down right in front of him, not caring about who may be out here. I morph into my beast then walk out into the water slowly, enjoying the cool freshness enveloping around my feet. It feels wonderful and reminds me of the lake back at the farm. Without thinking, I reach down and begin to swirl the water around with my powers, causing the wind to begin to pick up. The trees sway gently in the breeze, and a bright light engulfs me in the water. I offer my power to Mother Earth, and she receives it graciously, then I throw my hands up toward the sky and beg the gods for help. "Please save me! I want to go home!" I scream loudly, hoping that they'll hear my pleading cries.

A loud, thunderous cracking noise echoes throughout the woods when a large tree limb brakes free and falls to the ground. "What have I done so wrong!" I yell toward the sky, begging for mercy as my emotions begin to run rampant. The wind gets a little stronger, and I fall to my knees in the water. Then suddenly, everything stops, and I'm shoved back into my hellish reality.

With his face frozen with shock, Lazar is standing stiff as a board.

"I'm going to feed my beast. I'll be back," I tell him just as I begin to take flight, and he can only nod. I find some deer then quench my thirst for the time being, and Lazar is still standing where I had left him when I return.

Breaking free from his coma, he says, "Renee, you have great power!" Standing in front of me, he reaches out his hand then touches

187

my face, and the familiar feeling of being loved takes my pain away for just a few precious seconds.

"We'd better be getting back," I tell him, not wanting to be gone for too long because I don't want him getting hurt, but I'll take a beating for him anytime!

Lianna comes running outside, screaming at us, when we get back to the house. "Where have you been? They are waiting for you!" Aiden and Sebastian are back already, but they weren't supposed to be back until a couple of days from now.

Aiden rushes up to me after we get inside then slaps me across the face. "You should not venture out so late!" he yells at me hatefully.

I look up at him. "It's only a little after five p.m.! I can't just sit here and stay in my room all of the time!" I scream at him angrily.

"You do not talk to me like that! You will be punished!" he yells at me.

"Then punish me, you fucking prick! I'm not your slave!" I roar at him with a huge growl because I want to tear his throat out, hand it to him, and then watch him bleed to death! My rage is epic, and it is hard to hold myself back! Lazar is standing behind me and grabs the back of my shirt then yanks it, trying to tell me to be quiet.

"I will show you what disobeying is then!" Aiden screams at me then grabs me by the hair of my head and drags me down the hall with everyone watching me while I thrash around.

"Let me go!" I scream from the top of my lungs. I could probably break free from his grasp with little effort if I used my powers, but I'm going to take whatever he gives to me just to show him that he won't break me so easily.

Aiden drags me outside to the tree in the backyard, rips off my shirt, and then ties my arms around it tightly. Lazar and the others follow, rushing outside to see the show. Aiden grabs a skinny tree branch and rips it from one of the trees then begins to thrash my back with it. It hurts like hell, but I don't make a single peep. He is really angry now because he wants me to beg for mercy. So he hits me even harder, and the pain is god-awful! I manage to take his abuse, and the only thing that is coming out of my mouth is my heavy breathing.

"Scream, you defiant child! Scream!" he cries out angrily, yelling at me from the top of his lungs.

I growl at him with all my built-up fury and rage, wanting him to know that I mean business, and my fangs are exposed because I want to bite him. He looks at me with hate-filled eyes then punches me in the face, knocking me into the bark of the tree. I take his blow then look back at him, and he is coming at me again. He proceeds to punch me one right after the other, and I'm bleeding from my nose and have some cuts on my face from the bark of the tree and his fist. Blood drips off my chin as it bleeds out of my wounds.

"Stop it, please!" Lianna screams at Aiden, so he wheels around to look at her.

"She will learn to obey!" he yells at her, mad with rage.

Now I know what life must have been like for Ezekeial all those years—constantly having to please this monster to keep from being punished all the time. He must have gotten what he wanted because he throws the switch down then releases the rope from my arms, and I fall to the ground. "Lazar, get her cleaned up!" Aiden orders Lazar, pointing his finger at him.

"Yes, sir!" he replies nervously then runs over to me to peel me off the ground. Everyone else goes back inside the house, whispering among themselves.

"Why did you test him like that? You shouldn't have done that, sweetheart!" he scolds me when he helps me back to my feet, but I stay quiet.

My face is a mess, my back feels like it is on fire, and Lazar almost has to carry me back inside. We pass the group while he helps me down the hallway to the stairs leading up to my room, and they're all staring at me, bloody and beaten.

Getting into my room, Lazar says to me, "Renee, I will not be around for a couple of days, so you must behave yourself!"

"Why? Where are you going?" I question him, worried about him leaving me.

"The moon will be full soon, and when it's time for my beast to awaken, they lock me up in a cage down in the basement until it's passed. They fear my wolf because one bite from me can kill them.

189

So once a month, I have to stay down there for a few days until the full moon is over."

"Why can't you control your beast? Set it free whenever you please?" I ask him, not really understanding why he can't control it.

"I don't know how to control it because no one has ever taught me how to! It takes over with rage when it's in full force, and I submit to its desires," he answers, looking at me with those soft brown eyes of his and fear written across his face.

Once he helps me clean up my wounds, he wraps my back up with some bandages. "At least you have fed today, so you should heal up quite nicely!" he whispers to me softly, smiling. His soft touch is comforting, and I want to hold him. But I know that if they see me do this, they'll take him away from me. I can't risk losing him for any reason because he is all that I have here. I do want to see what his beast looks like though!

"I must go," he tells me, staring deep into my eyes, then gives me a sad face and leaves the room when Lianna walks in.

"You must join us for dinner tonight, so please come easily because I cannot bear to watch the torture of any more punishment!" she says, not making any eye contact with me.

"Is that what you let him do to Ezekeial all of the time? You should be ashamed of yourself for letting him be treated like that because a mother should always protect her children! Not to just stand back and allow them to be tormented and abused! I couldn't stand there and watch my son or daughter be beaten like that and not try to help them!" I scold her, almost livid. I can feel hatred welling up inside me, picturing Z as a little boy tied to that tree and being whipped. She looks at me, and her eyes begin to well up with tears. "I thought so!" I blurt out then give her an angry soft growl.

Lianna gazes into my eyes. "That is what happens when you disobey him, so please, do not anger him anymore!" she pleads with me, but I look away from her because the sight of her makes me sick, thinking about her letting him do that to her son.

"I'll be down in a minute because I need to change my clothes. Will that be acceptable?" I ask her with another growl, and she nods vigorously, happy that I'm obeying Aiden's wishes.

I get to the table, and all eyes are on me. "You will drink your blood tonight," Aiden demands me.

"I can't drink it. I'm sorry," I reply. Everything goes silent, and no one moves. Even Sebastian seems nervous and uneasy.

"What makes you think that you cannot drink it?" Aiden questions me, giving me the evil eye, and I can see that he is getting fired up again.

"I like it straight from the vein! Don't you like to go out and hunt? It sets my soul free—the thrill of the hunt, the midnight sun shining down upon my face, and the sounds of the night as the evening unfolds," I explain, drifting away to my glorious memories of being free.

He stares at me, lost in thought because he knows that I'm right. "We do not hunt here because it is strictly forbidden! We cannot risk being seen, and no one has hunted here for years!" He loses himself in thought yet again, and I can sense his anger diminishing. "Ezekeial has pampered you way too much by letting you do whatever you want to! Things are not like that here, so you must abide by the rules. And hunting is out of the question!" he tells me sharply.

Luckily, I make it through dinner without incident. It is getting dark, and I watch the sun go down from my balcony, thinking about what may be going on at the farm right now. I'm still really angry with Z, but I miss him terribly. I want to be in his arms, having him run his fingers through my hair and talk to me softly. I begin to weep, just wanting to die, because I'll never be able to deal with this new life of mine every day. I can't see myself having sex with Sebastian for the rest of my life either because I don't even like him. My broken heart is dragging me down further into the nothingness and spiraling me down into a bottomless black pit of despair. I have to marry Sebastian this Saturday, and my constant agony consumes me because I can't escape this nightmare! If I try to leave, Lazar will probably be punished terribly or even killed. Not to mention, Aiden told me that if I left, he'll hunt me down for however long it takes for him to find me. I don't care about myself, but I don't want anyone else getting caught up in the crossfire. I'll never have a peaceful existence, and I want them dead. But I can't just kill them, for surely, there will be horrific consequences from that heinous act. Plus I just can't go out and kill anyone because it is not who I am!

Saturday comes, and I can only grieve in silence at what I'm about to do while standing in front of the mirror, gazing at this hideous dress that I'm zipped into, dying to just disappear. Lazar is going to be downstairs for one more night, and I really miss him being around because I don't have anyone else whom I can talk to. The bustling around of the whole ordeal is getting my senses all jacked up. My heart is pounding, my palms are all sweaty, and I can hardly bear the thought of all this. There are only supposed to be a few people here, and I'm going to be meeting these so-called Elders of theirs. The thought of crawling into bed with that awful Sebastian has got me on edge because I've never been with anyone other than Ezekeial, and he is the only one whom I want to be with.

Lianna leads me down the hall into the huge room that I was in on my very first day here, and it is all prepped for the occasion. My heart is going to burst right out of my chest, and I can't breathe from the tight collar of this damned dress around my neck, choking me. So I keep tugging at it, trying to loosen it up, but it is not giving.

"Are you ready?" Lianna asks me once we get to the room.

I want to say *no*, but I can't because the show must go on. "I guess," I tell her unhappily, hanging my head down low. She leads me down to the walkway, the music begins to play, and the operation commences. Looking at Sebastian while approaching him, I can tell that he is undressing me with his eyes, and a wave of cold chills crawl along my spine. I hold my head down during the entire thing, not looking at anyone, because it is taking everything I have not to start bawling my eyes out. It is all over within half an hour, and I am now Mrs. Sebastian Dragkarr. I can't help but begin to cry because I've always wanted my last name to be Dragkarr but not with Sebastian. As Sebastian and I leave the room, all I can think about is Z and what I would give to be with him right now. My life, as I know it, has been taken away from me, and I know that it will never be the same.

I'm escorted to another room. "Renee, the Elders are in here, and you must behave!" Sebastian orders me with a sharp tongue then opens the door, and the two of us step inside. Sitting at a beautifully handcrafted large wooden table are four decrepit, withered old pale-white men. They look like something who has just walked straight out of a horror movie!

"Well, well, we finally get to meet you!" one of the things say to me, smiling a horribly disgusting smile, but I don't move or speak, watching the thing while it looks me over, almost drooling.

"Aren't you a vision of beauty!" says a different one this time, and I almost bolt out of the room when it gets out of its chair then walks up to me because its appearance is fowl and grotesque. This one is even creepier than the others because it is horribly disfigured, and I can't even begin to imagine how it ended up looking like that!

"I am Valdimire, and I am two hundred fifty-four years old!" he tells me cheerfully as if he is proud of it. "We are very pleased to meet you!" he continues to say, and I'm ready to get the hell out of here before these abominations decide to do unspeakable things to me because I can sense they have evil intentions. Not to mention, I'm sure, by the way they look, they sure as hell don't get much action in the bedroom!

"Have you been able to use any of your powers?" he asks me point-blank.

"What powers? I don't have any powers!" I question him, feeling surprised, because I don't want him knowing anything about my secret powers.

"My visions have shown me that you have great power, and I am sure that, by now, they should be making themselves known. Maybe you should try practicing with them to awaken them because they just might need a little help rising to the surface," he suggests as if he is trying to coax the truth out of me.

"I don't have a clue as to what you're even talking about! I don't have any powers!" I cry out in frustration, trying to convince him that I'm worthless to them. He stares me down with a squinty eye, studying me, and then turns around and walks back to his chair.

"They will come in time," he says when he begins to take a seat then looks at me with a twisted huge grin plastered across his face, and thank you, sweet baby Jesus, when I'm led out of the room then told to go upstairs.

That was the biggest creep factor ever, except for what I'm about ready to have to do because they tell me to go up to my room and wait for Sebastian.

The night has ended, and it is time for the grand finale. I feel like I'm going to pee all over myself. My heart hasn't stopped pounding, and my nerves are shot. I run to the closet to take a few gulps of tequila from my secret stash, hoping that it'll help numb my sorrows and anguish. Plus I keep seeing Ezekeial's face every time I close my eyes, and I'm sinking further into the darkness of the abyss with grief and can't be saved. I gaze at the wedding ring that has been placed on my finger, and it is not at all what I've been dreaming of. My heart was set on something like the one that I had seen at the mall last year, and it sinks in agonizing disappointment as I stare at the one that I'm wearing now. None of this is what I had ever dreamed of for myself nor expected. *Damn you Ezekeial!* I begin to cry because my life is crumbling down all around me, so I take a few more swigs from my bottle and then put it back, not wanting them to know that I have it.

I take off this horrible gown, throw it over on the couch, and then put on my jammies in hopes that he doesn't come. I look at my phone and see that it is blown up with messages once again, and they range from the very first day that Z had left me up until just now. I haven't even looked at or even messed with my phone since I had erased everything in the morning on day 1. They're all from Z, and I can't bear to read any of them. So I just go stick my phone inside my suitcase, trying not to think about it.

Suddenly, it happens. I hear a knock at my door, then Sebastian walks in, smiling from ear to ear. My world has just completely shattered, staring at him in disgust, knowing what I'm going to have to do with him.

"Are you ready, my wife?" he asks me happily when he begins to tear off my clothes and then his own. He throws me down on the bed, and I just keep thinking to myself, *Please just get it over with!* His heart is racing, and he is really excited. He jumps on top of me then begins to do his thing, and it is not at all like my usual lovemaking. It is absolutely awful! Sebastian is all over the place, and then he bites me. "*Ouch!*" I scream out from the sudden shock and pain, but he

194

seems to like it then does it again. He has bitten me twice, once on the arm and once on the shoulder, and this is definitely not normal for me and is completely unexpected.

He finally gets done then lies beside me, panting. "You need to get more into it," he tells me crossly. I give him a hard stare then turn over away from him because I just can't do this. He pulls me over on top of him, wanting me to give him some affection, but I just can't do it. "You had better try harder to please me, or you will be punished!" he tells me hatefully. "I am your husband, and it is your duty to make me happy," he growls angrily, but I don't say a word, trying to control my temper, dying to have this hellish nightmare come to an end. Luckily, it is only a few minutes later, and he falls asleep.

Lying next to him, I can't stop thinking about Lazar because I'm desperately needing someone to confide in. Sebastian is fast asleep. So I move a little, trying to sneak away without getting caught, and he doesn't even flinch. I manage to sneak out of the bed, get dressed, and make it out into the hallway. So I peek into the room before I close the door, and he is still snoring loudly. The door to the basement is in the kitchen, so I head toward the kitchen as quietly as I can, trying not to make even one sound. Getting in the kitchen, I spot the door that leads to the cellar, walk over to it, and then open it up slowly. It smells musty and damp down there, but I can't really hear anything. So I peek my head inside the doorway, listening for any signs of life while straining my ears, but still nothing. To hell with it because the worst thing that can happen to me is I get killed!

I make my way down the stone staircase, and it seems to wind around forever. Even though I can see everything in the dark, a small light shining at the bottom of the stairs is a welcome sight. Once I hit the bottom, I'm standing on top of a stone floor that appears to be covering the entire area. I see a shadowy long hallway in front of me, with a few lights placed along both sides, and there appears to be a door at the end of it. I can see some bars from where I stand, so I creep farther into the hallway and spy a set of metal bars to my right, plus what appears to be another set on the other side of these. I'm guessing these are two separate cages by the looks of it. Then I hear it—a slow, rhythmic heartbeat, along with the sound of resting breathing—while I stand motionless. I decide to follow the sound, which is at the first set of bars, and they're made up of thick steel, along with a large, heavy metal gate to match. The eerie illumination of the light and the ominous atmosphere are bone-chilling.

I accidentally hit one of the metal bars while nosing around, trying to pinpoint the beast inside. Looking over quickly to see if I've awakened it, I see it jump up, then it races over toward me with lightning-fast speed, growling softly. It has a hold of my arm before I realize it, and I try to jerk it away. But at that very same moment, it bites my wrist. Everything happens so fast that I don't even have any time to react! I pull my arm free then examine the damage. I have a bite mark across my wrist. But it is only bleeding a little, and I'm not too concerned about it. I know Lazar has said that his bite can kill a vampire, but as of right now, I'll welcome death with open arms. It would be a sweet release from this hellish nightmare and an easy way out.

It is standing quietly, almost motionless, sniffing the air, trying to catch my scent, then it cautiously approaches the bars to where I'm standing. It stops only inches away from the bars, and I can almost make out its entire figure. And I'm stunned because he is magnificent! He has the stance of a man but just a little bit different. He is taller as his beast, and his body is full of brown and grayish hair. I can see the sharply defined muscle tone around his chest, belly, arms, and legs; and he is definitely well-built. His hands have long black claws at the ends of his fingers, and his head is the shape of a wolf. Its pointed ears are twitching and moving around, trying to hear me, and its canine eyes stare me down with great intensity. He has his teeth barred just a little bit but really isn't acting too threatening.

"Hello, Lazar," I say to him softly. He must be quite surprised because he cocks his head a little then backs away from the bars a few steps, so I move in closer. I'm not expecting it when he throws himself up against the bars, slamming into them. So I step back slightly but hold my ground because I want to tell him everything that has happened to me, and I don't care if he is in there or not!

I sit down in front of the cage, so he crouches down on the ground and tries to reach me through the bars. I touch his fuzzy hand. He jerks it back and then sits up, staring at me with wild, crazy eyes. They're a brilliant goldish color, with some orange around the outside of the iris.

I look him straight in the eye. "I just need someone to talk to, please! There's no one else here but you!" I beg of him, beginning to lose my emotions, and I'm pretty surprised when the wolf takes a seat on the floor then watches and listens to me quietly.

I begin to tell him all about the wedding, the creepy old men, and the horrible night of sex that I've just had. Then I tell him that I'm starving because they won't hardly let me eat anything and that my beast will need some blood soon. The wolf sits and listens to me ramble on for quite some time without stirring, and other than my own complaining, I can hear the sound of him breathing and his soft rhythmic heartbeat. He is calm, and his aggressiveness seems to have disappeared while he sits silently still, listening to me. It is comforting just to be close to him, and I'm glad that I have him to confide in.

I scoot a little closer to the bars, tempting him, wanting to see just how far I can go before he lashes out at me again, but he doesn't move. My wrist has stopped bleeding. So I reach out to him then grasp one of the bars, expecting him to go ballistic, but he doesn't. He slowly moves his head toward my wrist then licks the blood from it. I begin to cry, so he stops then looks at me and gives me a soft whine. I reach over with my other hand and grasp another bar, dying to touch his head and to run my fingers through his fur, so I slowly move in on him, testing my limits. He is frozen in place, not moving, and I can hear the slightest increase of his heartbeat. So I reach between the bars then hold my hand up to his nose, waiting for him to attack me. He looks at me intently, not really sure what to do. So I push my limits even further and touch his nose with my finger, but he jerks back and jumps away from me. I continue to hold my ground while he slowly approaches me once again and cautiously puts his muzzle next to my hand. I reach up and run my fingers along his nose, and I can sense the swiftly change of emotions coming from him when I gently rub his fur. I reach up farther along his head, running my hands and fingers around his ears and face, then he breathes out a sigh of pleased contentment and makes a low groaning sound.

I pull my hand back, but he looks at me, begging for more. So I rub my hands around his neck and scratch it gently. His fur is so soft, and it reminds me of my favorite blanket back at the farm.

"I knew you'd be in there," I whisper to him happily. He is enjoying the rubdown that I'm giving to him, and his tongue is hanging out of his mouth while I lavish him with my affections. I begin rambling on some more, then he licks my face when I'm least expecting it, and I hold back a laugh because it looks like he is smiling at me. He grabs my wrist, the one that he has bitten, then looks over it and whines. "I'll be fine! The worst thing that can happen is I die," I say, smiling at him, but he doesn't like my comment whatsoever because he growls a low, deep growl at me.

I feel better with being able to get my thoughts off my chest, but I know it is getting late. So I glance down at my watch. I hope that Sebastian hasn't woke up, finding me missing, and is running all around the house, looking for me.

"I better go. It's really late, and I don't want that jerk looking for me," I tell Lazar. I kiss his nose. "Good night, Lazar." He makes a groaning noise, telling me good night, before I make my way back up the stairs. And I thank the gods when I get back to the room because Sebastian is still sleeping, so I slink into the bathroom to wash Lazar's scent off me the best that I can, trying to be quiet. I'm not expecting it that, when I step out of the bathroom, he is standing outside the door, waiting for me.

"What are you doing?" Sebastian questions me sleepily.

"I just had to pee. Do you think I might have something to eat?" I ask him, and a surprised expression flies across his face.

"Renee, it's after midnight. It can wait until the morning," he tells me as he grabs my injured wrist then pulls me to bed, and I'm hoping that it is healed up by the morning.

I wake up before Sebastian and quickly check out my wrist. There is not even a red mark along my skin, and a huge wave of relief washes over me. Sebastian begins to stir, and I panic, thinking about having to have sex with him again. But he calms back down then rolls over. *Thank you, sweet baby Jesus!* I scream out inside my head.

But my peace doesn't last for very long though because he wakes up shortly afterward, then that was that—another day of pure hell!

I'm finally able to get up to get dressed. He has scratched me all over and has bitten me again.

"Go get some breakfast," he tells me cheerfully as he climbs out of bed. "You will need your strength for later."

I don't waste any time throwing on some clothes, then once I'm out in the hallway, I see Lazar practically running toward me. He grabs my wrist and looks at it. "I'm fine!" I assure him, smiling, and he smiles back at me then walks me down to the dining room.

There are all kinds of food spread out all over the table, and I'm dying to eat. But Lianna and Aiden are staring at me with intense, watchful eyes.

"How was your night?" Aiden asks me with a smirk slapped across his face.

I lock eyes with him. "I don't kiss and tell."

He doesn't like my comment but goes on about his business.

"Go on, grab some food!" Lianna orders me, smiling happily, so I pile up my plate then take a seat. Sebastian comes in a little bit later then sits down next to me, happy as a lark. He leans over then kisses my cheek, and I'm just about to lose myself but manage to hold it together, smile at him, and then finish eating.

A few more weeks pass by, and I'm getting weaker every day. I haven't fed at all in the past month, which is not like me, because I usually try to feed every two weeks or more.

I had gone out one night from the balcony, but when I returned, Sebastian was waiting for me, enraged that I was out hunting. They've blocked up the entire doorway, so now I can't even go outside on the balcony or even peer out the windows. Sebastian is constantly all over me, and I can't stand it! I haven't even been able to hang out with Lazar, but Lazar knows the limits and leaves me alone, not wanting to catch anyone's eye.

I'm sitting in my room, enjoying this time alone, then I decide to look at my phone. It is completely full of messages, so I begin to delete them, one by one, but stop because Z has sent me one this morning, and I can't help myself when I open up my voice mail to listen to his message, needing to hear his voice.

"My love, I am so sorry, and I miss you so much! I love you. Please call me!" he pleads with me.

Tears begin to stream down my face, and I want to call him so badly. But I know that I shouldn't because if Sebastian hears me talking to him, it'll all be over.

I don't hear him walk into the room, and he grabs my phone right out of my hand then slams it against the wall, breaking it.

"You had no right to do that!" I scream at him, absolutely enraged, and I'm about to lose control because I can't do this anymore!

"You do not need that phone!" he yells at me hatefully.

"It had all of my stuff on it! All of my music and pictures from home were on that!" I'm so pissed and upset that I want to take him down.

"Well, you do not need all of that anymore because you need to focus more on your womanly duties!" he growls at me with angry eyes.

"I want to call my mama!" I scream out as loud as I can. "I haven't even gotten to speak to my family at all! You get to see yours every day!"

Sebastian stares at me, at a loss for words, then he says, "You better quit screaming, or you will be punished!"

I begin to growl under my breath. "Then punish me, asshole! I fucking hate it here!" I'm screaming, along with growling, from the top of my lungs, livid with rage. Everyone comes rushing into the bedroom while I'm running around rampant, screaming and crying.

"Does everything around here have to be a family affair? Can't you freaks mind your own business!" I yell at the onlookers, and they all gasp in shock.

I'm tearing up the room, trashing the place, and going ballistic. I begin to growl and roar as loud as I can, freaking everyone out.

"Renee, calm down!" Aiden demands me.

"Screw you! I hate this place, and I want to go home!"

I roar and scream some more, then Aiden comes running after me and strikes me with his fist. I turn around and jump on top of him then sink my fangs into his arm, and the next thing I know, Aiden and Sebastian throw me down to the ground with the both of them trying to hold me down. I'm still roaring and growling, but when I begin to howl loudly, Lazar comes busting into the room. "Renee, you need to calm down!" he urges me with worried eyes.

"Forget all of you!" I cry out angrily.

I'm roaring so loudly that I can feel the vibration from it all around me, and everyone covers their ears, not being able to stand all the noise. Something strikes me on the back of the head, and I almost black out. But I'm not giving up so easily! I can feel them wrestling me around, so I begin to thrash around violently. Then Aiden grabs the poker from the fireplace and strikes me repeatedly with it along my back, so I turn around, swipe it right out of his hand, and then smack him on top of the head with it. He becomes enraged and jumps on top of me, pinning me down, and I'm beginning to lose my steam trying to fight them. Sebastian and Aiden whip me with one of their belts, and it is total chaos because I just keep on going. I yell and scream, throwing whatever I can get ahold of, and I want to use my power but hold it back, not wanting to expose it.

"Get her down to the basement and throw her into one of the cells! She can sleep in there for the night!" Aiden screams angrily.

Sebastian hits me across the back of the head with something really hard. I'm not sure what it was, but it almost knocks me out. I submit, wanting the quiet time down in the basement. Not to mention, it is going to be the full moon tonight, and Lazar will be going down there to lock himself up. Sebastian wrestles me down to the basement then throws me into the cell right next to the one that Lazar was in last month.

I yell at Sebastian, "I want some food! Get me some food, you jerk!"

Looking at me with cold eyes, he replies, "You will not be eating anything tonight! Hopefully, the wolf does not tear you apart!" He walks out of the cell, shuts and locks the door, and then looks at me one more time before he leaves me.

A little while later, I hear someone coming down the stairs, and my heart skips a beat when I see that it is Lazar. He walks into the cell next to mine, so I sit and watch him quietly. But he doesn't look at me or even speak to me. He begins to take off his clothes, just like what I've done to him several times before, and I must say I'm liking what I see! He has well-defined abs and muscle tone, is a little pale, but is still sexy as all get-out! He turns around, walks over toward the gate, places his clothes outside of the cage, and then shuts the door tightly. He turns to face me, stark naked, and smiles enormously, and I can't help but smile back at him but don't dare make a peep because I don't want them to hear me. We just sit and wait patiently, enjoying each other's company. But I can't help myself when I begin to scoot over as close to him as I can get with the bars sandwiched between us, and he does the same. He looks at me, and we lock eyes. His sweetness is making me forget all about the nightmarish hell that awaits me.

Lazar reaches over and touches my face then runs his hand and fingers along my head, and his loving touch soothes my broken soul. I rest my head against the bars and let him feel my body, needing this sweet, loving attention so badly, and even though I can't see outside, I can sense it getting darker and can feel the night coming on. I want to be free and fly through the night sky under the light of the moon, just like I used to, and hunt whenever I want to when my beast needs fed.

Lazar gently massages my back and runs his fingers along my spine, and his tender touch is giving me the erotic chills. I can't hide my growing excitement when my heart begins to pound, and I begin to breathe heavily. Lazar is getting pretty excited himself then begins touching me and caressing my body a little harder. All is quiet, and I can only hear the two of us, our bodies giving ourselves away. He is looking deep into my eyes, so I reach over, place my hand around the back of his head, pull him to me, and then kiss his lips. We wrap our arms around each other the best that we can from between the bars, then while I hold onto him tightly, I begin to cry.

He pets my head and whispers in my ear, "Calm down, sweetheart. Just calm down. I will hold you all night!"

While I cry, he holds me within a loving embrace, rubbing me all over, trying to comfort me, and whispering sweet nothings in my ear. It must be getting late, and the midnight sun must be shining brightly upon us because Lazar releases me. "I have to get back right now!" he cries out frantically, pulling away from me.

Lazar lies down on the ground several feet away from me, and I can see something beginning to happen, along with all the familiar sounds of bones breaking, skin tearing, and small whimper of pain as it all climaxes. He stands up once his transformation is complete then slowly creeps in closer, looking for my acceptance, so I reach my arm out to him. He is cautious when he approaches me, but it doesn't take him long to rub his head against my hand then pull me in closer to him with his large clawed hands. I scoot as close to him as I can, wanting his fur to rub up against me, and he is breathing heavily, dying to have me closer but not being able to. I can't get any closer to him, so to hell with it, this is happening! I don't care if he kills me because death will be a quick release from this hellish nightmare! I remove my clothes. Then walking over to the cell door and using my power, I unlock it. I leave my cell then stop in front of his, and he is quick to come over to where I'm at while I stand before him, waiting to either be killed or to be welcomed into his furry arms.

"Do you want me to come in?" I ask him, smiling, and he nods, begging for me to open the door. So I open the door, and he backs away when I walk into his cage. I don't care if he strikes me dead because I'm ready for death and welcome it with open arms. But he doesn't move and watches me with intense eyes as I step inside then holds his arm out to me, so I touch his hand. Lazar motions for me to take his wrist into my mouth because he wants me to feed from him, so I look him in the eye and say, "Are you sure?" A freakish, beastly smile creeps across his face, and he nods. So reluctantly, I pick up his wrist with both of my hands then bring it up to my mouth. He is waiting patiently for me to begin, so I take it into my mouth and slowly bite down. He lifts his head up and then pulls me around, bringing me into his chest, and the feelings are all too familiar. I begin to tear up from his comforting embrace, thinking about Z.

Lazar places his muzzle against my cheek while he holds onto me tightly, so I take my time, not wanting to rush the wonderful feelings that I'm having right now within this precious moment in time.

He pulls me slowly over to the far wall then braces me up against it. So I release his arm, then he places it around my waist and gently holds onto me. He moves me into position then takes me, and the pleasing sensations are amazing! I lose myself within these fabulously new sexual sensations, loving every minute, while he licks my back slowly and rubs his face against mine and then begins to lick me around my neck and shoulders. This is unlike anything that I've ever done before, and it sends my body into absolute sexual madness! He is thrusting into me harder, and his soft fur is rubbing all over my bare skin, adding to the intense erotic sensations that I'm feeling. I have to say that this is absolutely epic! No wonder they make it taboo for the two species to mingle because someone wants to keep this their own hidden secret!

Lazar's stamina is amazing, and I can't hold myself back any longer when I have one of the greatest climaxes of my entire life! Lazar rubs his sleek muzzle along the back of my neck and licks my cheek once he finishes, trying to keep from making any noise, because we sure as hell don't want to get caught, and I think we've done a great job of it! Once our love affair is over, he slowly releases me, panting heavily and drooling quite a bit, so I turn to face him then run my hands around the top of his head and along his ears and neck.

"I have to tell you that that was the best lovemaking I've ever had!" I whisper in his hear, and he smiles at me then pulls me against him again, giving me a good squeeze and rubbing his face against mine. "I need to go back over there before someone decides to come down here," I tell him, feeling a great sense of urgency. He nods and licks my face one more time, then I get into my cell and put on my clothes just in the nick of time because Sebastian comes down, bringing me a plate of food, staying as far away from Lazar as possible.

Lazar growls deeply at him, so he hurries up and drops the plate down in front of me on the floor then bolts back up the stairs like a streak of lightning. I smile at him then grab the plate and offer him something to eat, but he won't take it.

"Thank you, cutie-pie. That was great!" I tell him happily while I eat my food, and he gives me a snorting "you're welcome" then sits with me for the rest of the night. I fall asleep next to him while he runs his hands and fingers along my body, and it feels amazing to be loved like this again.

Waking up, I jump away from him because someone is walking down the stairs. Lazar is still wolfed out and moves into the far corner then growls loudly, so I try to act like I've been terrified all night when Sebastian comes down to retrieve me.

He lets me out of the cage. "You need to take a bath! You smell terrible!"

I smile over at Lazar while I follow Sebastian, and he gives me a huge beastly smile then nods. Sebastian takes me up to my room, then I draw the tub water as hot as I can stand it, dying to dive in.

He comes in to check on me. "You are a mess. Get cleaned up!"

After I clean myself up, I check out the aftermath of my beating from the day before. My body is healing rather well, but it is not going to last for long.

CHAPTER 18

My Living Hell

My hell continues almost every day, and I'm getting weaker as the time passes because my body can't heal as quickly as it usually does. Aiden and Sebastian are constantly beating me and starving me, and Aiden has begun raping me, sometimes with Sebastian standing and watching. Sebastian lets his own father rape his wife but doesn't even try to stop him! I know that Lianna knows about this, but she does nothing to bring me any relief. And Lazar can't help me either. Occasionally, I'm able to see him, and we've made love several more times. It is the only time that my pain goes away, and getting lost within his loving affections sets my soul free. But it only lasts for a short amount of time. I've been here for about five or six months now, and I've completely lost track of time. My body is riddled with bites, scratches, and whiplashes and is black and blue from the constant abuse. The pain is almost unbearable at times, and I just want to die. My heart still mourns for my vampire lover every day, and my soul cries out for its other half. I break out my bottle of tequila when my pain is at its worst, but it is almost gone. And I lose myself more and more every second of every day. I'm slipping into a dark depression, falling deeper and deeper into the black abyss and begging the gods to release me from my constant hell. I wonder every day why the gods have chosen me to be this special someone, having all these spectacular gifts that have caused me nothing but heartache and pain. My family and I aren't anything special, just your average, ordinary, everyday Americans trying to earn a living and muddle our way through our pointless existence. It is definitely not a blessing at all!

"Why have you not gotten pregnant yet!" Sebastian screams at me when I get up from bed. I can hardly move from all the wounds and bruises covering my body, and I'm sure that I have a few broken ribs and bones from all the abuse. Plus I'm so hungry my stomach never rests. I just look at him because I don't even want or have anything to say. The despair is overwhelming.

"I need some food, Sebastian," I tell him, pleading with him.

"You do not need anything to eat! You are not even pregnant!" he replies with angry eyes. I can hardly keep my eyes open from feeling so weak, so I lie back down. "You are worthless!" he screams at me hatefully, and at this point, I really don't care because I'm begging for death as I slip into the nothingness then fall asleep.

"Renee…Renee…wake up!" I hear a familiar voice whispering to me. It is Lazar, and he is shaking me. "I have some food for you, but you will need to come down to the kitchen."

I look up and see that it is dark outside. "What time is it?" I ask him.

"It's after ten fifteen p.m.," he replies, helping me get dressed, then leads me down to the kitchen.

"Where's everyone at?" I question him, surprised the whole house is empty.

"They have all left and gone somewhere. Please, just eat something while you have the chance!" he begs me.

There is food all over the kitchen, so I grab a roll from the counter while he grabs some slices of meat and eats a few pieces.

"Eat as much as you can because I don't know when they will be back," he tells me nervously.

But just when I get ready to take a bite out of another roll, I hear, "What are you doing!" It is Aiden, and he is screaming in rage. He runs over to me then punches me right in the face, and I drop to my knees.

Lazar rushes to my aid and stands in front of me. "What are you doing! She needs some food!" he screams at him angrily.

"Get out of my way!" Aiden orders him.

"No! I will not!" Lazar yells back at Aiden just when Lianna and Sebastian come running into the kitchen.

Sebastian begins to beat on Lazar, and Aiden is hell-bent on beating me, then they begin to drag us outside. "You both will be punished!" Aiden shouts angrily. But I'm so weak that I can't even fight, and Lazar is weak himself because he has been trying to satiate my beast but tries to fight them off anyway. They drag the two of us over to the tree outside then place Lazar and I across from each other with our hands touching. They tie us up to the tree.

"Hold on, sweetheart! I'm right here with you!" Lazar whispers to me softly, trying to hold onto my hand.

A few minutes later, Aiden comes out with his whip then begins to lash us across the back, first me, then Lazar. And it seems to go on for hours. My body is numb from the pain, and I slip into the darkness once again. *Please take me! I can bear no more!*

"Please stop!" Lianna cries out, choking on her emotions. "They were just getting some food!"

"They should not have been stealing the food!" Aiden shouts at her.

"Please, Father, let them be!" Sebastian pleads with him. But there is no mercy for us because Aiden throws the whip at him and tells him to hit us, and then it will all be over with.

Sebastian has never whipped us before, and he looks at his father. "I will not do it, Father! They need some food, and you will not let them eat!"

Aiden is furious but walks away, ordering Sebastian, "Put them both down in the basement! Take Renee to the back room this time because I have something special for her! She will never steal any food again!"

Lazar and I get taken down to the basement. They throw him into his usual cell, but this time, Sebastian takes me to the door at the end of the hallway. I'm in and out of consciousness, feeling myself being dragged around, and I can hear the door open. We walk in, then Sebastian flips on the light. I can barely see, but when I look up, I can make out a large, strangely shaped rock sitting on the floor in front of me. It is kind of squared but rounded to a dull point on the top, right in the center of it, and I can see leather straps fastened to each corner. I guess the best way to describe it is to say that it resembles a square pencil with a dull point, standing about three feet high. Sebastian flips me over on my belly then places me on top of the rock. I can't touch the floor, and my legs and arms are dangling downward.

"Take off her clothes then tie her down!" Aiden orders Sebastian when he enters the room, so he obeys and pulls off my clothes, leaving me lying naked on top of this medieval torture rock.

Sebastian begins to spread my legs apart but hesitates, and I can sense a twinge of sympathy welling up from within him. But he continues to spread them apart anyway, wraps the straps around them, and then tightens them down, continuing to my arms. He pulls all the straps tightly down, and an excruciating, agonizing pain explodes throughout my entire body. It is almost unbearable, but all I can do is just lie here while the straps pull me firmly against the dull point of the rock. It is sticking right into my abdomen, sinking in as far as my body will allow it to go. My arms and legs are pulled so tight that I can't even feel them anymore after only a few minutes, then Aiden proceeds to punch me in the head with his fist, causing my face to slam against the rock, bloodying my nose and cutting my cheek. *Please, God! Take me! I don't care if you have the devil himself collect me. Just take me away from this awful place!* I cry out silently inside my head. Aiden lashes me with his whip a few more times, claws my backside, and then finally stops.

"We have to go, son, because we have an early flight in the morning, and we need to get to bed. Those two are not going anywhere! I will have someone let them out late tomorrow night," Aiden tells Sebastian, then they leave the room, flip off the light, but leave the door hanging wide open.

I can't feel my body anymore, and the darkness is swallowing me up. I'm sinking further into the depths of despair, and I don't want to come back as the world disappears all around me when I begin to pass out from this excruciating, ungodly pain.

"Renee! Renee!" I hear a voice calling out to me from beyond. "Renee! Wake up!" I hear Lazar crying out. "Please, sweetheart, wake up!"

I can hear him, but there is no way in hell that I can even communicate with him. I begin to hear all kinds of commotion commencing behind me when the sounds of clanging, screeching metal, growling, roaring, and then echoing of something cracking engulf the room. There is more noise, and then I hear metal groaning as if it is being forced to bend. There is a large crash. The sound of rocks falling and metal screeching can be heard once again. Then suddenly, someone is in the room with me, and I can hear them panting heavily. I feel the soft touch of a furry hand untying the straps from around my arms and legs, then I get lifted away from the top of the rock ever so gently. And I can smell and feel the blood from my back as it runs down my skin. They cradle me in their arms, and I realize that it is Lazar. He has turned into his wolf by his own free will and has broken out of his cage. He sits down on the floor, trying to catch his breath, and rocks me gently.

"Please kill me. I can't go on anymore. Please do it now," I manage to whisper to him, and he begins to whine then slowly rises to his feet, still cradling me in his arms. I can feel the gentle stride of him walking as he carries me out of that room. Then we're climbing the stairs all the way to the top, and I can feel him hit the last step. I see flashes of light while he makes his way down the hallway, so I manage to look up and can see that we've made it to the front door. It opens up slowly. Lianna walks in, and when she turns around, she sees Lazar standing right in front of her.

"Oh…my God!" she screams out loud, petrified by the wolf.

He growls at her then thrusts me out to her, telling her that we need to get the hell out of here with his bodily gestures. His beast is slowly diminishing, so he speaks to her. "Get her out of here now!"

She gasps when she looks down at me. "What have they done to her! This poor girl! She does not deserve any of this! She belongs with Ezekeial, not here!" Lianna begins to sob, and I feel her grab my hand then squeeze it. "I am going to make this right!" Lazar holds me tightly against his chest, and I can hardly breathe but welcome his love.

"Please, Lazar, will you get her cleaned up? I need to make a few calls," Lianna tells him nervously, so he nods then takes me to my room.

Lazar draws me up a bath then places me in the tub as gently as possible, trying not to cause me any more pain. The water burns my torn and tattered body, and every open wound is screaming in pure agony. I know the damage must be bad. Lazar pats my skin gently with the washcloth, trying to wipe away the dried-up blood, and ends up climbing in the tub with me.

He rocks me back and forth and kisses my face. "It will all be over with soon, baby!" he whispers in my ear. "I love you," he tells me, and I can hear him weeping. I begin to tear up too, and I so desperately want to throw my arms around him and hold him against me but I can hardly move.

He finishes wiping me down, picks me up out of the tub, wraps a towel around me, and then lies me down on the bed. I manage to look over at him. "I love you too, handsome," I reply in a breathless whisper.

Lazar runs over to me, places his hands around my face, and then kisses me. He is crying again, and I can feel his tears hitting my skin when they fall from his eyes.

"Just let me die, Lazar. I'm ready."

The look of complete shock flies across his face. "I can't let that happen. Drink from me!" he orders me as he places his arm against my mouth, trying to shove it in.

"I can't because you'll die! You've already given me too much of yourself!" I scold him in another breathless whisper.

"Then I will die!" he cries out angrily, so I turn my head to the side, trying to escape him.

Lianna barges in, "What are you doing? Hurry up, get yourselves dressed, and get her things packed! We need to be at the airport within the hour because the plane is waiting! I need to get her paperwork and passport before we leave!" she runs back out of the room then tears up the hallway as she races down it.

Lazar dresses me in a warm, soft, and stretchy jogging outfit and then goes to get himself ready because he is coming with me, like it or not! I hear him getting my stuff ready, but I don't really have much left to even take back because Sebastian has torn up most of my clothes, along with almost everything else that I've brought with me.

"Let's go!" Lianna demands. So Lazar picks me up, and Lianna carries my bag, then we get into the car to head to the airport.

Chapter 19

Coming Home

For the last few months, Satan's health has deteriorated greatly. His once-beautiful coat has gone totally dull, and he has lost a substantial amount of weight. He barely moves around now, just stands motionless, with his ears pricked straight up, listening for her. Sometimes he bursts out into a gallop across the pasture, bucking and kicking, letting out horrible screams as if he is in pain. Today has been the worst, by far, because he has fallen down and will not rise. With him thrashing around, tearing up the ground around himself, and all the while, making horrible noises, Ezekeial stands over him, and he knows that something must be happening to her. This horse is a part of her somehow and feels her agonizing pain. He unexpectedly springs to life then rises to his feet, almost knocking Ezekeial down, and the giant beast is almost growling at him in rage, with his eyes fixated on him.

"I'm going to go get her right now, big fella!" Ezekeial tells him softy. The stallion groans, walks away from him, and then suddenly falls again but, this time, doesn't move. Dutchess stands over him, nudging him with her nose, because she is worried that this may be his last breath. Ezekeial can't bear any more of it because he wants her home *now*, and the stallion needs her back as well. Something terrible has happened, and worry starts to overwhelm him. He doesn't care who he may have to kill in order to bring her home, but he will do it! Anger wells up from deep within him, and he begins to roar at the sky. Then walking over to Satan, he looks down at him. His breathing is shallow, but he is still alive. So he pulls on his legs, drags him into his stall inside the barn, and then closes the door. Filling up a large bucket with water then setting out a bowl of sweet feed, he heads to the house. Dutchess follows him anxiously because she is nervous, and she knows that Satan is very sick. Her belly is heavily swollen from pregnancy, and she is about to have her foal very soon.

"I am going to go get her! I will not leave her there another moment!" Ezekeial tells her angrily. She neighs in approval and shakes her elegant head. Then swiftly turning around, she trots back to the barn.

Ezekeial turns on his laptop because he is getting the next flight to Romania no matter what time it is or how much it costs, and as he begins to type in the information, his cell phone rings. It is sitting on top of the island in the kitchen, so he bolts over to answer it. To his surprise, it is his mother. "Hello, Mother! I am so glad that you are calling!" he answers while he dashes back to the computer.

She is talking frantically. "We are on our way to America right now, so I need for you to meet us at the airport where our plane always lands. You must drive your truck to the plane! I'm bringing her back to you, and I have everything already taken care of!"

"Mother, what is going on? Is everything okay? Please tell me that Renee is okay!" he pleads to his mother, and he is really worried now because something is very wrong.

"I cannot talk right now, and I must go! We will meet you there in about twelve hours! Goodbye, my son!" She hangs up, and he is left with nothing but silence.

Ezekeial's mind begins to run wild, and he is totally freaking out. He begins to cry from happiness and fear, worried about what Renee will be thinking when he picks her up from the airport and hoping that she will be able to forgive him for what he has done to her. This is going to be the longest twelve-hour wait ever! He runs upstairs to fix Renee's room back up because he has been holding up in there every day since she has been gone, and he has gotten it a complete wreck.

Cleaning has helped take his mind off the wait, then he decides to go and check on Satan before he leaves for the airport later. The barn is quiet, so he flips on the lights. Dutchess is standing in the stall, looking tentatively over at Satan. He is lying motionless, his breathing is shallow, and he looks like death warmed over.

"Please, boy! Hold on for a little longer because she is coming home!" His eyes fill up with tears knowing that he has caused all this, all because of his own cowardice. He should have stood up to Aiden and declared his love for her. He fears that she will probably never forgive him for this, and his heart pains from the very thought of it. He reaches down and rubs Satan along the neck. "I am so sorry for everything!"

He still has a few hours left before he has to be at the airport, and he needs to get himself cleaned up. Since he has come back from Romania, he hasn't hardly shaved his face or cut his hair, so after he gets back to the house, he begins to groom himself with his mind spinning in circles, worrying about seeing her, but thrilled with the thought of her coming back home. There is hardly any food in the house, and he knows that Renee will be starving. So he plans on taking her shopping before they drive home from the airport.

Anticipation is setting in, and he is getting really anxious, and once the time has finally come, he begins to make the agonizing drive to the airport, feeling happy, tense, worried, and scared all at the same time. His nerves are on end, and his pulse is racing. Ezekeial has brought her coat along, just in case, because it is the middle of December, and it is really cold. He knows that she didn't have one on when they had left because it was early spring when they had gone to Romania. Hopefully, Lazar has taken good care of her because he told him to make sure that she was well-fed. He knows that things will not be the same as they were before, but he is willing to do whatever it takes to make it all right once again.

He sees the plane as he slowly pulls into the airway. His heart shifts into overdrive while he drives closer to it, and his mind is racing out of control. Ezekeial's mother meets him out in the parking lot before he even gets out of his truck. "Hello, Mother. What is happening?" he questions her, demanding answers. Ezekeial scans the area, searching for Renee, but she is nowhere in sight. "Where is she?" he questions Lianna, beginning to panic because his mother's expressions read of pure horror.

"I need to talk to you first," she answers, looking away from him.

"What is it! Tell me! What have they done to her?" he cries out loudly, dying to see her.

"I had to bring her back because she belongs to you. She will never belong to anyone else! I am so sorry! I never meant for anything like this to happen! She did not deserve any of this!" Lianna screams out loud, weeping.

"What the hell is wrong!" Ezekeial yells as his anger rises almost over the top.

"They have hurt her really bad, son. I need for you to just take her back to your farm and do not stop until you get there!"

Ezekeial begins to get out of the truck because he wants to see her this instant! He slams his door then urgently begins walking toward the plane, knowing that something is definitely wrong. Just when he approaches the plane, he spots Lazar climbing down the steps with something cradled in his arms.

"Mother, what have they done!" he roars loudly, not being able to contain himself.

Lazar is quickly approaching him, but he rushes over to him in a flash, dying to know what has happened. Renee is wrapped up inside a blanket, and he can only see her face.

"What has happened to her?" he questions Lazar angrily.

"Is your truck unlocked?" Lazar asks Ezekeial, not even stopping, continuing to walk toward his truck.

"Give her to me!" Ezekeial screams at Lazar, almost livid.

"I will not! I want to put her in the truck myself!" Lazar growls loudly at Ezekeial, and this is a huge surprise to him because Lazar has never acted like this before!

Carefully, Lazar opens the door on the truck while Ezekeial watches him impatiently, wanting to rip Renee away from his arms. He hops into the back seat and lies her down across it, placing her head in his lap. Then he caresses her head with his fingers and runs them through her hair. "You are back where you belong, sweetheart. I'm so sorry that I couldn't help you anymore."

Ezekeial is listening in, wanting to hear what he is saying, while Lianna is almost sitting on the ground, breaking down, crying. This is not at all what he was expecting.

"Just let me die, Lazar. I'm in so much pain. There's nothing left for me," Renee whispers without moving.

"As you say, 'It's not happening'!" he replies, smiling at her, then rubs her head some more.

Ezekeial is getting more furious and anxious by the second, then he hears, "I love you," as Lazar bends down and kisses her face, and that sends him over the edge.

"Do not touch her anymore!" Ezekeial screams at him, but Lazar just looks at him then growls a hateful, menacing growl while flashing his wolfy eyes at him.

This throws Ezekeial into madness, and he runs over to Lazar, getting ready to pull him away from her, when he hears, "Just let him be!" Lianna yells at him, stopping him dead in his tracks, so he wheels around to look at her. "He has been with her through all of this, so let him have his time! He has never left her side, a faithful companion when there was no one else there for her!" Lianna's gaze shifts over to them. "They have a special bond that no one will ever break, and I wish that I had someone as special as that in my life!" she tells Ezekeial, choking up once again, then slowly walks away toward the plane.

Ezekeial stands alone in the parking lot with his eyes welling up with tears, because he knows, exactly, what she's talking about, and his heart pains from the thought of it.

"I will always be with you! Don't ever forget that!" he hears Lazar tell Renee, then Lazar bursts into tears. "I must go now, and please be forgiving." He leans over and kisses her cheek once more then gets up slowly, trying to be as gentle as possible. Lazar whispers something in her ear and then walks up to Ezekeial. "You should have never left her there! I would give anything in this world to have someone as special as her love me as much as she does you! She could never love me like she loves you. That's the only reason why I am letting you have her back!" He turns away from Ezekeial then walks back toward the plane, growling softly under his breath.

Shocked by the whole unexpected turn of events that have just unfolded, Ezekeial walks to the back of the truck and looks in on her. Renee is not moving, except for trembling from the cold. "You are safe now, my love, and no one will ever hurt you again!" He hops behind the wheel, grabs her coat, lies it over her shaking body, and then drives away, wanting to hurry up to get her back home.

Driving home, he can't stop thinking about Lazar because he has never been so aggressive toward him like that! *What happened over there?* It was all just so crazy! It seems like the drive back to the farm is taking forever, an endless journey through time, and he hasn't heard a peep out of her at all. And he is dying to see her and touch her because the waiting is pure agony!

Pulling into the driveway, he shuts off the truck then turns around to look at her. Still not a single word or sign of life coming from her, he begins to get worried and rushes to get her out of the back seat of the truck. As soon as he picks her up, he knows right away there is something very wrong. There is no weight to her at all, and he can feel her bones protruding through her clothes. "Let us get you into the house. Your bed has been waiting for you," he whispers to her softly.

Renee is as limp as a rag doll, and he holds her close, wanting to give her his warmth. He tries to be as gentle as possible while carrying her upstairs then lies her down on her bed. Her skin is very pale, and she has dark circles underneath her eyes. And once he begins to take off her hoodie, he sees right away all the claw marks, bite marks, and slashes along her arms.

"Oh my God, baby! What have they done to you!" he screams from the top of his lungs. Ezekeial begins to remove the shirt that she is wearing but has to lie her down to walk away because the sight of her horrific abuse is almost too much to bear. There is hardly any untouched skin left on her body because, practically, every inch of it is all black and blue and riddled with wounds and slashes. He steps back in pure rage and shock while putting his fist in his mouth then bites down onto it to keep from screaming. Tears begin to stream down his face, and massive guilt scorches him from the inside out.

He pulls off her pants to see what else they have done to her and gasps, not being able to believe his eyes. Her inner thighs are full of bite marks, the dragon tattoo on her side is almost peeled away from her body, and scratches and bruises are running up and down every inch of her skin. Rolling her over, he can see the familiar slashes from the whip that Aiden had used to beat him with, and with this, he has to get up because some of them are so deep the bone is exposed. Running out of the house then through the yard, he roars from anguish and pure fury. He stands in the yard, panting heavily, then begins to roar again. But some of her wounds are still bleeding, so he needs to get it stopped and turns his attention back to getting her cleaned up and nursed back to health.

Drawing up some bathwater then pouring some Epsom salt into it, he places her in the tub. The searing pain from the salt causes her to whimper a little bit, and tears begin to stream down her face. Ezekeial begins to cry while trying to wash her thoroughly without inflicting any more pain to her, but it is almost impossible. And he can still smell Lazar's scent on her and won't be satisfied until it has been scrubbed away.

"What have I done to you!" he whispers to himself while he washes her, choking on his guilt and grief. "I am so sorry, my love! I was getting ready to come get you when Mother had called because I cannot be without you any longer!" He kisses her cheek but can still smell Lazar's scent on her, so he grabs the washcloth and gently wipes her face some more.

"Just let me die, Lazar. I'm so tired, and the darkness calls to me," she says in a breathless whisper then begins to cry weakly and shake violently.

Ezekeial runs his hand across her head then wipes the tears away from her eyes. "I am here for you, my love! Please do not leave me!" he pleads with her, choking on his tears. He finishes washing her up then picks her up out of the tub. There is no meat left on her bones, and her stomach is growling insistently. "I never thought this would happen to you!" He pulls her close to him then hugs her against his body for a few minutes, trying to warm her up.

After Renee stops shaking, Ezekeial rubs some cream on her terrible wounds then wraps some bandages around her belly, across her breasts, and around her back, covering up the deep slashes that have been whipped into her. He places her underneath the covers of the bed and pulls her fuzzy blanket over the top of her. "I must leave you for a minute to run up to the barn," he informs her then makes a mad dash outside.

Ezekeial had a sick calf a couple of weeks ago and has some leftover IV bags filled with electrolytes and nutrients lying inside the fridge up in the barn, so running like the wind, he grabs them frantically then bolts back up to the room. She hasn't moved and has started shaking again, so he works quickly to get the IV started, not wanting to waste another minute. She moans a little when he inserts the needle into her arm. Then getting that done, he hangs it from the bedpost and then removes his clothes and gets under the covers with her, holding her up against his warm body, trying to ease her trembling with his body heat. Her lips are turning blue and purple, so he wants to warm her up as quickly as possible. And while he holds her in his arms, a ginormous sense of relief blankets over him, knowing that she is right here with him once again. He has had to take sleeping pills just to get to sleep every night because he can't go to bed without her, so having her back home, lying next to him, is absolutely wonderful! Watching her while she sleeps, he spies the wedding ring that Sebastian has placed on her finger, and in an angry rage, he pulls it off then throws it across the room. "You belong to me forever and always, not to anyone else!" he growls angrily then snuggles up to her even more.

Renee is beginning to warm up, and her shaking slowly subsides. But he can barely hear her breathing, and her heartbeat is almost nonexistent. He rubs her head then runs his fingers through her hair, ecstatic that she is back home with him, feeling content for the first time in months.

Waking up in the middle of the night, he notices the IV bag has gone completely dry, so he grabs another one to replace the empty one. Renee is looking a little bit better, her color is beginning to come back, and he can see that her wounds are slowly healing. But she needs some blood to help her heal faster, so he cuts his arm with his fang then tries to open her mouth, wanting to get the blood into her system. But she isn't having any of it and begins to fight him, so he stops. "You must feed, my love! This will help you heal!" He tries again, but she won't drink from him and squirms around, trying to get away. "Please, take it," he whispers to her. But she still won't feed, so he leaves her be. "Maybe later," he tells her softly.

Ezekeial leans over and kisses her lips and then presses his face to hers. "I have missed you so much!" he says happily as he lies back down then covers the both of them up. Curling himself around her, he drifts back to sleep then falls into the sweet nothingness of slumber.

The sun rises, and its penetrating rays shine brightly through the windows of the French doors. There is a thick layer of frost covering the ground from the chilly morning air, and when Ezekeial wakes up, he looks at Renee right away. He can hear her heartbeat sounding more normal and steadier, and her breathing sounds less labored. Good, the IV is working! He grabs another one then attaches it. But there is only one left, so once it is gone, he is going to force her to take in some sustenance, whether she wants to or not!

"I must be going into town to get some food for you! I know you will be wanting some, as you say, 'groceries,' soon!"

He gets up then begins to get ready to go into town, but before he leaves, he wants to make out a list to make sure that he doesn't forget anything. Grabbing his list then hopping into the truck, he heads toward town. His spirits are lifted, and it feels wonderful to be going shopping for her. He needs to grab her some clothes, too, because there wasn't much of anything left of her stuff, just that one small suitcase and duffel bag, but there wasn't much in it, only containing her broken phone, her paperwork, and a few shirts. He decides to take the cell phone to the store to see if they can fix it.

Ezekeial makes a day out of his trip and picks up everything and more from what is written down on his list. They were also able to repair her phone, so he stops to pick it up before he heads back to the farm. He decides to turn on her phone once he gets in the truck, wanting to make sure it works, plus feeling curious about what may be on it. He sees all his text messages and voice mails that were never read. There are missed calls from her mother and a few other people who she had never gotten, so he definitely needs to have her call her mother as soon as she is able to. He opens up the pictures app then begins to look at them, and when he comes across the pictures of himself that she had taken right before they had left for Romania, he begins to weep. He continues to scroll through some more of the photos and finds a few of Lazar, along with a couple of selfies of her and Lazar. Ezekeial begins to get crazy-mad with jealousy, along with feeling hurt, but it's his own fault and he can't be angry with either of them.

Getting back to the house, he brings all his groceries and supplies in then rushes up to check in on her. She is all snuggled up with her fuzzy blanket, the way that she has always done before, and looks pretty content while resting peacefully. She is healing up quite nicely, but she still needs some blood.

"Renee...Renee," he softly calls out her name, and she stirs a little but not much. It is after 5:30 p.m., and it is getting dark outside already. "Renee, you must feed," he says to her again.

"I'm tired," she barks in a forced breath.

"I know that you are tired, my love, but you must feed!" Ezekeial pleads with her again.

Pulling her up and away from her blanket, he cuts his arm, attempting to get her to drink from him once again, but she begins to push him away. This time, he shoves his arm into her mouth, forcing her to taste his blood. She is much too weak to fight him, and while he lets the blood run down her lips, she slowly opens her eyes and looks at him. Then startled and freaked out, she jumps right out of his arms all crazy eyed, with her eyes darting around, trying to catch her bearings. "What the hell!" she cries out loud, confused and in utter disbelief. "I must have died! Thank you, sweet baby Jesus!"

CHAPTER 20

Starting Over

I can taste the blood in my mouth and awaken from the peaceful slumber of the dark abyss, and Ezekeial is cradling me in his arms. "What the hell!" I cry out in disbelief. "I must have died! Thank you, sweet baby Jesus!" I've jumped right out of his arms, and my body is screaming from the terrible pain because every move is excruciating.

"You need to feed, my love," Z tells me with an intense gaze.

"How long have I been here?" I ask him, trying to wrap my head around what is going on.

"Since yesterday afternoon," he answers, watching me closely.

I scan my surroundings, making sure that I'm actually back at the farm and not in that terrible house, then breathe a huge sigh of relief when I realize that I'm definitely back at the farm. I lose my emotions and begin to cry, and Ezekeial reaches out to grab me. But I jerk away from him because he is the one who caused all this!

"Please, I hope you can find forgiveness in your heart for me. I was actually going to go to Romania myself yesterday to come get you because I cannot stand being away from you any longer, but Mother called me right when I was getting ready to purchase my ticket!" he explains with sadness and guilt in his eyes, and I'm not really sure what to say because I can only stare at him, feeling a mountain of mixed emotions. "I have missed you terribly, and the guilt has been ripping me apart! I was going to kill them if they tried to stop me!" he continues. But starvation consumes my every thought, so I don't really care what he has to say right now.

"Where's Lazar?" I ask him, and a shocked expression flies across his face.

"He left with my mother, why?" Z questions me.

"Hopefully, he's okay! They told him that he'd be punished if he didn't stay with me and keep me on the property. Maybe I should call him!" I say, feeling great concern for Lazar. But I think Ezekeial is getting a little ticked off, so I drop it. I'll just have to call Lazar sometime when he is gone.

"Please, you need to feed," he tells me while reaching his arm out to me, wanting me to feed from him. "Take it," he commands me, but I can hardly move because my body hurts terribly. I try to reach out to grab it, but I'm in way too much pain. So he scoots in closer to me, getting ready to place it up to my mouth.

"STOP!" I cry out as loud as I can when he begins to wrap his arms around me.

"What is it, my love?" he questions me, looking confused, as tears roll down my cheeks, remembering his coldness right before he had left me in that horrible place.

"I can't," I tell him in a whisper then look away from him. I know Z is hurt by this, but I don't care because this is all his fault!

"I am so sorry!" he pleads with me. "I can never tell you enough! I will never let anyone touch you again because you will stay with me forever! I will kill anyone who tries to take you from away me!" He is getting really upset, but I just sit and listen to him, still mad as hell, not speaking or offering him any kind of comfort. He is dying for me to give him some attention, but I just can't right now because my anger and mixed emotions for him are holding me back. "Please, feed from me now!" he barks at me, getting pissed off, and I love it!

I just ignore him and let him get even angrier while I look out the window, trying to spy Satan out in the field, but I don't. So I get up on unsteady and weak legs, wanting to get a better view outside. I can't even hold myself up, and I fall down. Z doesn't waste a second to peel me up off the floor. "Where's Satan?" I ask him, and he gives me a strange look.

"He is in the barn," he replies crossly because he is dying for my attention, and I'm not submitting to him in any way.

Z reaches over to touch my face, but I turn my head away because I can still picture him leaving me behind like I never even mattered, just as plain as day. "Why am I here? The farm isn't my home because you had made that perfectly clear before you abandoned me! I need to go back home to Missouri!" I cry out, almost screaming.

Z loses it. "I am so sorry! I did not mean any of it, but it was the only way...the only way..." He can't finish his sentence.

"You mean the only way that you could leave me behind with those damned monsters!" I scream at him hatefully, and he cowers down, knowing that he has done something horribly wrong. "Do you know what I've been through? Well, of course you do! Look at my fucking body, Ezekeial! Look at what they've done to me!" I'm livid! He looks at me, stunned, because I never cuss like that, then begins to cry, holding his arms out to me, begging for my forgiveness. "I don't want to hold you! How can I want to comfort a man who threw me away after making think he loved me so much? Everything was just a lie, and I can't believe you did that to me! All of this is your fault!" In a mad rage, I rip the bandages off my body. "Look at me! I'm a hot mess! My body is in total shambles!" I can't help myself as I carry on, needing to get my feelings off my chest before I burst while Ezekeial is bawling his eyes out. "I want to go home to my family because I sure as hell don't want to be here with you! Besides, you don't want me here anyway! Why did you even bother bringing me back here!" I yell at him angrily, and he is stunned. An expression of pure shock flies across his face. "Where are my car keys? I'm going to go home right now before you let them come get me again! I never in my life ever expected anything like this from you!" I'm able to get up with being so angry then walk shakily over to the closet with him watching me fiercely. I open it up then begin to grab something to wear.

"Please, come sit down! You cannot go like that!" he pleads with me, still crying.

"I don't give a shit! This isn't my home, and I want to go home right now! I miss my mama and family! I couldn't even call them because your brother broke my phone! I trusted you with my everything, and you took me over there then left me like I was nothing but your used-up piece of trash, you fucking asshole!" I'm yelling as loud as I can, wanting to make sure that I get my point across to him while he grovels and begs. This hits him hard, and he rushes over to me while I'm trying to put on some clothes.

"You cannot leave me! I never meant to hurt you so much!" he cries out with tears streaming down his face, wanting to embrace me. Z reaches out and grabs me then pulls me against his chest, and I can't help myself as I melt in his arms and begin to cry, releasing my emotions. I want to just submit to him, but he has hurt me so badly that I can't. So I force myself to pull away from him, but he won't let me go. I struggle a little bit, but there is not a chance in hell that I can break free from his vice. So I end up submitting to him. I know I'm a complete failure, but what else am I supposed to do?

Ezekeial begins to rock me in his arms, holding onto me tightly. "I know you cannot forgive me right now, but please, just let me hold you for a while!" he begs me, dying for my love and affection, so I let him hold me because I don't really have a choice anyway.

He carries me back to the bed and lies me down, and I can't even begin to describe in words how agonizing the pain is. Plus I'm lying here naked, an absolute freaking mess.

"I will get something for you to put on," he tells me then quickly runs to his room and grabs me one of his T-shirts. Z wants to dress me, so I let him because besides the terrible pain, I'm feeling totally exhausted and worn down.

"I love you so much. Please do not leave me!" he whines, rocking me in his arms. I'm helpless against this amazing, comforting feeling because I feel so safe and warm while I rest my head against his chest, along with his chin pressed against the top of my head, and he is rubbing it gently across my scalp, whispering softly in my ear. I love this feeling that I haven't had from him in months, and I'm a prisoner within his loving embrace. So to hell with it, I'm going to let him hold me! I'm getting so sleepy while he rubs my head, and I'm in heaven right now, enjoying every minute of it.

"Please feed from me," he says to me again then puts his wrist up to my mouth, and I want to deny him the pleasure. But I pull it into my mouth, release my fangs, and then bite down slowly. I'm so hungry!

As I feed from him, he presses his face harder against mine, making me feel absolutely wonderful. His blood slowly satiates my hunger, but without warning, pain explodes all over my entire body! I jump right out of his arms then fall on the floor, with the sounds of bones breaking and things tearing inside my body radiating all around me. I break out in a drenching, cold sweat then begin to thrash around from the excruciating pain. I'm shivering uncontrollably, and I cry out because it hurts so badly! My muscles are squirming underneath my skin, and things deep down inside me are moving and slithering around because my body is trying to heal itself. I scream out from the agonizing pain, begging the gods to make it all stop.

"I am here. Calm down, my love!" I hear him say as he places his hand on the top of my head, trying to comfort me, but the pain is unbearable!

My stomach begins to cramp up, and I double over from the immense pain. Z is trying to hold onto me, wanting to comfort me, but I feel like I'm about to throw up. So I manage to make it to my feet, race as fast as I can into the bathroom, and then hug the toilet after I lie my head down on the seat. The cool touch of it feels wonderful against my clammy, feverish face, but the relief is short-lived.

Z comes rushing in right behind me then kneels down beside me. "I am here, my love! I am here!"

I can hear him choking back his tears while he rubs his hand along my back, caressing it softly, then I begin to throw up and hang my head over the toilet. But there is nothing really coming out. Every dry heave sends searing pain inside my abdomen, and I, suddenly, feel a strange sticky wetness run down between my inner thighs and can smell the scent of blood. I dry heave once again, and more liquid runs down between my inner thighs. Another wave of cramping hits me, and I grab my belly with one of my hands, leaving the other one clinging to the toilet, bracing myself from the excruciating, god-awful pain. Z is still kneeling beside me with his hand pressed into my back, terrified.

With another dry heave, I feel something expel out of me. It is warm and feels like gooey jelly as it slides down the inside of my inner right thigh. I panic and move, causing it to break free from my thigh, then it falls onto the floor between my legs; afraid, I freeze in place. Ezekeial lets out a small gasp then plants his fist against his mouth, and I already know what has happened before I even look at it.

All my pain has subsided, and I only have a mild achy feeling while scooting back away from the toilet then look down. There, on the floor in front of me, lies a dead fetus. It is perfectly formed, with fingers, toes, and all, and his skin is blue from being lifeless. A tear runs down my cheek because they've killed this innocent baby by not letting me eat and from the constant abuse. "I'm so sorry, little fella," I whisper when I lean over him, and I wonder whose baby this is and how far along I was with Sebastian's words running through my mind: *Why aren't you pregnant!*

Z is staring at me with an expression of pure horror and shock plastered across his face, and I'm furious when I gaze over at him. Without thinking, I get up on my knees, then reach over, and punch him in the jaw. "This is all your fault!" I scream at him angrily.

He tries to pull me over to him, but I pull away then scoot up against the bathroom wall, staring out into the nothingness. Could this have been Lazar's baby? I go numb, losing myself in my own thoughts.

"What have I done!" Z cries out while staring at the lifeless baby lying on the floor.

"Everything!" I answer him hatefully while trying to get to my feet, but I keep sliding around on the fluid that is discharged from my body.

"Please let me help you!" he shouts at me while he quickly hops to his feet.

"Just stay the hell away from me!" I growl at him loudly.

"I will take him and bury him beneath one of the trees out by the lake, okay?" he asks, looking for my approval.

"That would be really nice of you," I answer in a soft voice, looking down at the baby one more time.

Ezekeial grabs one of the small hand towels from the closet then wraps the baby in it. "I will be back shortly, my love, and I will clean all of this up when I return. Go take yourself a nice hot shower, and I will grab another shirt for you to put on."

Tears are streaming down his face, and there is blood and bodily fluid all over the bathroom floor. It is one hell of mess, along with myself, so I take his advice and pull off my soiled shirt then climb into the shower. The scalding water burns at first, but then it begins to soothe my aching body. I'm totally exhausted and hungry, and I still can't believe that this has all just happened. But I can't cry anymore because my tears are all dried up. I see him cleaning up the mess on the floor, and he has placed a clean shirt, along with a fresh towel, next to the shower door.

As I grab the towel then step out of the shower, I can see my body's reflection in the mirror and can't believe how terrible it looks because it is absolutely grotesque and disturbing! Not being able to bear the sight of it any longer, I put on his shirt then begin to walk wobbly over to my bed.

"Let me help you to bed," he says while holding his arms out to me, and I submit to him, needing to be held and longing for comfort after that hellacious ordeal. So I allow him to scoop me up then carry me to bed.

Ezekeial sits down on the bed, cradles me in his arms, and then begins to rock me gently once again. He pulls me against his chest, and the warmth of his body against mine offers me the solace that I've been craving because I need him now more than ever. "I am so sorry, my love! Nothing that I can ever say or do will ever take any of this back," he says while rubbing his face against mine and kissing my cheek.

Z covers the both of us up then offers me his wrist again, so I willingly take it because I need his blood to heal me. I can tell that this is giving him some of the attention that he has been dying for, so I close my eyes and let him rock me to sleep. I've missed him so much and haven't felt this good in months, and I don't ever want to be hurt like that again!

"I love you, my love," he whispers to me while he slowly rocks me, sending me into a warm, snuggly, and heavenly bliss. I release his arm, then he wraps it around me, and I can feel and hear him sobbing. I feel so content while lying in his arms, and I don't ever want this peaceful moment to end. So I nuzzle my face into his chest and pull on his shirt, trying to get as close to him as I can. He begins to caress my head then run his fingers through my wet hair, and I drift to sleep, feeling absolutely wonderful for the first time in months.

Waking up in the middle of the night from terrible hunger pains, I decide that I must have some groceries. I'm still lying in Z's arms, and he is fast asleep. So I slowly try to move off him without waking him up. He stirs a little, but I manage to get to my feet without disturbing him. I feel so much better after everything has passed, and the blood that Z has fed to me has helped me out tremendously. I cautiously leave the room then head downstairs, hoping there is some food down in the kitchen. Jackpot! He has stocked up the whole kitchen with food! I leave the light off, grab the peanut butter off the counter, and then open it up. Grabbing a spoon, I dive in and begin shoveling it in my mouth, lavishing in its fabulous taste. Then I take the milk out of the fridge and pour myself a huge glass of it. Oh, man! I haven't had any of this stuff in forever, and it tastes amazing! I gulp my milk down, open up the fridge, and then rummage through it. There is some lunch meat in there, so I tear into it, not being able to stop myself. I see that he has picked up some of my favorite doughnuts, so I grab a few of them then cram them into my mouth, overjoyed with the fabulous taste of them. I'm ravenous! I turn around, and Z is watching me while I bust into all the food, going crazy with my feeding frenzy. But when he steps out of the shadows toward me, I have a flashback of Aiden striking me in the kitchen, so I cower down next to the stove, throwing my arm up at him, waiting for the blow.

"It is okay. It is just me!" he tells me then reaches down and pulls me back to my feet. "I will never strike you!" Z assures me as he pulls me against his chest, dying for my attention, but right now, I'm starving!

"Please, just let me eat! I haven't had any food like this in months!" I whisper to him while gazing into his intense green eyes.

He nods and looks away from me then puts his head down. "Eat all that you want to, my love, because I am not going to stop you," he whispers to me, and I can sense his guilt and shame, knowing that these terrible things have been done to me because of him.

I gaze into his eyes once again, touch his face, and then run my fingers through his hair. "Thank you," I whisper softly and then continue on my quest for food, shoveling in everything I can get ahold of. I see him watching me, smiling with satisfaction, then he leaves me alone and goes back upstairs. I eat until I'm full, grab some juice, and then head back upstairs myself.

"Did you get enough to eat?" he asks me when I walk into the room. He has taken a shower and is lying in bed with just his shorts on.

"Well, I think so! There may be a piece of bread left for you to eat in the morning, but I can't say for sure," I reply, and Z laughs. He looks good enough to eat, but I'm not ready for any of that yet.

"I have missed you so much!" he says as he grabs me up then drags me into the bed beside him. He wraps his arms around me, and from my contentedness of a full belly, I close my eyes and begin to drift away into the dark abyss. I feel him running his hand along my neck and arm ever so tenderly, then he kisses me on the cheek, and I can hear him begin to weep once again. "I am so glad that you have come home to me," Z whispers.

The morning comes, and I want to see Satan terribly. Ezekeial is still soundly sleeping beside me, so I rise slowly, trying not to wake him, then slither out of bed. I tiptoe as quietly as I can over to the open closet to find some clothes to put on, and as I pick out some clothes, an amazing sense of relief and peace overwhelms me because I'm feeling so much better today! Not wanting to make a lot of noise in the bedroom, I creep down to the downstairs bathroom to get dressed. My boots are still sitting where I had left them before I went to Romania, next to the side door, so I slip them on, step out onto the porch, walk around the house, and then head up to the barn. I manage to make it up to the barn door without getting caught, and I smile when I hear a loud whinny coming from the inside. It is Dutchess, and she hears me approaching.

Once I step into the barn, I'm appalled with shock and utter disbelief because Satan is lying on the floor of his stall, motionless. I can hardly hear him breathing, and his heartbeat is barely audible. Dutchess seems to be asking me for help while she stares at me with great, intense emotional distress. I walk into the stall then sit down beside him, and my beautiful stallion is a complete disaster! He has lost so much weight, and his coat is dull and unhealthy. I move in closer, lift his limp head up off the floor, and then place it in my lap.

I caress his muzzle gently. "Please, big fella, stay with me," I beg him, but he doesn't move. "I'm here with you now, and I've missed you so much! I've thought about you every day. Wake up and talk to me!" I cry out unhappily, almost in tears, while I run my hand along his neck and around his ears, whispering comforting words to him.

Satan begins to come to, so I lean over to grab the water bucket then scoop some water in my hand. I pour as much of it as I can into his mouth, and I can hear him trying to swallow it. So I scoop more water into my palm, allowing him to sip it slowly. "That's good, big fella! Let's get you some more water!" I cry out happily. I place the bucket over by him, then he raises his head and begins to drink out of it. This seems to perk him up, then he looks at me with his soft dark eyes. He nods a little, and I laugh at him, wanting him to get up. I place my hand on his head, rub his ears, and then run my fingers along his neck, and he begins to move around but doesn't get up. "You need some food," I tell him while looking around.

I see a small bucket of grain over on the other side of the stall, but before I can even get up, Dutchess grabs it and brings it to me. "You're pretty smart, my lady!" I tell her, giving her a huge smile. Dutchess is heavily pregnant, and I can hear her foal's heartbeat pumping strongly inside her belly. It is very close to time. She gives me some horse talk and then walks over to me and nudges my head with her nose. I stick my hand down in the grain and pull out a handful from the bucket then force it into his mouth. Satan accepts it easily, and I manage to get him to eat almost all the feed in the bucket. "That's good, big fella!" I whisper to him with a big sigh of relief.

I feel myself becoming really tired and drowsy, so I lean my head against the stall wall then close my eyes. Before I know it, I can feel myself drifting away into the realm of darkness, feeling at peace knowing that I've been reunited with my long-lost spirit—this mighty beast who came to me from the flames of the fire not so very long ago.

*****

Satan rises to his feet carefully, not wanting to step on her. He has missed her so much, and just having her back with him overjoys him. The two of them share a special bond unlike any other, and he has been lost without her. Renee is sleeping peacefully, and he wants her to get her rest. Suddenly, Ezekeial rushes into the barn, screaming for Renee.

"Renee! Renee! Where are you?"

Ezekeial sees that Satan has gotten up, so he walks over to the stall. And there she is, lying against the wall, out cold. He begins to walk into the stall when Satan dashes forward, stepping in his way. He wants Ezekeial to leave her right where she is at because he hasn't gotten to see her in months and has missed her something awful.

"Please, Satan, let me take her back to the house. It is cold out here, and she needs to be in her room," Ezekeial explains to the mighty black beast.

Satan snorts in disapproval because he is not going to let him take her away from him ever again! Walking over to her, he nuzzles her face gently with his nose, wanting to feel her. Her face is cold, and he can see her shiver ever so slightly.

"Please, I promise to you that she will be just fine! I will make sure she comes out here and sees you tomorrow!" Ezekeial pleads with him.

Satan decides that Ezekeial is right because she should be inside, so he steps back out of the way, letting Ezekeial get to her.

"Thank you, boy! I am going to take good care of her," Z tells him with tears in his eyes.

Satan gives him another snort and then walks over to Dutchess and rubs his head along her bloated belly, still very angry with him. Before Ezekeial leaves the barn, he gives him some more feed and water then picks Renee up and takes her back down to the house.

*****

I wake up, and I'm lying on the bed in my room. Looking at the clock, I see that it is already 4:37 p.m. "Man, where did the day go?" I say quietly to myself. I'm still in the clothes that I had worn outside earlier this morning, so I decide to go downstairs to grab a snack because I've got a rumbly in my tumbly something fierce! I don't see Z, but the food is calling my name!

I happen to glance out the back door while rooting around in the kitchen and notice that my car is gone. "Where in the hell is my boo!" I scream out loud without thinking. My heart jumps right out of my chest, and I haul ass outside to the driveway, searching for my TA.

Oh...my...God! Where's my car! I run over to the little red garage in the driveway then rip the doors wide open, but still, there is no boo! I'm ready to go in an all-out rage! *What did that mofo do to my car!* Without realizing it, I'm growling like anyone's business, and I'm so pissed I can't stop growling.

"My love, what is wrong?" I hear him say behind me, so I swing around, mad as hell.

"Where in the hell is my boo! What did you do with her?" I'm about to come unglued!

A huge smile flies across his face, and I want to rip it right off him. "Hold on, I will go get it," Z says to me as he walks past me.

I'm panting heavily from being so mad because I just can't believe it, and I'm pacing around, ready to blow, thinking about tearing Ezekeial to shreds! The next thing I know, he is pulling up in the driveway with a fully restored Trans Am just like my boo! I stop dead in my tracks, frozen in disbelief and awestruck because it is absolutely beautiful!

"Is this my car?" I ask him when he walks over to me.

His smile is over the top. "Yes, this is your boo."

I run my fingers along the driver's side fender lovingly like I always do, smiling from ear to ear. I've calmed down from my livid rage and can't take my eyes off it. The paint job has totally been redone, all the pinstriping is brand-new, and the magnificent rising phoenix on top of the hood is as stunning as ever! The honeycomb wheels have also been redone, and they glisten in the sunlight. I open the driver's side door then sit down behind the wheel, and I'm speechless because the entire inside has been totally overhauled too! The seats have been recovered with new black leather and are trimmed out with gold. Plus a rising phoenix has been embroidered on each of the seats right in the center, adding to the awesomeness factor. The radio has been upgraded as well so that I can plug my phone into it, and the instrument panel is still the original but has also been redone.

"It's absolutely beautiful!" I tell Z ecstatically.

"I could not stop thinking about you, and I felt like you were here with me while I was working on this car. I've redone the whole engine, and basically, it's all brand-new! I have done this for you, my love, and I hope that you like it," he says, smiling happily. And by the way he is staring at me, I know he is dying for some attention from me for the great thing that he has done. Even though I'm still upset with him, I can't help myself and get out of the car then wrap my arms around him. "Thank you, Z. It's amazing!" I tell him, overjoyed, hugging him tightly. I'm thrilled!

My stomach begins to growl. "Sounds like someone is hungry!" Z says then begins to laugh.

"Yeah, that would be me!" I reply when I shut the door on the car, still looking at it while I walk toward the house because I can't peel my eyes away from it!

Rooting through the fridge, we find some food then take a seat at the kitchen table. A newspaper is sitting next to me, so I thumb through it. And Z is looking at a different section of it while we eat.

"I'm going hunting tonight," I tell him, and he looks over at me, surprised.

"Are you going to be able to? I am coming with you!" he demands me with a fierce stare.

"I'm going to have to because my beast needs fed. Plus I'm ready to fly! It's been a long time! I'll want to go alone, and I'll be just fine. I flew off from the house one day, so they blocked up the balcony so that I couldn't go out again, then I was beaten severely. I was basically locked in my room twenty-four hours a day after that, except for when we'd go into the office to help out with the business! Lianna would drive Lazar and I over to the Dragkarr building, we'd put in our day, then be taken straight back to the estate." With that, he drops his newspaper and stares at me with those beautiful green eyes of his.

"I am so sorry, my love. No one will ever hurt you like that ever again."

"I know they won't because I'll kill anyone who ever tries to beat me or hurt me again!"

His eyes are fixated on me, but he is at a loss for words, not sure what to say. I rise from the table then grab the bottle of tequila out of the cabinet next to the fridge where I've always put it. Lost in my own thoughts, I pick up my headphones and cell phone then go sit down on the porch swing outside. I've always used this as my thinking chair, and I'm so glad that Z had gotten my phone fixed. I have everything on it. Plus the only way that I can see Lazar is from the few pictures that I had taken back at the estate.

I open up my playlist, turn on my tunes, and then begin to scroll through my pictures. There they are—the few pictures that I had taken of him and me when we were able to get away from those monsters. Memories begin to rush through my brain like a wild, angry storm brewing out of control, and I wonder how he is and where he is at. I hope they didn't do anything bad to him after he and Lianna had gotten back to Romania.

I see Z coming outside from the corner of my eye, then he sits down next to me. So I hurry up and close my photo app, trying to act like I'm scrolling through my music, searching for a song. I take a giant swig from the bottle then look over at him, and he is staring at me intensely. He reaches out, wipes the tears away from my cheek, and then pushes my hair out of my face. I take another giant gulp out of the bottle then look away.

"I do not know how you can drink that stuff like that!" he says, looking surprised.

"Yeah, well, it was the only thing that could help dull the pain and to help me escape my hell for a while," I explain.

Z's eyes begin to well up with tears. "Then why are you drinking it now? Are you in pain?" he questions me.

"Nope, I just need a drink, that's all. Thoughts and memories are crashing through my brain, and I just need to get away for a while," I reply then look over at him. "The terrible memories don't just disappear, Z," I add, and he nods, not saying anything else while he stares me down. I take a few more drinks then decide to head back in.

It is getting cold, and I'm ready to feed before it gets too late. But as I get up, Z grabs my hand, pulls me over to him, and then sits me in his lap. He wraps his arms around me then pushes the swing back and forth slowly. He presses my head into his chest, and the feel of his warm body and embrace is so wonderfully inviting.

"I love you so much, and I never meant to hurt you."

Z pulls my face up to his then kisses me on the lips, and I kiss him back, wanting more but not letting myself give in to him. He kisses me again while he rubs his fingers around my face and through my hair, but I abruptly stop him.

"I need to go hunting," I tell him sharply then hop up out of his lap quickly. I still have the bottle of tequila in my hand, so I take another giant swig of it as I walk into the house. I place it back inside the cabinet then head up to my room. After locking the door behind me, I begin to take off my clothes then step into the bathroom, wanting to check out my bruised and beaten body. It is still a mess, but it is healing rather well and quickly, considering how bad it had looked before. I breathe a huge sigh of relief, pleased that I'm beginning to return back to my old self once again.

I release my beast for the first time in months, and I must say it hurts like a mofo! It is magnificent in all its glory, and I can't wait to take to the sky. The night is calm and chilly, but I don't care while the shimmering moonbeams envelope me, beckoning me into the night sky. I open the French doors then breathe in the cold evening air, savoring this fantastic moment. It has been so long I almost feel like I'm going to be punished if I fly off, feeling a great sense of worry and anxiousness, and I know that Z is watching me from somewhere. But I don't care because it is my time right now, and I need to be alone. I flap my wings back and forth, noticing that they're a little stiff, but they'll be okay once I get my blood pumping. I leap into the sky and take flight, feeling absolutely amazing right at this very moment, free from everything, and the welcoming release can't be any greater.

I cruise around for a while before I do anything, taking my time and enjoying the flight. The moon is high, and the night is crystal clear. I see the deer below, so I dive in to get my fill then savor every minute of it, not wanting it to be taken away from me. My beast gets satiated for the first time in months, and the phenomenal feeling emanates within my entire body while savoring the pleasing satisfaction of fulfillment. I can feel a wave of emotions rising while I stand here, looking around, thinking back on the past, and I begin to cry, unable to choke back the horrible memories that keep crashing within my mind's eye over and over again. I drop to my knees then throw my hands over my face, trying to calm myself down. These emotions lie deep within my soul, and the sweet release of my pain is inevitable because it must be set free. I can't hold back my intense feelings and emotions any longer as I lose all self-control and have the biggest nuclear meltdown of my entire life.

I pull myself back together and rise to my feet then make my way over to the lake. There is a small marker next to the tree where Z had buried the baby boy, so I stand here for a minute, recollecting on the memory of the other night. A tear runs down my cheek while I gaze down at the tiny grave site, thinking about how much my life has been forever changed. I turn around, walk down to the water, and then step into the glassy surface; and almost immediately, it begins to vibrate all around me. Gentle waves dance around my ankles, and a bluish glow surrounds me. So I walk farther out into the water, up to my thighs, then raise my hands up to the sky to give thanks to the gods for saving me and for setting me free, releasing me from my torturous hell. Glittering, sparkling flakes rain down upon me, then I stick my hands into the water, offering my power to the gods and to Mother Earth. Watery hands rise out of the depths then caress my face, gesturing its thanks, but doesn't take any of the little power that I have left. The glow fades, and I've been kissed by Mother Earth and by the gods themselves. Tears fill my eyes from happiness while I walk out of the water slowly, and once I'm completely out, the chill of the freezing air nips at my wet skin. Satan and Dutchess are standing behind me, waiting patiently for me to give them some loving, so I scratch both of their necks then turn to Dutchess and slide my hand along her swollen belly. I can feel the foal moving around inside her.

"He's going to be a big one!" I tell her then chuckle. She nods and snorts in agreement, and I laugh. "I'm glad that I'm not you at this point!" She and Satan both snort loudly then give me some horse talk. I laugh at them while I rub the both of them down some more. "I love you, two bunches!" I tell them, embracing this precious time that I'm having with them. Satan nudges me with his nose, and Dutchess runs her muzzle along my side. "Well, I'm ready for a nap, you two! I've gotten my belly full, it's late, and I'm cold! I'll see you two tomorrow, okay?" They nod, then I walk back down the pasture with them. I know Z is stalking me from somewhere because I can feel his presence plus smell his scent wafting through the chilly night air.

Getting to the barn, I wave the horses good night then fly back up to the balcony. I open the doors, put my beast to sleep, and then lock the doors behind me. I want to make him grovel and beg for his affection because I'm not going to give into him so easily! I turn on the faucets to draw up my bathwater as hot as I can stand it, light my candles sitting around the bathroom, shut off the lights, hop into the tub, and then lie back. This day has been epic, and I want to savor it up until the very last second for as long as I can.

I hear footsteps coming toward me, but I don't open my eyes. Z must have gotten in here before I had gotten back because I can feel his piercing stare watching me, waiting for me to look at him, and I can sense his terrible longing for my affections. "Take off your clothes and get in because there's no point in you standing over there and staring at me all night," I bark, still not opening my eyes, and I can sense his thrilled excitement as he begins to remove his clothes.

Z gets in behind me, sits down, and then gently pulls me up against his chest. My back is facing him, but I don't turn to look at him and can feel his manhood rising to the occasion against my lower back within seconds. Z wraps his arms around me then holds onto me tightly, rubbing his face against my head. "I want you so badly," he whispers in my ear.

Oh, you're going to get it after I make you beg first! I think to myself, smiling. He is running his fingers along my back, massaging me softly, and his gentle touch and soaring excitement are making me feel pretty frisky myself. But I ignore his advances while I relish in his wonderful affections. His sexual excitement must be becoming almost unbearable because he is practically hunching me in the tub, but I just smile to myself while I hold my ground, not giving into him.

Z climbs out of the tub, picks me up without any effort, and carries me to the bed. Then after sitting me down delicately, he begins to kiss my lips. As I kiss him back, he cups my face with his hands. "I love you," he tells me, staring deep into my eyes.

I don't say a word to him and continue kissing him on the lips then pull him down on top of me, wanting him to take me now. He slowly and gently thrusts himself inside me then begins to make amazing love to me. The pleasing sensation of having him sets me on fire because I've missed this from him for so long. Z takes his time, wanting to enjoy this moment that we haven't shared in so long, and he finishes rather quickly but I flip him over on his back, wanting more. I finally get what I want then lie down on top of him, panting.

He rubs my back and runs his other hand along my side. "Thank you, my love. I have missed that," he tells me in a soft whisper.

I smile while kissing him on the lips. "You're welcome and thank you." I dismount then lie next to him, resting my head on his chest, feeling a little disappointed with myself for not making him beg more.

"Did you get enough to eat earlier?" he asks me.

"Yep! I feel ninety-nine percent better!" I answer, knowing he was watching me the whole time.

"That is good! I am glad that you are feeling better!" he replies, grinning happily.

"It was wonderful to be free, doing as I please," I tell him while I run my fingers along his chest. "I can't even imagine what your life was like there because I know it was terrible. I snapped at your mother one day and told her that she should be ashamed of herself for letting you be treated the way that you were. After I was whipped for the first time, I knew it was what Aiden had done to you your entire life. I wouldn't give him the pleasure of my fear, and it made him so angry that he beat me even harder. But still, I didn't make a peep. He punched me in the face a few times before your mother chimed in and yelled at him to stop. She should've protected you at all costs no matter what! He did stop, only because he knew he'd been defeated, making him hate me even more. I felt empowered after that, with making him so angry.

"I want to take him out to that tree one day, tie him up, let him starve for a few weeks, and then rock his world with that whip! Then I'll rip his dick off and shove that little prick down his throat and watch him choke on it while Sebastian watches with me. I'm going to take that psycho strip him down, throw his ass on top of that torture rock down in the basement, tie his legs and hands down as tight as I can get them, then whip his whole body with that same whip, just like they did to me! And before I'm done with him, I'm going to cut off his balls and scream at him, 'Why can't you get me pregnant!'" I realize that I'm having a slight ranting fit, so I cut it off and bite my tongue.

"I will gladly help you out with that, my love," Ezékeial says, trying to choke back his tears.

I don't know what he is thinking about after my little rant, but he grabs me up then pulls me tightly against him. I can feel him trembling a little, so I run my hand along his face then rub his head. "I love you, Z." He bursts into tears and holds me even tighter, kissing my face all over. I must have hit a huge nerve with my little speech, but once he pulls himself together, he mounts me then begins to make slow, passionate love to me once again, delicately caressing me all over and kissing me endlessly.

"You are amazing, my love, and I will never let you leave me again!" he whispers to me then sends me into a heavenly, sexually erotic bliss.

I give him all the love that I can, wanting to soothe his pain, and he makes love to me off and on during the rest of the night, wanting to satiate his long-awaited sexual desire. I submit to his every wish, wanting him even more.

CHAPTER 21

Loving Him

Morning comes, and as always, I'm starving. It was a long night—a great night but a long one. Ezekeial is still sleeping soundly, so I put on my sleep shirt then head down to the kitchen. I feel like having some pancakes for breakfast, so I dig out the pancake mix then begin whipping up some groceries. It feels so great to be able to be back in the kitchen and working! I get the griddle out to begin cooking some bacon and sausage, and I can't help but look outside and stare at my shiny new car sitting in the driveway.

"Good morning, my love!" Z says, coming up behind me, startling me.

"Hey there, sexy beast!" I reply, turning around to look at him.

He walks over to me, picks me up off the floor, and then gives me a huge hug and kiss. I laugh at him and kiss him back. "Is there something interesting out there that you keep looking at?" he asks me with a big smile.

"You bet your ass there is because I'm dying to take my boo out for a spin!" I tell him, grinning happily, and he smiles then laughs out loud.

"Why not go after we eat?" Z suggests.

"Hell yeah, I'm game!" I cry out excitedly, and he laughs at me some more then kisses my lips.

I finish cleaning up then race upstairs to take a quick shower, or so I thought, because Z ends up in the shower with me, and we have yet another round of wonderful lovemaking.

"Okay, Mr. Frisky, I'm going out for a drive! You're going to have to cool that thing down for a while!" I tell him as I dry off, and he is grinning from ear to ear, eating up my comment.

We get dressed, and I don't waste one second to make a mad dash out to the car before I get snatched up then have to take off my clothes once again. I slide in behind the wheel, and Z is quick to hop into the passenger's seat. I break out my phone, turn on one of my favorite tunes (Metallica's "Whiskey in the Jar"), and then fire up the car. It sounds phenomenal, purring like a kitten!

"Wow! She sounds great!" I tell him excitedly, and he is staring at me just like a little puppy madly in love. So I place my hand on the top of his head then run my fingers through his wet hair. I gaze into his eyes for only a split second, grip the steering wheel, and then take off slowly down the driveway; but once we hit the pavement of the open road, I stomp it!

The ride is fabulous, and my car is freaking awesome! "I love it!" I scream out loud with pure joy, and Z is laughing at me, pleased that I'm ecstatic about my amazing car. I stop at the gas station to fill it up, then Z goes in to pay for the gas.

"Nice car you've got there, pretty lady," a strange man says while approaching me then gets way too close.

"Thank you," I reply when he stops in front of me, almost on top of me.

"What are you doing?" Z asks the guy angrily.

"I was just admiring your rides," he answers with a creepy smirk.

I can see the jealousy and rage well up in my vampire's eyes. "Come on, lover, let's go!" I say to Z, wanting to get the hell out of dodge before this guy meets Jesus today.

The guy walks away, then Z hops into the car. "I cannot leave you alone for one minute!" he scolds me with an angry face, and I laugh at him.

"Jealous much?" I ask him, and he looks over at me, shooting me his "whatever" face. So I smile at him, chuckling to myself.

It is late once we get back to the house, and he runs upstairs. I hear his cell phone ringing over on the counter, so I rush over to answer it. And my heart stops when I see that it is Lazar calling. I snatch it up quickly, dying to talk to him.

"Hello, Lazar?" I ask in an excited whisper.

"Renee, is that you? I have missed you so much, sweetheart!" he cries out ecstatically. "I've tried calling you before, but he won't let me talk to you!"

I am not shocked by this at all. "Let me go outside so that we can have some privacy, so give me a minute," I tell him, hauling ass out the kitchen door.

"Okay, I will wait," he replies, sounding anxious.

Satan is waiting for me outside, so without wasting any time hopping on his back, we make our way up to the tree line. "I've missed you a lot too!" I say happily, with my eyes welling up with tears.

"How are you doing since you've gotten home?" he asks.

"I went hunting last night, and it was so wonderful to be free again! I've been so worried about you! What happened after you and Lianna had gotten back?" I question him, hoping that he is okay.

"She set me free, baby! She gave me all of my paperwork then set me free before they came back from their trip!" he explains, sounding overjoyed.

Satan and I stop by one of the trees, so I slide off his back then sit down next to it. "Oh my God! That's great, Lazar!" I shout out ecstatically, beginning to cry for his happiness.

"It was all because of you why she set me free, all because of you! Thank you so much, sweetheart! I love you!"

"I love you too! I'm so happy for you! Get out there and find your place in this world because you deserve it!" I tell him, feeling so thrilled for him.

Suddenly, Ezekeial explodes out in front of me, screaming. "What are you doing! Why can you not talk to him in front of me!" he growls angrily, and he is pissed!

"You won't let me talk to him, that's why!" I yell at him.

"Why are you sneaking around!" he questions me hatefully.

"Because I don't want to feel like I can't say what I want to say to him with you staring at me!"

"What is going on with the two of you!" he continues to question me.

"Sweetheart, it's okay. I can talk to you again later. I love you so much!" Lazar tells me.

"Did he just say that!" Z screams at me in pure rage, staring me down. "You two were together, were you not? Was that child that came out of you his?" he asks, almost about to lose his cool, and I hear Lazar gasp.

"I don't know! How could or would I even know whose baby it was? I was raped, beaten, and molested by your brother and stepdad, and the only one I had to offer me any comfort was the wolf that your books and manuscripts made out to be the scum of the earth! Only in the short amount of time that I was able spend with him, was my pain, misery, and grief relieved, and my suffering put to bay! I didn't have anyone at all when you left me there! No one, except the love and affections of my special wolf! The faithful companion who was always by my side, getting beaten and whipped with me from trying to sneak me something to eat! He tried to satiate my hunger, letting me feed from him, while they starved me! He saved me from the house of monsters that you'd left me in! I don't regret nor am I ashamed of anything that I've done because he's my guardian angel! The man whom I thought was my guardian angel, lover, and best friend lied and deceived me since day one, knowing the entire time that we'd been together and never saying a single word about it, knew he'd be taking me there one day, leaving me behind to rot with them! He gave me away to his brother without hesitation, knowing I'd be forced to marry him! You didn't seem to mind that I was going to be sleeping with your brother once you abandoned me like a fucking piece of discarded trash! I begged and pleaded with you to just let me stay behind because I knew something was wrong, and it was you, Ezekeial Michael Dragkarr, who knew, the entire time, what was going to happen to me. But you took me to Romania anyway, knowing that hurts me more than any of the hell that I've had to endure! I didn't even care if I lived or died! I love Lazar and always will, and there will always be a special place for him in my heart. And you nor anyone else will ever take that away from me! When it all came down to it, the wolf was willing to give his life for me, but my vampire lover was a fucking coward, leaving me behind like I didn't even matter! If that child would have lived and turned out to have been Lazar's, I would have protected my little 'werepire' at any cost! I would have given my life for him!" I've dropped the phone sometime during my emotional outburst. I knew Lazar had heard everything that I've just said to Z, so I leave it lying on the ground. Satan nudges my arm and bows down, so I climb onto his back, then he and I walk away, leaving Z standing alone. I don't look back, and I ask Satan if we can just trot around the property for a while.

*****

Ezekeial knew that Renee was right. Everything she has just said to him is the harsh, terrible truth. He knew the entire time she was going to be left at the estate, and he did leave her behind like a selfless coward. Walking over to his phone, he picks it up. "Thank you for saving her," he tells Lazar, feeling horribly ashamed of himself. "I was a coward, and there is no excuse for what I did to her."

"You need to make it right because she will forgive you! She loves you more than she could ever love me because she belongs to you, and she will always be yours no matter what!" Lazar tells him, choking on his tears. "I will always love her. Renee is a very special woman, and what we have will always be ours. You should be on your hands and knees begging for her forgiveness and also being extremely grateful that she still loves you! I must go. Goodbye, Ezekeial," Lazar says abruptly then hangs up the phone.

*****

Satan drops me off at the door. "Thank you, big fella. I love you," I tell him as I walk away. Then after getting inside the house, I dig around in my camo backpack, searching for my car keys. But they're gone. I know, for sure, I had put them in there after we had gotten back earlier, but Z must have taken them.

I grab the tequila out of the cabinet then make my way upstairs. I expect to see him waiting for me when I hit the landing at the top of the stairs, but he is nowhere in sight. I'm glad because after our huge fight, I don't even want to look at him. Closing and locking my bedroom door behind me, I head into the bathroom then begin to fill up the tub because I plan on soaking and drinking the rest of this terrible day away. I light my candles then climb into the tub with my bottle in hand. The hot water feels wonderful, and the booze is drowning out my sorrows. Lazar keeps popping into my mind, and I think back to the wonderful lovemaking that he and I had made because it will always be the best ever. The erotic memories of the soft fur of his wolf rubbing along my backside, the licking of my body with his magical tongue, and the silky-smooth feeling of his muzzle when he rubbed it against me send a wave of sexually charged chills all over my body. Right now, I wouldn't mind having him here with me, doing it all over again.

My water is getting cold, so I decide to get out and dry off. My fuzzy blanket is lying on the bed, so I wrap myself up with it and embrace the familiar feeling of being with Lazar as its pleasing soft-ness rubs against my naked body. I take another big gulp from the bottle then place it on top of the nightstand next to my bed. After snuggling into my blanket, I close my eyes, waiting for sleep to find me, but just as I'm about to drift away, someone sits down on the edge of the bed. *Oh, man! Here we go!* I scream inside because I can't get away from this guy!

"I am very sorry for everything that has happened, and I want you to know that I can accept anything that you have to say to me and will not argue with you about it," Z says to me in a timid voice.

"I need my car keys, please," I tell him hatefully.

"You have been drinking and do not need to be driving!" he shouts unhappily.

"Just leave them! I need to go home for a while, and I plan on leaving in the morning!" I bark at him coldly.

"Please, you cannot leave me! I need you here with me!" he whines.

"Look, you said you wouldn't argue with me! I just need to get the hell out of here for a couple of days, and I'd like to go home to visit my family," I tell him bluntly.

Z gets up, leaves the room, returns my keys by placing them on the nightstand, and then leaves me to myself. I take another swig from the bottle, snuggle back into my blanket, and then try to go back to sleep. The next thing I know, he is crawling in bed with me then pulls me against his chest, spooning me. He is holding onto me so tightly that I can hardly breathe.

"You're choking me!" I cry out angrily, so he releases me from his grasp then begins to sob while he touches my face and rubs me all over.

I'm getting really annoyed with him, so I cover up my head with the blanket then scoot away from him. But he pulls me back then tries to kiss me. "Please, Z, just stop!" I yell at him angrily, just about to lose my temper.

"Please, I need you! I want you!" he whines. "Feed from me, please! I need for you to!" he begs desperately. This guy is relentless, begging for my affection! "I am so sorry! I know I cannot be upset with you about anything that had happened there!" he tells me, choking on his emotions while stroking my back.

I can feel myself becoming aroused by the wonderfully soft blanket being rubbed against my bare skin, along with his whining and begging, so I turn to face him then look right at him. And I can see him just as plain as day through the darkness of the night with my night vision. I can't help but love this man with all my heart and soul, even after all I've been through and the things that he has done to me. To hell with it! If he wants me to feed from him, I will, so I grab his arm and sink my fangs into it aggressively. He jumps but doesn't pull it away, and I don't really take in anything because I really just want to cause him a little pain, along with taking out some of my frustrations. Z begins to rub himself against my thigh, sending shivering tingles into motion all over my body, so with not being able to resist his advances, I turn my backside to him, allowing him to have me. I still have his arm in my mouth and won't let it go just to aggravate, but he seems to like it. So I hold onto it tightly with my fangs. He has his free arm wrapped around me, holding onto my waist and pulling me against him. But I can't hold onto him anymore, so I release his arm. He immediately spins me around, and I'm looking right at him as he pulls me in closely and kisses me on the lips. I kiss him back, then he sits up in the bed, picks me up, and places me on top of him. He pulls my face to his then begins to give me the most passionate kisses ever. Rubbing his face against mine, he slides it down along my cheek to kiss my neck. He is rocking me back and forth in his lap, and the pleasing sensations are absolutely amazing! We both climax at the same time, and this just seems to set him on fire because he picks me up then lies me on my back, kissing me everywhere. Z is going crazy, drowning me with his affections and rubbing himself all over me, getting hard once again, and I love every minute of it!

"I love you so much, my love, and I want to be the best lover that you will ever have," he tells me in a breathy whisper.

So that is what this is all about! He is worried that Lazar is a better lover than him. I hate to break it to him, but no one has anything on the wolf! This is still wonderful, and I'll never tell! It is another night of fabulous lovemaking, and I'm absolutely exhausted! Z has finally fallen asleep, and I'm so glad because I need to get some rest myself! I wrap my fuzzy blanket around myself, and it doesn't take long before I'm out like a light.

I call my mama to see if we can come for a visit right after waking up, and she is ecstatic. So I tell her that we'll be leaving today and that we'll be in some time later tonight. Z is still sleeping, so I go into the bathroom to take a shower. But of course, he is up like a shot and is in the shower with me in no time.

"Are you going to go to my mama's house with me, or are you staying here?" I ask him, and he looks at me, stunned.

"I thought you were just saying that because you were mad at me," he replies.

"Nope, it's happening! I've already called my mama and told her that I'm coming. I haven't seen any of them in months!" I gripe while he runs his fingers along my belly.

"I will go anywhere that you go," he says, happy as a lark, so I let him do his thing, then we finally get out of the shower.

Z leaves the bathroom to get dressed, and while I'm standing in front of the mirror, drying my hair so I can straighten it, I see my birth-control pills lying in the top of my drawer. I haven't taken any pills since before I went to Romania and have had a lot of sex these past couple of days. "Shit!" I say out loud.

"What is it?" Z asks me, walking into the bathroom.

"Oh, nothing. I can't find my hair ties," I reply, lying to him. I dig in the drawer and see them lying at the bottom of it. "Here they are!" I cry out happily, so he leaves the bathroom without asking me any more questions. Well, it is too late to worry about it now because I can't start taking them after all this! I'll just have to keep an eye on myself.

After I get ready, we cram all our stuff into Z's truck then head to Missouri to visit my family. It is about 7:30 p.m. when we make it to my mama's house.

"How have the two of you been?" she cries out ecstatically while running up to me then latches onto me. She goes over to Z and gives him a hug. "I haven't seen you guys in months, and no one's returned any of my calls!" she gripes with a frown. "Renee, I made you some cupcakes! I know you're hungry!"

Z begins to laugh. "I thought the first time we went shopping together I was going to need to go back to the farm to get my trailer!" Everyone laughs while they all greet us with lots of hugs and kisses.

"I'm going to dive into your cupcakes, Mama!" I tell her with my mouth watering, thinking about her fabulous cupcakes, so I don't hesitate to bolt inside. Z gets our stuff out of the truck then carries it up to my room, and it feels wonderful to be back home because I didn't think I was ever going to see it again.

"Ezekeial, do you know how to work on engines and stuff?" Kent asks him.

"But of course, do you need something fixed?" Z asks him, smiling.

"Yeah, I've got this old skid steer that I need to get fixed."

"Well, we can take a look at it tomorrow," Z replies happily.

"That would be great! I'll dig out some warmer stuff for you to put on because it's cold out there!" Kent tells him, grinning from ear to ear.

"I would really appreciate that!" Z replies happily.

"You guys should see what he did to my boo!" I tell them excitedly as I grab my phone. "He redid the whole car, and it's absolutely fabulous!" I had taken some pictures of it before we left, so I pass my phone around to show everyone my new beast.

"Wow, it looks great!" Kent says with wide eyes. Everyone is nodding in approval while I scroll through my photos, beaming with pure joy.

Mama has some leftovers from supper, so Z and I clean them up. Well, I should say that I've eaten most of them. We visit for a while and then go upstairs because it is getting late, and I'm still worn out from the night before. "Man, I'm exhausted!" I say to Z while I get the bed ready. He smiles at me, and I'm thinking, *Oh, shit! Here we go again!* I pull the covers down, then we both climb into bed. He must have read my vibe because he keeps his hands to himself and just pulls me close to him. It feels great to be lying in my old bed, and the feeling of being home soothes my weary soul. We both fall asleep, and I finally get some much-needed rest.

Morning comes, and my mama whips up a huge breakfast. Reese, Charlene, and I are all sitting and chatting at the dining room table, waiting for the groceries to commence. Z and Kent are already working on the loader outside.

"I have to get to work," Reese says unhappily after she rises from her chair.

"I'll see you all tonight!" We all tell her goodbye, and as she heads to the door, she says, "Renee, did I ever tell you that your Z is really hot!" Everyone looks at me and gives me a huge smile.

"Well, he is certainly a delicious piece of eye candy! Not to mention, his wonderfully sexy accent!" I tell her with a big smile, and we all crack up laughing.

"I'm so jealous of you!" she gripes then walks out the door, shaking her head.

"Food's ready!" Mama yells out, so I tell the guys outside then rush to grab myself something to eat. I'm starving! Z comes in and cleans up, fixes a plate, and then sits down next to me.

"You girls seem to be having a good time in here! We can hear your laughter all the way outside!" Kent says to us, and I smile at him and then look at over at my mama and Charlene, giving them a wink. They crack a smile then begin to eat their food. "I think we may get that damned loader fixed today!" Kent chimes happily.

"If not, we will get it tomorrow," Z tells him.

Everyone eats, then I help my mama clean up. "I'm going for a walk," I tell her as I head for the door.

"Okay, see you in a little bit!" she replies, smiling. I grab a couple of cupcakes then make a mad dash out the front door, wanting to make a trip down to the creek to check it out.

Strolling down the road toward the creek brings back so many memories. I make my way along the path then all the way down to the water's edge, reminiscing about the first time that I met Z. The day is cold, but it feels fabulous to be out and about. The crystal-clear water in the creek is rushing past me quickly from the winter weather, and the sound of the running water is so calming and relaxing, soothing my weary mind, body, and soul. My mind is clear for the time being, and I set myself free from everything in the peacefulness of this therapeutic moment. I amble down the bank, following the path of the flowing water and jumping over the watery puddles as I go.

"Where are you going, my love?" I hear his heavenly Romanian voice ask. So I turn around, and Z is standing only a few feet behind me.

"Just getting out for a while because it's really nice out today," I answer.

"Yes, it is very nice," he replies, smiling. He walks over to me, scoops me up off my feet, and then cradles me in his arms like a baby. "This place is full of many memories, my love," he says as he kisses my cheek.

I smile at him. "Yes, it sure does hold a lot of memories!" I agree then kiss him back. He kisses me once more and then sets me down.

"We are almost done with the loader, then he has his tractor that I am going to help him fix," Z tells me, smiling.

"Oh, no! Not another tractor!" I say to him jokingly, remembering the last time he had to work on his tractor. Z laughs at me and shakes his head. "I'm glad you can help him out!" I tell him happily.

"Yes, I like helping him!" Z grabs my hand. "Come, let us get some lunch because I know that you can eat something."

"You've got that right! I'm starving!" I reply, and he chuckles at me as the two of us walk hand in hand, taking our time heading back to the house to grab some lunch.

It is late, so we're all turning in. I've had an awesome day, and I'm so glad that Z has been able to help Kent get his loader fixed. Hopefully, the tractor will be an easy fix as well.

"I'm going to take a shower," I tell him then begin to undress, and I can tell by the look in his eyes that he is coming in with me. Reese is gone, so I know we won't have to worry about her.

I lock the bathroom door after Z files in behind me then hop into the shower. He is begging for attention, and I'm more than willing to give it to him. He is all over me, and I submit to his every desire. I almost laugh out loud thinking about his jealousy issues, trying to be the better lover.

"You make me so happy, and I want for you to be happy also," he says to me after he finishes.

"I am happy! Just don't ever expect me to go back to Romania with you ever again!"

Z shoots me an angry eye then pulls me to him and embraces me tightly. "That is not funny!" he scolds me.

"I thought it was!" I reply, snickering a bit.

We crawl into bed, and he is already ready for round 2. Damn, this guy is wearing me the hell out! "Why don't we go hunting tonight?" I suggest when he begins to hop on top of me. "I want to make love with our beasts tonight under the midnight sun," I explain.

"I love that idea!" he replies happily.

"Let's go!" I cry out excitedly.

We hop out of bed, carefully make our way downstairs, and then take off outside. "What a beautiful night it is!" Z blurts out when the two of us begin walking across the field.

"Yes, it sure is!" I agree, looking up toward the night sky and admiring the beauty of the full moon. We walk all the way to the other end of the cornfield and into the tree line. It is pretty cold, but it is not going to last for long once we get undressed and awaken our beasts.

"Let us eat!" he says to me just as he begins to take flight. I'm ready to fly myself, so we take off into the starry sky then, shortly after, spot the deer.

We feed until we're completely stuffed and then make our way over to the clearing. Once we land, Z doesn't waste any time walking over to me, then he grabs me by the waist to pull me in closer. I run my hand along his chest then along his head.

"I am going to make the best love to you ever," he whispers to me softly, and I smile to myself, thinking about this silly sex war that he has going on.

"I'm ready for you!" I reply while raking my claws along his belly, then he begins to kiss me all over, rubbing himself up against me. Z's wet excitement begins to run down my thigh, so he turns me to face one of the trees, wraps his arms around me, and then thrusts himself inside me from behind. He slowly moves me up and down, rubbing his tail all over me and kissing my back as he does so. The sensation is fabulous, and I don't want it to stop! He begins to kiss my neck then rubs my head with his chin as his beastly body covers me at every angle. He is beginning to pant, and I can't hold back any longer because this amazing sexual encounter is driving me totally wild! Ezekeial knows that I've finished then thrusts himself into me harder, sending my spectacular climax over the edge, and as I cry out, he climaxes himself, releasing a loud growl from the pleasing sensations. This wonderful lovemaking comes close to the wolf, but who am I to judge?

I kiss his lips. "That was great, baby. Thank you!"

This really makes him happy, so he grabs me up and squeezes me tightly. "I am glad that I can please you like that!" he tells me, beaming happily.

"You have no idea how well you've just pleased me!" I reply then nibble on his lower lip. He smiles from ear to ear, eating up my comment. And once we get back in bed, he wants to go again, so we make love one more time. And I'm completely done for.

"Z, I'm exhausted! I'm going to sleep!" I gripe, wanting to go to sleep. He kisses my lips then rolls over, leaving me alone for the time being, so I curl up around him and finally get to relax in bed.

"My love, do I please you enough?" he asks me out of the blue.

"If I'm not pleased enough, then I've got some serious problems! You please me more than enough!" I run my fingers through his soft hair, and within minutes, he is snoozing away. Finally, sleep, here I come!

Waking up the next morning, I find myself alone. Looking at the clock, it is 10:45 a.m. Man, I really needed that! I lie here for a few and then decide to get up, ready to begin the new day.

"Good morning, sleepyhead!" Charlene says to me when I stroll into the kitchen.

"Good morning to you too!" I say, smiling.

"There are some brownies and snacks all over there. Just get whatever you want to eat," Mama tells me happily, so I begin shoveling in everything in sight then grab myself a big glass of milk.

"Man, Renee, are you pregnant or what?" Charlene questions me, and I stop and freeze in place.

"Why, no. I've always eaten like this!" I reply, feeling uncertain about her comment.

"I think you're eating more than usual," she points out to me.

"Well, I'm not pregnant. I just love to eat!" I explain, still feeling very uncertain with my own words.

"We're going into town. Would you like to come with us?" Mama asks.

"Sure! I'll go!"

We grab our stuff then load up in the minivan. Kent and Z are up in the field, working on the tractor. So we stop, and I get out to walk over to them.

"Good morning, baby. I'm going into town with my peeps," I tell him then kiss him on the cheek.

"Okay, we should be done by the time you all get back. I love you," he tells me, smiling.

"I love you too!" I repeat then rush back to the van.

We sing and talk all the way to town, laughing and enjoying our day with one another. Mama wants to pick up some food for dinner, but the store is so busy. It is pure chaos trying to shop! People are darting all over the place with their grocery carts, while others are poking around.

"Do you want those Cornish game hens and wild rice that you love so much?" Mama asks me.

"That sounds great, Mama!" I cry out excitedly because her Cornish hens and wild rice are awesome! "I'm going to run to the bathroom," I inform them as I begin to walk away.

"Okay, we'll be around here somewhere," Mama replies, so I run over to the women's section to grab a pregnancy test. It has only been about a week and a half since I've been back from Romania, and I doubt if the test will work. But I figure that it can't hurt to check it out.

I pay for the test at the pharmacy then make my way to the bathroom, and as I'm walking down to the last stall in the bathroom, I begin to feel nervous while reading the instructions. I have to wait two minutes before the test results will show up, so I do what the directions explain, set the timer, and wait, scared to death.

The timer goes off, and it reads positive. *Oh, no!* I begin to panic, not expecting anything like this to be happening, so I sit on the toilet, trying to calm myself down, not wanting to expose my secret. My face feels flushed, and it takes some time for me to gather myself back together. But I realize that I shouldn't be so upset about this news because I haven't been taking my pills. I decide to wait for a couple more weeks and then try another one, so I wrap up the used test with some toilet paper, toss it in the trash, clean up, and then head out to find my mama and Charlene.

"Did you need anything before we go?" Mama asks me when I join them.

"I think I'm good, Mama! Thanks!" I'm still worried about that test, but what can I expect? I had lots of sex, with no birth control at all, and that equals baby!

We bag up our stuff then make our way back to my mama's house. "You girls have been gone all day!" Kent gripes when we walk inside.

"Well, it takes forever just to make a trip to town and back!" I explain.

"I am glad that you are back because I thought I was going to have to come and find you!" Z says to me with a big smile.

"Nope, I'm back! I wasn't abducted or anything like that!" I say then laugh, thinking about the night that weirdo had gotten ahold me. Z looks at me intently, then he smiles really big.

Mama begins supper, so Charlene and I break out the old Uno cards.

"Let's play!" Charlene cries out excitedly.

"Okay, but you know I'm going to win!" I tell her, chuckling, and she laughs.

"Yeah, whatever!"

We play until supper is ready, while Z has been watching TV with Kent. Mama calls to us, telling us that it is time to eat, and her groceries are spectacular! I forgot just how much I've missed my mama's cooking, but I try to control myself by not eating too much.

"This is really good!" Z tells my mama. "Thank you for the wonderful dinner!"

"I'm glad you were able to help Kent get those things fixed out there!" she says to him, almost drooling.

"It was easy. No problem!"

"Mama, your birds are the bomb!" I tell her happily, and everyone nods in agreement.

"When are the two of you leaving?" Mama asks, so Ezekeial looks over at me, not sure what to say.

"I think we'll head out in morning," I reply. "It's a long drive back to the farm."

"I'm so glad that the two of you came to visit! I was getting really worried when I hadn't heard from you!"

"Well, shit happens, and sometimes life can get really messed up and crazy!" I tell her, then she nods.

"Amen to that!"

We all head to bed for the night, and I'm so ready to lie down. Z and I take a shower then climb into bed. "I hope you have had a good time with your family," he tells me.

"Yeah, it's been really great! I'm glad you came with me," I tell him as he snuggles up beside me.

"I have had a nice time as well. I am glad that I came with you, my love, because I cannot be without you," he tells me, going into foreplay mode. Z kisses my lips then runs his fingers along my face and through my hair, and he is dying for some more lovin'. So I return his kisses as I place my hands on his chest then run my fingers around his muscles.

"Did I ever tell you that you have a killer body, Z?" I say while I draw around his muscular abs.

"Why, I do not think so! I am glad that you like it!" he replies happily, and I can see him smiling in the dark, eating up my compliment.

"I don't just like it. I love it!" I tell him, grinning. I know this is turning him on, so I reach down and rub on his member, giving it a gentle squeeze. That is all it takes, and before I can react, he is mounting me quicker than the speed of light. We make love once more after that and then go to bed. Lying beside him and gently running my fingers around his chest and belly, I wonder how he'd react if I told him that I was pregnant.

"Good night, my love," he says then gives me a kiss.

"Good night, Z," I repeat then return his kiss. Sleep finds us once again, but I wake up in the middle of the night, starving. Hoping I can sneak out of bed and out of the room without waking Z up, I quickly bolt downstairs to raid the fridge. I grab some food then sit down in the living room, trying not to make a peep. Sitting in the dark with only the light from the outside shining in, I can hear the sound of a hoot owl calling out into the darkness. Feeling curious, I stand up then walk over to the front door. I look out of the front-door window then gaze up into the night sky. The sky is bursting to life from the twinkling shine of the tons of stars dotted up in space, and I watch some clouds slowly drift across the moon. Finishing up, I quietly go back to my room.

"What have you been doing?" Z asks me when I try to sneak back under the covers.

"I needed a snack," I reply, and he chuckles.

"My love, I do not know where you put everything that you eat! You are a bottomless pit!" he tells me sleepily. "Come, snuggle up to me," he orders me, reaching out his arms. My vampire doesn't need to tell me twice, so I jump over to him. "Did you get satisfied?" he asks.

"Yeah, for about an hour," I answer, and he laughs at me some more then pulls me against his warm body, tangling me up within his loving embrace.

We pack up and head to the truck, say our goodbyes, and then hit the road.

"Are you needing anything to eat?" Z asks me when we get into town.

"Nope, I'm good, but I might take a nap though," I answer, still feeling sleepy.

He looks over at me. "Lay your head down on my leg and rest for a while."

"Okay, I think I will!" I say, so I lie down across the seat then place my head on his leg. I wake up about two and a half hours later when he stops for gas, and he has his hand on my belly, rubbing it gently.

"Your stomach is getting hungry! It is growling like mad!" he tells me, chuckling.

"Yeah, I sure could eat something right now," I agree as I slide across the seat of the truck.

We go inside, and I use the bathroom then grab some food. I grab some doughnuts, chips, chocolate milk, and cookies to snack on.

"Do you want a doughnut?" I ask Z after we've been on the road for a while. He nods, so I feed him a few doughnuts.

"You had better save the rest for yourself because I have plenty here to eat," he tells me, and I smile at him then kiss his cheek. Only a few more hours to go, we'll be back at the farm! Thank you, sweet baby Jesus!

We pull into the driveway, and the TA sparkles from the ghostly rays of moonlight shining down upon it. We grab our gear then make our way into the house, and it is so nice to be back at the farm because I've missed it! I want to see the horses, so I dash outside then race up to the barn. Dutchess is lying on the ground in her stall, and I'm thinking that she is going to be having her foal tonight. She is breathing heavily, and she looks like she is in a great deal of pain. Man, we've gotten back just in time!

I walk over to her, and by the look in her eye, I can tell that she is scared. So I kneel beside her and rub my fingers along her muzzle then along her huge bloated belly. She groans from my comforting touch, and I can feel a contraction coming on when she begins to tense up, then she moans when it commences.

"Well, someone's going to be a mama today," I tell her while I rub her sleek neck.

Z walks into the barn and approaches us. "We have come home just in time!" he tells me while he inspects Dutchess.

"Yeah, we sure did!" I agree, still rubbing and caressing her neck. She moans again, so I put my hand on her belly, trying to rub out the contraction. Dutchess presses her head against the floor, pushing as hard as she can, trying to birth her foal, and about ten minutes later, I can see the foal beginning to appear as it is being born. Satan paces around nervously while he watches, and I can't wait to see our new edition. Z runs over behind her to pull it out, and I continue to rub on her stomach, talking to her softly.

"I told you he was going to be a big one! What do you think we should call him?" I whisper to her while she continues having more contractions. The baby finally comes out and is lying on the floor. I see Z doing something, but I'm not sure what as Dutchess slowly rises to her feet then turns to meet her new baby. Loving her new foal already, she gently nudges his face then gives us a pleased little bit of horse talk. He is absolutely gorgeous and looks just like them! He is jet-black, with long scrawny legs.

I look at Dutchess. "What do you think about Hightower?" She looks back at me and gives me a hard stare. "Not sure, huh? Well, we can think on it."

Satan walks over to them to check out his new edition. He is well-pleased, looks over at me, and then gives me a loud neigh.

"Yes, he's beautiful, big fella!" I tell him as I stroke his long neck.

"We will leave the three of you alone so that you can have your time now," Z tells them then grabs my hand. The foal is already up, drinking milk from his mama, and I'm ecstatic!

"Good night, beautiful black beauties!" I tell them happily as we leave the barn. "That was great, Z!" I tell him excitedly.

"Yes, my love, it sure was!" He holds onto my hand then leads me out of the barn and back to the house.

We take a shower when we get upstairs, and I give Z a nice rubdown in the shower. "That feels nice. Thank you!" he says to me, loving every minute of it.

"You're welcome," I tell him happily. I turn off the shower, ready to get out, then when I begin drying off, he scoops me up then carries me to the bed.

"Do you need something to eat?" he asks me, grinning from ear to ear.

"Nope, actually, I feel fine!"

He gives me a curious eye. "I am surprised!" he replies then begins to kiss me, dying for some affection, so I give him what he wants then lie in bed, ready for sleep. I cuddle up next to him wrapped up with my blanket and easily drift away into the realm of Slumberland.

A few more weeks pass by, and life is returning back to normal around the farm. We end up naming the new foal Hightower, and he is the cutest little fella ever! I worry about when those monsters from Romania are going to come back for me because I know it is inevitable that they'll try to come get me at some point, but I don't know what else to do! I've contacted a few lawyers to see about getting a divorce from Sebastian, but it has all led me to a dead end. I have another pregnancy test to take, but Z never leaves me alone long enough for me to have any privacy. And I'm pretty sure there is a child growing inside me, but I would like to just verify it. I don't really know how to tell Z about it because I can't find the right words to say. Plus for some strange reason, I just can't bring myself to tell him! Sometimes I think I can feel something moving around inside me, and it is really a strange sensation.

"I need to run to the farm store to pick up a few things. Would you like to come with me?" he asks me.

"No. I think I'm just going to stay here to get something ready for dinner," I reply, glad to finally get some me time.

"Okay, I will be back in a little while," he says then gives me a kiss. "I love you!"

"I love you too!" I tell him before he walks out the door. Yes! Finally, I can take this damn test!

Z leaves, but I wait a good fifteen minutes before I go up to my bathroom. I open up the test and do as the directions say then turn the timer on for two minutes. The wait is nerve-racking! Finally, the buzzer goes off, and I look at it. Big surprise, it is positive! I wrap it up then discard it in the trash where I know he won't see it. My heart begins to race, and my brain goes into overload. *Now what do I do?* I go downstairs to start on my supper, and my mind is spinning out of control. "I'm going to need a lot more peanut butter and crackers!" I tell myself out loud then bust up laughing.

I hear the truck coming down the driveway, so I get my shit together, trying to act normal.

He drives up to the barn to drop off his supplies then returns. "I am going to have to go out in the morning to check on all of the cattle," he explains.

"Do you need my help with that?" I ask him.

"No, I think I can manage just fine!"

"Okay, I just thought I'd ask! That ol' bull you picked up the other week doesn't seem very friendly."

"No, he is not at all nice," Ezekeial agrees then looks away, thinking about that not-so-friendly beast. We eat supper, and I can't stop thinking about the little life growing inside my belly. I hope I have a son, and I would like to name him Maximillian.

"My love, let us take a bath together tonight," Z says to me after we eat.

"Okay, let me get this stuff all cleaned up first!" I put on my headphones and turn on my playlist, listening to my tunes while I clean up the dishes. Finally finished, I draw the bathwater, light my candles, and then dive into the soothing steaming water. Z comes in after me then climbs in behind me, so I lean back and lie my head against him then sigh from the relaxing contentment.

"You might want to watch out for that old bull tomorrow because I think he'll attack you if you're not careful," I warn Z.

"I will be just fine! I have had cattle for quite some time!" he gripes, getting aggravated with me, while he washes me with the washcloth.

"I think we need to get bigger tub!" I cry out unhappily when his elbow hits the inside of the tub.

"This one is big enough!" he tells me, chuckling, then hugs me tightly. I switch him places to wash his back. "That is nice." He sighs when I begin to rub his back, massaging his tight, tense shoulders. I rub them a little harder and squeeze on the muscles around his neck. They're really stiff, so I try to work them out the best that I can. He lies back and lets me have my way with him, lavishing in all the affection that I'm giving to him. This guy needs constant attention; he lives for it. But as long as I give him some every day, he is as happy as a lark!

We get out and hop in bed, then he lies on his belly, wanting some more. I grab my lotion, climb on his back, and then begin to work my way around his husky build, caressing him softly. He is in heaven right now, and I'm glad that he is enjoying himself so much. Z turns over on his back, leaving me sitting on top of him, so I begin to rub my hands and fingers along his chest, doing the same as I had done to his back. He is looking at me, but I can't read his thoughts. Then without warning, he pulls me down to him and wraps his big arms around me. "I am so lucky to have you," he tells me while staring deep into my eyes.

"Yes, you are, because I wouldn't do this for just anyone!" I tell him, giving him a big smile. He smiles back at me and kisses me on the lips then holds me again. "What's wrong, Z? I know you well enough to know that something's bothering you," I say, seeing the worry written across his face.

"I just worry, that is all," he answers.

"What about?" I question him.

"I know they will be coming for you someday, and I do not want anything to happen to you! I will kill them if they come!" he cries out loud then loses himself within his own thoughts.

"I'll be more than happy to help you kill them!" I agree.

"I know you will!" He kisses me then slides me down beside him. "I will let you rest tonight, my love," he says, smiling at me, then kisses me on the forehead, and I'm so exhausted that I almost fall asleep before I even hit my pillow!

*****

Ezekeial feels restless and can't fall asleep while his mind runs wild, thinking about Aiden and Sebastian coming to take Renee away from him. He listens to her breathing and the slow, steady beating of her heart while she falls deeper into sleep. Then something else can be heard, so he moves in closer, trying to hear whatever it is. Straining his ears, listening intently, he moves down her chest then to her abdomen, and there it is—the sound of a faster beating heart with quicker movement! It is not hers but something else. He doesn't move, listening to it and straining his ears even harder, wanting to make sure that he is actually hearing it! She is carrying his child and hasn't told him. Maybe she doesn't know, but he doesn't believe that. So he decides that he won't let her know he has discovered her secret, waiting to see if she says anything to him. He beams with happiness. A tear falls from his eye because this is what he has been wanting so badly, and it is really happening! He runs his hand around her belly. "No one will ever harm either of you," he whispers softly then kisses her on the cheek and runs his hands around her face. The love he has for her is eternal, and no one is going to take his family away from him! He gets as close to her as he can then puts his face next to her cheek, rubbing his nose against it. She lets out a soft growl under her breath, and he laughs. "I love you too!"

*****

I wake up, and he is gone. The clock says 9:56 a.m., so I get up to begin my morning routine. I fix some breakfast then walk up to the barn, carrying Z a plate of food, and he is trying to get the cows through the rails so that he can vaccinate them. It is a tough job, especially when they don't want to cooperate.

"I have some food for you!" I shout out to him over all the commotion. Z looks over at me and smiles, stopping his chores for now, then grabs his breakfast.

"Thank you! I am getting pretty hungry!" he tells me cheerfully.

"How many do you have left?"

"Quite a few. It has been a slow process this morning, and that bull keeps getting in my way!" he gripes, and we both look outside at that mean ol' bull.

"Well, I can help you round him up then put him in the arena if you want to."

Z's eyes shoot wide open. "No, absolutely, not! I will be fine, so just stay away from them!"

I am not sure what to say. "Well, okay then! I'll just go back to the house!" I reply then shrug my shoulders.

"Please do! I do not want you getting hurt from trying to help me out here!" He walks over to me then kisses me on the cheek before he goes back to work.

I spy Satan and his family standing in their stalls before I leave the barn, so I go over to pet them. They all neigh loudly at me as I approach them, run up to their stall doors, and then stick out their heads, dying for some attention. I pet each one of them for a few minutes and then walk back down to the house. Looking back at the barn, Z is standing in the doorway, watching me intently, while I close the gate.

After lying some frozen meat out for supper, I decide to look up some stuff about pregnancy on my phone. I read about what you should and shouldn't do, things that a pregnant woman should eat, and what to expect during the different stages of pregnancy. I really need to go see a doctor. But I'm not ready to tell Ezekeial about the baby just yet, and I can't get away from him long enough to even make an appointment. I'm so involved in reading the information I don't even hear him come in.

"Did you hear me?" he questions me, and I look up, not expecting him to be standing there.

"No, what did you say?" I ask him, with my heart pounding.

"I need to run back to the farm store to get a few more things. Do you want to come with me?" he asks.

"Sure! I guess I can ride along!" I say to him happily because I think he is wanting me to come with him, so I decide to go. I erase the history on my phone while we drive to the farm store, and I can see him watching me out of the corner of his eye. I stick my phone in my bag then watch the scenery flash past us while we make our way to town.

"Have you gotten that bull done yet?" I ask him.

"No, I am saving him for last because he is going to be trouble, I think."

I laugh. "Yep, that guy isn't going to go down without a fight!" Z looks over at me and smiles then grabs me by the arm and pulls me over to him. He puts his arm around me and gives me a hug. "I am going to get him done no matter what!" he assures me, chuckling.

I smile at him then kiss his cheek. "I know you will!"

Getting to the store, we gander around, looking at all the different things that they have. They have all kinds of neat things here: boots, tack, shoes, clothes, toys, collectibles, food—you name it!

"I'm going to grab the things that I need," Z tells me while I look around.

"Okay, I'm going to check out all of this stuff!" I reply happily.

He walks away headed to the back of the store, so I mosey around, going through the clothes then look at the shoes. My eye catches a bright-red halter hanging on a rack, so I pick it up. "This would be a good color for Hightower," I say to myself.

"Do you talk to yourself all of the time?" Z asks me as he walks up next to me, smiling.

"Yeah, but I usually never get an answer back."

He laughs. "Do you want to get that?" He points to the halter in my hand.

"Do you think this color will look good on Hightower?" I ask him, and he chuckles at me.

"My love, I think it will look just fine on him. Come, I have got a lot of work to do!" he says, wanting to get back to the farm.

Z buys the halter with the rest of his supplies, then we head back to the house. "I think I need to get a job! I hate not working and feeling like such a mooch!" I tell him, thinking about the baby, because it is not going to be cheap for all my prenatal care, not to mention, the cost of the baby's upkeep. I'm going to have to buy diapers, wipes, and all the necessities associated with being a parent.

Z shoots me a crazy look. "Like hell you need to get a job! You do plenty at home!" he barks angrily.

"I'd like to make my own money! I went to college and can probably find a decent office job somewhere close to the house," I explain.

"Renee, you do not need to get a job. I have plenty of money! We are not hurting for anything at all!" he barks bluntly.

"But—"

"I do not want to hear any more about it! You will be at home with me!" he yells loudly, so I drop the subject then look out my window.

We get back to the house, and he drops me off then drives up to the barn. So I go inside to begin fixing dinner. The day has already flown by, and it is getting pretty late. I turn on the TV in the living room then turn on the sound system because I can Bluetooth my phone to it and play my music, listening to it while I cook.

The food is done, so I begin to walk up to the barn to tell Z that it is time to eat. It is almost dark already, and it is beginning to really cool off. I watch him walk out of the barn, going after that mean ol' bull, when all of a sudden, the bull slams into him, throwing him up against the barn like a rag doll! I take off, running as fast as I can to get to him, because the bull starts trampling all over him and is trying to gouge him with his horns. Releasing my beast, I hop onto its back, grab ahold of its neck with my claws, and then rip its throat wide open. Blood pours out of its wound, but it still isn't going down! I jump off it to check on Z, and he is lying motionless on the ground. I can't believe my eyes when the bull heads toward him once again, so I run into it, knocking it off its feet. I punch it in the head as hard as I can while it thrashes around, trying to get back on its feet. Then crushing its skull, it suddenly stops and goes limp, not moving or breathing, so I know that I've finally killed it. Running over to Ezekeial, I assess the damage, and he is pretty mangled up! It looks like the ol' bull has gouged him with its horns a couple of times and has stomped the shit out of him. He is an absolute hot mess!

Satan runs out of the barn, then Dutchess and Hightower. "I need for you to help me get him back to the house," I tell them as I begin to peel Z off the ground, and they nod then rush over to me. Satan lies down on the ground, and Dutchess braces herself against Z while I push him on top of Satan's back. I manage to get him on top of Satan's back, then he rises to his feet slowly. Dutchess stands on one side of Satan while I stand on the other, walking carefully back to the house.

We get to the porch. "Okay, I need for you to help me get him all of the way inside," I say to Satan. So he carefully climbs up on the porch, and I open the side door. We walk him over to the couch, then he drops down enough to where I can push Z off him. "Thank you, big fella!" I tell him, hugging his neck tightly. "Will you please make sure that the gate is closed and locked for me?" I ask him, so he nods and walks back outside, then I can hear his heavy galloping as he makes haste back to the open gate to close it.

Z is a mess, and he is bleeding profusely. So I rip off his shirt then cut off his pants, needing to see the extent of the damage that has been done, and that ol' bull sure did a number on him! I race to the bathroom to grab a few towels, some peroxide, and water then begin to clean him up, washing the dirt from the gaping holes in his abdomen from the bull's horns. One is closer to the side of his lower-right waist, and the other is next to his left hip. His legs are black and blue from being trampled, and he has tons of cuts and bruises along his back and chest. "You're a mess!" I tell him as I wipe him down. He is out cold, but I'm still talking to him anyway.

I dash over to the pantry to grab some gauze and bandages that he had stocked up on from when I had come back from Romania, then suddenly, he grabs my hand just as I'm pouring peroxide into the wound from one of the horns. "Just don't move!" I demand him in a sharp tongue. "You've been literally beat to shit!" I say and can't help myself from chuckling. Z just looks at me then lies his head back down on the couch pillow. Some blood begins to run out of the wound that I've just cleaned, so I lick up his side with my tongue, cleaning it off. He just stares at me with a blank expression, so I say, "I can't let that good shit go to waste!"

He tries to laugh at me, shaking his head. "You are one in a million, my love."

"I know! I've got to keep it interesting. Otherwise, life would be way too boring!" I reply. Then staring him down, I tell him, "Oh, by the way, you'll have to go buy yourself another bull because the last one just went and met Jesus."

He looks at me with wild eyes. "Are you okay? What did you do?"

"Let's just say that he messed with the wrong beast! Yes, I'm fine!" I chuckle at him, not realizing that I'm bleeding from my lower back. The bull must have gotten me when I jumped off him.

"My love, you are bleeding!" Z tries to scream at me but can hardly get the words out from the excruciating pain.

"It's fine! I can take that little bit of pain any day!" I assure him while I pull myself around to look at my back. It is a pretty deep gash, and it is bleeding profusely.

"You need to get that taken care of this instant!" he cries out angrily, getting himself really worked up.

"I need to get myself taken care of. What about you? You're a hot mess!"

"Get yourself taken care of this instant!" he screams at me from the top of his lungs then grabs my arm.

"Fine! Here's the water and the towels! I'm going to go upstairs to take care of myself!" I stomp off through the house, getting angrier by the minute, mumbling some cuss words to myself.

I get the bleeding stopped then wrap up my whole waist with gauze and bandages. I can feel the baby moving around, so I know he is doing just fine. His heartbeat is strong, and the rhythm sounds good. When I begin to run back downstairs, Z is trying to climb up the stairs. "Why don't you just stay on the couch!" I yell at him hatefully, getting really pissed off at him.

"I need to make sure that you are okay!" he tells me, panting heavily, and his heart is pounding as he fights to get up to me.

"Oh man, you're such a pain in the ass!" I gripe angrily.

"I am fine! You are the one that needs some help!" he scolds me, so I grab ahold of his arm then help him up the stairs to my room. He flops down on the bed and lies down, still panting heavily, trying to catch his breath. "Let me see your back!" he orders me, so I slowly pull down my bandages. "Turn around!" he screams at me. "I want to look at you all over!"

"Okay, what's your problem? I'm fine!" I growl, but he just shoots me a dirty look and then lies his head down on the bed and closes his eyes. "I'm going to run you some bathwater so that you can get cleaned up, then I need to go out to the barn to clean up the mess that I've made of your bull," I tell him as I run into the bathroom to turn on the water.

"No! You just leave it because I will clean it up tomorrow!" he yells at me furiously.

"Whatever! Just come in here and get in the tub!" I demand, pointing at it. I turn off the water then help him in. "Drink from me!" I order him.

"No! I will not!" he replies sharply. "Drink from me, damn you!" I hold my wrist up to his mouth, getting ready to tear it open for him, but he grabs it and shoves it away.

"I will not! Just go get me one of the bags from the fridge!" he screams at me, so I give him one hell of a dirty look then leave him to go downstairs. I spy the sleeping pills he was using before I came back from Romania, so I take three of them out of the bottle. "I'll fix you!" I tell myself out loud as I grab him some of his dead cow in a bag, pour it in a glass, mix the three pills into it once I crush them up into a fine powder, and then take it up to him.

Z is lying in the tub, with his head resting against it. "Here you go! Dead cow in a bag!" I say, giving him the dirtiest look ever.

"Thank you," he replies when he takes the glass from my hand. He drinks all of it, then I begin washing the dirt off his face and arms. Z keeps staring at me but doesn't say a word, and I don't dare make any eye contact. "Do you need some more?" I ask him, and by the way he is looking at me, I can tell that he is getting really sleepy.

"No, that is all," he answers, trying to fight to keep his eyes open.

"Let's get you into bed," I tell him, wanting to get him under the covers before he falls asleep, so I pull the covers down, help him into bed, and then hold him up while I wrap some gauze and bandages around his wounds before I let him lie all the way down.

"I love you," Z says to me as he passes out.

"I love you too," I repeat, getting him situated, then cover him up. He is fast asleep in no time, and I'm going to go cut up that ol' bull whether he likes it or not! There is no sense in letting it go to waste, and I know that when he wakes up, he'll definitely be way too sore to even attempt cutting it up!

It is late and really chilly out tonight. I've brought everything with me that I'll need to dress the bull with, and I'm so ready to get this show on the road. I tie a rope around Satan then around the bull's leg, thus dragging its dead carcass into the barn. I could probably pull it inside without all that, but I don't want to risk harming my baby. The other two horses watch quietly while we drag the bull inside, then I hook it up to a winch to pull it up with so that I can easily cut it up and clean it. I put a small steel stock tank underneath it so that nothing from it will get all over the barn's concrete floor then decide to drink whatever I can get from it as to not let that go to waste either. There is not much blood left inside it, but it fills my belly, then I commence to dive into the surgery. I gut it and then begin to skin it. He is pretty big, so it is going to be a long night! There is a large, deep freezer out here inside the barn that is empty, so I'm going to bag him, tag him, and then stack him inside it.

I glance over at the clock in the barn, and it is already 1:42 a.m. I'm almost done, and I am so ready to finish this night up! Z will probably be out until late tomorrow morning, so I'm not worried about him waking up anytime soon. I cut the last bits of meat from the bone, bag it, and tag it. *Thank you, sweet baby Jesus!* I scream inside my head when I stack it with the rest of the meat. But I still have to clean up the leftovers to discard them, so I drag the carcass and the leftovers over to a large brush pile sitting out in the pasture then set it ablaze. The fire roars to life. I watch it as it burns with tired eyes, and the horses are still watching me while I work. I decide to take a seat in a chair by the large sliding barn doors, wanting to keep a close eye on the fire while it burns, but my eyes get really heavy. And without warning, I fall fast asleep.

*****

Satan, Dutchess, and Hightower walk over to Renee then get close to her, blanketing her in their warmth. She is out cold, and so is Z. So they stand against her, faithful companions, showering her with their love and affection while they keep her warm throughout the cold night. She snores loudly as she sleeps, and Satan nudges her face with his nose because he loves her very much and will do anything for her. The morning comes, and they are all still there, a large circle of beautiful black beasts surrounding their loved one until she awakens.

"Renee! Renee! Where are you!" Ezekeial screams out for her in sheer panic from not being able to find her. He races to the barn and sees the three horses all standing in tightly knit circle, and he is quite stunned when he realizes that they're protecting her from the elements, resting next to her. The three equines watch him as he walks over to them, staring him down with wide open eyes as if to tell him to go away and let her be.

"My love! What are you doing?" he questions her, but Satan pushes him back with his muzzle, telling him to back off. "You let me take her in this instant!" Ezekeial screams at him. "She is pregnant, and I do not want her out here!" Satan's head shoots straight up, and his ears prick forward, listening to his words. "I want her in the house right now! She should not have been out here doing this!" he shouts at the mighty beast. "I do not want anything to happen to my family!" Satan submits then rubs his muzzle against Renee's face. They all back away, letting Ezekeial scoop her up, then walk out toward the pasture to graze. Ezekeial gently picks her up then cradles her in his arms as he carries her back to the house, and she is out cold and is still snoring. He is a wrecked mess but doesn't care because he wants to get her in bed.

He lies her down on the bed then pulls up her shirt, wanting to hear the beating of his child's heart. Ezekeial lies his head down on her belly then strains his ears to listen for it. He can feel it moving around ever so slightly and also hears its strong, fiercely beating heart. Smiling, he kisses her stomach then proceeds to undress her because she is a mess and her clothes stink of death. "I cannot believe you did all of that! You are something else and never listen!" he gripes but smiles at her, shaking his head.

*****

After I wake up, I notice that it is after 2:00 p.m. *Holy shit!* I look around but don't see Z. I stink something awful, so I decide to take a hot bath. I feel a little bit achy after last night, so I add some of my bath salts to the water, brush my teeth, and wait for the tub to fill up. I hop in then lean back, resting my head against the back of the tub. Man, it feels heavenly!

I close my eyes and begin to drift away, content as I relax in the hot water, then out of nowhere, I hear, "What the hell were you thinking last night!" Z is standing in the bathroom doorway, scolding me.

My eyes fly open, and I focus them right on him. But I just stare at him for a minute. "Please, just leave me alone. I'm exhausted right now," I say to him softly.

He walks over to the tub then sits down beside me. "Thank you for doing all of that, but I could have taken care of it myself." He kisses me on the forehead, but I lie motionless, not able to do anything. "Are you hungry?" he asks me.

"No. I just want to sit in this tub and soak for a while. How are your wounds today?" I ask him.

"They are healing well, and I will be as good as new by tomorrow. How is your back?" he asks me.

"It's a bit sore, but it'll be fine," I answer. Z just keeps staring at me. "What is it? Why do you keep looking at me like that?" I ask him, getting frustrated with him.

"I just think you need something to eat, that is all." He looks away from me then walks into the bedroom. "I am going to strip this bed. It is, as you say, a 'hot mess'!"

I can hear him taking the covers off the bed then walking down the stairs. He comes back in then remakes it with some fresh sheets. I just want to go lie back down at this point because I'm utterly drained of energy.

"Are you going to get out of there any time soon?" Z questions me when he walks back into the bathroom.

"I'm getting out now," I reply as I begin to stand up.

"Here, let me help you." Z picks me up out of the tub, helps me dry off, carries me into the room, and then sits me down on the bed. I grab my blanket then curl up with it. "Renee, you need to eat something! This is not like you!" he tells me in a worried voice.

"Fine! I'll get something to eat, and then can I please just relax?"

He smiles at me and nods happily, so I get up to head down to the kitchen with him right on my heels. "What do you want to eat, my love?" he asks me once we walk into the kitchen.

"Well, I sure as hell don't want any steak!" I tell him sarcastically, and he laughs out loud, shaking his head and grinning from ear to ear.

"You never cease to amaze me!" My vampire grabs me up then wraps his big body around me, holding me within his vice. "I can never tell you enough just how much that I love you!" Z releases me, then we rummage around the kitchen for something to eat. I make the both of us up a couple of fairly large sandwiches and some chips, then we sit down at the kitchen table. Z turns on the TV, so we watch it while we eat. "By the way," he says while looking at me with serious eyes. "Did you put something in my blood last night?" he questions me, and I want to tell him my secret but don't.

"No, why?" I ask him, playing stupid. He stares me down, giving me the I-know-you're-lying eye, but doesn't say anything else about it. So I continue eating my sandwich, trying not to smile.

Eating the sandwich awakens my hungry stomach, and I still want more to eat. Z is still finishing up his food when I get up to get something else. "I am glad that you are feeling better!" he tells me cheerfully.

"Yeah, I'm just a bit achy. I know you've got to be pretty sore! That bull beat the hell out of you!" I say while I rummage around for more to eat.

"I am not going to lie because I feel like I have been run over by a Mack truck!"

"I didn't mean to kill it, but he was pretty nasty!"

Z laughs at me. "No worries, my love. It is over with, done with! I am just glad that you are okay!"

Shooting me a funny eye, I look away from him toward the TV. *I wonder if he knows because he sure acts like it, and I'm sure that he can hear its heartbeat!* I think to myself. I grab a few cosmic brownies and some chocolate milk then head for the bedroom. "I'm going to go lay in bed and watch some TV for a while," I tell him.

"I am coming right behind you!" he tells me, hopping up out of his chair.

We head up to the bedroom, then I place my milk on the nightstand while he turns on the TV.

"Those horses kept you warm throughout the night! Did you know this?" Z asks me, and I smile from the thought of those sweet beauties huddling around me in the cold.

"Nope, I had no idea they did that! I don't remember anything after I sat down in the chair," I reply.

"It was sure a sight. I will tell you! They love you dearly!" he tells me, smiling.

"Yes, I know!" I say happily, turning to look at him, and he is just sitting in the bed, staring at me again.

"Come to me. I want to hold you."

I like the thought of that, so without hesitation, I crawl into his arms. He cradles me like a baby and rubs his face along the side of mine, so I wrap my arms around his neck and hold onto him tightly, pressing my face into his shoulder. This guy is such a big softy sometimes!

Z rocks me in his arms for a while and just holds me, not speaking a word, and I can hear the baby's heartbeat while I lie in his arms. And I know that he can hear it too, but still, I say nothing. It sounds strong and healthy, thank goodness, because I want him to be as healthy as possible. Every so often, I can feel it move just a little, and I know that everything is going to be okay.

Z lets me go, so I scoot over to the side of the bed, grab one of my brownies, and then take a drink of my milk, and he just watches me while I inhale my brownie, not saying a word. I can see him out of the corner of my eye, but I don't dare make any eye contact. I get up to brush my teeth then hop back in bed, snuggling up in my blanket and getting close to him. Z wraps his arms around me and pulls me in closer, neither of us speaking another word.

It has been almost three months since I was rescued from hell, and I'm beginning to worry more and more about them coming back to get me. I'm surprised that it hasn't happened yet, and I'm very thankful that they haven't shown up. The baby is starting to get more active, but I still haven't said anything to Z about it. Plus I still haven't seen a doctor, which I'd really like to do. Spring is right around the corner, and I'm hoping that Ezekeial begins to get busy with his farm stuff. So I find a few numbers to some local ob-gyns close to home and save them in my phone.

"I am going to go check on the herd. I will be back in a little while," Z says to me. "I think, on Friday, I am going to go to the sale barn to pick up another bull. Do you want to come with me and pick one out?" he asks me with a huge smile plastered across his face.

"Not really. I could care less if I see another one ever again!" I say, crossing my arms, and he laughs at me then kisses me on the head.

"That is fair enough!"

After Z heads out to the pasture, I make my move. I call the doctor's office to see if anyone will take me in on Friday, and with a great stroke of luck, they have an opening at 10:00 a.m.

Chapter 22

The Baby

"Hello, my name is Renee Cox, and I have an appointment today," I tell the lady at the front desk.

"I need your insurance card and ID. Here's all of the paperwork that you need to fill out too, sweetie," the lady at the counter says to me in the friendliest manner.

"Thank you!" I reply.

She smiles at me, then I go sit down to fill out the paperwork. I'm still covered under my stepdad's health insurance, thank goodness, so I have that part covered.

I get everything filled out then hand all of it back to her. "The nurse will be with you shortly," she says to me, still smiling.

They call my name, and I begin to freak out, getting myself all nerved up. "Hello, Renee. I'm Dr. West, and is this your first pregnancy?" the doctor asks me kindly. I don't want to say anything about the miscarriage, so I keep it to myself.

"Yes, this is my first," I answer.

"Well, let's get this started!" he tells me cheerfully. "I'll have to examine you first. Do you have any idea about how far long you are?"

"I'm about three months pregnant," I reply.

"Well, we'll do an ultrasound today to see how the baby's doing and check out the size of it. We may even be able to tell what sex it is! How does that sound?" he asks me, and I'm smiling from ear to ear.

"That sounds wonderful!" I say excitedly.

He gives me the exam and then tells me to pull up my shirt so that we can take a look inside.

"What does the father think about this, may I ask?" he questions me.

"I haven't told him yet because I wanted to get everything checked out before I tell him. I'm sure he'll be happy about it. It's just that I'm scared enough as it is and want to keep it a secret for now."

"I completely understand! First-time pregnancies are really scary, and every woman has their own way of dealing with it. Now let's check this baby out!" he tells me happily.

So I pull up my shirt, then he squirts the lube on my belly, getting prepared, and then begins to roll the wand around. His nurse stands with us too and smiles when the baby pops up over the screen. My heart is pounding, and I'm scared and excited all at the same time!

"Well, if you look here, you can see it. The hands, feet, head, heartbeat, and size all look perfectly normal, except I think that this one may be going to be a big one! It looks like you'll be due around the middle of August, early September. I can even tell you the sex if you'd like to know." He looks up at me.

"Yes, I'd love to know!" I'm dying for his answer as my pulse flies through the roof with excitement and anticipation.

"It looks like you have a baby boy growing inside of you, Ms. Cox!" he tells me then looks up at me and is smiling as big as I am.

"I'm so happy! I was hoping it was going to be a boy!" I cry out ecstatically, becoming emotional. "Thank you so much, Dr. West!"

"You're welcome! I'm happy that you're happy, sweetie!" he says then prints off a few ultrasound pictures and hands them to me. "I'm going to write you a prescription for some prenatal vitamins because I'd like for you to take them once a day, and we want to see you back again in four weeks."

"Okay, will do!" I tell him with joyous excitement. He leaves the room, so I gather myself back together, thrilled as ever.

I make my next appointment and plan on telling Z sometime soon about the son that he is going to have because I can't hide it from him for much longer anyway, although I'm almost positive he already knows. I stop at the pharmacy to get my vitamins before I leave for the house and make it home before he gets back from the sale barn, so I run my vitamins upstairs, hiding them, along with the pictures, inside the drawer of my nightstand. My little Maximillian is on his way, and I can't be any happier!

Shortly after I get home, I can hear the rattling of the trailer as he drives it up to the barn, and I sure hope this new bull is a lot friendlier than the other one! I begin preparing dinner and collect myself, getting on with my day, when I hear him pull the truck into the driveway then see him approaching the door. "Hey there, sexy beast!" I tell him when he walks inside. "What kind of monster did you pick up today?" I ask him, grinning, and he laughs at me.

"This one will be much better! I promise you this!" He comes over to me then kisses me on the lips.

"I sure hope so because there's no more room in the freezer for any more meat!" I say then bust up laughing.

Z smiles at me and shakes his head, chuckling. "How long will it be before supper is done?"

"Oh, I'll say about thirty-five minutes or so."

"Okay, I am going to go take a shower because it has been a very long day!"

"Sounds good! I'll be down here!" I tell him as I flip my pork chops. I'm so hungry and can't wait to eat!

The food is done, and Z is walking into the kitchen, wearing only his bed shorts. He looks good enough to eat himself, and I try not to stare at him. I set the food out. And as he fixes his plate, my stomach begins to growl loudly, so he looks over at me. "Have you eaten anything today?" he questions me.

"No. Not yet, why?" I ask him.

"Why have you not eaten anything yet?" he questions me, giving me the angry eye.

"Well, I've been busy! I went to the store to pick up some supplies that we were out of, and then I had to put it all away! I also washed some laundry! I've been going all day!" I explain, telling him a big fat lie, but he doesn't know that. I did grab a few things at the store while I was there!

"Well, get over here and eat because I know that you are hungry!" he barks at me in a sharp tongue.

"You don't have to tell me twice!" I tell him as I grab a plate and dive in!

After dinner, I get everything cleaned up and put away then make my way upstairs. "Calgon, take me away!" I'm pooped! I turn on the tub water and lose myself in thought while it fills up, my mind focusing on the baby.

"Renee...Renee?" He is talking to me, but I didn't hear a word he has just said.

I snap back, "Yeah, what is it?" I ask him.

"Where are you at right now? You have not heard a word that I have said!" Z is looking at me with questioning eyes.

"Sorry, I'm just tired, that's all," I explain while turning off the water. "Maybe I should go hunting tonight because I can't even remember the last time that I've gone out."

"No! I think you should wait!" he tells me, staring me down.

"No, I'm going to go right now since it's really nice outside. Why don't you come with me?" I look over at him, and a huge smile creeps across his face.

"Sounds good to me! Let us go then!"

We get undressed, awaken our beasts, and then head out into the wonderfully bright and inviting night sky. The evening is absolutely gorgeous! We fly over the property, searching for the deer, then spy the herd grazing below. We both get our fill, then walk hand in hand while we stroll across the open field. Z pulls me over to him then begins to rub all over me, wanting some attention, so I return his advances as I begin to rub my hands and fingers around his chest then moving them to his back and caress his wings closest to his shoulders. He puts his hands around my face then pulls me to him, kissing me softly on the lips and running his fingers through my hair. I feel his tail rubbing me between my thighs, and my senses burst to life. So I bring my tail around then begin to rub it along his manhood, driving him absolutely crazy! He begins to kiss me all over, and he is pawing all over me and rubbing me harder with his tail. So I do the same to him, and then without warning, he flips me around and thrusts himself inside me. My body screams with heavenly delight when he pushes it in deeper, driving me wildly insane.

Pure sexual satisfaction radiates from everywhere, and I cry out from the sensational pleasure of his amazing loving. This excites him even more, and he is out of control, rubbing me everywhere and kissing all over my back. I can't keep from finishing. Z begins to flap his wings, trying to thrust into me harder, and this sends me over the top. I cry out again from the heavenly sexual bliss of having another phenomenal climax, and he is loving making me scream. I can tell that he has finished when he begins to slowly come to a halt. So I turn around to face him then kiss him on the lips, and he kisses me back. Z pulls me against his chest, holding onto me tightly, so I massage his head with my hands and fingers then gently through his hair, enjoying this tender moment with him. He is pressing his belly against mine, wanting me closer.

"What's wrong, baby?" I ask him, sensing a sudden shift in his emotions.

"Nothing. I just want to be close to you because I love you so much," he answers then kisses my lips.

I want to scream out about the baby, but for some reason, I just can't do it! He wraps his tail around my waist then rubs it ever so delicately along my bare skin, and the pleasing sensation of his soft fur feels wonderful as it brushes against me. He releases me, then we fly back to the house, and I finish filling up the tub and hop in, feeling exceptionally gracious for the fabulous night that I've just had.

"May I come in?" Z asks me.

"Of course!" I reply, smiling, so he gets in behind me then pulls me against his body. I'm pretty sure that I can feel him sobbing, but I don't acknowledge it. "I love you, Z," I tell him while I lie against his chest, then he wraps his arms around me and holds me within a loving embrace. He plants his face in my hair then rubs his nose along my head, and we just sit like this for a while. So I wait patiently for him to release whatever thing he seems to be going through right now. The water is getting cold, and it is funny because he must have read my mind.

"Let us get out and go to bed."

We get out, dry off, brush our teeth, and then climb in bed. I roll over on his chest and put my arm around him, looking him dead in the eye. "That was the best lovemaking that I've ever had. Thank you!" I tell him as I kiss his cheek.

My words please my vampire lover enormously, and a huge smile creeps across his face. "I was hoping you would be telling me this!"

I chuckle while he beams happily then turn over on my back. Z turns over on his side and scoots close to me while he gazes deep into my eyes, but I close mine when I begin floating away into the black hole, drifting to sleep. I feel him place his hand over my belly, then he begins to rub it delicately. So I lie still and relax while he does his thing, wanting him to think I'm fast asleep. I know he can feel the baby because Max begins to squirm around from the pressure of his papa's hand. I hear Z laugh quietly as Max tries to wriggle free, and the sensation feels really strange when he kicks around. I want to throw my arms around him and tell him about the baby, even though he already knows about him. But something is holding me back, and I'm not sure why.

"No one will ever hurt you nor your mother! I will kill them!" Z whispers to baby Max. He takes his hand away from my belly, runs it along my chest, and then kisses my breasts. He then moves up to my face and kisses me on the lips, trying not to disturb me. Z gently cuddles up to me and places his face next to my shoulder, kissing it softly as he settles in. "I could never ask for anyone better to be by my side, and there is no other woman on this planet that can ever compare to you, my love," he whispers to me then, shortly after, falls asleep. His sweet words tug at my heart, and I can't help myself when my emotions break free and tears stream down my face.

A couple more weeks have passed by, but I still haven't said anything to him yet, even though he already knows that I'm pregnant. The telltale sign of an ever-growing baby bump is a dead giveaway, and I'm quite surprised that he hasn't broken down and said anything to me about it. The day begins just like any other day. I'm thrilled when my phone begins to ring, and it is my mama.

"Renee, are you okay?" she asks me, sounding concerned.

"Yeah, why?" I ask.

"Well, we've gotten a bill from the insurance company today, and it was for a doctor's visit that you went to. You're not sick, are you, sweetie?" she questions me.

Z has gone up to check on the cattle, so now is the perfect time to tell her about the baby. "Well, I had to go see an ob-gyn, Mama. I'm going to be having a baby boy around the end of August, beginning of September," I begin to tell her, and the line goes silent for a minute.

"So are you happy about it?" she asks.

"Yeah, of course! I'm just afraid to say anything to Z about it, and I'm not sure how to go about doing it," I explain.

"Why? Does he not want to have any kids?" she asks me, sounding worried.

"It's not that, because I'm sure he'll be happy about it. I'm just trying to work through some issues," I try to explain.

"Nothing serious, I hope."

"No, nothing like that. I'm just scared about some stuff, that's all. It doesn't have anything to do with Z. It's about other things that have happened to me, and I just don't know what to do." I want to confide in her about everything that had happened to me in Romania because she doesn't have a clue about me being married to Ezekeial's brother or about the miscarriage that I had, but I can't. My problems are just a little more complex than regular mortal issues.

"Well, whatever it is, I know you'll figure it out," she assures me.

"How much was the bill? And I'll send you the money to pay for it with," I ask her.

"Renee, it's nothing, so don't worry about it!" she replies.

"Well, I have another appointment in two weeks, and there will be another bill. I can't expect you to pay for all of this, Mama!"

"Right now, don't worry about it, okay! Just get yourself straightened out! I'm going to have a grandson! What do you plan on naming him, or have you even decided yet?" she asks me cheerfully.

"I'm going to name him Maximillian Ezekeial Dragkarr."

"I love it!" she screams out joyfully, and I laugh at her, feeling happy that she is ready to be a grandmother.

We chitchat for a little while longer, then we say our goodbyes. Once I end her call, my emotions get the best of me, and I break down, crying. *What am I going to do?* I need to get a divorce from Sebastian, and I certainly don't want them coming after me! I don't want my little Max being hurt or killed! My mind begins to run rampant, and I end up making myself sick. A wave of nausea hits me like a freight train, and I have to race into the bathroom to throw up.

*****

Renee didn't know that Z had come inside while she was on the phone with her mother. He stood at the bottom of the stairs, eavesdropping in on their conversation, choking back his tears while he listens to her talk about the son he is going to be having, and he absolutely loves the name she has chosen for him. He wants to run to her, dying to offer her some comfort, knowing that she needs him right now, but he can't. He knows that he is the one who has caused her so much grief and distress, and extreme guilt and shame tear him apart. He quietly sneaks back up to the barn and paces the floor, trying to figure out a way to fix his huge mistake. His cell phone begins to ring, and it is a number that he hasn't seen before.

"Hello, who is this?" he asks.

"My son, this is your mother! Aiden and Sebastian are getting on a plane as we speak to collect Renee! You must get her out of there!" she cries out hysterically, and his heart drops from shock.

"They are coming now?" he asks in utter disbelief.

"Yes, you must do something before they get there!" she screams at him frantically.

Livid anger and rage well up from deep within him. "This cannot be happening! I will kill them!" he screams into the phone then hangs up.

Ezekeial knows Renee won't stand down if she has to face off against Aiden and Sebastian, so he is willing to do whatever it takes to keep her and baby Max safe. Losing his family is not an option, so if he dies trying to save them, then so be it!

CHAPTER 23

Hard Goodbyes

Hello? Ezekeial?" Lazar says when he answers the phone.

"Lazar, I need your help! Aiden and Sebastian are on their way from Romania as we speak and are coming for Renee!" Ezekeial screams into the phone hysterically. "I cannot let anything happen to her or my son!" he explains, still screaming.

"Your son?" Lazar asks.

"Yes! She is pregnant with my son, and I cannot lose either of them!"

"What do you want me to do? I will do anything for her!" Lazar replies, getting worried, so Ezekeial and Lazar hatch up a plan to get Renee away from the house until Aiden and Sebastian can be dealt with. It may come with a hefty price, but Ezekeial is willing to pay it at whatever the cost.

*****

It is getting late, so I pull myself back together as I make my way down to the kitchen, needing to get dinner started. I know Z will be back from the barn at any time, and I need something to take my mind off all this craziness. I plan on talking to him about the baby once he and I get in bed this evening and to also show him the ultrasound pictures.

I notice Z's phone sitting on the island in the kitchen, which I'm pretty sure wasn't there earlier, but I don't give it another thought as I turn on the oven. My mind is going ninety to nothing while I wait for the oven to preheat, but it comes to a screeching halt once Z's phone begins to ring. My heart skips a beat when I see that it is Lazar calling. I'm not sure if I should answer it, but I really need someone to talk to. Lazar has always been the best listener, and I can't help myself when I answer his call.

"Hello, Lazar?"

"Hey there, sweetheart! How have you been?" he asks me cheerfully with that sweet voice and sexy accent of his. I can't hold back my emotions when I begin to cry, dying to spill my guts out to him. Suddenly, Z flies through the door and rips the phone right out of my hand.

"What in the hell are you doing!" he screams at me angrily. I'm taken aback by his abrupt outburst and freeze in place. "You are not ever going to be faithful to me because you cannot stop thinking about Lazar, can you!" Z screams at me from the top of his lungs, and his behavior and threatening demeanor are starting to frighten me.

"I just needed someone to talk to! He was the one who called your phone, so I answered it!" I explain, pleading with him.

"I cannot stand the sight of you! I cannot live like this!" Z tells me, still screaming. "They are coming for you, and I'm going to let Sebastian have you back! You disgust me!"

Z's hateful words cut me deep, and I don't know what to say when panic begins to set in. I begin to tremble when my adrenaline shifts into overdrive, and my nerves are completely shot. Z bolts out of the kitchen and races up the stairs, so I give chase, wanting to know what he is going to do. I'm appalled when he grabs my suitcases then begins to shove some of my clothes inside them, mumbling words in Romanian. Once he stuffs my suitcases full, he grabs my camo backpack and then races back downstairs.

"Please, stop! What are you doing!" I cry out in pure terror as I run after him.

He grabs my arm then drags me outside next to the TA. "You need to get the hell out of here and disappear, or else, I will give you back to them when they get here! I do not want to see you ever again! Go call Lazar and stay with him, you whore!" With that, he slaps me across the face, almost knocking me down, and I can taste the blood from my bloody nose when it runs down my face and into my mouth.

I pull myself up, holding on to my car, and the shit hits the fan! Thunder begins to rumble across the sky, the wind becomes violent as it picks up speed, and lightning explodes with blinding flashes like a massive firework display. "Don't you ever touch me again, or I will fucking kill you!" I scream at him then let out a loud menacing growl. With that, a bolt of lightning strikes the ground only steps away from me.

Z runs over to the car, throws my bags inside the trunk along with a black duffel bag, and then throws my backpack down at my feet. "Get the hell out of here, you whore! I do not want you here anymore!" he roars loudly.

I'm not risking little Max for any of this bullshit, so with my powers, I fire up the car and open the driver's side door. "You don't have to worry about me ever bothering you again, Ezekeial! I'll disappear from you forever!" I shout at him as I pick up my backpack then hop into the car.

I close the door and take off down the driveway, throwing gravel all over the place. Looking back in my rearview mirror, I see Satan running at full speed, trying to keep up with the car, and I can hear him calling out to me. His desperate cries rip me apart, so I tell him with my mind that I'll call for him when the time is right. Once I hit the pavement, I punch the gas, letting my anger take the wheel, and don't look back.

*****

Ezekeial falls to his knees, having a nuclear meltdown from what he has just done. "I am so sorry, my love! I hope that one day you can forgive me!" he cries out as he drops to the ground, holding himself up with his arms and hands. He is oblivious to anything happening around him when the mighty stallion charges him at full speed then runs into him, throwing him across the driveway.

Stomping his hooves around Ezekeial's head, he snorts and growls, throwing gravel all over him. "I had to do it! They were coming for her, and I cannot risk her or the baby getting hurt!" he screams at the raging beast before him. Satan paces around him, stomping his feet, wanting to smash in his head. "I did not want to do this!" Ezekeial pleads with the enraged black steed. Satan gives him a swift kick in the leg then gallops back up to the barn where his own family awaits and listens, wondering what has just happened.

Ezekeial picks himself up off the ground and slowly walks back into the house. He grabs the bottle of tequila out of the cabinet then goes back outside. He sits down on the porch swing on the same side that Renee always does when she is out here and begins to drown out his sorrows. Remembering his cell phone, he rushes back inside to retrieve it then returns to the spot where he had previously been sitting and opens up the find-my-phone app. He has her phone on his plan and can track her everywhere she goes, and he sees that she is on the move then waits to see where she stops at first because he doesn't want to lose track of her for any reason. The phone begins to ring, and it is Lazar.

"Did it work, Ezekeial?" he asks him, but Ezekeial almost can't answer him from choking on his grief.

"Yes, she is gone. My soul is lost once more," he replies then hangs up the phone. He has just made another terrible sacrifice, and he'll never be at peace with himself again. "They will pay for this! I will guarantee you this!" he cries out loud then drinks from the bottle. "I will kill you both!"

*****

I'm tearing up the highway and trying to wrap my mind around what has just happened! I can't believe he hit me! I didn't do anything wrong, and I'm stunned that he has just called me a whore! I'm so lost in thought that I don't even realize I'm almost out of gas. I pull into the next station and park the car a few feet away then break out into tears, not sure what to do. I don't have any money or place to go! He has done it to me again, and I can't hold in my grief while I sit here and just cry continuously. I get out then look inside the trunk at the luggage he has thrown into the car, but there is nothing other than some clothes and junk stuffed inside my suitcases. So I grab the black duffel bag that I saw him throw in along with them. It is filled with money and my paperwork from college, passports, etc. *Thank God!* I breathe a huge sigh of relief because, at least, I can fill up my car and find a place to sleep tonight!

I pull my car up to the pump then grab my backpack, and I happen to see my iPhone sitting inside it. I know that I'll need to get rid of it because they can track me with it, and I can't risk them finding me. So I'm going to disappear for good! I open the trunk to grab some cash out of the bag, stuff it inside my purse, and then go pay for the gas that I've just pumped. I leave the station then focus my attention to finding a store to pick up a new phone at. It is after 6:00 p.m., so I'm hoping that Walmart will still have someone working at the phone counter.

Luckily, the phone counter is still open, so once I pick out the one that I want, the boy at the counter hooks me up. My old phone gets turned off, and my new one gets activated. So now I'm off the grid! Reality checks in when I realize that I don't have a clue where I'm going to go, so I head over to the magazine section to see if I can find a map. I can't risk going home because I don't want my family being caught up in the crossfire, so I'll have to decide which way I want to go. I grab my map, along with a few magazines to read, hoping they'll help keep my mind occupied. While I browse through the road atlas, the one for Florida catches my eye, so I take it from the rack. I've always wanted to go to the beach, and since I'm wanting to disappear, this is the perfect opportunity to do so!

My stomach begins to growl angrily, so I also bag up some groceries before I head to the checkout. My mind goes wild while I walk through the parking lot, and once I get inside the TA, I sit behind the wheel for a few minutes, trying to pull my shit together. I know that I plan on heading south, so I fire up my boo, then she and I begin our journey into a new frontier.

I drive for about three hours longer then decide to find a place to stop for the night. Stopping at the next gas station to fill up the car, I spy a small motel down the road and decide to make that my resting place. Once I pay for the room and get inside, I already know that this isn't where I want to be at all, but there is no other choice for me. I throw everything that I've picked up at the store on the bed then grab the black duffel bag out of the trunk of the car. I make sure my room door is securely locked after I bring in the bag then set it down on the bed, wanting to check out the contents inside. After unzipping it, I dump all of it out over the bed, and there is a shit ton of cash, along with my paperwork. I begin to count the money, but there is way too much of it. I can't focus on what I'm doing when I begin to choke up, so I stuff all the money back inside the bag then hop into the shower. The warmth of the water feels wonderful as it runs down my back. But flashes of the shakedown earlier keep replaying through my mind, and I just can't hold myself together anymore. I lean my back up against the shower wall then slowly slide down it, hitting the floor of the tub. I start crying buckets of tears and can't stop because I just want to go home and sleep in my own bed. I want Z lying next me with his hand rubbing on my belly, feeling his new son move around inside me. I cry harder with every thought and pull myself into a ball, trying to comfort myself as I rock back and forth, wishing that I would've never answered that damn phone.

Eventually, the hot water runs out, so I have to force myself out of the shower. Drying myself off then wrapping a towel around me, I go lie down on the bed, still crying, alone and scared. I just keep thinking about what I'm going to do next because even once I get to Florida, where do I go from there? I run myself out of tears and can't cry anymore, and I know that my life will never be the same. My baby will never know who his papa is, and my heart breaks from the thought of it. Lying here, drowning in misery and sorrow, I fall into a restless sleep, dreaming terrible nightmares.

*****

Ezekeial has been sitting on the porch swing, lost within his own thoughts, choking on his tears when he happens to glance down at the phone and realizes that it is not working anymore. "Oh no! What did you do!" he screams out in disbelief. For the first time in his entire life, he hasn't gotten a clue as to where Renee is! He hops up, distraught and panicking, not knowing what he should do, because he wasn't expecting her to have her phone turned off! "Oh my God!" he screams out into the night. "This cannot be happening!" Standing on the porch, he sobs uncontrollably, fearing that he has lost his family forever.

The phone rings, and it is Lazar. "Where should I pick her up at?" he questions Ezekeial impatiently.

"I do not know! She had the phone turned off, and I do not know where she went!" he shouts hysterically.

"What! We won't ever find her now!" Lazar screams at him angrily.

"I know that! Do you not think that I do not know this!" Ezekeial yells as loud as he can, still disbelieving that this has happened. "I must go!" he tells Lazar abruptly then hangs up the phone. Hopping into the truck, he looks at the last ping on the map of the cell phone, hoping that she hasn't gone too far, because when he finds her, he's going to fix all this and never let her leave him again!

The drive seems to be endless, and time is passing by quickly. Renee could be anywhere right now, and he is beginning to panic! The last ping stops at the Walmart a few towns over, so he parks the truck and dashes inside because she must have gotten herself a new phone here. The phone counter is closed, but a store clerk is rearranging some of the movies in the next aisle.

"Excuse me, may I ask you a quick question?" Z asks the clerk politely, and the boy smiles at him.

"Sure, what can I help you with, sir?" he asks Z.

"Did you happen to sell a beautiful woman with blonde and brown hair a new phone earlier?" he questions the boy. The boy stares at Z but doesn't say a word. "Please, I must know. She is my wife and has been missing, and my family needs to find her!" he pleads with the clerk. The clerk stands quietly for a minute, trying to decide what to say to him.

"Well, yes. She wanted a new phone, so I fixed her up! I couldn't help but to stare at her because she had the most beautiful eyes and smile! You're a very lucky man!" the boy answers happily. "I sure hope you find her and that nothing's happened to her. She was really nice.

I did see her walk over to the aisle with the maps and magazines after I'd gotten her a new phone, but that was the last that I had seen of her," the boy explains, smiling, then goes back to what he was doing. Z stands in place for a minute, trying to gather his thoughts.

Ezekeial leaves the store and heads out to the truck, looking around for any sign that she may be nearby. He is at a loss and isn't sure what he should do now. The thought of her being gone scares him to death, and he can't seem to get over the way he had struck her out of his mind. Not to mention, the violent storm that had popped up from out of nowhere from her rage. She'll do anything to protect little Max, and he smiles, thinking about that, knowing that he'll be safe. He has never seen her as angry as she was earlier, and she would've killed him if it had come down to it. Starting the truck, he decides to drive around to a few other towns to see if he can spot the TA anywhere because it is late, and maybe she has stopped somewhere close by to rest.

His search for the car has led him nowhere, so he decides to stop at a roadside park to rest for a while. The sun has already risen, and he has been driving around aimlessly for hours. His mind races with the memories of everything that has happened up until this point, and he knows that all this is his own fault. If he would've just stepped up and took Aiden and Sebastian on from the beginning, none of this would even be happening right now. His eyes fill up with tears when he thinks about how all this could have been avoided if he wouldn't have been such a coward.

Ezekeial closes his eyes then drifts off into a restless sleep, his heart heavy with sadness. Then waking up a couple of hours later, he decides to head back to the farm because he doesn't have a clue as to where she may have gone and has high hopes that maybe she decided to go back home. Satan is still at the farm, and he knows that she'll come for him at some point. So when she does, he is going to fix this terrible mess.

Arriving home, his heart sinks when he doesn't see the Trans Am parked in the driveway, but he can sense right away that something is awry. He jumps out of the truck and notices the side door has been kicked in and that someone has been inside his house. The house is in total shambles, and there isn't one closet or cabinet that hasn't been torn into. Ezekeial races up to Renee's room to see what has been done to it, erupting with anger when he walks inside, because the bed has been ripped apart and all her stuff has been thrown everywhere. The furniture has been overturned, and her clothes and other items in the closet have been ripped from their hangers and strung about. The drawers have been pulled out of her dressers and nightstand, and the contents have been scattered throughout the room.

Ezekeial begins to organize her clothes and the papers that are all strewn about. Then noticing a few pictures lying on the floor, he reaches down to retrieve them and is stunned when he looks at them. They're the ultrasound pictures that had been taken at Renee's first doctor's visit. There, in those three pictures, is his little boy. He bites his fist, trying to hold back the agony of it all, and sits on the bedroom floor, staring at them, wondering if he will ever get to see him.

Jumping up, he realizes that he hasn't checked on his own bedroom. He has a safe placed within the closet wall that no one knows about, containing all his money and important belongings being locked away safely inside it. He rushes to his room then throws open the door, and thankfully, the safe wasn't found and is still unknown to anyone. But his room, otherwise, has been totally trashed. Nothing has been untouched. He doesn't care because all that is replaceable, unlike the items he has stored inside the safe. He knows it was Aiden and Sebastian who were here because he can smell them, and their reeking scent is vile! Looking around at the damage, he walks back into Renee's room then begins to clean everything up. It is going to be a very long day with having to reorganize the house, but he doesn't mind because having something to do will take his mind off the monumental problems at hand for the time being. He picks up the photos of little Max then places them right back in the nightstand drawer where they were lying next to, wanting to keep everything the way that she has left it, and slowly he begins the tireless task of cleaning up the house.

Finishing up the damage control, Ezekeial walks up to the barn. He wants to check in on the horses to see how they are doing. Satan is standing inside of his stall, staring out into the nothingness, longing for her. Dutchess and Hightower are grazing peacefully out into the pasture.

"Satan, is she okay?" he asks the morning stallion. Satan looks at him but gives him nothing. "Please, I am begging for you to let me know if she is okay!" he pleads with him. The steed is still angry with him after last night and doesn't comply, giving Z a glaring, squinty eye. He decides to give him a quick nod, gesturing that Renee is fine, so that Ezekeial will leave him alone. "Thank you. I am very sorry for everything that has happened because I know this is all my fault and that I can never take anything back. I will forever wait for her to return to me," he says, choking back his tears as Satan turns away from him, joining his family, not being able to stand the sight of Ezekeial for any longer.

*****

Waking up this morning is terrible! I had the worst night's sleep ever, and I feel awful! My belly is growling fiercely, and I only have a few snacks left. I decide to stay here for one more night, wanting to figure out where would be the best place to go, so I walk up to the office, pay for another night, and then drive the TA over to the store to pick up some food. I have quite the cart full by the time I've finished then load up the car. Getting back to the room, I settle in for the day with my groceries and maps, scouting out the different places to go in the US. I want to go somewhere close to the beach because I love the ocean, and from what I've gotten counted out from the bag of money, there is plenty inside it to buy a nice place. I can at least thank Z for that. I spread the map out across the bed, searching for Florida, then scan through it closely, waiting for something to catch my eye. Miami catches my eye, so I think this is where I'm going to make my destination point. It is a long way from where the farm is in Georgia, so I know it'll take a while for anyone to ever find me there. I feel satisfied with my decision then chow down on my food.

I fish out my new phone then begin checking it out, trying to see what else may be different on this new one as to the old one. I've kept my old phone, so I get it out too, wanting to look through my pictures. I scroll through them and see the ones that I've taken of Z, the day he was sleeping peacefully in bed. I can't cry anymore, but the sight of them tugs at my heart and sends waves of sadness throughout my soul. I open the phone numbers, and staring at his, I'm dying to call him but can't. At least I can look at it and know that it is here for me if I need it. Little Max is active today and is wriggling around nonstop, and I hope he doesn't hate me when he gets older, when I have to try to explain to him about his papa, because I couldn't live with myself if he didn't want to have anything to do with me. I turn on the TV, wanting to try to focus my mind on other things, but it is useless. I want to find a place with enough property so that Satan has plenty of room to run, although he may not want to leave his family for me, and I can deal with that. I wouldn't want to give up my family either, but I'll worry about that when the time comes. So for now, I need to get my shit together and get on with my life. It is going to be hard, but I have to do it because there is no other way. I also need to get settled so that I can find a new doctor for Max, needing someone to help me through all this. I'm scared and alone, not even having the comfort of my wolf to talk to. I have Lazar's number, but calling him will only create more issues that I don't need right now because answering the phone to talk to him has already caused me enough trouble. I lie down on the bed, feeling exhausted and worn down, and it doesn't take me long before I feel myself drifting slowly into the dark abyss. I welcome it, for tomorrow, my new life begins.

To be continued...

Join Renee on her new journey to discover where she ends up next! There is a lot more to come, so keep reading! I've thrown in a small sneak peek of the next book, so enjoy!

Forever and Always, My Love

Book 2: The Den of the Wolves

Hopping into the old Trans Am to begin my journey toward a new adventure, I'm hoping things will begin to look up soon. I miss Z terribly. But he doesn't want me anymore, and he had made that perfectly clear. It is just Max and I for now, but I'm happy with that, hoping this fresh start will lead me into greener pastures. My sights are set on Miami, so I turn on the map app from my phone then let it download the directions. Technology is a wonderful thing these days, and I embrace its usefulness. The TA purrs as we travel from highway to highway, and the sound of the engine soothes me while I travel onward. I hope Satan is doing well, and I wonder how the other two horses are doing also. I love them all, and it feels like a death in the family with having to leave them all behind.

I've been driving for about eight hours now. I stop occasionally to use the bathroom, to get snacks, and to fill up the car. I can almost smell the salty air as I get closer to my destination, and I welcome it with open arms. The trip, beginning from where I had left from, is about a ten-hour-and-fifteen-minute drive, so thankfully, I'm almost to my stopping point. I stop at another gas station just before I enter Miami to pick up some real-estate magazines that are sitting in the racks inside the store, wanting to see what is available, and the cost of the surrounding properties. I decide to rent a room for the night and settle in, looking through the magazines that I've picked up. The places aren't cheap around here, but I know I'll be able to find something suitable for me. I mostly want some land because I can always buy a camper or something for now to live in. I come across an ad for fifty-two acres out of town, with a fixer-upper sitting on the property.

"I think I'll call them tomorrow," I tell myself out loud, anxious to see what it looks like. It also says that it has some sort of ocean outlet behind the property that is included with land. Turning on the TV, eating some groceries, and then taking a nice hot shower, I snuggle under the covers, feeling a little bit better.

*****

Ezekeial is going crazy not knowing where Renee has gone to. Lazar has called him again, wanting to know if he has found her yet, and was incredibly angry when he told him that he hasn't gotten the slightest idea where to even begin looking. He goes up to her room and lies down on the bed, staring at her fuzzy blanket. He didn't grab it for her when he threw her clothes into the suitcases and wishes he would have. The daylight is fading, and it is another night alone, worrying about her and wanting her back by his side. He looks out across the night sky through the windows of the French doors and wonders if she may be looking at the same ones as well.

He gets undressed then wraps himself up into this blanket of hers, taking in her scent, and he can smell her favorite lotion that she puts on almost every evening while he stares out into the sky. Sleep doesn't come easily, as her face flashes within his mind's eye over and over again, following the feelings that he felt when he touched her belly and the feeling of his son moving around inside her. This is all so unbearable, and he wants this nightmare to end!

*****

I get up to call the number on the ad, anxious to make an appointment and dying to take a look at this property. I'm excited and nervous all at the same time! The lady has set up an appointment for around 1:30 p.m., and it is already 12:01 p.m. So I type the directions into my phone that she has given to me because I want to get there early to check it out for myself before she arrives. It is about a fifteen-minute drive from Miami City, just about like being back home and having the long drive to town, so it is nothing I can't handle. I smile, thinking about the many trips to town I used to take with my mama to go shopping.

I come to an overgrown driveway entrance and see the For Sale sign stuck down in the ditch line right in front of the worn-out, rusty old mailbox. After turning the TA into the driveway, I'm expecting some crazy lunatic to burst out of the tree line at any given time, chasing me down and screaming while wielding a machete in one hand, because the creepy atmosphere along the driveway is quite unnerving. It is lined with thorns and thick brush along either side of it, and I'm relieved when I can see a clearing up ahead as I pull in a little farther. I strain my eyes while trying to get a clearer view of the upcoming landscape, and I'm pleasantly surprised when the car pulls into the blinding sunlight of the clearing.

Upon entering the clearing, the property opens up into a lush large open field that has overgrown but can be easily cleaned up. There is a huge old plantation-style house slightly off to my right, so I park the car in front of the wreck of a house then get out. I look around as I walk toward the backside of the house, and I'm quite surprised with how big the backyard is! Along the outskirts of the backyard is another line of woods, and it seems to encircle the entire property. Then I spy what appears to be a path along the edge of the tree line, but I'll check that out later.

I'm dying to get a peek inside the house as I step up on the front porch, so I don't hesitate to grab the doorknob and to turn it, hoping that it is unlocked. To my surprise, the door swings open, so I cautiously take a few steps inside. The house is massive, and the floor plan is absolutely amazing! I'm standing in a large, grand foyer, and located along the walls on both sides about middleway of the room, two beautifully hand-carved wooden staircases flow up to the second floor. At the back of the room, underneath the two staircases, I can make out an entrance to a room, and I'm guessing that it must lead into the kitchen. Looking over to my left, a large entryway leads into a room, and to my right, another of the same entryways faces me. I decide to head into the room off to my left, and once I walk inside and survey the area, I know that this must be the living room.

Peeling wallpaper and the old wooden floor and debris strung about, along with the history behind the house, take me back in time to when I first peered into the window of the old blockhouse that my mama and Kent live in back home, and I smile to myself from the pleasant memory. Along the wall facing the foyer, a ginormous stone fireplace runs up the length of the wall then right through the ceiling. The place is in total disarray but has great potential!

I step out of the living room, wanting to check out more of the house, but I don't want to risk climbing up to the second floor. So I head into the room across the way and find that this is the dining room. It is exquisite and even has the last occupant's wooden dining room table and chairs left inside it, along with some matching furniture and hutches. The room circles around to the kitchen at the back of the house, so after I nose around in it, I go back outside into the backyard, wanting to check out the path.

The mouth of the path is overgrown, but I don't care as I barrel right through it then follow it as it twists and turns through the dense woods. I breathe in the fresh, fragrant salty sea air while taking this pleasant nature walk, enjoying the peacefulness and familiar feelings of being back home. Finally, reaching the end of the path, it opens up onto a white sandy beach with the ocean waves gently lapping at the shore. It is not exactly like being out at the beach, but it is still beautiful and is like having my own private oasis all to myself! As I begin to search the shoreline for some shells or other marine treasures that catch my eye, I hear a car pull in, so I rush back toward the house to see if it is the lady from the ad that I had talked to earlier today.

Until next time!

About the Author

Renee Barton has loved to read ever since she can remember. She was about thirteen when she got her first computer, and she used to sit behind it for hours, writing short stories, only to erase them shortly after.

Her life and the people who have been in it have inspired her to write this book because she believes that we can be anything or whoever we want to be within the pages of a book. Our deepest and greatest fantasies, experiences, and dreams can come true and be told through our eyes while we imagine ourselves living a different life. Reading and writing are great escapes from our hectic lives, and even though you may not have been able to have the things or live the life that you've always wanted to, losing yourself into a great adventure can be an amazing, sweet release.

Her book contains actual things that have happened to her throughout her entire life but also lets her live out a part of her life that will never exist. She has lived through plenty of trials and tribulations, struggling to muddle her way through life from day to day, but she knows that she is not alone. Never give up, and even when things may be at their worst, take a seat and clear your mind. Grab a book and set your soul free!

CPSIA information can be obtained
at www.ICGtesting.com
Printed in the USA
LVHW032341161121
703472LV00005B/177